THAT SUMMER IN FRANKLIN

THAT SUMMER IN FRANKLIN

LINDA HUTSELL-MANNING

Second Story Press

Library and Archives Canada Cataloguing in Publication

Manning, Linda
That summer in Franklin / Linda Hutsell-Manning.

ISBN 978-1-897187-89-0

I. Title.

PS8576.A563T53 2011   C813'.54   C2011-900076-8

Edited by Jonathan Schmidt
Copyedited by Kathryn White
Designed by Melissa Kaita
Cover photo © iStockphoto

Printed and bound in Canada

Second Story Press gratefully acknowledges the support of the Ontario Arts Council and the Canada Council for the Arts for our publishing program. We acknowledge the financial support of the Government of Canada through the Book Publishing Industry Development Program.

 ONTARIO ARTS COUNCIL
CONSEIL DES ARTS DE L'ONTARIO

 Canada Council   Conseil des Arts
for the Arts   du Canada

Published by
SECOND STORY PRESS
20 Maud Street, Suite 401
Toronto, ON M5V 2M5
www.secondstorypress.ca

For James

THE FRANKLIN STANDARD
Friday July 22, 1955
Page 1

FATAL ACCIDENT AT FRANKLIN HOTEL

Mr. Hugh Mourand, owner and operator of Franklin's prestigious Britannia Hotel, called police yesterday to investigate the death of Charlie Elliot, longtime kitchen employee of the establishment. Mr. Elliot was found crumpled at the bottom of the stairs in the hotel's kitchen. Mrs. Mourand, being the only one in the hotel at the time, said she heard nothing and found Elliot's body when she went into the kitchen to make tea, shortly after 3 P.M. It is thought that Mr. Elliot collapsed, possibly from a heart attack, and fell down the stairs, sustaining a fatal blow to his head. Mr. Elliot, who emigrated from London in the 1920s, had worked at the hotel since it opened and had no known relatives. The incident is undergoing police investigation, and an autopsy will be performed.

———————————————————

THE FRANKLIN STANDARD
Monday July 25, 1955
Page 8

OBITUARIES

Elliot, Charles, Thursday July 21, 1955. Suddenly at the Britannia Hotel. No funeral service. Interment Fairgrove Cemetery, Clark Road, Franklin.

HANNAH I

HANNAH WATCHES the windshield wipers swish-swish back and forth, late afternoon November rain jet-streaming off the car as she attempts to hold her expressway speed below the posted limit. Sometime this morning, and no one could tell her when, Hannah's seventy-seven-year-old mother, Edith, was found collapsed and unconscious in her dressing gown on Franklin's rain-drenched east beach. Hannah, called from her tenth grade English class and flung into this disaster, made her way to the office feeling as though she were moving through thickened air. The secretary was, of course, more than sympathetic when Hannah explained why she would need a sub for the rest of Monday and Tuesday as well.

It takes a good hour and a half to drive from Toronto to Franklin. How could this have happened? Hannah wants a blow-by-blow description. What time did her mother leave the house this morning? How long did she wander about in the wind and drizzle? Why didn't someone on the street notice her? Who found her collapsed on the stone beach, her pink, quilted housecoat matted with sand and seaweed? "In some degree of shock and hypothermia"—that's what the policewoman had said in an almost breezy tone of voice, as if she were giving the weather report.

The more she tries to concentrate on her mother and the crisis at hand, the more her past reinvents itself—contradictions bridging the almost five-and-a-half decades of her life. Duty versus escape. Memory versus selective amnesia. Roots versus branches. For the last forty years, climbing as far up and out as she could, hoping never to return, and at the same time, desperately wanting to.

This stress, in turn, brings on a massive dose of guilt. She hasn't visited her mother enough and has developed avoidance as a life skill. Dutiful Christmas trips always, a few days whirling in with presents, arriving in darkness, leaving in darkness. Short, compartmentalized visits bounded by time and her teaching life. Summer holidays rarely, always a legitimate excuse: summer school and courses that kept her feet moving up the pay-scale ladder, travel related to the curriculum, renovations to her tidy nest. These last few years when she does visit, she has refused to admit anything is changing, especially those silent but pervasive *ravages of time*.

Now her mother—the master organizer and money manager, typing and filing until just before her seventieth birthday, her mother, the supreme sacrificer, who subsequently grayed and with-ered into retirement—has become unpredictable and confused, no longer able to cope.

Not that there haven't been warnings, telltale indicators Hannah refused to acknowledge: too much dried-up food in the fridge, too many newspapers and magazines piled under tables, chairs, the bed. That indefinable yet distinctive smell, pulling everything downward, like shabby slippers shuffling across some unseen line. The few neighbors Hannah has spoken to over the years kept tabs on things, kindly taking out garbage and shovel-ing walks. One neighbor, who had last year quietly asked about a number in case of emergency, gave Hannah's school phone number to the police.

And the last forty years? An unwieldy number, forty, with neither the stature of fifty nor the glamour of twenty-five. Forty years: four decades, two score, too many. And more importantly, what to show for it? Her mother asked this every time she visited, every Sunday when she phoned.

Two sets of things have evolved over the years: those spoken and those not. Two slim volumes of published poetry, spoken, given autographed to her mother who never mentions them, although Hannah knows she has shown them to other people. Whenever she runs into neighbors, walking back with her mother from their customary Christmas Day trek along the beach, or after a hurried trip to the supermarket to stock up on staples, someone is calling, running over as she unloads overflowing plastic grocery bags from the trunk. "You're the poet." "How charming." "Wonderful to be so creative." "Such a rewarding hobby." Sincere comments she has to assume, but never acknowledged or commented on by her mother. And Hannah? Head of English at Charles R. Fenshaw Secondary School, highly organized and known to be old-fashioned tough on students. One year left until well-deserved retirement. With her mother, Hannah still slips into an abyss of uncertainty and neediness, wanting only to please yet having no idea how to begin, as if the forty years never existed, as if they are a book she is reading about someone else.

Her undergrad and graduate degrees and teaching, spoken—partially approved of by her mother, who feels two-and-a-half graduate years excessive, indulgent. That Hannah paid for those is beside the point. A waste of seconds, minutes, hours, days, weeks, all ticking furiously where they shouldn't be, misplaced and misdirected by Hannah.

Her love child, still unspoken—painfully and willfully erased, slipped in between the two volumes of poetry during her final year at graduate school, the result of a liaison with a certain professor with an open marriage sharing his expertise and bed. Complications and a Cesarean, dubbed "the operation," the reason for delaying her final thesis rewrite, the extra six months to recover, cover over—forget.

Now she knows the child, a boy, whisked away by his father to a relative in England, has been educated at Oxford: a Hardyesque chapter with a sixties up-beat ending—for the boy at least, a man now, almost thirty. The healing distance of years? Not possible.

Her less-than-satisfactory series of men over the years, unspoken—especially the latest, Russ, a writer she is sure is on the way up. He tells her she looks ten years younger than her age, envies but doesn't criticize her relentless exercise regime, and is marvelous in bed. Even though they've been an item for more than two years, Hannah is realistic about futures. He is almost fifteen years younger. Their relationship? Definitely unspoken, but then her mother doesn't ask anymore—a small plus in this sea of minuses.

This introspection verging on self-pity evaporates abruptly at the Franklin turnoff sign, the wipers swish-swishing clean the windshield, clearing Hannah's focus, reminding her that in the next ten minutes or so she will have to prepare herself. She hasn't been home since last Christmas. She fully intended to go for a few days this past summer but spent most of July sprucing up her place, and in August, took a ten-day cooking course in France. Class prep seemed to fill every minute once she was back. The fall semester roared in on her with teachers frantic over the new curriculum and cutbacks everywhere. Thanksgiving weekend she rented movies and didn't budge from the house. Now this.

The hospital sign leaps out at her right off the expressway, not where it should be, where it used to be, on the east side of town. She feels pulled into some surrealistic scenario—a sprawling new building, trees and landscaping impeccable, the Franklin Area Health Care Center information signs blaring across the immaculate black-paved parking lot, a wide wheelchair-accessible walkway, automatic front doors opening into a pristine foyer.

Into the hub of hospital busyness. Brightly lit halls lead off in three directions, an impressive reception area resplendent with

oversized foliage plants and gleaming leather chairs, all with that
unmistakable smell of antiseptic masking the edges of sickness and
decay. Hannah inhales sharply and approaches the front desk.

"I'm here to see Mrs. Norcroft, Edith Norcroft." The click-click
of the computer by an unsmiling receptionist who impartially taps
in the name, her long, polished nails identifying an unraveled life.
Hannah feels each tap touching exposed bone. *Edith with long
golden hair, Longfellow, The Children's Hour.* How inappropriately
appropriate.

"You're a relative?"

"Yes, yes. I'm her daughter. I…"

"Two thirty-two, Clarence Ridley wing. Check in at the nursing
station opposite the stairs."

Hannah has always had trouble with impartiality, usually trans-
lating it into accusation or, at the very least, suspicion. For a split
second she considers hauling out her birth certificate to prove who
she is, or giving reasons for why she wasn't already here, or explaining that what has happened isn't her fault. Instead, a numbness
washes over her, and she nods to the receptionist, already preoccupied on the phone, and walks as if into a thick fog to the elevator
where two orderlies are discussing last night's hockey game.

The second-floor doors click behind her, presenting two
halls, both smelling paint clean, both deserted. Clarence Ridley.
Politician? Benefactor? The farmer who owned this land?

"Excuse us."

A middle-aged man and woman push hurriedly past her off
the elevator. How long has she been standing here, rabbit-still,
impaled by the indirect lighting? The signs jump out at her now,
gold embossed lettering, *CLARENCE RIDLEY WING,* and in
brackets discreetly below, *Special Care Unit*. Hannah feels her heart
pound, her chest constrict. No, she says to herself, taking several
deep breaths. No panic attacks here. She checks to make sure no

one is watching, no one who might misconstrue her deep breathing, for whatever reason, and takes several more. The receptionist didn't say anything about "special care." She remembers her mother visiting a neighbor who was in Special Care years ago, when the old hospital had just opened a spanking new wing, in 1951 or '52. Her mother, who hardly ever visited anyone, had made an exception with Mrs. Brant down the street, a garrulous old woman so unlike Hannah's mother, it always amazed Hannah that their friendship evolved. The connecting link was flowers. Mrs. Brant ended up in Special Care after she broke her hip. "The end of the line for her," Hannah's mother said. "It'll be the poor house if they don't scratch up some sympathetic relative."

Hannah forces herself not to run down the hallway, to walk deliberately and professionally as if patrolling the hall between classes.

Each of the three nurses behind the nursing-station counter scrutinizes a document. Two conferring, one solo. Hannah tries clearing her throat and, when that doesn't work, opens and closes her purse a few times, then, feeling more and more agitated, paces the length of the counter and back. Two nurses leave. The third answers the phone. No one makes eye contact with Hannah.

"I'm here to see my mother, Mrs. Norcroft."

The nurse on the phone nods and keeps talking. One of the first two returns, obviously in time to hear *Norcroft*. "Dear little Edith," she says cheerily. "She's doing so much better this morning."

Edith, Hannah thinks. Mother certainly won't like that. "I'm her daughter," she says again, feeling exposed, practically condemned.

"Yes, yes," the nurse says, as if Hannah is already labeled. "The poet. Your mother rambles a bit and we think she's had a TIA, but she'll be so glad to see you." She beckons Hannah to follow.

A TIA, Hannah thinks. What the hell is a TIA?

The nurse waves her into a semi-private with its cheery yellow walls and pseudo Monets looking down from above both shiny metal beds. This thin, slack face with hair in disarray can't be her mother's. The adjoining bed is empty.

"Sleeping again, Edith?" the nurse chirps, leaning over her. "Wake up, Edith dear. You have a visitor."

Hannah stands awkwardly at the foot of the bed. A stroke. Is a TIA a stroke?

"Better sit down," the nurse says, pulling a stiff metal-legged chair close to her mother's head. "She takes a while to wake up but she'll probably know you, being her daughter and all."

Hannah sits down and lowers her purse to the floor. Later she remembers the *clunk* of it, the sound of her own accelerated breathing, her mother's slow rasping in and out.

"Mother?"

No response. Eyes still shut. Hannah looks up, but the nurse has already left. She glances over to the window to see a thin edge of sunlight slip through the clouds brightening the wall behind the beds, then back to the partially open washroom door, the added toilet-seat assist and the panic button cord-pull in full view. The closet door, however, is closed. Hannah jumps up to investigate. Two hooks, an upper and lower shelf. Where is her mother's pink, quilted dressing gown, her slippers? What about the house? Is it still wide open—a sitting duck for vandals, petty thieves? She should have gone there first. She intended to, but the hospital wasn't where it should be, where it used to be.

"Is that you, Hannah?"

Hannah wheels about and falls into the chair. "Mother, what happened? I'm so sorry. Are you in pain?"

Her mother's face lifts momentarily out of its gray slackness. "This is a fine kettle of fish," she says, in a voice almost her own. "I need a cigarette."

"No smoking in here, I'm afraid."

Her mother turns her head away. "You and that nurse," she quavers. One hand has mole-pushed its way outside the blanket, her nicotine-stained fingers clutching the satin edge. "Everyone telling me what I can't do, what I mustn't do."

Hannah stares at her mother's hand, gnarled with broken nails, several too long and curling inward. Her mother had such beautiful hands, nails always manicured and polished, tap-taping the hours on her Underwood typewriter. She gardened with two pairs of gloves, thin rubber ones inside a pair of flimsy white cloth ones. Hannah takes a deep breath and tries to think of something helpful or reassuring. All of this must be so humiliating.

"They mean well," her mother continues, sounding stronger, "telling me I'm too young to go into nursing, telling me there's a depression just around the corner. Well, I showed them, didn't I?" She turns back toward Hannah, her face fierce with concentration. "I showed every last one of them."

Hannah nods numbly—reaches out and places trembling fingers over her mother's gnarled fist.

"Same as when I met Harry. They all said he'd never come back, said I'd be sorry. Sorry is as sorry does. I wasn't sorry then, didn't have time to be sorry later." The face slackens again, baby-bird eyelids sliding down over clouded eyes.

"Mother?" No response.

The nurse looks in. "Gone again, is she? Doesn't usually last more than a few minutes at a time. Fresh coffee in the lounge. You look like you need it."

The coffee has that bitter, institutional aftertaste; the creamer the wretched sprinkling kind. Oprah intones on TV, her audience here a motley crew of wheelchair occupants, half of whom are asleep. The middle-aged couple standing over by the window is obviously in some state of crisis, their body movements like Morse code tapping out their trauma. The woman looks vaguely familiar, and Hannah, in no mood for old acquaintances, walks abruptly back into the hall, wanting a cappuccino, some Vivaldi, another chance at the last forty years.

Hannah drives along Main Street on the way to her mother's house, her sense of urgency overshadowed by dread of what she will find when she gets there. The street hasn't changed that much—probably too many empty storefronts, mall-mentality castoffs. Spindly trees have been interspersed with new heritage-looking streetlights. Cardinal's Ladies Wear is now a flower shop, and Pinser's, down at the heel for so many years, sports a Handy Hardware sign, definitely an improvement. But it's the Britannia Hotel that leaps out at Hannah, forcing her to flick on her turn signal and pull over.

The Britannia Hotel on the southeast corner of Victoria and Main, the scene of Hannah's first summer job, waitressing in the venerable dining room, tips hoarded for first-year university and freedom. The Britannia Hotel, now a Vintage Sundown Inn, beautifully restored with sandblasting and replica 1920s windows. I wasn't aware, she thinks staring at it, that the Sundown Inn chain went in for vintage anything. There are still the marble stone steps, though, the wrought iron railings, and the bas-relief Victorian couple over the huge double doors, he with suitcase, she with parasol, *Respite to the Weary Traveler* etched beneath: a momentary reminder of Hannah's youthful enthusiasm and innocence.

No one now believes what small-town fifties life was like—not with their smartphones and morning-after pills and rap lyrics. But it wasn't like *Leave It to Beaver* and *Happy Days* and all the other TV cardboard-cutout versions of the decade. The Britannia Hotel in 1955, the catalyst for her first-and-last date before university, was indifferent to the unforeseen trauma she witnessed there.

Hannah looks up at the three stories and inhales sharply. The hotel and that summer will always be synonymous with Charlie, a

Dickensian character, tireless in the kitchen, grateful for his pittance, always cheerful. She rarely lets herself think about what happened to Charlie that afternoon or the role played by Larry Mourand, the boss's hotshot sixteen-year-old son. It's erased, blanked out. She concentrates, instead, on the architecture. Baroque? No. Gothic. Southern Ontario guilt and gothic, a place she has no intention of setting foot in again.

COLLEEN I

A RAW NOVEMBER wind snaps sprawling shrub branches against the house as Colleen arrives for her Monday visit to check on her dad. As always, the smell of urine hits her the minute she unlocks the back door. Chaos. Everything is chaos now that her mom is gone: overgrown shrubs, backyard flowerbeds full of dried-up weeds. The unfairness hits her again as she stands inside the back porch, fists clenched, psyching herself up. Where will she, ye Gods, find her dad today? On the tiled kitchen floor, food-spattered in spite of Heda's weekly cleaning? On the hall stairs, piled up with empties and dirty clothes?

She has to deal with her dad and what's left of his life. She has no choice, never has had. Not when she was living at home and not since she married and never left Franklin: always the good little girl, forever-and-a-day caregiver, even though half the time she'd like to pound the bejesus out of him. For starters, why is he still alive? And why is Colleen left with all of it? If anything in this world was fair, her mom, not her dad, would still be here. Colleen used to dream what it would be like after he was six feet under. She and her mom could fix up the house, sell it. The neighborhood has gone all spiffy except for their old eyesore. Colleen's husband, Art, says board and batten over the Insulbrick would do wonders. Put fancy new appliances in the kitchen, gold faucets and a new tub in the bathroom, and, presto, double its value.

Her mom was all worn out by the years and working shitty shifts at the 7-Eleven, her beautiful auburn hair almost dull gray. Colleen yells at her sometimes when she's alone out at their farmhouse. You could have moved to one of those snazzy apartments, Mom. You could have gone on a bus tour to Florida, gone to night school, played the piano again.

No, her mom had to get herself hit by a drunk driver. The irony of it—twenty years ago, riding that excuse of a bike home from a late shift at the 7-Eleven—hit by a damn drunk driver.

Colleen stomps into the kitchen to slop more than enough disinfectant into a plastic basin. She's so ticked off, she could almost slosh the stuff down the front of her dad's pants. Elder abuse. She read about it in a magazine the other day, how adult kids beat up on their senile, elderly parents—some smart-ass, young reporter dishing out disgusting details she wished she hadn't read. She would never stoop to such things. Getting older has its advantages; it's toughened her, made her able her to block certain things out—almost forgive.

"I'm all washed up, Madge," her dad slurs as she steers him to the stairs, "should be taken out in the field and shot." How many times had he said that over the years? It's an old racetrack phrase, Lillian, her older sister, told her. When a horse can't run any more, they take it out in the field and shoot it.

"It's Colleen," Colleen reminds him as he staggers up the stairs and into the bathroom. She throws him clean pj's from a pile on the dresser, listens to him stumble into them. "Aim for the damn toilet bowl," she whispers as she pulls back the blanket and waits for him to appear and fall into bed.

She stops in the kitchen and stares at the table. Mostly when she comes into the house, she tries not to look at it. She's tried a couple of times to convince her dad to get rid of it. The legs are rusty, and the stuffing's coming out of one of the chairs. Her dad will have none of it. "What the hell would I want with a new table and chairs?"

It was 1969 or '71—she can't remember the year now—a summer afternoon, trying to be the helpful daughter. Her mom called from work and asked her to take lunch to her dad. Even though he's already snoring upstairs, she sees him sitting there, pissed as usual before noon. Good thing he was that day. Made it easier to get away from him groping her, thinking she was Madge. Good thing she didn't fall apart after or go all funny. Some women did.

Colleen hightails it to the living room to scrub the floor and sofa. In spite of repeated elbow grease and disinfectant, both it and the rug stink. When they finally get him into the nursing home, she's going to throw out the aging sofa, it and every pee-soaked thing in the house. Off to the dump. She'd love to burn it in the backyard, burn the whole damn house, all the junk and hurt: *Crazy Daughter Burns Family Home.* Nothing erases the odor, still that wet-diaper smell. If it was summer she'd open windows, prop open the back door with an empty case of twenty-four, let a breeze through.

She tiptoes past the stairs, tucks a graying strand into the thick knot piled on her head. She wears it like her mom now, ever since the funeral. Art loves it, calls her his Hepburn girl.

As Colleen pulls on her coat, her dad's snoring increases. He won't remember she was here, probably deny it like anything if she mentions it later. She glances at the stinking mess again. Thank God Heda's cleaning tomorrow. Outside, she kicks at a couple of dead weeds then turns and walks through the backyard to the old wreck of a fence, shrub branches pushing through rotting boards—one sad little red currant bush, missed when they transplanted the rest out at the farm.

Red currant jelly. She found more than fifty jars in the basement after her mom died. Every year while Colleen was at home, her mom gave most of it away to music students, neighbors, anyone who dropped by. Colleen had no idea she kept making it summer after summer. Jars and jars, wax still in place, her mom's neat handwriting on each label. Now Colleen makes the stuff—hears her mom's voice telling her to wash the berries, pick out the stems, hang the bag high enough to let the juice drain right.

Hannah Norcroft's mom loved red currant jelly. Where did that come from? Hannah Norcroft. Her best friend that summer of 1955 when they both waitressed at the Britannia Hotel. There's something she doesn't want to think about. Poor old Charlie and what happened to him. Her life has had too many traumas as it is—most of them not as awful as that. She shouldn't complain, not really. She doesn't most of the time. Just buries it all with the rest of her guilt and carries on.

High strung, smart-as-a-whip Hannah, her mom so grateful for Colleen's mom sending Hannah home with red currant jelly. Mailed a fancy little Thank You note, saying how good it was with roast chicken. Too weird, Colleen thinks, even now. Cranberries are for roast chicken; red currant jelly is for toast or Christmas tarts. Hannah Norcroft. Where would she be now? Probably well-off and successful.

Colleen blinks back tears and trudges to the back step, railing half off. She really should lose some weight. Not that she hasn't tried many times. Something always gets in the way, some disaster or other, and she ends up eating to work through it.

She pushes at the railing trying to force the bent nails into holes on the weathered post. For sale: older two-bedroom house, dry basement, needs some work. It drives her up the wall every time she rehashes that her mom actually bought the place—after Colleen left for Teacher's College, after an unexpected inheritance arrived. Not that her mom consulted anyone. Oh no, Mrs. Independent, keep-her-affairs-to-herself. Lillian had a fit about it, a long-distance fit over the phone. Colleen was up to her neck in midterms or practice teaching. The last thing she needed was her know-it-all sister telling her she should have done something. Like what?

Colleen gives the railing one more push and hurries to the car. Remembering is not what she should be doing. It's her only day off from the hardware store and she has a list as long as her arm. The November air catches the back of her coat, making her shiver. Get a hold of yourself, Colleen, she tells herself. Count your blessings.

Even with the car heater on high, her teeth chatter. Anyone who says being fat keeps you warm is wrong. She drives along Franklin's Main Street through the two-block business section. There's no place to park; well that's just an excuse really. She can't face going into a store yet, the smiles, the chitchat, the "how are things at the hardware store" routine. Instead, she turns south on Victoria toward the lake and finds herself, as always, parking down by the beach where, thirty-five years ago, she and Art worked out how they would break the news of their sudden wedding plans. She had missed two midterms because of morning sickness and all she wanted to do was forget the whole stupid course and be with Art. What a gorgeous, sexy maniac he was in those days. All that love wrestling and hand groping, mostly on park benches, occasionally sneaking into her room if the landlady was out. Nothing but rules in the fifties. She remembers being scared and thrilled by his attention, the fact that he was ten years older. It was worth the risk. Besides, Art was the first person to make her feel safe, really safe, as if nothing could ever harm her again.

In the end, they pretended their wedding plans were started a year earlier and, seven months later, wrote "preemie" in all of Artie's birth announcements. He was small, just over six pounds. Colleen stares at the tree's bare branches. Where have the last thirty-five years gone?

"What kind of stupid, feel-sorry-for-yourself trip is this?" she says out loud, gripping the steering wheel. A rerun of her soap-opera past. She will not feel sorry for herself. Her mom did enough of that for both of them. She finds her list, something she can hang on to: definite things to do, written down and ticked off one by one, start to finish, hour by week by year by decade. Her kids tease her about her lists and tell her she should put them all together as a book: Lists that Saved My Life, or Listing the Years. Could be a bestseller, they say. They don't know she has saved most of them in cardboard boxes, up in the attic—why, she has no idea—tucked away behind old curtain rods and boxes of keepsakes. When she dies—or when they put her in a home—they'll find them.

Traitor runs through her head again. She signed papers two weeks ago, the first step toward getting her dad moved into Sunset Lodge. Art has promised to help when they get the call to take him, though it's not like they'll get any warning. She'll have to call Art to come from the store, and he'll land in late while her dad's ranting about "what the hell is going on anyway?" Art will shuffle his feet and look embarrassed. Colleen will have to make something up. Why they have both showed up in the middle of the day to take her dad somewhere. What she'll tell him, she has no idea. Art will say nothing. Dealing with stress is not one of his strong points.

The next day after the store opens, Bill Dobson calls asking Art if he can make an emergency delivery to the Sunset Lodge kitchen. She hears Art mention a ten-piece place setting of Melmac dishes, chuckling as he hangs up.

"Some darned fool dropped a whole stack of dinner plates," he says, smacking his knee. "I can finally get rid of that confounded Melmac."

"Did you tell him it was Melmac?"

Art nods, grinning. "Twenty-five bucks for the lot, I told him."

Colleen says nothing. Art's generosity at the store has always been a sore point between them. Twenty-five bucks? She fumes silently. He'd probably have said yes for a hundred, or at least fifty. "The Lodge," she says out loud, "When are you delivering them?"

"Sometime after lunch, I guess. Why?"

"Perfect," Colleen replies. "We'll use it as a trial run for Dad."

Art stares at her, obviously trying to figure this out.

"We'll take him out for a drive and you'll just happen to stop at the Lodge."

"And that will…"

"Oh, Art," Colleen says throwing up her hands. "That will… get him used to driving there. Give us a chance to see how he reacts…"

"You know how he'll react," Art says dryly, "But okay. Makes no difference to me."

Colleen dials the number, hoping her dad's still sober, knowing if he is, he'll likely be in a rotten mood, complaining and pouting like a little kid.

"Thought you might like to go for a drive this aft."

"Guess I could use another case of twenty-four."

"Pick you up at one?"

"What's your damn hurry? Beer store's open until six."

"Art has to deliver an order. We'll have to make it one."

"Don't expect me to dress up."

That afternoon, as Art drives around to the Lodge's back delivery door, her dad's tirade is in full swing.

"Goddamned old folks home," he repeats, after Art returns. "You'll never catch me in a place like this."

"Some folks don't seem to mind it," Colleen manages to say. Any more would be an open statement of what's to come, Colleen the Jailor clanking her keys.

Art says nothing. They have a fight about this after they drop her dad back at his house.

"You could have backed me up."

"Um hmm."

"But you chickened out."

"I don't think so."

"What then? You were thinking of something else? You couldn't? That's it, you couldn't. You didn't want to. You didn't want to help me out."

"That's not true."

"Then what is? The fact that I've got a deadbeat father, drinking himself to death over some cockeyed memory of his wife? The fact that he's living in a damn cesspool, expecting everyone to look out for him, pity him, clean up after him?" She's into it now, sounding more and more like her dead mother.

Art pulls the car over onto the shoulder. He takes her hand. "Colleen," he says quietly. "We'll get through it."

Colleen turns away. Something is always waiting to attack her life, always has been, probably always will. Her chest tightens and she feels herself slipping down into blackness—a familiar place that pulls at her, blanking out common sense, wrapping her in how stupid and no good she is. Just before the blackness sucks her in, she flings herself against Art, pressing her face into his shoulder, sobbing and hanging on to him as if he is keeping her from drowning. He strokes her head over and over, nuzzling his rough face against hers.

"I think I'm okay now," she whispers, finally. She attempts a smile and blows her nose. "I found a red currant bush back by the fence at Dad's yesterday."

"We don't need any more of those," Art says, starting the engine.

"I know. And you know what? I remembered Hannah Norcroft and her mom and the red currant jelly."

"Have you told me about this before?"

"Yes, yes. It was a long time ago—the summer we both wait-ressed at the Britannia." She doesn't want to remember this, especially right now. Instead she concentrates fiercely on the scratch on the glove compartment door, the ragged windshield wipers, the crack in the corner of the windshield.

"I could take you home now," he says. "Instead of back to the store."

Colleen stares out the car window. Just the sound of home dims the events trying to reinvent themselves in her mind. I could tell him he's deliberately changing the subject, she thinks. "I could get supper ready, then," she says instead.

Art puts the car in gear, spinning the wheels in the gravel as he speeds up. Colleen closes her eyes. She knows the Britannia is not something he wants to talk about. More than once when she's in a piling-up-disasters mood, Colleen has told him about the accident at the hotel that summer day in 1955. Not what she knew really happened, only what the papers said. No mention of Larry Mourand, the boss's son-of-a-bitch, arrogant son. Just poor old Charlie. That's how she's dealt with it over the years. She keeps the rest of it buried under all her other life disasters.

The car stops, and Art turns off the ignition. Colleen opens her eyes to see the stone farm house, solid and reassuring in the afternoon light.

BRITANNIA THEN

NATHANIEL BOWEN, who built the Britannia in 1926 when Franklin still had aspirations of becoming the provincial capital, kept his hotel operating right through the Great Depression and Second World War. He died, suddenly, of a heart attack in 1945, many said because his only son, groomed to be heir, was killed at Dieppe. Less than three months later, businessman and entrepreneur Hugh Mourand, looking to relocate from Ohio to Canada, spotted Mrs. Bowen's "for sale" ad in a Cleveland newspaper.

The Franklin town council had already met about the impending fate of the Britannia. She was down at the heel, and Earl Pinser, on the council at the time, thought they should ensure that the building be preserved, not modified or modernized like that ugly new addition on Franklin High. Harold Clark, an ex-army colonel from the First World War, said that considering the historical importance of the hotel to the town, Mrs. Bowen should give preference to local buyers, "Franklin blood," as he called it. Sarah Finn, an antique dealer and the only woman on council, said persuasion was always more effective than force, and that whomever became the owners should be welcomed into the community and encouraged to carry on the Britannia's tradition. This was met with "hear, hear" from the men, generally at a loss to respond to the flamboyant Mrs. Finn, who wore large hats and gloves to council meetings and who, while she was campaigning for council, rode the garbage trucks to personally check out complaints of discrimination between rich and poor areas of town.

The Mourands were definitely not Franklin blood. As soon as they arrived, the hotel was closed up tight for a week. Everyone speculated as to what they were doing. Earl Pinser, good hardware man that he was, was sure they were taking inventory. Harold favored vermin and insect extermination, as God knows who had been holed up there for the last few months. Mrs. Finn said it really wasn't any of their business, and she was sure the Mourands were assessing the situation and making new plans. When the doors opened again, it was to a series of out-of-town workmen and goods going in, and considerable piles of plaster and old carpeting going out. Franklin old timers and the town council, except for Mrs. Finn, remained tight-lipped and watchful.

Mrs. Finn waltzed in the first day, the brim of her hat collecting plaster dust, her leather boots clicking on the foyer's hardwood floor. She found Mr. Mourand in the back office, papers and boxes everywhere.

"I'm representing town council," she said, extending a gloved hand, "and I'd like to welcome you to Franklin."

Hugh Mourand stood, his six-foot-three frame towering over the diminutive Mrs. Finn, his large hand enveloping hers. "Delighted to meet you, Mrs. Finn, my pleasure indeed. Deandra and I plan to rejuvenate the old place, turn her back into the gem she once was."

"The council will be pleased to hear this," Mrs. Finn replied. "The Britannia deserves to be the town's centerpiece again."

"I can't take you through right now, but as soon as we get her shipshape, I'll invite council in for a tour."

"Excellent, Mr. Mourand, Franklin Council will be right behind you." Mrs. Finn turned to leave.

"I'm sure my wife would like to meet you," Mourand added. "She's finding the adjustment from city living a bit difficult."

"Tell her to drop in to my antique shop, Finn's Collectibles. It's on the same side as the Britannia, one block west."

Mourand nodded and, flashing what would come to be his trademark smile, returned to the clutter on his desk.

Mrs. Finn triumphantly reported to the next council meeting that the Mourands were following closely in the Bowen tradition and that the Britannia would be a town showplace again.

By the midfifties, when Colleen Miller and Hannah Norcroft worked there, the hotel was functioning at full capacity, both Rotary and Masons holding weekly dinner meetings in the recarpeted dining room and an ongoing clientele of traveling salesmen, business men, and itinerant laborers booking into the renovated single rooms upstairs, a number of which contained original Victorian furniture. The Mourands kept the third floor for themselves with private stairs down to the second-floor hallway. There, in one of the storage rooms next to the kitchen stairs, Charlie had his room.

Years before, whenever Charlie had arrived, and no one knew for certain, Mrs. Bowen had converted this storage room into his living quarters. He ate his meals in the kitchen and, as far as anyone knew, used the basement facilities. Mrs. Bowen was adamant Charlie stay on when the place was sold. Rumor had it, she made it a condition of sale.

Hugh Mourand, who still maintained his US connections, was a shrewd businessman with a seemingly bottomless pocket. He quickly made himself known about town, dropping in at every shop on the main drag to introduce himself, charming the women and impressing the men. He wore stylish suits, often a cravat at his neck, his wavy salt-and-pepper hair a tad longer than stylish for a man his age. He joined Rotary and promised generous amounts to local charities, gaining the confidence and support of even the most conservative small-town thinkers.

Deandra Mourand, known as Daisy, wore filmy, slightly out-of-date dresses with trailing sleeves and layered skirts. She frequented Sarah Finn's antique shop, and Sarah made sure only the best information about the Mourands was circulated. Deandra Humphrey had danced with the American Ballet Company until a knee injury forced her to change employment. She told Sarah that she met Hugh when working as an assistant bookkeeper in a classy Chicago hotel. There were several miscarriages before little Larry was born in 1939. Although a sickly baby, he grew rapidly into a lanky boy, tall as his father by the time he was sixteen. His mother doted on him and told Sarah Finn he was a perfect son. With his father's wavy hair and his mother's aquamarine eyes, he was dubbed the Personality Kid by the locals at Roamer's restaurant.

Larry charmed his teachers, excelling each school year with little effort or work. He could be arrogant and easily riled up, though, and following too many fights on the way home from sixth grade, Daisy had taken to driving and picking him up in the Lincoln Continental. Few dared taunt him, and the one or two he favored were occasionally allowed inside the luxurious vehicle on the way home. Up until fifth grade, he liked to parade around the hotel foyer after school, sporting his Matchbox Models collection, stored in a wooden cigar box. He learned quickly that male patrons loved to admire the tiny cars and trucks, holding them up to inspect their detail and authenticity, often slipping him a quarter for his trouble. Later, he took to building model airplanes in his father's office, bringing them out for appreciation once finished. Since ninety-five percent of the weekday clientele was male, his audience was ongoing. Mourand watched the boy, feeding his air of superiority and shooing him upstairs only when Daisy insisted.

Once the boy turned fourteen, however, Mourand had Larry spend Saturday mornings behind the foyer counter, learning to deal with the public, getting a feel for the business. Dressed in a custom-made suit, his blond hair slicked back, he charmed everyone. Traveling salesmen kept telling his father the boy was born to sell, while itinerant workers, usually at the hotel for a week or so, tended to flatter him and call him Sir.

By 1955, Larry was a sixteen-year-old pro, suave and confident, charming older women and leaning easily into his father's smooth sophistication. Friday afternoons after school, he often swaggered down the main drag, smoking a Philip Morris pilfered from his dad's pack, looking for girls to chat up, returning home only when he knew supper would be ready. His found his mother's continued coddling an embarrassment and figured he was old enough to do whatever he wanted.

That summer in Franklin proved to be a turning point for almost everyone at the Britannia Hotel, and as turning points often are, it was random in its choice of victims and relentless in its consequences.

HANNAH II

AS HANNAH PULLS from the curb, watching the Britannia disappear in the rearview mirror, she clearly remembers the beginning of that summer of 1955. Tenth-grade final exams and her mother going on, as usual, about how short of money they were and how many times did she have to remind Hannah to apply for a summer job at one of Franklin's local stores. Respectable places, she called them. On Friday, the morning of her last exam, Hannah promised her mother she would get up her nerve to go in and ask at Cardinal's Ladies Wear or Pinser's Hardware. The pay was nothing to write home about, but the work was steady.

Just before she headed out the door for school, her friend Colleen called and tipped her off about the Britannia Hotel waitressing job. "The other summer waitress just up and quit," Colleen said, "so you'd better snap to it this aft. Mr. Mourand says first come, first served."

Hannah still remembers how she couldn't believe her luck and how she planned to get the job before telling her mother.

Walking home after the grueling two-hour French exam, she fantasized how she would look in her uniform, form-fitting but not too much, professional looking and business-like, how she would chitchat with all sorts of interesting patrons, travelers from distant and exotic places as far away as the United States, and how she would smile and be efficient and pocket huge tips.

She dithered over what to wear and, in the end, chose her striped dirndl skirt and white blouse with its Peter Pan collar. Businesslike yet feminine. The afternoon was a scorcher, and by the time she rode her bike all the way to the Britannia, her blouse was pulled out with telltale underarm perspiration marks, her brown ponytail halfway down her neck, fine loose ends sweat-glued across her forehead. She leaned her bike against the hotel wall and pulled out the elastic, catching the errant ends into some semblance of order. After tucking in her blouse as best she could, she walked sedately up the marble steps, pausing in front of the imposing oak doors to take a deep breath.

Once inside, she froze, the grandness of it all overwhelming her, the foyer's coolness wrapping her in stale smoke and cooking smells. Huge portraits, shiny leather chairs, the polished hardwood floor all seemed too cold, too intimidating. She couldn't do this.

"You must be the girl Colleen recommended." Mourand smiled, the silver in his wavy hair catching the afternoon light, his paisley cravat emphasizing his jaw line.

"Hannah Norcroft," Hannah said, catching her breath. She willed herself toward him, her saddle shoes squeaking on the hardwood floor. "I'm here about the waitressing job."

"Fifteen dollars a week is what I pay." Mourand reached across the counter, his hand sparkling with several rings.

Hannah took his hand reluctantly. She had no experience shaking hands with men, and besides, he wasn't at all what she expected.

"Astrid, who's the cook here, says to show up midmorning tomorrow," he continued, gesturing toward the dining room. "Good time to get a feel for the place. It's always less busy on the lunch shift." He tapped the counter with his fountain pen. "Check in first with my wife, Deandra, for your uniform. She's always here at noon, usually in the back office." The phone rang and he turned to answer it, smiling and motioning her out with his other hand.

On the way home, Hannah worked on ammunition for her mother. The Britannia Hotel was the apple of Franklin's postwar eye. People her mother considered respectable and important would be there—Rotary Club members and ladies of the Knights of Columbus.

Hannah spent the rest of the day at home, cleaning. She cooked macaroni and cheese for supper, one of the few recipes her mother allowed her to make. After they ate, while her mother relaxed with her after-supper cigarette, Hannah broached the subject.

"I know it's a fancy hotel," her mother replied, taking a long drag on her cigarette, "but you never know who is going to stay there."

"Colleen made more than double what I'd get in any downtown store—including tips, between sixty and seventy dollars a week last summer."

"I see," her mother said patronizingly, "wearing some low-cut blouse, no doubt."

"Mother, they wear uniforms."

"I see."

"Well, can I?"

"You're fully able, if that's what you're asking me."

"I'll give you half each week."

Her mother's efficiently short nails tapped the kitchen table.

"Let me help," Hannah persisted.

"I'll agree," her mother said finally, "if you put half away for university."

"All my tips and most of my fifteen dollars a week."

Waitressing meant hard work and long hours in the fifties. Six days a week, afternoons off, but no weekends. No minimum wage, no sick leave, no grievance committee if anything went wrong. And they loved it, she and Colleen, thrived on it that first month, except for Larry. Larry turned out to be a proverbial thorn in Hannah's side.

Looking back now, Hannah knows that, really, the good times far outweighed Larry and the trauma he inflicted. They were young and earnest and worked like dogs. The cook, Astrid, was a sergeant major, large boned and relentless. Waitresses before Colleen and Hannah nicknamed her the Viking. Charlie was her physical and emotional opposite, diminutive and gentle, always there to help, always giving an extra hand. Hannah's initial well-being had a lot to do with Charlie.

Astrid told them he came originally from Scotland, was orphaned in London, and came over as a Bernardo boy. When Hannah asked about this, Astrid explained that a Victorian Englishman, Dr. Bernardo, took in homeless and abandoned boys in London, and sent them to learn farming at a training center he established in Canada. How Charlie ended up in Franklin, no one knew. He had a room upstairs, food from the kitchen, cigarettes from Astrid. In return he tirelessly cleaned pots and carried out slop, did all the extras. The first day Hannah worked, Colleen said, "Charlie's gold—the best." When introduced to Hannah, he blinked and coughed slightly. "Welcome Lassie," he said, reed-thin voice, hand partially covering his mouth: a Charlie characteristic. Colleen said one of his front teeth was missing. He helped out far beyond whatever call of duty he was bound to, often shooing the girls away, "Charlie'll finish it, Lassies," so either or both could leave. Colleen said he came with the place when the Mourands bought it ten years before.

Enough, Hannah says to herself, as she turns her car onto Lakefront Road. Mother's house is what I should be thinking about. Mother's house and how am I ever going to deal with all the years and all the baggage.

The next morning, Hannah is still picking through and throwing out, one part of her wanting carte blanche to evacuate everything, while some niggling voice keeps insisting she look through every pile, every box, every closet. Just in case.

Yesterday her quest was to find a particular photograph taken early in July 1955 with Astrid's Brownie camera: Hannah and Colleen and Charlie, on his birthday. Not to be found. This whole sorting business is a nostalgia trip she doesn't need. After lunch she'll make one last visit to the hospital and then home to reinvent her life—try to decide what to do. How long her mother can stay in the hospital is a disconcerting unknown. The doctor, when she finally pinned him down yesterday, was vague and hedged regarding her mother's incapability. Her prognosis? Not good. That much was and is obvious. She has had, they surmise, a series of small strokes, TIAs, an acronym that trips-up the tongue. She certainly cannot return to the house alone. There isn't money to hire twenty-four-hour nursing care, and Hannah still has one more teaching year before she could even consider retirement. Not that she had, not until this happened.

She imagines moving back into this little house—her room with its fifties dresser and faded chintz curtains—trying to keep tabs on her mother, locking the door with a key at night, shadowing her during the day. And if she slipped out again—scouring the neighborhood, standing on the stone beach, scanning up and down, out into the water, wind and terror cutting through her? Circumstance has spared her this; guilt eats at her freedom.

She finds the blouse in the back of her mother's closet, buttons still missing, washed but not ironed, its full peasant sleeves permanently creased. Her first and only summer date. She was under house arrest for the rest of the summer after that escapade—sign in, sign out, no movies, the library once a week on her day off. Her mother wringing her hands at Hannah's perceived indiscretion,

accusing her of wantonly losing her virginity, probably being pregnant, eliminating her opportunities, throwing away university and
the good, postwar fifties life. And Hannah saying nothing in her
own defense, explaining nothing, revealing nothing, storing her
mother's verbal attack in her memory banks, fuel to further widen
the chasm between them, ammunition to keep her away once she
left. The blouse reminds her that some part of her will always, to
some degree, be here.

What happened that evening with Gordon Ellis initiated the
art of not saying, of sitting in proximity to her mother while, at
the same time, creating enormous distance. This, the summer of
1955, is when Hannah devised the technique. Years of honing and
refining turned it into second nature, an almost tangible substance
between them.

Hindsight is so annoying. His twenty-year-old self-assurance,
his loaded tone of voice, wanting to walk her home, push her bike.
Push you over sweetheart, Hannah thinks, roll you over in the
clover. His agenda's time line speeding up. And Hannah unknow-
ingly aiding and abetting, being primed like a sweet young thing
ripe for the plucking.

She stands in front of the same mirror, watching her forty-year-
older reflection. What did she look like in those days? Her mother
had no camera so it is only her imperfect memory lens struggling
to identify her energy, her untapped sexuality.

She could have handled it later, even in university—told the
jerk where to get off. Looked after herself. Not because of but in
spite of her mother's ongoing admonishments. Be careful. Careful is
as careful does. A vacant maxim pitted against that yearning to find
out, to push into the unknown: dating, petting, going steady. Rules
were paramount then. Hannah remembers a colleague's teenage
daughter quizzing her about the fifties, the impossible rule-ridden
fifties—almost sentimental now, viewed with nostalgia. Not at the

time, though. Then it was like life pressing against her, daring her to try it out.

In those days, she thinks, folding the sleeves neatly under and putting the blouse in the "to keep" pile, we all pretended we knew everything and were terribly bored by it. When *Lady Chatterley's Lover* was secretly passed around, Hannah distinctly remembers not believing what she read: Mellors and the flowers and his rising member. She refused to believe it, afraid somehow that, if she did, something evil would rub off on her.

Colleen Miller was her best friend and confidante that summer, not that they spent much time together except working at the hotel. Whatever has become of her? An old-fashioned phrase as if fate or the Gods held control, as if, especially if you were a female in the fifties, you were expected to become someone, preferably a Mrs. someone, tucked safely away from a lusting male world. Both sexes lust now, Hannah thinks ruefully, even grade nines, but most of the guys still get off scot-free. Two teenage mothers in her twelfth grade English class, haggard little things, adult responsibilities pitted against Saturday nights out with friends, colicky babies versus exams. Colleen was adamant about not marrying. Ireland. Singing. She was a natural on stage. She aspired to being a diva. Forty years later—a retired diva by now.

The closet smells of dust and nicotine and her mother's perfume. Hannah spots something scrunched up behind several pairs of shoes: a skirt or rather *the* skirt. Hannah puts it up to her waist and slowly turns in a circle. "So what happened to you, Gordon Ellis?" she says out loud. "The corporate world, high-tech salesman, law?" Letting him walk her home that night was one thing. Allowing him to use her mother's car to take her to the drive-in, entirely another.

Hannah lays the folded dirndl skirt on top of the blouse and stares at the closet. The shoes wouldn't still be here. Patent ballerinas, black and shiny. Bought as being good for dances she was never allowed to attend, for visiting they never did—worn only that once.

If Hannah's mother has indulged in anything, it's shoes. Pairs and pairs lined up in the closet, boxes neatly piled, three dozen or more in four adjacent stacks. Hannah finds the errant ballerinas flattened under the farthermost pile. Small and narrow, impossible to get on now—feet spread with age, feet and ear lobes. Feet she already knew about. Giddily high-dancing pumps, some delicious color or style she couldn't part with, lugged from boarding house to apartment to town house. These were Cinderella shoes, and she had metamorphosed into the ugly sister, big toed and bunioned, struggling to squeeze too much into too little. Ear lobes she had read about in the doctor's office, likely twenty years ago, in one of those "did you know" articles about the small aberrations of aging. Ear lobes were said to double in length between forty and eighty. That evening, in the privacy of her own home, Hannah carefully measured each ear lobe, securing the vital statistics in the bottom of her jewelry case. July 14, 1972, ear lobe from bottom cartilage to tip, half an inch. Check in fifty years—heavy earrings would make it worse. She determined never to wear any, then forgot and did anyway. People living longer—hoards of old men and women, shuffling in their overgrown shoe sizes, ear lobes flapping in the wind. It was time for coffee.

The recently scrubbed kitchen still has that dead cigarette after-smell. Hannah has noticed it more and more over the years, once on a retrieved bedspread and later on a certain cashmere sweater she loved. Both taken home and washed and washed again, the stubborn dry ash smell refusing to let go until, thoroughly frustrated, she bundled them in plastic and deposited them in a donation box.

Coffee here is the instant variety. The old aluminium coffee pot is missing its innards, and it seems an unnecessary extravagance to

buy a new one for these few days. There's real milk though and some
Vivaldi on the portable cassette player she had the foresight to bring.
She plans to take it to the hospital and play Chopin for her mother,
something positive, something she will, hopefully, remember.

Coffee in hand, Hannah picks up one of the shiny patent
leather shoes and stares out the bedroom window toward the lake.
Bare branches of the old willow bend inward against the onshore
wind. Attempted date rape, that's what it was. And who was to
blame? A tough call now. Gordon egged her on and she followed,
waited for him all dolled up, found the extra set of car keys so they
could go to the drive-in.

From the perspective of fifties mores, anyone then would have
put the blame squarely on her. He was just hoping to sow some
wild oats. She thinks about her teenage moms, caught like flies on
life's sticky paper, stuck there with reality and dirt flecks. She was
lucky, really, physically strong and aggressive when shoved down
onto the car seat—furious and fighting back. They came here to
watch a movie, after all. Miss Purity Flour. That's what he called
her on the way home. And Gordon? Did he have a last-minute
moment of foresight? Possible, but unlikely. More likely it was her
thrashing, which caused the speaker to smack his forehead, that
cooled his ardor, as they would have said in the fifties, softened
him momentarily so that his thinking shifted above his waist. She
was a minor after all. Not so with Professor Hendricks, however.
She remembers assuring herself that she knew what she was doing.
He was the first older man she felt a kinship with, a father figure:
Anthony Hendricks teaching John Donne in her fourth year, thesis
advisor in her grad years, father of her never-to-be-seen-again son.
Self pity. Closed book. Get on with it.

Was she becoming her mother, bitter and jaded about men?
Her mother. Hannah checks the time. She's fifteen minutes behind
her schedule. Self-indulgence, that's what she's been wallowing in.

She grabs the fated Purity Flour outfit and tosses it all into a get-rid-of-it bag.

Five minutes later, windows fastened, heat down to minimum, suitcase more or less packed, Hannah locks memories inside with the front door key and prepares for the cosmic shift to hospital and daughterhood.

COLLEEN II

THE ACCIDENT that happens on Friday, only days after Colleen's visit, is what saves the whole thing, clears the way for Colleen's dad getting into the Lodge. They all call it "the accident," not just Colleen, even though no one else in the family has read about denial.

Colleen tells herself that denial isn't necessarily a bad thing. Denial that she was pregnant before she was married fooled her in-laws, even kept her in her mom's good books. Denial that she gave up everything for Art. Not hard when the kids were small. Gave up everything and gained everything. That's what she tells people. Denial that Art isn't perfect, that his kindness and love don't always make up for their ongoing money troubles.

Her dad's accident, when it happens, works perfectly as denial. Colleen's dad is the only grandpa her kids know since Art's dad kicked the bucket from a heart attack before Artie was two. Since her mom died, Colleen has tried to paint the best picture possible. Her dad has had a hard life; always worked at a job he hated; lost his wife too soon; should have played sax in a first-class band. It's so easy with the accident. He fell down the stairs, toting a beer, shades of forty-some years ago, only this time, Colleen wasn't there to get glass in her leg, or to be told by her mother it was from a broken jar of red currant jelly. She's carrying on where her mother left off.

Colleen's at home when Heda calls. "He's had a fall, Mrs. Pinser. You'd better get right over here."

Another break-the-speed-limit trip into town. "Drunk yesterday, drunk today," she whispers, thumping up the back steps.

Conscious or unconscious, Colleen can't tell right off. Drunk and breathing, though, crumpled at the bottom of the stairs, a split in his forehead, beer stench and broken glass everywhere, a murder-mystery pool of blood on the floor. A crisis always puts Colleen at her best: 911, a blanket, the kettle on.

"Dad? Can you hear me?" No answer. His face too white, just the faintest sign of breathing.

Heda is fussing behind them. "Oh, Mrs. Pinser, I'm so sorry, so sorry."

"Heda? You go on home."

"You can manage?"

"The ambulance will be here in a minute."

Heda grabs her cleaning pail and rags and is out the door almost before Colleen takes another breath. First aid. She looks at the cut running from his forehead into what's left of his hairline, a dead straight slice, skin peeling back, bone showing. Colleen grabs the stair rail, takes a deep breath. The bleeding has nearly stopped so he must have been lying here for a while. A knock at the front door. Colleen tears through the living room to answer it. They hardly ever use the front door, the cracked cement stoop practically right on the sidewalk, the open door giving neighbors a full-out view of the living room.

"He must have fallen down the stairs," Colleen says as they angle the stretcher past piano and couch. "The cleaning lady found him about fifteen minutes ago." She is sure they will ask why he is still living alone, but they don't. Their questions are short and to the point.

"Your father?"

"Yes."

"How old is he?"

"Eighty-one."

"On any medication?"

She pauses, wondering if she should say something about his drinking, not wanting to, thinking they will notice.

"Blood pressure pills, anything like that?"

"No, no pills."

They roll and strap him onto a backboard and then to the stretcher.

"Are you coming with us in the ambulance?"

"I've got my car."

"Does he have a hospital card?"

"I have it."

"Meet us in Emerg."

Whisk, whisk, whisk, out the door and gone. Colleen grabs a bathroom towel and throws it over the blood. Only then her stomach heaves; her hand shakes. They should have moved him into a nursing home ages ago. Stubborn old fart even when he's sober, insisting he can manage. How dare anyone think he can't? She calls Art at the store but it's Friday, and of course he's busy with a customer, and she won't explain the whole mess, or even part of it, to Jake, who answers the phone afternoons. "I'll call back," she says.

Colleen is out the door and into the car, revving the motor so hard it stalls. Damn thing needs servicing. The ambulance is out of sight now, but she can still hear the siren wailing. She turns north, knowing that even though it will likely roar right through, she'll hit every red light.

In the years between her mother's death and the accident, they've moved the Franklin Area Health Care Center from the east side of town to the west side, up by the expressway. Such a to-do in the papers: Franklin competing with neighboring Port Turner for location; local politicians shaking fingers at one another, each accusing the other of some political crap. Art was so fed up he told Colleen he had a mind to cancel the *Franklin Standard*.

When she reminded him it had always been like that, that even in high school, Port Turner was the only other town team to beat, Art, always quiet and reasonable in public, went into a before-dinner rant. Even though he has never raised his voice to her personally, never in almost thirty-five years, she still freaks out when he does this. It's usually over something in the dumb newspaper, but she always feels like she is right back at the top of the stairs, sitting in the dark, her parents shouting, a giant knot in her stomach.

At Emerg, after Colleen gives a nurse the run down, ignoring the fact she begins with "Oh my, Mr. Miller again," she panics, trying to remember whether she locked or even closed the front door. They've told her to wait while they stitch him up and x-ray his head and spine. The waiting room has the usual bored-looking crew; no one looks in terrible pain or ready to faint. Colleen finds a spot where no one can watch her and thinks about what she will tell the kids. Definitely not that he was drunk and fell down the stairs—something more respectable. It's not that she deliberately uses denial. It comes naturally from years of practice.

She remembers clearly, a number of years before, managing to read through two library books about adult children of alcoholics. There were actually books on the subject, accounts of other people worse off than she was. Or so she thought. She overheard someone in a grocery checkout line whispering to her friend how much one of these books helped her. It took Colleen weeks to get up the nerve to go into the library.

She hadn't been to the Franklin library since high school, when it was still on Main Street. This place was new and huge, with so many books. She went back twice before she actually found what she wanted. She sure wasn't going to ask and make a fool of herself. It was hard enough actually taking them to be checked out.

It had to be in the eighties sometime. Artie and the girls were out of the nest and the twins still in grade school. Colleen remembers she hid the books in the bottom of her sweater drawer and read them after the twins were asleep. They were easier to read than she expected, especially the parts where different people told what their life was like, past and present. She still can't imagine people doing this, spilling out secrets and horrors they lived with day to day. Over and over she read lines she could have written herself. She found she was codependent, linked forever to the way her parents did things, the way they thought about things. She already knew she was too eager to please everyone, that she probably denied things rather than facing up to them. The hardest part was that she likely passed this on to her kids. And so many of these people talked about being depressed, of falling into a black hole. Colleen said the words over and over: black hole. Her mom always said Colleen was down in the dumps. "You down in the dumps again? With such a good man, you shouldn't have a worry in the world." But she did, and when things overwhelmed her, she fell, sometimes in a split second, like a trap door opening, down and down into nothingness, into a terrifying black hole—the perfect thing to call it.

She tried to talk to Art about what she read, but he said he'd never been good at that psychology stuff and it was only a book, after all, and maybe not true. Colleen knew it was true—every single word. Even though it upset her, it made her feel better somehow, less alone.

A baby starts crying and Colleen realizes she hasn't phoned Art. Her change pouch has fallen open inside her purse and she finds only nickels, dimes. She could dump everything onto the floor. A quarter, where the hell is a quarter?

She sees Art before he sees her, sees him running from the parking lot, sleeves rolled up, no coat or jacket. She meets him just outside the automatic doors. The wind hits her face, stops the tears for a moment.

"Is it bad?"

"He knocked himself out—has a cut on his head."

Art puts his arm around her shoulder and guides her back inside. They sit in the far corner, his hand on hers.

"Mrs. Baker called the store. She saw the ambulance come for him."

"She and the whole damn street."

"It's not your fault, Colleen."

She nods, while everything in her screams the opposite. Everything is her fault, every single stinking thing—always has been, always will be. The black pit is right there, waiting for her. She squeezes Art's hand and forces herself to watch a few dry leaves spinning down the sidewalk, the baby still crying in the other room, her own breath in and out.

"I've put a call in to the nursing home," Art says quietly. "Left a message telling them what's happened, that we can't let him go back to his house."

"What are they going to do? Tell someone to die? We should have put his name in months ago." Her mother again. She takes a deep breath. "Sorry."

"It's going to be all right, Colleen." How many times has he said this to her over the years? All right—the answer for almost everything that had happened or might happen. But they had made it so far, almost thirty-five years. Lists and babies and gardening and love kept her head above water most of the time. She was sure that once she had been married as long as she had lived at home, everything would be all right. Twenty years to cancel twenty years. They had a night of nights on their twentieth wedding anniversary;

she called it the Good-bye Black Pit Party: champagne and grapes and sweat that left them worn out and hung over the next morning. Wonderful, but it didn't change anything.

"Mrs. Pinser?"

Colleen jumps up. Art follows her to the emergency reception desk.

The nurse leans forward with that all-important we're-in-charge look. "He's in Special Care, 245 Clarence Ridley wing, but not to worry, Dr. Montgomery says the concussion isn't serious and no broken bones."

"She obviously doesn't have a clue that he was too drunk to break bones," she mutters to Art as they wait for the elevator. "Or that this is the third time this year he's been stitched and sobered up."

"Could be they've put him in Special Care hoping he won't go home," Art says. "Maybe it's already arranged. Dr. Montgomery should know; he signed the forms for the nursing home."

"Right," Colleen replies, stepping into the thankfully empty elevator. "And he said when Dad was safely tucked away, no alcohol would be allowed. I'll believe that when I see it."

"Second floor?" Art asks.

"Yes," Colleen says, pressing the button, "and I still didn't get a straight answer about guests. Do they frisk guests?"

Art smiles and takes her arm. Colleen bristles. He's not the one who's been dealing with her dad. His friend, Bill Milligan, for instance, is always carting beer to the house. ˌ

"Not something to worry about ahead of time," Art reminds her as the elevator comes to a stop. "We'll cross that bridge when we come to it." This is one of Art's favorite little sayings.

"Straight along the fence line"—one of Colleen's favorite comebacks.

At first, Colleen doesn't see the woman standing with her back to them in front of the elevator doors. "Excuse us," Art says, pushing past her.

"He's in 245," Colleen whispers. "Down at the end of the hall so he won't wake the dead." No answer, which probably means Art doesn't hear or doesn't want to talk about it. If she wasn't so freaked out, Colleen might try her "he said, she said" routine. She read about it in a women's magazine article one of her daughters gave her: *If your male partner doesn't or won't answer your questions, try answering your own question out loud. Multiple-choice answers lower your stress and give him possible replies.* As corny as it sounds, it seems to work, once in a while, anyway.

Even before Colleen sets foot in the room, she knows how her father will look. All cleaned up, his forehead stitched like a Halloween scar, an intravenous tube in his arm keeping him doped and quiet. Last time it was his chin, and the time before… Her mom would have been seventy-seven this year. She swallows and leans against the side of the metal bed. Art's arm slides around her waist. "Need a chair?" She nods.

Her dad is right out of it, sweating off alcohol, full of painkiller. When he comes to, which hopefully won't be until after they leave, he will go into a roaring tirade. He has always been a quiet drunk until he's drying out. Dr. Jekyll and Mr. Hyde, her mother used to whisper when he was out of earshot.

Years ago, in the old hospital, he screamed and cussed for three days in a row. She and her mom took turns sitting with him, sick with worry, sure he must be in some awful pain. Asking the nurses was useless, and they never could get hold of the doctor. Afterward, her father said they made it up. Goddamned women exaggerating, as usual.

A young nurse tiptoes in behind them and puts her hand on Colleen's ample shoulder. "Fresh coffee in the lounge, Mrs. Pinser," she whispers. "He should be almost himself by morning." Colleen nods. All the nurses know, most are kind, especially Maureen Searp, someone she's known since high school.

Art is already out the door. This always ticks Colleen off, as if he's in a hurry and doesn't care. The nurse pats Colleen's shoulder and nods her to leave; Colleen is careful not to scrape the chair legs as she pushes herself up.

Art hands her the coffee, such as it is. Not great, but then they usually drink instant at home anyway. Art steers her to the window, and she looks out at the parking lot where a few diehards light up for their break.

"You were way ahead of your time, never smoking," Colleen says, watching a young orderly cup his hands over his unlit cigarette while a second throws yet another dead match to the ground. Small talk. Something to keep her mind occupied.

Art isn't listening. Colleen knows he's upset and worried about her, about her dad. But he never shows it—just stands there, staring at his feet or over her shoulder. If they were at home, she would snap at him and then later feel terrible. "Art?"

"Did you say something?"

"It isn't important."

He looks hurt now and worried, like a kid bawled out by his teacher.

"My turn to say it's all right," she says, giving his arm a squeeze. "I don't think we need to stay."

BRITANNIA THEN

HUGH MOURAND made sure nothing tarnished the Britannia Hotel's first-class reputation. The first hint of trouble in the men's room, usually on a Friday or Saturday night when locals as well as hotel clientele crowded the place, stopped the minute he appeared in the room, his tall frame and penetrating eyes effectively demanding any troublemakers leave. One nod and they obliged. Knowing Mourand always worked late in his office, the barman, Jake, who also acted as bouncer, would signal with a buzzer under the counter.

Girls who cleaned were instructed to report any suspect evidence or activity in a given room. Mourand's power was cloaked in charm, and he spoke only once to unwanted guests who seemed to leave without a whimper. His control was civilized and absolute.

The waitresses were told in no uncertain terms that if they didn't do exactly as instructed, in both the dining room and kitchen, they would get their walking papers. "Lots more where you girls came from" was one of Mourand's favorite quips.

Hannah, knowing everything depended on this job working out, memorized every task and how to do it. She was efficient at school and at home. She could do this. Her nervousness? She was always able to control that, to appear somewhat distant but always polite. It worked with teachers and the few people she knew in

town; it would work for this how-did-she-ever-luck-into-it summer
job.

It was on her first day that Astrid told Hannah about the trek to
the employee's washroom and how it was set up to keep trips short
and sweet. "Not likely you'll dillydally once you're down there," she
said. "Not with spiders and rats and banging pipes."

"No rats," Colleen whispered to Hannah afterward. "It's her
idea of a joke."

Colleen couldn't say she liked the basement of the Britannia. It
was old, that's all. Hannah followed her through the empty dining
room, out into the foyer, and past the front desk. The back hall was
paneled wood, darkened with age and poorly lit. At the far end,
past Daisy Mourand's office, was the door leading to the basement.

"But what if someone is already down there?" Hannah asked.
"Like Charlie or Mr. Mourand or, even worse, hotshot Larry?"

"If this top door is open, someone is down there," Colleen said.
"It's no big deal." She could see Hannah was nervous, picking her
way down the worn steps, hanging on to the not-so-smooth railing.

"What if the light's not on?" Hannah continued, staring at
the light bulb hanging in front of them at the bottom of the stairs.
Dusty cobwebs dangled between its twisted cord and the overhang-
ing beams.

"It's always on," Colleen said matter-of-factly. "We keep our
uniforms down here 'cause it's the only place to change."

At the bottom of the stairs, the same fancy paneling continued,
out of place somehow with the rough cement floor. "Neat, eh,"
Colleen said, running her hand along its tongue-and-groove surface.
"Pretty fancy for a basement."

"The place reminds me of Edgar Allan Poe," Hannah whispered.

Colleen paid no attention to this and pulled up on the door
latch into the bathroom. "You have to lift up like this when you
pull," she said, "so the door bottom doesn't scrape when it opens."

She pulled on the door, the racket echoing down the long, dark hall. "See, it's not too bad." Colleen pulled the beaded chain on the hanging bulb. "Hooks for our uniforms, sink, toilet, paper towels, lid on the garbage, and extra you-know-whats in the paper bag on the shelf for that time of month."

Hannah nodded. She had never been down in an old basement like this. It smelled moldy and seemed to go on forever into darkness. It was not a place she would choose to go.

Colleen knew Hannah did go down there to change in and out of her uniform every morning and evening and every afternoon, so she could hole up at the library and read—dullsville to Colleen. She could have razzed Hannah about it; her sister would have razzed Colleen if she was such a square, but Hannah was different, shy about a lot of things, and she was Colleen's best friend that summer. The whole thing was better left alone.

Later that week, Colleen filled Hannah in on all ongoing hotel gossip, including the possibly dangerous Larry. "Steer clear of him," she said. "He's sixteen, arrogant, and probably thinks we're fair game." When Hannah looked puzzled, Colleen grabbed her arm and whispered, "Someone as well endowed as you needs to be careful." Hannah nodded and tugged at the front of her uniform. "Look superior," Colleen went on, "and keep your tips in a safe place." She ended by saying Hugh Mourand usually checked the dining room either early in the morning or near closing. "When either of them comes poking around," Colleen said firmly, "just leave. If there's someone in the kitchen, go there. If not, clean the panes on the foyer doors."

HANNAH III

HANNAH MANAGES to make it to Franklin again on Sunday morning, a good time, as traffic is lighter than usual. She spends the morning sorting and arrives at the hospital early afternoon to visit her mother. As soon as the hospital elevator doors open, she hears screaming, long, drawn out male screams punctuated with threats and curses. It terrifies her so, she almost retreats into the elevator. Dante. The madhouse scene from *Amadeus*. She breathes deliberately in and out, walks gingerly along the hall toward the nurse's station.

The same nurse who whisked her into her mother's room less than a week ago sticks her head out from a room at the end of the hall. When she sees Hannah, she rushes toward her, smiling plastic reassurances. "Not to worry, not to worry." She steers Hannah into her mother's room, shuts the door, and smiles again. "I'm sure your mother would love to hear that fancy music. She asked about it this morning." Another plastic smile and she's gone.

Hannah takes the portable cassette player out of her bag and plugs it in. "Chopin," she says to the nurse who is gone. "The fancy music is Chopin." Even *Fantaisie Impromptu* can't block out the screams, and her mother is still sound asleep.

The medical profession hasn't really changed that much over the years; the equipment and techniques have improved but not the communication. What on earth is going on in that room? Someone in mortal pain—fallen out of bed, broken hip, broken back?

Hannah doesn't deal well with screaming, never has. Her mother never, ever screamed, and only one teacher in high school did. Mr. Barton, who taught grade nine math in an overflow building down the street from the high school, held there when the first addition was being built. Even then, in the corporal-punishment fifties, Barton's behavior would never have been tolerated in the main school building. Mr. Barton threw chalk at guys who clowned around. The day he picked up and shook little Jerry MacIntyre, desk and all, screaming death threats and suspension, Hannah, two seats behind him, fainted.

Screaming, after it reaches a certain pitch, becomes gender neutral, Hannah thinks. Her mother has not fluttered even an eyelash, and Hannah sits down to wait. To wake or not to wake? If she wakes on her own, her mother is more likely to be coherent, so the nurse has told her. That the screaming hasn't already roused her amazes Hannah.

"Your mother has developed a degree of dementia," the doctor told her during an all-too-brief telephone consultation the day before. "Nothing serious, but it does affect her short-term memory." This doctor, a total stranger to Hannah, sounded patronizing, with "being an ignorant woman you could never understand the complexities of all this" overtones in his voice. Hannah, brilliant in defending her dissertation and eloquent during staff meetings, was rendered almost monosyllabic; and only after she hung up did she think of all the pertinent questions she intended to ask. Now she wonders if dementia and deafness are connected.

The screaming stops momentarily, allowing the music to wash over her. Her mother moves slightly, her mouth twitching as if in a dream. This frail, stunted little body was once so full of fire and resolve, so determined to steer her daughter down the right path, make sure she was accepted into the right university. Would another university have made any difference to Hannah's life, to her one and only fatal sexual indiscretion?

Her labor was a draconian nightmare. Professor Anthony, bless his academic male heart, sent and paid for a taxi to take her to the hospital, not willing to actually risk accompanying her there himself. They discussed and decided this before the fact, at his cottage, during an earlier weekend in front of a blazing fire.

"Have a bag packed," he advised her; and she refrained from saying, of course you would know. "Time your labor pains" he went on, as if she was a child, for God's sake. Her thoughts at the time as she sat bulging and uncomfortable; vulnerable and not admitting to being terrified. Now she thinks how she was such a child, certainly to him, twenty years her senior. She stopped being disgusted with herself years ago. It accomplished nothing, and she has a good life now.

The screaming resumes, putting her right back in the labor room, she and three others: one an Italian woman who shrieked Mama Mia and clapped with every contraction. Hannah, taught from childhood to suffer in silence, to keep a stiff upper lip, endured excruciating five-minute contractions for almost twenty hours, staring mutely at the ceiling, eventually wishing she would die. Four sets of laboring women and three sets of nurses came and went; one more-abrupt day nurse threatened to make her get up and walk and admonished her for still being there. During the third shift, the floor doctor, a specialist who happened by, and three interns gave her vaginal examinations in fairly rapid succession. She was hanging on to the metal sides of the bed frame by then, her head pressed into the sheet, tears running over the bridge of her nose.

Behind her but not out of earshot, the three of them carried on a clipped conversation.

"It's an elbow."

"Too small."

"A toe?"

"Doesn't feel right."

"Who's her OB?"

"Morgan, but he's away."

For the last half hour, Hannah tried willing herself to faint. She fainted from fear several times, unjustified fear she was told later. Apparently she did not faint from pain. They continued talking as another contraction twisted inside her. Starting dull and in the lower back, it spread rapidly like a liquid fan, sharp and fast around her pelvis, wrenching her gut until every nerve in her body was caught in its vortex, until she screamed silently and endured by focusing somewhere at the back of her sweat-soaked head, anywhere but where she was.

Someone sat down beside her, put a hand gently over hers. "We're sending you for an x-ray." A nurse. "We think you may have a problem." Hannah burst into tears.

After waiting a half hour in the hall during visiting hours, and then enduring a second unpleasant shaving prep followed by a not-too-gentle x-ray, they finally knocked her out for a Cesarean. The rest was history.

Her mother makes a little snorting noise that abruptly changes Hannah's thought gears. The screaming has stopped; the Chopin nocturne nears its finale. Hannah reaches out to take her mother's hand, wondering how she endured her labor. No husband, no family. Like mother, like daughter. Her mother never mentioned her labor or that she was in Winnipeg when she gave birth—Winnipeg in Arctic-cold January. When she was small, Hannah always thought she was born in Franklin, took it for granted. She remembers asking one Christmas after a card arrived—love from Aunt Harriet, Uncle Clarence, Carol, and Brian. She must have been old enough to read. She asked if they could visit her aunt and uncle sometime. Her mother only pursed her lips, said Winnipeg was much too far away, that her sister's family had their own lives. She lit another cigarette.

When she was in grade eight and finally allowed to be at home without a sitter, Hannah found her birth certificate, folded up and yellowed in a satin-covered, heart-shaped chocolate box, stuck in the bottom of a large wicker basket full of un-ironed clothing. She was looking for a particular skirt and became enthralled finding things she hadn't worn in years—a dress from grade one or two, a bonnet and pinafore, baby-sized. She found it in the bottom of the basket, wrapped in pages from a 1940 *Winnipeg Free Press*, as if never unpacked. Her mother wasn't due home until after eight that evening. Hannah still remembers checking first the clock and then, to double check, the empty roadway in front of her house. Such boldness, such prying without asking, would have dire consequences. When she carefully unfolded the fragile paper, she found in the appropriate blanks: *Hannah Ester Norcroft, 8 pounds, 2 ounces, born at 11:15 a.m., January 11, 1940, Misericordia Hospital, Winnipeg, Manitoba.* Her hands shook as she carefully folded first the certificate and then, once it was safely inside the box, the old newspaper. Winnipeg. She found an atlas in the living room and located the city.

After that, Hannah tried a few times to ask her mother more about where she was born. Her mother was a master of verbal diversion, anger or tears being her two diversionary tactics. "I purposely don't want to remember," she would say, lighting another cigarette. "It has nothing to do with our life now." Or worse, her mother would burst into tears and disappear into the bedroom, locking it from the inside. Hannah retreated, too, to her own room or outside, and later when her mother reappeared, it was as if nothing had happened, as if those words and minutes had been permanently edited out. After a few attempts, Hannah promised herself never to ask again.

She still has relatives in Winnipeg, she supposes, her mother's younger sister, Aunt Harriet, and her husband, Uncle Clarence—if they are still there—and their children, her cousins, a girl and boy. They would be grown by now.

"So nice of you to visit," her mother warbles, staring up at her now. Hannah is sure her mother doesn't have the slightest notion who Hannah is.

"It's Hannah, Mother."

"Hannah, it's so good to see you."

Social etiquette, like a fine-meshed sieve letting everything else sift through, is still there, giving shape and logic to conversation.

Two nurses bustle in. "Time to rise and shine, Edith. Get you cleaned up for the day." Hannah watches her mother, sure she will sneer or grimace or, at the very least, give them her highly pained look. Instead, she's all puppy, nodding, reaching out to them, eyes momentarily twinkling.

"Sorry to interrupt," one says. "We're a bit behind this morning." Hannah sees Maureen Downey on the nurse's small black-plastic nametag, She remembers a Maureen, Maureen Searp, who came on the bus from Heron Landing or Billings, one of those places up on Spider Lake, a country kid, brilliant in math, terrible in English. She and Hannah helped each other, noon hours in the library.

Hannah watches her mother's rag-doll frame propelled between the two nurses into the washroom. Maureen—if it is Maureen—has put on weight, is slumped into herself, most likely from too many years of hauling heavy bodies in and out of bed. Her almost-gray hair is short, not stylish but sensible considering her profession. The other nurse is younger, thin blondish hair pulled back with a red elastic. More likely a nurse's aide, but impossible to tell these days with no regulation uniforms.

"In you go, Edith dear. We'll have you fixed up in no time." The bathroom door closes.

Could that really be Maureen Searp? Her voice sounds matronly, a confidant on the rounds, an I-could-do-this-in-my-sleep sort of voice. If it is Maureen, surely she would have said something to Hannah; but after almost forty years—maybe not.

That morning, Hannah found a school picture hidden inside the front cover of a July 1958 magazine. She opened the cover and there it was, her grade twelve picture from that year. She had trouble even finding herself—one of the taller girls, third row up with the boys who, forced into such proximity, were either snickering or looking excruciated, waiting to quickly extricate themselves from her proximity. Hardly any of her showed, just a white Peter Pan collared blouse, the ends of her straight hair crimped into a haphazard pageboy, a forced smile.

Next weekend she'll look for Maureen. She never would have made it through algebra without her. The country kids were a breed apart, partly because most of the town kids, permeated from birth with their own inherent lineage and self-worth, looked down their noses at them. Hannah didn't realize this at the time, of course, knew only that her unfailing ability to punctuate and draw the right conclusions gave her high marks and tacit acceptance into this tight town enclave—in spite of the fact that she worked one summer at the Britannia Hotel, in spite of the fact that she had no father. Killed in the war is what she told everyone, complying with her mother's wishes. "Don't you ever tell anyone," her mother said, more often than necessary. "Don't you dare say a word."

Hannah watches the two nurses maneuver her mother over to sit her on the bed. "Since you're here," Maureen says almost conspiratorially, "we thought we'd try her in the wheelchair."

Hannah wonders, momentarily, if Maureen assumes they know each other and is simply starting up where algebra left off. "No breeding," she hears her mother say. "No breeding and too familiar." After one of the few school affairs Hannah managed to drag her mother to, a fundraiser of some sort, Maureen rushed up with her mother, a toad-shaped woman smelling of woodstove smoke. The conversation was stilted, especially that of Hannah's mother who responded to the "glad to meet youse" with a less than enthusiastic air. Hannah liked Maureen and wanted her mother to, at least, be civil to her friend's family. Hannah mentioned this to her mother on the way home, tried to suggest another way of looking at it, something slightly less caustic. Her mother would have none of it.

"I'm not raising you to hobnob with that kind of riffraff," her mother quipped.

"But she's nice and she helps me with math."

"That's fine and you'll just leave it there."

Hannah instinctively pulled further back into herself—an ongoing survival tactic—more reserve, more self-control; another reason, of course, why she fit so easily into the town kids enclave.

"I'll take her for a stroll down the avenue," Hannah says, smiling at Maureen.

"Anywhere in this wing," Maureen replies, nervously tucking a blanket over Hannah's mother's knees. She hurries out almost abruptly as if her friendly quota has been used up or perhaps, more likely, because she didn't understand the comment. Amazing how chance meetings, planned meetings, and human encounters in general promote chat, even conversation, but rarely communication. Maybe next time, Maureen—if it is Maureen.

The wheelchair has a wonky wheel that squeaks relentlessly. This is their second loop down the hall through the lounge and back. Her mother has settled into herself, neck melted onto her shoulders, head almost upright, peering past the freshly painted walls, the bustle, silent now except for her nicotine-stained fingers that tap-tap on the metal arms of the wheelchair.

Hannah has stopped at the far end of the hall so her mother can look out the window. The parking lot below is filled with shiny up-to-date and not-so-up-to-date cars and sport utility vehicles; Hannah is amazed how many. She thinks of mentioning this to her mother, how statistics say more and more people are opting for the safety and comfort of a sport utility, not just families but retired people, single people like herself. What would this mean to her mother? If Hannah had a utility vehicle, perhaps she could take her mother out. Out from where? Not from here, but from that as yet nameless location—the dreaded nursing home, long-term care facility. If she stands on the far right side of the window and peers south, Hannah just catches the back of Sunset Lodge—formerly the Poor House, the House of Refuge and Respite, where the old and unwanted sat out their final days in small, institutionalized rooms with metal-frame beds and stiff-backed chairs. The doctor assured her the Lodge had been modernized, streamlined—the ideal place for her mother in spite of the waiting list. He made the statement as if it were a directive, as if Hannah would automatically know how to access admission procedures, as if she should have already done it.

Once back in the room, Hannah turns on the Chopin a second time. Years ago she had caught her mother more than once waltzing to it, a bit sherried up late on a Saturday night, holding a long silky scarf at arm's length.

Hannah sits now on the hospital bed, holding her mother's wrinkled hands, swaying them gently back and forth to the music.

"I'm always chasing rainbows," her mother cuts in, a little off key and a few beats behind. "Watching clouds drifting by," Hannah carries on for her, checking first that the door is shut.

"My dreams are just like all my schemes," Hannah's mother joins in. "Ending in the sky." They both stop then, Hannah because no more words will come, only memories and regrets, and her mother because she appears to have focused and is staring clear eyed at Hannah.

"Those damn rainbows," she says, faintly squeezing Hannah's

hand. "They were always disappearing."

Hannah puts her hands tentatively one on either side of her mother's thin cheeks, leans forward and kisses her forehead. "How about a drink," she says, picking up a glass of juice. "A celebration after our first excursion."

As her mother noisily slurps a few drops of juice, Hannah hums a bit of Chopin—an anxiety suppressant. What she has to do now is say good-bye and leave. Almost everything else is negotiable: whether the Lodge will soon have an available opening, what she will do with the house, the furniture, her past. She doesn't like holding her mother's life in the palm of her hand, of being the one left to make these decisions. She feels herself wallowing in the unfairness of it all. No, she says silently as she wipes dribbles from her mother's chin. No wallowing. She pats her mother's back and kisses her on the cheek. "I'll be back next week and don't worry, the house is safe. I locked it up tight."

She plans a fast getaway—down the elevator, out to the car, onto the expressway.

"Hannah?"

Hannah is at the door.

She pivots, leaning on the doorframe. "Yes, Mother?"

"You're sure everything is all right?"

"Yes, Mother."

"And you'll be back?"

"Yes, Mother."

"Don't worry about the rainbows."

Hannah throws her a kiss and bolts for the elevator.

Hannah grabs the weekend *Globe* from the front step of her Toronto house and unlocks the door. Esmeralda jumps from the back of the couch, purring and rubbing her silky side across Hannah's calf. Hannah dumps the paper on the couch, scoops up the creature.

"Sweet cat," she says, rubbing her face into the feline's thick, ginger-colored coat. "Dear sweet friend. I'll get you some food and then I'm off for a quick run."

She pulls on leggings and a sweatshirt; breathes in the sanity and order of being alone, independent; grabs her watch, water bottle, shoes and goes out into the last of the sun on the back deck to lace them up.

"Home safely then, are you?" Roger is beside the back fence, emptying a bucket into the composter.

"Oh hi, Roger, I just got in. How are Annie and the baby?"

"Wonderful. And you? How is your mom?"

Hannah doesn't want to talk about it really, but Roger is such a dear man. A new-age husband and father, sharing in everything, concerned about everyone. "She's a little better than I expected but the house is a mess." Hannah does a few stretches.

"Bet you want to get running," Roger says, back on his own deck. "We'll catch you later."

"Thanks for asking," Hannah calls as he disappears inside.

If she runs long enough and far enough, everything falls away. Those good old endorphins kick in, a self-generated, nontoxic high, better than alcohol and, in many instances, better than sex. Fewer complications, no obligations except to herself.

She runs down to the end of her street and along the periphery of the park. She used to run through it but not any more, not even here in this relatively safe neighborhood north of Eglinton, with a girl's private school abutting her backyard—too many newspaper horror stories, to say nothing of her mother's dire warnings still there, always hovering. Forty years ago, it would have been safe. Her mother was ahead of her time, or maybe nothing had fundamentally changed. Back then, you expected men to be predatory, unpredictable sexual brutes or sexual gentlemen. It made no difference. Every girl knew what they were after. *The Music Man*. Imagine that popping in, Hannah thinks. It was Colleen Miller who talked her into auditioning for the chorus of *The Music Man*. Was it eleventh grade? Colleen who was happy just to pass; Hannah going on five hours sleep for the two weeks prior to the show, as well as its six-day duration. It was exciting, though, being in a real production, prima donnas, set disasters and all. Exciting but not totally consuming, not like it was for Colleen. Colleen's endorphins kicked in when she was on stage, when she was no longer herself. Next week, she would drive down past Colleen's parents house, see if it was still there.

Hannah rounds the corner past the playground where some kids, too big for the swings, are horsing around, cigarette smoke wafting from their scarcely weaned faces. Not easy being a parent these days. She watches Annie and Roger in wonder—young, both working, Annie on maternity leave for six months—their enthusiasm and plans, with investments already in place for little Jessie.

When she steps out of the shower, Hannah already smells the lasagna. She pulls on an old tracksuit, then remembers the stuff from her mother's, still in the car trunk—one of the save-because-it-might-be-useful piles. Leave it, she says to herself. Get it tomorrow after school. She knows she won't, knows it will likely still be there Friday morning when she's leaving for school. She scrawls a note to herself—take stuff from trunk—and clips it to the fridge door, along with five or six others, now obsolete.

Two messages on her machine: Julia, saying call as soon as you get in. She can talk to Julia tomorrow at school. Russ, saying call as soon as you get in. She doesn't have energy for Russ this evening, not even Russ on the phone. One of the nice things about getting older, sexual energy can be compartmentalized, saved up, and savored instead of squandered relentlessly at any given opportunity. Russ is terribly intense, a novelist between books. He works part-time at her favorite bookstore down the street. He said he knew she was a poet the minute she walked in the door. Great line. He's nice to have around, but not all the time. She can't, for instance, see herself taking him to a school function—well, maybe her retirement party next year, if it lasts that long. He is forty-one but looks younger, a boyish thirty-five perhaps. They have long, intense discussions about poetry, he calling even her defense of Ondaatje or Atwood old-fashioned, she out-arguing him by sheer weight of years, of accumulated information. Even better sex—usually in the dark or semi-dark, as she is increasingly uneasy about perceived wrinkles on her highly trim, regularly exercised body. She expects to be eventually usurped; the potential for eligible competition multiplies with each passing season. She recolors her hair monthly, takes her hormones, and enjoys the feast.

There's a clip on the news about Winnipeg, a heavy November snowstorm, people leaning into the wind, traffic jams and fender benders. She should look up Harriet and Bill's address—her mother's younger sister, Harriet Taigg, from Winnipeg. The only time to go there would be in summer. How many to-do-on-Friday things did she have to remember now? She should make a list, but she hates lists. She is forced to make them at school: lists for directives, lists for secretaries, lists for curricula. Not at home; here she lives in a list-free environment.

COLLEEN III

COLLEEN WAITS until after supper on Monday to visit her dad, hoping he'll be dried out, determined that if he isn't, she'll simply get back in the elevator and leave. Art has made her promise. He's finishing overdue sales taxes from the store, one of those "ten days or we'll take action" letters that will have him working until after midnight. The twins are cramming for some test, already complaining about grade twelve and too much work. Colleen smiles, remembering those days. She can't say much; all she thought about then was the next audition and the next show. Having kids when you're thirty-six has its advantages though; she's more laid back, taking things as they come. The three older ones have fits about her so-called lack of rules now, especially the two with kids of their own. Ongoing choruses of "when we were that age you never let us" bounce off the twins who say nothing and still plead hard done by with any rules she sets.

The hospital is quiet tonight, no ambulance at Emerg, the halls empty. Colleen stops outside the elevator, tunes in, ready to bolt. There are muffled voices from the nursing station, TV on in someone's room, snoring from opposite ends of the hall. She tiptoes along, ready at any moment to take off back to safety.

"Colleen?"

It's Maureen. Hopefully she can fill Colleen in, give her a better idea of what's going on. "How is he?"

"A lot quieter." Maureen always has called a stone a stone.

"Should I wake him?"

"I wouldn't."

"Has he asked for us?"

"For Madge."

"I think I'll just take a peek." Maureen doesn't have a clue. Other people's lives wash right over her—it's probably how she's managed to put up with nursing all these years. A grown son taking over the farm, a daughter teaching full-time, never a money worry in her life. It's probably not that simple, but right now, it suits Colleen.

Her dad looks younger when he's asleep, less wasted. The sleeping monster who doesn't know he is. Intravenous has given him some color in his cheeks, filling out the increasing number of lines in his neck, although the spidery veins she is now used to seem to stick out more down the sides of his nose, right past his jaw bones. She's noticed those same spidery lines on other drinking buddies, even neat-as-a-pin Mr. Milligan.

She has no idea how they will actually get her dad inside the nursing home and, for a moment, wishes he had broken something, an arm maybe, some definite reason why he couldn't look after himself. She sits down at the foot of the bed, determined to stay only long enough to be able to tell him tomorrow that she was there, that she stayed for awhile.

The wind is up, smacking leaves against the darkened glass. Colleen stares at the bed and, for a moment, sees her mom, not her dad, tubed and sleeping. She remembers going all numb when the cops had called from the hospital. "It looks bad. You'd better hurry." Art, of course, was working late at the store, the three kids at summer camp. Scrambling for keys in the hall sideboard drawer, she made a run for the car. How many times did she pester her mom to call when she was working, not to ride that rusted old bike with no gears when it was getting dark? Funny, she remembers thinking, how you can still drive when you're half out of your mind with worry. Almost like a robot with the car shooting dead straight and your body ignoring everything else. Thank God the Franklin Hospital was still on the east side of town then.

It was almost too late by the time she arrived. Through the Emergency doors, puffing from fear and the thirty extra pounds she lugged around. The nurse, all professional and whispery, led her past the Do Not Enter doorway into that yellowed old hall, everything smelling like medicine and cleaning solvent. As soon as the nurse slipped an arm around her plump shoulder, Colleen knew she was in for it. She immediately thought of how she'd always wanted to take her mom to one of those fancy Toronto musicals, get her piano tuned, have a good old heart-to-heart with her this summer. The light was too bright in the hospital room, bright and almost cruel. Her mom lay tubed and bandaged in the bed, one of those life-support machines showing her heartbeat, blip-blipping off and on, off and on, and then, after hardly any time at all, before she could even ask questions, off. She'd been there less than an hour—too late to call Art. Too late.

She was a brick at the funeral and managed, after a lot of sweat, to write a few lines to read, standing up at the front of the funeral parlor and getting through it without crying. "You're still an actress," Art had whispered afterward, giving her arm a squeeze. It helped that her dad was actually sober, mind you, one of the few times in the last twenty years.

Twenty years. Where have they gone? It still amazes her that her dad's eighty-one-year-old frame ticks on in spite of everything. She lugs a casserole over once a week but has given up crabbing at him when she finds half of it moldy on the counter, usually under a stack of dirty dishes. Once in a while, Bill Milligan orders in fish and chips or pizza—using whose money she doesn't ask—the pizza boxes and greasy newspapers there or not there, depending on whether Heda has been in to clean. Bill Milligan, with his trimmed moustache and military manners, only makes things worse, loaning her dad money until his old age pension arrives, bringing beer to the house. "Ah yes," Bill always says if she drops in when he is there. "Mrs. Pinser, the merchant's wife." The fact he is hanging-out with the merchant's wife's old man doesn't seem to bother him. It has a lot to do with the piano. Bill chords loudly and not too well. Enough to get them both singing though, often full out by two in the afternoon.

In the first year after her mom died, the power was shut off twice and the telephone once.

"You should march over there and tell him who's boss," Janet said. Thanksgiving weekend—she was home from college, the nineteen-year-old mind at its best.

"Not that easy," Art replied quietly. Colleen knew that Art had already offered to sort out house expenses with no luck in convincing Frank that he could: "I can damn well do it myself. What the hell are you talking about?"

"Well, he's going to freeze to death or set the house on fire if you don't do something," Janet added. Supertramp was on full blast while she copied chemistry notes.

Artie, the oldest, who might have sided with his mother, was already down in Costa Rica. Pam, sixteen and barely able to hear over the noise of the popcorn machine, just shrugged and went for butter.

Colleen, who already knew she was pregnant but had only told Art, slumped down on the couch beside him. "Why don't you all work out a step-by-step plan, maybe a written script for me to memorize?" She pressed her face into Art's shoulder.

Janet turned the volume down. "Isn't there some agency that could help, someone you could phone?"

"Oh, let's tell everyone," Pam snapped, dumping the popcorn

into a bowl. "Advertise on the radio that we have a falling apart, alcoholic grandpa." She flounced into the TV room and slammed the door.

"Colleen?" It's Maureen's voice. Colleen half opens her eyes, sees her dad asleep in the hospital bed. "Visiting hours are over."

Maureen is back behind the nursing station when Colleen appears, feeling out of it and more than a little embarrassed. She must have dozed off. She wants to ask Maureen what the doctor really said. Did he say anything about the nursing home? How long can her dad stay here?

"Guess who's in 232?"

"What?"

"Edith Norcroft. Hannah's mother."

Fast gear change. "Hannah Norcroft? Are you sure? I haven't seen her in years." Now she can't remember what she was going to ask Maureen.

"She was here. Hannah Norcroft. This afternoon. Looks like a model. Where's she been all these years? Finally come back to do something about her mother."

"Hannah Norcroft's mother?"

"TIAs. Dementia."

Colleen nods. "I have to go. Art gets all worried. Say hello to Hannah for me if you see her again."

Cold rain pelts down on her, almost sleet, Colleen thinks as she starts the engine. "Damn damp," she says aloud, shivering inside her coat. The parking lot glistens and looks almost shiny enough to skate on. A million years ago when they were young, she and Hannah went skating all the time, almost every Friday night. Hannah Norcroft. Looks like a model. Not married or still going by her maiden name? A couple of her daughter's friends do. Not me, she thinks. No dusty old Miller for me.

Without knowing why, she turns left on Gerald and then says

what the heck and turns down past the skating rink. It's not on her route anymore, not since Artie was in hockey. The twins are all basketball and soccer, thank God, and wouldn't give hockey the time of day. Being a hockey mom at fifty wasn't something she wanted to deal with. Having to hang out at the rink was hard enough the first time around.

The place is deserted, a monster-movie pile of ice-snow melting in the rain. She slows down and pulls into the parking lot. Franklin Memorial Arena has been spruced up with two additions since the fifties.

She and Hannah went skating almost every Friday night from Thanksgiving to Easter, except for the time the student council organized an end-of-school bash there, the week before Hannah started at the Britannia.

Staring at the shadowed building now, Colleen remembers leaning into each step that June night, her blades cutting in with all the others, ice air cold on her face. The old PA crackling out Elvis: "Down at the e-end of Lonely Stre-et… Heartbreak Hotel…" Duck cuts, strides, angora sweaters—wonderful, nostalgic stuff, except, even after all these years, the kicker is there, the reason she never skated again.

Colleen's adult kids, especially Pam who went to Teacher's College and took psychology, bug her off and on about going into some kind of therapy, dealing with the past traumas, as Pam puts it—especially if she's been down in the dumps when one of them calls. "There is help out there you know, Mom," they say. As if it was something you could ask for at a drugstore counter.

"May I help?"

"Well, yes. I'm looking for something to get rid of black holes."

"I'm not sure…"

"I've tried babies and baking, even St. John's wort, but it hasn't helped. Not in the long run."

Colleen stares again at the darkened walls. Why is it that memories never go away? Always waiting to jump out at you, take you by surprise. If Maureen hadn't mentioned Hannah, she wouldn't have driven past the rink, wouldn't have stopped here. Hannah, who tried to teach me how to smoke, Colleen thinks, smiling. Right there, beside that wall.

Did you stop smoking, Hannah? Maybe she hasn't. Maybe she's switched to cigars. Pam and Janet tell her it's fashionable these days. Hannah went to Queen's, no, the University of Toronto. Colleen always pretended she didn't care about university. Pfft. What did it matter? She was going to be an actress. She only went to Teacher's College to stop her mom from having a freak out: "An actress? You'll never make a living doing that." Being a teacher would be something steady to fall back on. The College was up in Marborough, and she boarded with a stiff old English couple who posted rules in the front hall. The classes were boring and hard with the stupidest routines, as if they were all still in second grade. It was an endurance test, and Colleen lived only for Art's Sunday visits. Everything seemed out of control, about to fall apart, and then Art would stride in, red hair slicked down, and all the pieces fell into place, his rough shirt and musky smell changing the scene, the set, the whole play. She told herself that going out with him was just a lark. An older man—good experience for her acting career. And marriage? She told everyone, all through high school, that she would never get married.

Never say never. Colleen wonders who said that. Why is it that, so many times in life, we do exactly what we say we won't do, what we hate. Sometimes she is sure everything is mixed up together, especially love and hate. She rants at Art about this, that he loves her only to hang on to her, that if he really loved her he would let her go, tell her to go. It's a useless argument, especially since Art won't argue one way or the other. He bottles up when she rants—waits until she has worn herself out, then quietly says he loves her. And the damn thing always works.

Tires squeal on the next block. Colleen turns on the car. She wheels around in the empty parking lot and hits it for home. She went through this poor-me stuff after her mom died—thought she'd gotten it out of her system.

Art is still at the computer. Colleen sticks her head in the door. "Coming to bed soon?"

"How was he?"

"Asleep."

"Another fifteen minutes and I should have it licked."

Colleen throws him a kiss, knowing she can easily double or triple the time. Downstairs the dogs are already curled nose to tail in the TV room. They watch her through almost closed eyelids as she turns on the kettle. "It's all right," she says smiling. "I won't make you go outside again."

Two hours later, Sleepy Time tea and deep breathing haven't helped. Colleen blames the full moon. Art has finally fallen into bed, dead asleep while she breathes in and out no more than twice. She slips out of bed and tiptoes into Artie's old room. Through the window she watches long cloud pieces slice across the moon, cutting its face in half, then in quarters.

Was there a moon that June night, Hannah? The ice was fast, everyone whirling round and round, past the clock, the scoreboard. In those days, Colleen couldn't wait to get out of the house on Friday night, out and away from the war zone. That Friday her dad came home half cut, "Laid off till hell freezes over," he announced with bravado. Madge went at him with her usual tirade, and he retreated to the basement and a stash of beer. While Colleen was upstairs getting ready, he locked himself in the bathroom. When she and her mom finally pried open the door, there was blood from hell to breakfast. The doctor who came to bandage his wrists called it an accident and said it would do her good to go skating, mix with her friends. So she did. But even now, after all these years, the thought of skating makes Colleen feel like throwing up.

Post traumatic stress syndrome. There's a mouthful. Finding out about adult children of alcoholics is up in the top three surprises of her life. That there's a name for it and there are other people in the same boat, that she waits for the next disaster in her life like people in war-torn countries wait for the next bomb. It seems too far-fetched. Her life isn't in danger, nothing blows up except inside her head, terror of her own making, not bodies and blood and all that awful stuff on TV news. If she had her life to live over, maybe she'd join one of those overseas organizations, get right out there on the frontlines, see and feel some real danger, real death.

Her dad is such a bully, even though he pretends not to be, almost seems unaware that he is. As long as she lived at home, he was kingpin in everything, morning till night. After they were first married, Colleen used to see how long she could go without talking to him. Not that he noticed. As far as he was concerned, she disappeared as soon as she wasn't heading into the arms of show biz. She kept track for a while, a calendar on the inside of the closet door. Six weeks was the best she ever managed. Over the years, she has tried, always long distance of course, to talk to her older sister Lillian about him. Lillian says things like, "I don't remember it being that bad" or, "you always did have such an imagination."

Before high school, Colleen remembers hiding at the top of the stairs when her dad's drinking buddies were over for a game of poker, listening to him go on about Madge in her younger days, the story bigger and better as empties piled up under the kitchen table. "She sure was a looker," her dad would say, "the day she came in to buy music paper at Boddington's late in the fall of 1935." He was assistant store manager during the week, saxophone player in Jerry Hilton's Swing Band on weekends. Saxophones were all the rage; Benny Goodman was hot stuff. Frank told his buddies how he nearly convinced a third-year music student's mother that a Conn saxophone would make her son famous just before he caught sight of Madge: her terrific smile, hair piled up in a glory on the top of her head. He lost the sale but married Madge three months later.

Colleen can't remember her dad looking anything but old. He was only forty-one in 1955, but getting wasted every weekend for the last twenty-five years has given him a hollow-eyed, sickly look. In high school, Colleen never invited friends over, sure that once they found out, she would be cut out of any group.

Art laughed when she told him this, when they were dating and pouring out secrets to each other. "Your dad's a charmer. Maybe he drinks a little too much. No one notices." Colleen noticed and still despairs, but she has stopped hoping for the impossible.

How many times was he laid off for boozing on the job? Too many. It was almost better after he stopped working. Of course that's when her mom started her one-after-the-other shitty jobs. She couldn't have kids in for lessons anymore, not with her dad there. And who was going to hire a piano teacher? Minimum wage, convenience store sweat-jobs—in there with the high school kids. At least because of her age, she usually got better shifts.

Colleen sits on Artie's bed and stares at the hall light reflecting off the varnished door frame. The Friday night that her dad locked himself in the bathroom, Colleen used a crow bar to pry open the door. The jamb has never been properly fixed—pushed together with plastic wood and painted over several times. Colleen can still run her fingers along the rough edge where the wood split apart. When her father goes into the Lodge, that door frame will be the first thing to go. She wants to smash it into a thousand pieces. Even after all these years.

Moonlight flickers on and off the far wall, momentarily lighting up Artie's bulletin board and his grade-twelve class picture. Colleen

stares at it and wonders if her class year books would still be somewhere at her dad's house. Evelyn and Hannah were her best friends
then, as much as anybody could be. All of them skating round and
round that night. Evelyn Vandeuzen, Dutch Reform Church. And
Moira Jackson, pretending she was Marilyn Monroe. Most of the
girls would have nothing to do with Moira. When they went on
about her being a brazen hussy, Colleen usually tried to change the
subject. She knew Moira's dad was worse than her own. She'd seen
bruises on Moira's legs and arms when they changed for Phys Ed.
Moira would try to stay in the shadows, tossing her silky blonde
hair back and forth as a distraction. Amazing how you can live in
a town all your life and lose track of so many people. Of course,
they may have moved away, skedaddled out of Franklin like Colleen
thought she was going to. A small twinge of regret niggles at her
and disappears.

What if she had left—found herself a life somewhere else? She
was so sure she would back then. Escape. Her sister did. Colleen
is the brick, that's what Lillian says in her annual Christmas card.
Colleen remembers reading that children of alcoholics either get
out for good or can't. They get stuck forever in the alcoholic nest.
No use blaming Art, although she does sometimes when she's into a
rant—goes on at him for keeping her here, forcing her to deal with
it all. She always was the one who dealt with it. Her mom would
wring her hands, play her piano, cry. In the end, Colleen was the
one who took charge.

Even in high school, she felt trapped, caught on a one-way
street with no exit; and when her dad was disgustingly drunk or
her mom had cried for two hours straight, she wished she could go
crazy. Curled up on the floor at the end of her bed, she thought of
it as a possible way out. Not as bad as killing yourself, or as selfish
as taking off like her other sister did. In high school, the choir sang
carols every Christmas at the old "mental place" on Carver Street,

out near the town limits. Colleen remembers how the place terrified Hannah, who fainted while they were waiting in line backstage, before they even sang. Colleen found it fascinating, drawn to the idea that these people were locked in here, safe from the outside world. It wasn't until she saw *One Flew Over the Cuckoo's Nest* that she changed her mind. Even as an adult she has thought about it, in dark moments. It wouldn't be as awful for the family as suicide. It would be something she couldn't do anything about, something to fall into so she wouldn't have to cope—with herself.

Colleen realizes she is standing in the cold bedroom in the moonlight like a middle-aged fool, tears running down her cheeks. Crying over what? Spilt milk, her mom would have said. No use crying over spilt milk.

When she slips back into bed, Art rolls over, his hand finding her ample breast. He snuggles against her, holding her tenderly, loving her even as he sleeps. She concentrates on his warmth and listens to his slower breathing, a steady puff on the back of her neck.

BRITANNIA THEN

EARLY IN JUNE, Larry started helping himself to small amounts from the till. Sure that part-time desk clerk Moira would be blamed and tired of bumming a cigarette here and there from his father's packs, he figured he was entitled to buy his own. Larry knew if he asked for a larger allowance his mother would have one of her tizzies, and that he, in the end, would be the loser. Luckily, a month later, his father remained tacitly silent about his son's pilfering. Of course, legally he wasn't allowed to buy cigarettes, but if he slipped in the back door of Sloan's Smoke Shop and Pool Hall, he knew Max, the owner, would sell him a pack.

He'd seen his dad open the till enough times on Saturdays, knew the key was on a hook under the counter. What he didn't realize was that at the end of each week, on Friday evenings before Moira left and after Daisy herded her son upstairs away from what she called the dubious Friday night crowd, Mourand always tallied up.

That Friday night after helping himself to five bucks, Larry was ensconced in front of their new Motorola TV watching *Dragnet* and waiting to sneak out for a quick smoke; Mourand sat, as usual, in his office, balancing the books.

"What the hell...Moira?" Mourand had the cash neatly stacked in denominations, a tally sheet beside him.

"Yes, Mr. Mourand?" Moira had just applied some more Chanel
No. 5 and waltzed over to his desk, leaning into her cleavage to
observe his calculations.

"Till's short five bucks. Again."

Moira opened her eyes slightly wider and moved behind
Mourand, brushing her breasts against the back of his suit jacket.

Mourand looked toward the door and, seeing it closed, pivoted
his chair and pulled her onto his lap. "Innocent, I assume."

"Pure as a baby lamb." She leaned into him and curled a piece
of his hair around her finger. "It's that naughty son of yours, and
you know it."

Mourand ran his finger across her cleavage. "Positive?"

"I've caught him, more than once, ducking out from under
the counter. He waits till I go to the can. I swear." She giggled and,
standing up, gave Mourand's arm a poke.

Mourand smiled and, pulling a bulging wallet from his pocket,
placed two crisp twos and a one on the respective piles.

"My lips are sealed," Moira said, throwing him a kiss as she left.
She was on her way somewhere; and for whatever reason, Hugh
Mourand seemed to provide potential opportunities. No one except
Colleen knew much about her; she kept to herself after hours and
emulated Marilyn Monroe on the job.

It's unlikely Mourand ever confronted his son, and Moira knew
enough to gossip discretely. Saturday morning she took Colleen
aside and warned her to watch out for Larry. "Keep your money
stashed in a safe place," she whispered. "The Personality Kid's been
taking cash from the till. Mourand didn't raise an eyebrow when
he found it missing. That kid gets away with murder. God knows
what the little SOB will try next."

Colleen nodded and thought, one more wretched thing to deal
with this summer. The other summer waitress had quit after one
week, and now, Colleen figured it might have had something to

do with Larry. He'd better not try anything with her. She needed every cent she earned.

HANNAH IV

IT'S 8:15 A.M. on Friday and Hannah is on hold with the Sunset Lodge in Franklin. The air is too dry in her cramped, book-dusty office. Her box was crammed with mail this morning: another educational directive, minicourses in stress management, a list of TGIF locations until Christmas, a bunch of other stuff. She tucks them all under *Elements of Style* and flips open her teacher's Daybook. It's old fashioned to call it that now but she doesn't really care. Her first class is at ten and she has a pile of test papers to mark. A Writer's Craft class at one with the grade twelves, such a joy, several with potential. After class, at three, a meeting to discuss remedial grammar courses for ninth grade—obviously scheduled before disaster struck. She'll be right in rush hour traffic by the time she leaves for Franklin. Had she gone over her week on Monday, she could have rescheduled. She writes *short meeting* under the entry.

"Mr. Preston? Yes, it's Hannah Norcroft speaking. I was wondering about the admissions form you mentioned last week. Where do I get it and when do I need to hand it in?"

"Ms. Norcroft, yes. There is a detailed form, and I will fax it to you. Hopefully, you can drop it off late this afternoon or tomorrow morning at the latest."

"It will have to be tomorrow morning, Mr. Preston. I'm in Toronto teaching and won't be in Franklin until this evening."

"Ah yes, Toronto. Your mother is a Franklin resident?"

"Yes, yes, she's lived there for most of her life." He doesn't remember talking to me, Hannah thinks.

"Oh, Ms. Norcroft." Hannah hears him shuffling through papers. "Of course. I would mention that our candidates must be able to walk into the Lodge in order to qualify, although walkers and canes are allowed, so it is somewhat a technical point."

This would have alarmed Hannah except that on Wednesday, when she phoned the hospital, someone cheerfully informed her they had her mother up walking between two nurses and expected her to manage with a walker soon.

"My mother's using a walker now," she says, trying to feel hopeful.

"Also, there is an interview."

"An interview? What kind of interview? My mother has had a series of TIAs and…"

"Not to worry, Ms. Norcroft. A technical point and we're flexible here at the Lodge."

"But there is a waiting list, is there not?" Hannah is trying not to feel confused. "Just because my mother manages the interview doesn't mean there's an opening."

"Exceptions can be made under extenuating circumstances," he says. "And we will discuss it when the time arrives."

All definitely indefinite, Hannah thinks after she hangs up.

The day flies by with its usual disasters. A girl faints halfway through a first period chemistry test, and the assistant principal, Don Peters, who knows Hannah has a spare period, requisitions her to sit with the girl in the sickroom. She hasn't had any breakfast, she says, and stayed up half the night studying. When she bursts into tears, Hannah tries to comfort her, remembering her own long-ago confusion and embarrassment at fainting and coming to on the classroom floor, everyone staring down at her.

Even though she marks right through her lunch period, Hannah doesn't get the test papers finished, which means finishing them over the weekend. Not that she minds. She's done it for years, but never in Franklin, never at her mother's. Hannah's life is highly compartmentalized, and she has spent years perfecting it.

Three teachers are late for the afternoon meeting so it drags on in spite of Hannah's good intentions. Several are openly skeptical of a solution, and everyone has a different approach as to how they should begin. It's almost five when Hannah finally throws her briefcase into the car's back seat.

The parkway is jammed because of an accident in the express lane. She can see ambulance and police lights flashing up ahead as soon as she eases into the right-hand lane. She tunes into the traffic station where a brassy, urgent-sounding announcer rattles off the latest clog ups and fender benders. "Ambulance on the scene at Lawrence and Kingsway in the northbound lane, traffic moving slowly; avoid this area if you can." Hannah tries JazzFM. Oscar Peterson—yes. All she needs now is a slow Scotch and Russ. The traffic stops and starts.

When she called Russ on Monday evening, he said he had finally made a breakthrough on the ending for his novel and couldn't see her for the next few weeks. He's so sweet and sincere about it, but she can't help thinking it may be the final curtain ready to fall. No use being unrealistic, and besides, until she gets her mother settled into the nursing home, her weekends are on hold. Russ was understanding about that, too, but his parents are in their early seventies, off on a six-month holiday, walking through England and Wales. The commonality factor is zero. The traffic finally starts to move at a steady pace.

It's almost seven by the time Hannah reaches the Franklin turn-off sign, a crisp clear evening with a plethora of stars. In the parking lot, she slumps down in her seat to stare up at them, trying to psych herself up to go inside. She hopes Maureen isn't on. They haven't really spoken, anyway, and Hannah is in no mood for reacquainting.

As she heads out of the car into the bone-cold November evening, it always fascinates her how the unfamiliar so effortlessly becomes familiar. In the doors, up the elevator, Clarence Ridley pointing the way. No one is at the nursing station and she slips into her mother's room unobserved.

Other than her hair, which has been washed but not set— *something I would never do in my right mind,* she hears her mother saying this—Edith Norcroft asleep looks much more like herself. Hannah makes a mental note to bring a dressing gown and slippers and wonders if they've been walking her mother down the hall barefoot. She should have thought of this last Sunday when she visited. She feels suddenly in over her head with no one to help. What must the nursing staff think of her? What will they think? Her mother's voice, and here she is dishing it back to herself. She doesn't remember seeing another dressing gown and slippers at the house, and she has forgotten to ask about those that her mother arrived in.

Hannah sits down beside the bed. Her mother is lying on her back, one wrinkled arm across her stomach, the other flung carelessly out to the side, palm up, almost as if she is dancing in her sleep. Hannah puts her hand over her mother's wrist, feels the steady pump, pump of blood through her veins.

A nurse she hasn't seen before comes to the door, nods, and leaves. At least they'll know I was here, Hannah thinks. She stays another few minutes, then feeling suddenly exhausted and starving, makes a fast exit to the parking lot.

Garland Street has become a full-fledged fast food strip, one of those anywhere streets found in every small town. Hannah stops to grab a hamburger and a small chips, an indulgence she allows herself once in a while. The place is full of kids and the staff looks too young to be there, but they're polite and the food quality is acceptable.

The house smells even staler than she remembers, probably because she's tired. Her sense of smell and hearing accelerate in relation to her degree of exhaustion. She turns up the heat, dumps her briefcase and suitcase on the floor, and falls into a chair to attack her feast. On the counter opposite, stacked upright against the fridge, are a couple of outdated cookbooks, some magazines, and a *Reader's Digest Condensed Book*. Growing up, Hannah was rarely allowed to cook, and when she did, she usually made a mess of it. Her mother always hovered, checking this, correcting that. Hannah feels her shoulder muscles tense just remembering.

She notices her mother's red address book tucked in between two cookbooks. A razor-edge memory jolts through her: Uncle Clarence and Aunt Harriet.

Her mother was always so secretive when Hannah was growing up. So many things were off-limits: most of her mother's bedroom, especially anything on or in the dresser, the contents of her purse, and the red-covered address book with fancy gold-embossed lettering. In public school, Hannah was sure her mother had the names and phone numbers of all her teachers, who she regularly phoned to check up on her. In high school, it was secret lovers from before and even after Hannah was born: dark exotic gentlemen who looked like movie stars. Hannah stares at the red cover now and feels guilt at the thought of opening it. This is silly, she says to herself. Taigg, H.

Under the T's: Thatcher's drug store, Mrs. T., phone number only, and then, Taigg, Clarence and Harriet, 297 Partridge St, Winnipeg, Manitoba, 204-938-4226.

Hannah gets up and paces into the living room and back. If she does phone, what will she say? Probably the wrong thing, as she is not good at this. What would be the logical thing to say? Who she is and that she would like get to know them, now that her mother is ill? How do you strike up a conversation with a relative you've never known? What if she phones at an inconvenient time? What if they're not well? They could both be dead. They could be out and she might get an answering machine or, more likely because of their age, no answer. She picks up the phone and dials the number.

Aunt Harriet answers, and after Hannah says who she is and why she is calling, the silence lasts long enough to convince Hannah she never should have phoned, that it is all a mistake.

"Well, I must say you've taken me by surprise, my dear. I've been sorting through a box of family photos and I'm looking at you and your mother just back from the hospital."

Hannah's turn for silence. The background, which has been in shadow all her life, suddenly lights up. Her mother at Harriet's, standing by the steps on the lawn—no, no, it was January, standing in the living room, holding a baby, holding her.

"Hannah dear, are you still there?"

"Yes, yes. I'm sorry, it's just that…" Hannah feels as though the breath has been knocked out of her. Breath and words and coherent thought.

"I've been finding it so hard since Clarey went, and tonight I thought I'd take a little trip down memory lane."

"Clarey?"

"My husband Clarence, dear. We buried him six months ago today." Her voice trails off.

"But your children, my cousins. They were with you? Helped you?" This wasn't what she expected. How to ease herself out of this. A grieving woman she can do without. One disaster is all she can handle right now.

"Oh, I shouldn't be loading you down with my troubles. You've probably got enough on your plate. How is my Edith?"

"She's…she's in the hospital, I'm afraid."

"Poor dear. Is it serious?"

"Yes…no. She's had a little stroke."

"Oh my. Should I send a card?"

"I'm sure she would like that."

Silence again. Hannah has no idea what to say next.

"Why don't I just bundle up a bunch of these photos and send them to you?"

"If it's no bother…"

"No bother at all. You're my sister's flesh and blood. Dear little Hannah. We both worried about you so."

"You'll need my address?" Hannah asks. Even sitting, she feels her knees shake.

"I'll just send it there to your mother's address on the Lakefront Road. Give my love to Eadie, Edith I mean. We always used to call her Eadie."

After she says good-bye, Hannah sits for a long time holding the red address book, running her fingers over the gold-embossed lettering.

Over the years, in stressful situations, Hannah has developed a coping strategy. In situations where she feels out of her depth, the many times she has felt betrayed or hurt, she has rationalized that when faced with the bottom line, she is always alone therefore, therefore…Do this. Think that. Go for a run. Watch a movie. This short conversation contradicts everything; pulls the proverbial rug out from under. "We both worried about you so." People she didn't even know. Why didn't they call then? Why didn't they visit?

Hannah feels her face getting wet and she stomps around the kitchen, tidying up, setting a mug and bowl out for breakfast— things she normally never does until the next morning. Maybe they did call. How would she know? In those days, getting no answer would be likely. After that summer working at the hotel, Hannah practically lived at the library, working there when she wasn't reading or studying. Her mother slaved long hours, overtime, for Hannah. And to ask why they didn't visit was stretching it. People didn't travel in the fifties, even the sixties, that much. They probably couldn't afford it. They had two children or three. Hannah wished she had asked for pictures of Harriet's family.

After her tidying frenzy abates, Hannah impulsively goes to the Victrola. Converted into a plant stand, it sits under a high west-facing window. Last week, Hannah threw several dead plants into the back flower bed. Poor wizened up things, long gone from lack of water. More evidence her mother had not been herself for some time. The only one with any life was a spider plant. Hannah trimmed off several of "the babies," as her mother called them, and stuck them into a glass of water in the kitchen window. In a couple of weeks, she will add them to the main pot. The spider plant is dry again but it looks healthier. As she sets it into a pot of water in the kitchen sink, Hannah smiles at her own concern—another of her mother's imprints.

The old brocade cloth covering the Victrola is spotted with cigarette burns and water stains. Hannah can almost hear a seventy-eight thump into position on the turntable, part of her mother's Saturday night ritual—a ritual eroded by time, brown record jackets scattered between overflowing ashtrays, an empty sherry glass.

Hannah carefully removes the dusty cloth and holds it up by two corners. What was it in its real life? A tapestry of some sort, elaborate rose pattern on a once-thick burgundy backing. Maybe Aunt Harriet would know. She has to sit down then, the throw falling lopsided onto the Victrola.

As corny as it sounds, everything has changed, shifted with that one phone call. The whole damn foundation, and she isn't ready for it. She can't remember not hanging on to her loneliness, wrapping it around her, layer upon hurt layer. It has always suited her; she has grown to depend on it.

She folds the tapestry back and raises the Victrola's lid, the jointed metal support arm squeaking into lock position. A record is on the turntable: Chopin's *Fantaisie Impromptu*. Lying alongside,

half on, half off the record, is a faded rainbow-colored chiffon scarf.
She picks it up thinking it's not as long as she remembers. She drapes
the scarf around her neck and winds up the Victrola, relieved that
the brass crank on the side still works. It occurs to Hannah that she
could play all these old records, one by one, as her mother did. She
wonders where the Victrola came from? From her grandmother's
family? Her mother would never have been able to afford to buy
one. When she opens the bottom door housing the record collection, a half-filled bottle of sherry tips out. Harvey's Shooting Sherry.
Her mother has good taste.

In the china cabinet, Hannah finds a sherry glass. It's dusty and
at the bottom, a dried-up drop of sherry no bigger than a dime.
She will regret this in the morning. She knows it and doesn't care.
She rewinds the crank and, sherry in one hand, scarf in the other,
twirls and sings, refilling her glass as she replaces one record with
another. Bing Crosby, the Ink Spots, Vera Lynn. Once through the
pile, she returns to Chopin.

I'm always chasing rainbows,
Watching clouds drifting by.
My dreams are just like all my schemes,
Ending in the sky.

She sings lustily to the end of the piece and falls onto the couch
dizzy and quite tipsy. "That's what you should be with sherry," she
giggles. "Tipsy. And you're wrong, Mother dear. For the first time
in your life, you're wrong. Rainbows don't all end in the sky."

Hannah wakes at 3 a.m. with a splitting headache, moonlight
casting a long angled shadow from the turntable arm onto the
window ledge. She staggers to her feet and, pulling the curtains,
turns off the lights, worrying in her muddled state that someone
might have seen her, not realizing until the next morning that the

window not only faces the wrong way but is too high up for prying eyes. She barely remembers falling into bed, pulling the comforter around her.

In the morning she feels even worse, head pounding, stomach like a soggy sponge full of swamp water. The kitchen clock says ten past eight, an hour late for her usual caffeine fix, and of course, she has forgotten to bring any real coffee. She pulls off her sleep-creased clothes and climbs into the old claw-foot bathtub, pulling the curtains around her. They're torn in several places, moldy in others. Ah, yes, the joys of home, she says to herself. The hand-held showerhead housing has, long ago, broken out of the wall, leaving two big screw holes, spouting moldy bits of drywall dust. Good thing she doesn't have allergies. Spraying water on herself with the old green twist-on shower hose leaves something to be desired, she thinks. Unless you're showering duo, which makes her think of Russ. Somehow, it's all right to be naked with him in the shower. Besides, Russ is no Adonis, bulgy around the middle from too much sitting in front of the computer. He doesn't exercise except tussling in bed with her, which, he says, is all the exercise he needs. It's a good line and, besides, if he were in better shape, she might have been too intimidated to go to bed with him—well, for more than the first few months, when their electrical energy fields were at an ongoing explosive level. Dear, dear, Russ. She wonders if he has written her into his new novel. That would be flattering. She's written poems about him, intense, erotic lines she hasn't been able to show him. Enough about Russ, she says aloud. Get on with it.

She knows there is nothing but instant coffee here, and her stomach simply can't hack it. She'll do takeout. After dressing quickly, she remembers she needs to collect clothes for her mother: slippers, which she can't find, a dressing gown with the hem coming down, and a pair of men's pajamas. Is that what her mother wore?

Men's pajamas? It seems unlikely, but Hannah cannot find a night-gown, and her stomach is having small acidic seizures.

When she sees the crowded parking lot at Tim Hortons, she drives around to line up at the drive through. Listening to the inside chat is definitely not her style this morning. She's wearing dark glasses, and now in the cold light of dawn, she can't believe she actually got drunk on her mother's sherry. When she finally gets her black coffee and low-fat carrot muffin, she decides the parking lot of Sunset Lodge will be her breakfast place.

She parks facing the building and tries to remember what it looked like in the fifties. Then, the high school choir came and sang here. One glance through the door at the wheelchairs full of bent, old, glassy-eyed men and women and she fainted. That evening, her mother's explanation was less than satisfactory.

"The poor house," she said in a disparaging tone of voice. "God preserve me from the poor house when I get old."

She hears her mother say it, out loud, as if she is in the back seat. Hannah turns on the radio. She retrieves an old *Cosmo* maga-zine from under the passenger seat to put under the application form. She should have brought her briefcase; no, she should have filled the form out at the house on the kitchen table. She stares momentarily at the pouty, cleavage-heavy model on the cover. Hannah knows she's probably too old for *Cosmo* but she gets it every once in a while anyway. "One Hundred Ways to Drive Him Wild" and they don't even list the good ones. Probably twenty-year-olds writing the articles, getting all their information from friends, none of them experienced enough to know anything but the basics.

"Enough of this," she says out loud, and placing the Lodge form on the magazine, she uses the steering wheel as a tilted desk top. The form is long and complicated and tedious with questions she has no idea how to answer. Things like, *How many bowel move-ments does the candidate have on an average day? How many times a day does he/she urinate?* Hannah answers what she can and, signing on the dotted line, shoves it into the provided envelope.

She has to admit the foyer of the Sunset Lodge is tasteful. To the right of the entranceway, a cozy living room arrangement of sofas, love seats, and chairs. That they look too new and never used does cross her mind, but she is determined to keep an optimistic outlook. No one is at the front desk, but Hannah glimpses several women in a room behind. A stylishly dressed, middle-aged woman bustles out to greet her. "Just doing some faxing," she says. "Short staffed. You know how it is."

Hannah nods and hands her the envelope. Better here than with the patients, Hannah thinks. The woman tosses the envelope into a nearby basket. Hannah is sure she hasn't looked at the name. "It's for Mr. Preston," Hannah says. "I teach in the city and he said I could drop it off this morning."

"Um hmm," the woman nods, turning her back. "He'll get it Monday." She disappears through the door again. Hannah wants to ask a few questions, maybe get a short tour.

A white-haired woman bent over in a wheelchair appears around the corner at the far end of the hall. She laboriously maneuvers herself toward Hannah, clutching a piece of paper and muttering to herself. When she reaches the front desk, she looks up. "Ring that damn bell, will you?" she chirps, banging her fist against the side of the counter. "Get them lazy bums off their asses."

Hannah rings the bell and makes a fast exit. She wonders if they have private rooms. If not, is it possible to choose one's roommate? It doesn't matter, she thinks to herself, getting back in the car. It's a fait accompli—sealed, delivered. From somewhere back in public school days, when they still had morning bible readings, or from some university course, she hears "and the Lord put a mark on Cain." He killed his brother. The mark of Cain. Hannah feels it pressing like a cold steel-like brand on her forehead.

THAT SUMMER IN FRANKLIN

When she arrives at the hospital and Edith is not in her room, Hannah panics. She's fallen, broken her hip, choked on something, died. She runs into the hall and sees her mother in the walker, a nurse on either side, wearing what looks like her own pink dressing gown—and the slippers, although Hannah cannot be sure. Her mother has a do-or-die look on her face, fierce concentration. "One foot forward, lean on the walker, then the other foot, now a little rest." Hannah realizes one of the nurses is softly saying this, over and over. Hannah withdraws to the bedroom and waits.

A nurse rushes in and grabs the wheelchair. "Change of vehicles," she says, rushing back out. Hannah looks around the corner in time to see her mother collapse like a half-deflated balloon into the wheelchair. "Your daughter is here," the nurse says too loudly, wheeling her in. "All the way down the hall and halfway back today. Didn't we Edith?" The nurse gives her a spaniel pat on the head. "Nearly lunch time, and then you can have your nap." Hannah's mother slumps further down into the wheelchair. The nurse reaches behind her and pulls out a strap. "We'll just put on your seat belt, Edith, so you don't go racing off."

Hannah helps her mother with lunch, vegetable soup, most of which spills onto her bib. Her right hand, which she normally uses, flops by her side, and she makes no attempt to use the left. Hannah puts a piece of bread into it. Edith squeezes the bread fiercely then lets it fall. "I talked to Aunt Harriet last night," Hannah says, after she has tried with only moderate success to give her mother some tea. "Your younger sister, Harriet."

"Not a good cook," Edith says, actually focusing on Hannah.

Hannah takes a deep breath. Progress. "I talked to her on the phone in Winnipeg."

"Too dear," her mother says, frowning.

"It's okay. I can afford it."

Edith sits up, suddenly, pounding the arm of the chair. "Please,

please, oh please." She is almost in tears.

"What is it, Mother?" Hannah grabs her mother's hands. "Are you in pain? I'll get the nurse." She rushes out, only to find the nursing station empty. "Nurse?" she calls, not knowing what else to say. "Nurse?"

A nurse sticks her head out from a room at the end of the hall. "Be with you in a minute. We're just finishing Frank."

"But my mother is in pain. I think something is wrong."

Hannah runs back to her mother now, slumped down in the chair again, eyes closed, a yellow puddle on the floor beneath.

Hannah sits down, every nerve in her body jangling. She stares past her mother, waiting for the nurse to appear.

She had to go to the bathroom, she thinks. I could have taken her. Why didn't they tell me? "This is horrible, an indignity," she whispers, leaning over to take her mother's hand. "I'm sorry, Mother. I'm so sorry." Her mother opens her eyes, momentarily, and then closes them again. Like peek-a-boo, Hannah thinks. If I can't see you, I'm not here.

The following week, Hannah decides to take her mother out for a ride, a trial run before the move to Sunset Lodge becomes a reality. She brings something familiar, the raincoat she bought her mother two Christmases ago. It is snack time and Edith is up and in the anchored wheelchair.

"And how much did this cost, pray tell?" her mother quips, staring at the coat as if it were brand new.

"I've always said the color suits you," Hannah replies, ignoring this and trying to be upbeat. "Dusty rose."

Edith stares out the window.

"And here's the matching scarf," Hannah continues, draping it around her mother's neck. Her mother loved that scarf and wore it often.

She fingers it now, holding one end to the light. "I shouldn't be wearing your scarf," she replies, trying to pull it off.

"No, no, Mother. It's yours. You wear it."

Edith sighs and sits back, closing her eyes as if to avoid further discussion.

Hannah takes a deep breath and pulls the running shoes out of her bag, shoes she insisted her mother buy last year for walking, especially along the beach. They look as though they have never been worn, not one grain of sand caught in their deep-notched treads.

"Snack time, Edith," a young nurse's aide appears in the doorway carrying a tray with two Oreo cookies and a small glass of apple juice.

Hannah watches dumbstruck as her mother pulls one cookie apart, eating the filling first, eyes twinkling. She is so taken aback she has to stand up and look out the window. Her mother never ate Oreo cookies. She never touched a chicken drumstick with her fingers and always cut bananas into a bowl before eating them. She never pulled apart anything she was eating.

When the nurse's aide returns, she helps get Edith into her shoes and the raincoat, pushing it partially under her bottom as Hannah does up the buttons. It seems a bit large now. "Thanks," Hannah says as she put a dab of rouge on her mother's cheeks. She looks quite dapper with her hair set earlier in the week.

"Will you be able to get her into the car?" the aide asks.

"I hadn't thought of that," Hannah replies, feeling again out of her depth.

"I'll come down with you," the woman says cheerfully. "It can be a bit intimidating the first time."

The aide shows Hannah how to position the wheelchair up against the open car door, how to encourage her mother to push herself up to a standing position and hang on to Hannah's shoulders so she can pivot her body around and lower her old buttocks onto the seat. Her mother sighs and puffs and settles into the seat like a slowly deflating balloon, wrinkling down until the seat belt touches her chest.

"Have a nice ride," the young woman calls, as Hannah climbs into the driver's seat.

"Hannah?" Edith says after they are driving only a few minutes.

Hannah is trying to decide between the beach and the park. "What is it?"

"Are we going home?"

Hannah feels a knife cut through her. She takes a deep breath, steadies her hand on the wheel. "Not today, I'm afraid."

Her mother settles even further down into the seat and closes her eyes. A few minutes later, she is sound asleep. Half an hour later, having driven up and down the length of Franklin twice, out to the beach, and half way to Port Turner and back, Hannah survives the ordeal of getting her mother back into the wheelchair and up to her room. She leaves feeling thoroughly discouraged, wishing someone else, anyone else, could take over and deal with everything.

COLLEEN IV

AFTER TWO WEEKS in hospital, Colleen's dad is pushing to go home. Friday evening, she and Art and the twins talk, yet again, about how they are going to deal with it.

"Tell him a pipe burst," Steve says, grinning at her. "The place is flooded."

"Have you heard anything definite from the Lodge?" Art asks, helping himself to more stew.

You look tired, Colleen thinks. Dark circles under your eyes. You shouldn't still be working such long hours.

"Colleen?" Art gives her an are-you-all-right look.

"I did actually get through to someone earlier this week. Whoever I spoke to said the processing of his application was pending."

"Bureaucracy," Cal cut in. "Bet if you were the mayor's wife, you'd get him in fast enough."

Sunday, Colleen is right in the middle of making curried hamburger when they phone from the hospital to say her dad has fallen and may have broken something. Steve and Art take over supper; Cal has already left to pick up Grandma Pinser, who lives in a classy senior citizen's place near the lake. Colleen pulls her old beige trench coat over her sweatshirt, grease-spattered from the frying pan. Her hands smell like onions.

"If I'm not back, go ahead without me," she calls as she grabs the keys and hurries outside. He would have to fall today, she thinks, and then, at almost the same time, God I'm selfish. It's unusually warm for November, and as she heads outside to the car, she breathes in an end-of-fall smell, leaves and flowers not already frost-dead filling the afternoon with glorious scent. She kicks at the leaves, and Tiff, one of the golden Labs, sprawled out in the sun, thumps his tail. "How could he break something in the hospital?" she mutters as she opens the car door and climbs inside. She sees him in a heap at the bottom of the stairs, nothing broken, too drunk. His bones are most likely brittle she thinks. He hasn't eaten a decent meal in forty years let alone drunk any milk.

The hospital parking lot is jammed, and Colleen drives round and round trying to find a spot. Sunday afternoon and everyone and their Uncle George is here to visit. Her mom used to say that and laugh, saying she didn't even have an Uncle George. When Colleen finally spots a space between a pickup truck and a minivan, it's a squeeze to get in, but she makes it. Open less than six months and the parking lot is already too small.

The elevator is packed, the hall a zoo, and her dad's bed empty. She waits at the nurse's station, tapping her fingers on the counter, listening to family chat all around. Today of all days with Grandma Pinser coming. Colleen has been fussing in the kitchen most of the day, even making chocolate zucchini cake.

Colleen thinks Art's mom is almost perfect. When her own mom was still around, she tried not to let it show. Madge Miller, already sure she was on the short end of the stick all her life, went into her wounded routine at the drop of a hat. "Go ahead, have dinner with them if you want. It's only the third time this month." Back then, the Pinsers lived in their hundred-year-old brick house in the right section of town, huge old maple trees up and down both sides of the street, and yes, it was nicer going to dinner there. The biggest dining room table Colleen had ever seen with more than enough room for them all. Dinner at Colleen's parents always set her nerves on edge. Her dad was either too drunk or too grouchy, the house too small for three noisy little kids, her mom going back and forth between cheery hostess and hard-done-by wife.

When they were first married, even up until after they had the first two kids, Colleen kept track on a calendar, trying for an even score, but the Pinsers were always having family drop in, Rosie's sisters from Toronto, cousins from the States. They'd get a phone call and Art would say, "We'd really better go." It wasn't exactly a chore and, especially after Rosie was widowed, it meant a lot to her. Art was the good son while his older brother Bill, who ran off to California years ago, was a drinker. Whenever Art mentioned this, he always looked as though it might be partly his fault. "William," his mother said, the few times it came up in family conversation, "William had a bit of a problem." Art said his brother was a double for his dad. In looks only, he would add quickly, usually turning away.

A nurse finally shows up and sends Colleen down a floor to the Cast Clinic, a waiting room full of people with casts and braces and crutches. At least there is someone at the desk.

"Frank Miller?" she asks.

"Down the hall that way and to the left. Next to x-ray."

It is snazzy, this new facility. Looks like it should be efficient. How many times had she walked down those yellow-painted halls in the old place—with her mom and then without her, finding her dad muddled and swearing, getting dried out and patched up one more time?

Her dad looks gray and obviously drugged, the beginning of a large purple bruise on his forearm, another on the side of his forehead.

"Dad?" Colleen says. He smells like hospital now, not like

Frank Miller anymore. "Dad, what happened?"

"Madge?" her dad says, opening his eyes.

"It's Colleen."

"Tell Madge she has to sign some goddamned form before they'll fix this arm of mine."

A nurse appears.

"Mrs. Pinser?"

"What happened? How could he possibly break something?"

"He fell out of the bed, Mrs. Pinser."

"What about the railing? Weren't railings up on both sides?" Colleen wishes Art were here. She's gearing up to say something she'll regret.

"He said he was trying to reach a glass. He must have grabbed the lever by mistake. We think he blacked out momentarily and fell sideways onto the floor." She hands Colleen the clipboard and form.

"Should I wait upstairs?" Colleen signs and hands it back. "Do you know how long it will be?"

"Dr. Montgomery hasn't seen the x-rays yet, but as long as there are no complications, they should have the cast on within the hour."

Her dad has a roommate, a huge old guy who wheezes every time he breathes, coughing and spitting into a pan at almost every other breath.

"Doctor says I got the pneumonia," he says, as if she has already asked.

"Did you see my dad fall?" she asks.

"I seen nothin' lady, like I told the nurses. One minute he's in the bed and the next minute he ain't." He hacks a couple more times, then, on purpose she thinks, closes his eyes. Arrogant old fart. If he does know anything, he's keeping it to himself. There's always the chance that her dad told him to keep his mouth shut. Frank was probably doing something he shouldn't, the story of his life.

She sits by the empty bed for a few minutes before going out to the hall. His wheezing is too much for her nerves. After thumbing through all the out-of-date magazines in the lounge, she wishes she had brought the mystery she was trying to read. Janet left her a box of them at Thanksgiving, said they were good for relaxing. Colleen wasn't sure she would ever get on to reading a whole book. She read nothing the first five years of her marriage, too whacked out from diapers and housework.

Even after she was married and pregnant with Artie, Colleen was still sure she would manage to teach the two years out of five the Teacher's College guidelines required for a permanent certificate. She would teach full time later. Three babies in four years ended that pipe dream. "Three will be quite enough, don't you think?" her mom had said. Colleen laughed and said that was the plan, which it was, but then after her mom died, Colleen couldn't seem to stick to anything for very long. She signed up for a ceramics course at night school, then quit after the first week. She tried Aquafit at the Y and hated it. She watched TV, ate too much, and blimped out. Art surprised her that year with a weekend to Niagara Falls—on their anniversary, ushered off by their teenage children with the nudge-nudge, wink-wink routine. Colleen relaxed for the first time since her mother's funeral, relaxed and forgot her diaphragm, and nine months later, Cal and Steve came into the world. The Niagara kids, Art would say, grinning and always looking a little embarrassed. One for each set of falls. After getting over the shock, it was a comfort being pregnant again, life to replace life. She never dreamed she would have twins.

An orderly wheels her dad past the lounge; she can't see how much of his arm is in a cast. She follows and the orderly pulls the curtain between the two beds. She would have if he hadn't.

"Does it hurt much?" Colleen asks after the orderly leaves. The cast from his elbow almost to his wrist has his arm in an uncomfortable-looking, bent position.

"It's a damn bother," her dad replies, a little groggily. "How will I open a beer when I get home?"

Colleen takes a deep breath. "Maybe you won't be able to go home—right away, I mean."

"Well, I'm not coming to stay with your zoo, if that's what you're suggesting."

"I'm not suggesting anything."

"You're not going to put me in that damn home, are you?"

Colleen turns too quickly, feels her face redden.

"That's it, isn't it? You're going to lock me up in that damn old folks home."

"Nothing's been decided yet."

"I can see right through you, you know. Just like your mother. Jesus Christ, just like your mother."

Colleen feels her fingernails hard on her palms. "I think we should leave it up to the doctor." She stares at the floor. "I have to go now."

"Since when can a goddamned doctor throw you out of your own home?" he yells after her as she bolts down the hall. She can hear him all the way to the elevator.

Colleen hits the gas out of the parking lot, screeching to a stop at Garland Street. Instead of turning toward town, she goes left and onto the expressway, speeding up way over the limit, her dad's words pulling her back through the years: "Jesus Christ, just like your mother, picking up the pieces, looking after things." And who should I be like, she thinks. You? Ye Gods, should I be like you? She can't see now for tears, the windshield blurring.

That's what he wanted. She was supposed to be what the wheels of fortune hadn't let him be: a showbiz wonder, the headliner on some theater marquee, a natural, a star on the way up. That's what he told everyone, went on and on about it, but never once came to see her in a show. Always said he would and then headed down to the pub and never made it—not in grade eight when she sang "Oh Bethlehem" at the Christmas concert, not in high school when she had a lead in one play after the other. Her first drama teacher told her she had sawdust in her veins; she loved being on stage, turning into someone else, if only for a little while. When by chance that same year her science teacher explained most butterflies only lived a few weeks, she put the two together. She would be alive on stage, a butterfly. But only for a few weeks and then die, back into the crap of life. She almost flunked her final year in high school because of it. First Maria in *The Sound of Music*, and after barely scraping through midterms, she won honorable mention at the regional high school drama festival. She collected anything she could about New York: method acting, rags-to-riches stories, backstage extras to instant stardom. Her mom put a damper on it, not in so many words, but with hints, constant little barbs: Teachers always had jobs. Look at how the Winters' kids loved her when she babysat. Do New York later. Colleen called it Plan B. If some theater agent didn't discover her—Plan A—and she made it into the one-year Teacher's College course, why not?

When a car speeds past and cuts in ahead of her, she slows down. She realizes she doesn't even have her purse, her license. She goes off at the first Port Turner exit and drives back to Franklin on the old two-lane highway.

They're just starting dessert when she comes in the door. She can smell the chocolate. She sticks her head into the dining room, a happy grin in place. "Be there in a min," she says. "Just going to the Ladies first." She races upstairs to the bathroom and presses a cold, wet face cloth over her eyes. Into the bedroom, tracksuit off. She needs something showy, an instant butterfly outfit.

Five minutes later, dinner plate in hand, Colleen makes her entrance, blue shimmery top, dangling earrings, hair tousled with a little mousse. She knows her family is watching, especially Art,

all hoping it hasn't been too rotten. She smiles and tells Grandma
Pinser her blue rinse is divine.

"Well?" Steve asks. He is more outgoing, more like Colleen.

"He broke his arm," Colleen the butterfly says. "I stayed until
the cast was on and they brought him back to his room." She smiles
and takes a large mouthful of chicken.

"Was he upset?" Art asks. She knows he thinks there is more.

"He was a bit grumpy," Colleen says, getting another large
mouthful ready. "But you know Dad."

The conversation carries on from there, and Grandma Pinser
tells Colleen what a good cook she is, and the boys go on about
school, and Art, as usual, says little. He is watching her though. He
knows she's faking it; he's seen the butterfly routine before.

Steve takes off up to his room to play a computer game and
Cal gets Grandma's coat and the car keys. Hugs and good-byes are
fast and over too soon. Colleen feels herself slipping, the pit waiting. Falling in means she won't have to cope, like stepping off a
cliff, straight down. She speeds up, clearing the table and filling the
dishwasher before Art knows what she is doing. He stands in front
of the couch reading the Sunday paper, a little habit that sometimes
she ignores, more often ticks her off.

"Why don't you sit?" Colleen says on the third whirlwind trip
between the kitchen and dining room.

Art doesn't hear or seems not to. She is never sure which. She
slams the pots into the sink, scrubbing and rinsing furiously. Any
minute now and it will be too late; she'll crash like a race car driver,
going full out, right into the black wall. She'll wish she hadn't later,
but right now, she doesn't care.

BRITANNIA THEN

LARRY BEGAN hanging around the dining room half way through Hannah's second week at the Britannia—eyeing her and making sure he found opportunities to walk up behind her or corner her, making lewd suggestions only she could hear, or telling his father whenever she took too long serving a customer or messed up an order. He had already tried once to grab her breast. When she raised a hand to slap him, he laughed.

"Better be nice to me," he whispered in her ear. "You don't want to get fired, do you?"

He'd already been in checking the dining room with Mourand, his father even calling him an "assistant manager." But it was obvious that Larry couldn't care less about learning the business. He was the boss's son and he swaggered around as if he already owned the place. Mourand had tried to instruct him on the finer details of the job: how to hold glasses up to the light, how to check for water spots, how to run a handkerchiefed finger along the banister for dust and check under a table for crumbs. On his rounds with Mourand, he was hardly able to suppress his boredom. As the owner's son, Larry made it clear that he had other things on his mind, more important things—like leering salaciously at the waitresses.

It seemed the waitresses were not Larry's only target. Twice when Hannah came into the kitchen hauling a heavy tray piled with dirty dishes, she had interrupted Larry elbowing Charlie up against the metal sink. The first time she didn't think much of it. The second time she noticed that Larry was in Charlie's face, and the old man seemed frightened. She saw Charlie reach into his pocket to pull out what looked like a couple of bills. Larry grabbed them and was out the back door in a flash.

"You shouldn't be giving him your money," Hannah blurted out, edging the tray onto the end of the metal counter already piled high.

Charlie forced a smile. "Nothing to worry about, Lassie. The boy needed extra cash."

"That's ridiculous," Hannah replied, staring at him. "He's the owner's son. He has more money than all of us combined. Your money is your money. Did he say he'd pay you back?"

Charlie shrugged and plunged a load of dishes into the soapy water.

Initially, Hannah found Larry an annoyance more than a problem. Usually Astrid shooed him out or his father called him to go upstairs. Something intervened and he left. Until one particular evening, the first time, as it turned out, of many. Hannah retreated to the kitchen twice and out to the foyer once. No one was at the front desk, but she could hear Mourand and Moira talking in low tones in the back office. Telling herself he was only a year older than she was, for heaven's sakes, she marched back into the dining room, Larry inching closer as she set clean napkins at each table. Colleen had left early, and Astrid was likely outside in the alley having a smoke with Charlie.

Hannah knew she should try to think of something to say to him, politely tell Larry to cut it out. She wasn't good at small talk, however, and he could pretty well do as he wanted.

When she turned to trace her steps yet again into the kitchen, he moved in on her, his shock of wavy blond hair falling to one side, his know-it-all look staring her down. In his hurry, he knocked over a chair and, catching Hannah's white starched apron strings with one hand, grabbed at her buttocks with the other. She turned abruptly, mute with fear and indignation. Whacking her one arm against his, she elbowed him hard in the chest with the other. "Buzz off," she whispered as he grunted and let go. "Bitch," she heard him say as he beat it out of the room.

Hannah picked up the chair and stood white-knuckling the back of it until she stopped shaking. She guessed he could be after her tips and, if Colleen was right, intended to feel her up even more. But why? For a moment she wished she had taken a retail-store job—safer, duller, way less money.

After retying her apron, she pushed in the chair to finish setting tables.

It was bad enough trying to do her job properly while trying to avoid Larry in the dining room. Far worse were rumors that Larry had discovered a way of spying on the girls when they were changing in and out of their uniforms in the downstairs washroom.

It wasn't so bad first thing in the morning because the dining room opened at seven and both she and Colleen were down there together. The afternoon and evening were different matters.

Several times, when she was changing for her afternoon sojourn at the library, Hannah felt that someone was watching her. At first, she simply talked herself out of it, thinking she must be imagining things, reliving some scene from a novel or movie, being ridiculous. She'd scan the walls and ceiling and, buttoning her blouse as she went, dash out the door, up the stairs, feeling the afternoon hall light flood over her. Safety. That was before she noticed the knothole above the sink mirror. It was in shadow, and at first, she thought it solid. When she stood absolutely still, however, she could hear a faint creaking behind the wall, as if someone standing on something was watching. She pulled on her blouse and, grabbing her pedal pushers, beat it into the toilet cubicle to finish dressing. After that, if she was alone, she always dressed inside the cubicle. She thought of saying something to Colleen but it seemed ridiculous, and Hannah was too shy, too worried Colleen would laugh or prove her wrong. Besides, she knew from what her mother said, what she overheard at school, sexuality was evil, something to avoid at all costs.

The very next evening, unbeknownst to Hannah, Larry came on to Colleen for the first time, the same staring routine, followed by what he seemed to think was a subtle kind of stalking.

"Shouldn't you be somewhere else?" Colleen said, banging silverware onto a table.

"Dad told me to check things out," Larry replied, looking officious.

"Check away," Colleen snapped back. "Everything's shipshape."

Larry grinned and made an elaborate pretense of checking a glass or two, then moved a table closer to Colleen.

His stupid antics bugged Colleen more than they alarmed her. She knew everyone was out of earshot, but at that point, she never dreamed he would make a move on her.

As she reached up to dust the banister leading to the second la-di-da seating area, Larry dashed forward, pinning her against the wood railing. She could smell his cigarette breath as he grabbed the front of her uniform, clumsily pressing his hands against her breasts. Her retaliation was swift and instinctive. She twisted around and kneed him hard in the groin, her hands slapping his face and shoulders.

He buckled, momentarily, groaning and muttering, "Bitch! My dad will…," as he ran from the room. For days after Colleen relived the incident, terrified Larry would make up some cock-and-bull story to get her fired. She had to have this job no matter what. She wondered if Larry had tried to paw Hannah, worried that if he hadn't, Hannah would think Colleen, with her constant stream of high school admirers, egged him on. She thought about talking to Moira about it, but there was never an opportunity, and Moira, being older, more experienced, and apparently involved with Mourand, wouldn't necessarily understand. Maybe, she thought, Larry figured if his old man could have Moira, he should have dibs on the waitresses. Like father, like son.

The following afternoon when Colleen caught Larry trying to muscle Charlie out of his meager pocket money, she slammed her tray on the counter and yelled at him to leave Charlie alone, sending the kid packing out the back door.

That evening she talked to Hannah about it. "I'm sure he was muscling Charlie out of money," she whispered as they were waiting for Astrid to bring more potatoes to the steam counter.

"I caught him too," Hannah replied. "And I told Charlie that his money was his money."

"Hurry up now, girls," Astrid cut in. "Don't be chatting when there's work to do."

Before she actually discovered it, Colleen had suspicions that Larry was skulking around in the basement. On sunny afternoons when the dining room was closed and the waitresses had two hours to themselves, Colleen always changed into her bathing suit, heading down to the beach to soak up sun and forget her life for a while. Even though she felt wary, changing in the basement washroom was practical, fast, and—she had no other choice.

In mid-July, on a particularly fabulous beach day, she had stripped off her clothes and was pulling up her bathing suit when she was sure she heard someone breathing. She yanked up her suit and, grabbing the chair, pushed open the cubicle door. "Get lost, weirdo," she hissed. The door banged back, the sound echoing over the wall and through the darkened basement. Silence. As she pulled on her blouse and shorts, Colleen scanned the walls and, finding a dark circle above the mirror, pulled the chair over to get up for a closer look. "You're cruisin' for a bruisin'," she hissed. Retrieving a wad of toilet paper, she stuffed it into the space. Colleen listened again but the basement was quiet, only the faint creaking of someone upstairs breaking the silence. Larry was long gone, having beaten it up the stairs with her first remark. After that, Colleen always checked and replugged the hole each time she went to change.

Female employees in the fifties had few options. Harassment was common; reprisal almost nonexistent. Whatever each girl thought about Larry, she kept to herself, neither willing to share information with such sexual overtones, not wanting to be seen as being morally loose, storing it as far back in her mind as possible. This summer job was there and each would see it through to the end, no matter what.

HANNAH V

THE WEEK RUSS calls to say he has finally finished the first draft of his novel and couldn't they plan a weekend away to celebrate, Mr. Preston phones from Sunset Lodge to announce there is an opening and Hannah can move her mother in that Friday.

"I've spoken to your mother's doctor," he begins, "and we've decided that the interview, usually a formality anyway, can be carried out just prior to admission."

"Could this possibly be deferred until Monday," Hannah asks, trying not to sound petulant.

"There is a substantial waiting list," Preston replies abruptly, "and I don't need to tell you how fortunate it is that this opening has occurred."

"I did have other plans," Hannah says, attempting to make her tone sound urgent.

"I see," Preston clips back. "I should tell you that unless there are extenuating circumstances, the Lodge's policy is to hold the room for two days only."

Hannah has a momentary impulse to ask if pent up sexual energy constitutes extenuating circumstances but instead says, "I'll make arrangements to be there, then."

Russ has already booked them into The Sighing Poplars Inn, a wonderful little place northeast of Toronto where they've been before.

"Not to worry, Babe," he says, and lowering his voice, "I probably need to rest up to be ready for you."

"I should be able to make it by mid-afternoon, I think." Hannah shifts in her chair and tries not to visualize Russ sprawled on the bed.

"I'll be waiting."

"If I can't make it by three, I'll leave a phone message at Mathers' Store."

"That'll set the gossips buzzing," Russ chuckles. "I always tell them you're my agent and we're having a business meeting in a phone-free zone."

"Your agent?" Hannah stifles a laugh.

"It gives them something to talk about," Russ continues. "Not much going on in that neck of the woods." The store, where they often pick up supplies, is in the small village south of the inn.

"Should I bring wine?"

"I've already bought Champagne and some vintage Scotch."

"I'll try not to drive too fast."

Hannah gets a sub for her last period and for Friday. She manages to make it onto the expressway before all the jam ups. Her goal is to reach Pinser's Hardware store before it closes. She really needs a good cup of coffee first thing in the morning.

Franklin's main street is relatively sleepy by the time she arrives shortly after five. The hardware store looks deserted, and as she walks in expecting a wash of déjà vu, she is instead assaulted by extensive remodeling and upgrades. Handy Hardware standards she assumes. They have kept the hardwood floors, though, all sanded and polyurethane, and one of the beautiful old wooden counters.

"Looking for anything in particular?" Hannah looks up to see a good-looking redheaded teenage boy approaching.

"Well, yes, I am as a matter of fact. A new coffee maker. Not too expensive but one that makes a decent cup." She wonders how much this smooth-faced boy knows about coffee.

"We have Cuisinarts, KitchenAids, and Sunbeams right now," he says, beckoning her to follow him down an aisle. "The Cuisinarts are kind of pricey. KitchenAid is good, but most people have been buying this little Sunbeam model." He points to it on the shelf. "It makes six cups and lets you pour a cup before the whole thing is perked."

"Crucial," Hannah replies, nodding. "I need that first cup of coffee pronto, as soon as I smell it."

At the counter, he slips the coffee maker into a Handy Hardware bag and runs her credit card through the machine.

"Visiting Franklin?" he asks, handing her back the card.

"I'm here to see my mother," Hannah replies and, not wanting to elaborate, turns abruptly to leave.

"Have a nice evening," he calls as she opens the front door. She is struck by his professional air and efficiency. Out of the corner of her eye, she notices a familiar-looking man rearranging stock in the front window. Someone she has seen recently? Unlikely, as the only other place she has been is the hospital.

As she turns into the driveway, the little house on Lakefront Road seems even smaller, a shrunken shadow in the November twilight. Hannah realizes she has not been back to the house on a Thursday evening in years. She tries to remember when the last time would have been—when she was still in grad school, perhaps, or some summer after she started teaching. Any summer for that matter. She was always taking courses, bettering herself, keeping busy, doing, doing, doing. Trying to live up to her mother's expectations. And her mother now? Stopped almost dead in her tracks, terms of reference evaporated in the twinkling of a TIA.

The house seems less alien, partly because Hannah has become used to it and partly because she has rearranged things, adding a few familiar items from home: a tablecloth, some candles in the living room, decent-size towels, and now the coffee maker.

Everything in the old kitchen reminds her of her past. It would make a good fifties movie set she thinks, oilcloth on the expandable chrome-legged table, checkered linoleum flooring, a set of copper-bottomed frying pans hanging over the stove. As memories attempt to flood in on Hannah, she concentrates on tomorrow's visit and where she will tell her mother they are going. In an optimistic, won't-this-be-fun voice, she will mention another car ride—definitely not the destination. The destination is like a dark looming shape, like the Marshalsea in Dickens's *Little Dorrit*.

She sits down with her cup of freshly brewed coffee and, opening her briefcase on the floor, pulls out a medical dictionary she wangled from reference at the school library. She's been meaning to research this since the nurse first mentioned the dreaded acronym TIA.

Opening to the index, she locates the page: *TIA: transient ischemic attack*. This condition, she reads, is described as an episode of *cerebrovascular insufficiency* and is often linked to a *partial occlusion of an artery*. Not finding this terribly helpful, she forges on and, when she finds that the cause is likely *atherosclerotic plaque* or an *embolism,* she almost gives up. Who writes these dictionaries? Who has to use them? Poor overworked med students and nurses-in-training. She takes a deep breath and goes on, only to balk at the line that tells her symptoms vary depending on the site and degree of *occlusion.*

She looks up *occlusion,* a blockage in a canal or vessel, and *dysphasia*, an impairment of speech. She's getting into overload now and skips over *atherosclerotic plaque,* checking instead *embolism* which seems to be some kind of abnormal circulatory condition where an *embolus* scoots along in the blood stream and then gets stuck somehow.

She underlines *embolus* and goes back to the E's. A foreign object or air or gas or a piece of *thrombus*. Ye Gods, thrombus. No wonder doctors don't tell you much. Thrombus she finds are little *platelets,* small bits of blood that have fastened themselves to the inside of a vein. It's not a medical dictionary, it's a medical maze.

She reads all the passages a second time and stops to think them through. A TIA is caused by a partial blockage to a blood vessel, like a mini stroke: blurred vision, dizziness, weakness, impairment of speech, unconsciousness. Her mother was walking on the beach—a sunset, leaden sky, slight drizzle? Everything blurring, then dizziness, reaching out to steady herself, knees buckling, crying out, a strange sound perhaps mistaken for a gull's cry, tripping finally and blacking out on the stony beach. Who found her? Someone walking a dog? Kids down skipping stones after supper? A strange pink pile of something in the distance, almost like a body, almost like her mother. The quintessential question remaining forever unanswered. Why, dressed in her dressing gown and slippers on a cold November evening, did her mother go walking on the beach?

She pours a second cup of coffee and tackles *dementia*.

Several kinds are listed, the most likely is senile dementia, although the doctor called it progressive dementia. *Senile dementia, see senile psychosis.* Good practice for developing dictionary skills, she thinks—might be an interesting assignment for an English class.

Senile psychosis is described as a mental disorder that leads to a *generalized atrophy of the brain.* This, in turn can result in memory loss, impaired judgment, a state of emotional apathy, and periods of confabulation, all of which are irreversible. The rest of it is not that difficult. The condition is irreversible, more often happening to women than men and it runs its course, getting progressively worse. The definition ends by saying there is no known cause of brain deterioration but that several theories are being studied. A vaguely hopeful conclusion to an abysmally hopeless condition.

Hannah reads the paragraph a second time and runs her finger along the word confabulation. To confabulate. To talk, to chat. It makes her think of Edgar Allan Poe; she has no idea why, more likely Hardy or Thackeray. It's a pretentious sounding word, unusable in today's writing, except as dialogue for some pompous soul. She should ask Russ. Hey Russ, want to confabulate? He'd take it as a come on for sure. That is definitely not what is meant here.

She retrieves her Oxford dictionary and looks up the word.

Confabulate – 1. converse, chat. 2. Fabricate imaginary experiences or compensations for the loss of memory.

She sits for a long time staring at this second meaning. It explains so much, says so much. She wants to shake its hand and say thank you. Why hadn't she thought of looking up dementia before her mother landed in the hospital?

The trouble with life is, she thinks, no one tells you when to change gears. Months ago, maybe even last year, her mother started saying and doing things that were just slightly out of synch, comments and actions possibly suspect. Hannah ignored them at first, reacted badly to several, and on the few occasions when she tried to contradict her, her mother staunchly defended her own point of view.

The banana peels in the toilet were a case in point. Her mother phoned the school on a Thursday morning. Hannah was teaching *Macbeth*. "It's an emergency call," the secretary said over the intercom. "I'll transfer it to your office right away." At least they're a good class, Hannah thought, giving them something to do and tearing down the hall to her office. They won't go into instant chaos mode.

"Hello?"

"Hannah?"—panic in her mother's voice.

"What's happened? Are you all right?"

"There's water, water everywhere. I can't stop it."

"A broken pipe?"

"I don't know, I…"

"What about the turnoff in the basement?"

"I can't seem to find it."

"Have you called a plumber?"

"A plumber? Oh, a plumber. No, I haven't."

"You have a plumber? Someone you use for emergencies?"

"Yes, of course I do." Back to sounding like her mother.

"I think the turnoff is right behind the hot water tank. You know, in the far corner of the basement."

"Yes, I'm sure that's where it is. I'd better go."

"I'll call you at lunch to make sure you're okay."

Hannah remembers how confusing that conversation was. She forgot where the water turnoff was? And the plumber—she forgot which plumber? That must have been it. They used several different plumbers over the years; her mother listed them in the red address book, probably crossing off each old one before writing in the new one. Later, Hannah read on the bill, as repairs and maintenance were billed directly to her, that the toilet was plugged. *Bananas skins plugging toilet* was scribbled on the invoice. When she asked her mother about this on the phone, she flatly denied it. "The most ridiculous thing I've ever heard," she said. "I would never do such a thing."

The "I never had a boyfriend" was the worst. Hannah still regrets what happened. Christmas last year, after they walked along the beach, her mother, not as interested in the spectacular ice formations, was telling Hannah about some grisly news item, a war atrocity, a report of child abuse, not the kind of thing her mother used to dwell on. When Hannah tried to change the subject, Edith sighed and said she knew Hannah had such a busy life, work and boyfriends and all. This seemed quite out of context, especially the boyfriends comment; and Hannah, feeling she was expected to respond, did mention Russ and how nice he was, a writer with his MA in history. This seemed to unleash some torrent in her mother, who turned on her and said how lucky Hannah was, all her life with a good job and no family responsibilities, no children and always a boyfriend.

"Not like myself," she added, "never a boyfriend or a husband. Not one in my whole life."

Still stinging from the no children comment and totally confused and angered by the words that came out of her mother's mouth, Hannah stood on the beach, Christmas Day in the cold wind, and totally lost it. "What about me?" she yelled. "If you never married or had a boyfriend, how the hell did I get here?"

Her mother reached out to Hannah, now blinded by tears, and tapped her gently on the arm. "I didn't mean to upset you dear. Have I said something to make you cry?"

"No, no, it's all right," Hannah replied, attempting a superficial recovery and wrapping an arm around her mother's bony back. "It's the wind, you know. The wind makes my eyes run."

In recollection, the incident, although branded into her brain still, always seemed impossible. It made no sense—until now. Confabulation.

Hannah feels suddenly whacked. She retrieves the cassette case she takes to the hospital and hunts in her briefcase for Joni Mitchell, one of the few popular-type folk singers she likes—a hangover from her grad student days. Joni Mitchell turned up as loud as possible, and after putting some of her own half-frozen spaghetti sauce in a pan on the stove, she impulsively decides to have a shower to relax—not a wise plan. In fact, it turns out to be worse than the first time she tried.

This time, the rubber twist-over-the-tap sprayer keeps spurting off, interrupting what shower effect she is managing to get. Also, squatting like an orangutan in the old claw-foot bathtub is not her position of choice. As she towels dry with one of her own oversized bath towels, Hannah decides she will call a plumber next week to see it he can put in something better. A tub-enclosure shower would be the best, but she isn't prepared to go that far. Not yet.

She makes pasta and gets candles from the living room. She has a glass of white wine while a couple of bakery rolls warm in the oven. This place needs a microwave. When everything is ready, she switches from kitchen light to candlelight. The spaghetti sauce is not half bad, one of the few culinary skills she has managed to acquire. After two glasses of wine and dinner, she closes her eyes and listens to Joni sing about her man from Mars. He is, in a way, Russ, with his writing and bookstore job and healthy parents. She'll be singing that song one day, listening to the silence so full of his sounds. She'll be fifty-five this year; Russ is forty-one. If they married, on their tenth wedding anniversary, she would be getting the old age pension and he would be just over fifty. She wonders about his mother. Is that what she is to Russ, a mother, that old Oedipus thing in full bloom? God she needs him, especially tonight. If it weren't so cold she would go for a run, run it off. She blows out the candles and pours another glass of wine.

Hannah does go for a walk the next morning, a cold drizzle peppering the black waves that lap against the stony shore. She is, of course, trying to locate the place where her mother fell, as if finding it—some telltale indentation in the smooth washed stones, some pink thread caught—would be an answer to appease her guilt.

Back at the house, she phones the Lodge to ask if she can see the room ahead of time. Can she bring some of her mother's things: pictures, bedspread, a chair perhaps? Pictures are acceptable and a bedspread. A chair, if it is not too large; she should probably see the room first. All clothes need identification, and the nurse recommends one of those permanent marking pens. Also, Mrs. Norcroft will be in the Controlled Access Wing and the nurse gives Hannah the number code to activate the door. Be careful on your way in, she says cheerily, sometimes there's a happy wanderer waiting.

Controlled Access Wing? Hannah feels as if the wind has been knocked out of her, a wire cage closing in. The doctor didn't say anything about controlled access, a conspiracy between him and the polite but obviously devious Mr. Preston. Her mother is going to be locked in, locked up as if in prison, an insane asylum. Padded walls and hypodermic needles.

This, then, is what it's like to get old, independence peeling off in strips, both inside and out: memory, freedom, choice. Floating off in layers finer than those of skin, imperceptible to both victim and observer. Not everyone, Hannah says fiercely to herself, not everyone ends up this way.

Hannah decides to take a painting to the Lodge, one of two faded watercolor scenes depicting what could be an English countryside. Hannah is sure there was only one of these in the house while she was living at home and wonders, momentarily, where the other came from. She knows her mother liked this painting. In high school, if Hannah caught her staring at it and asked, her mother would invariably say it was just a painting, nothing to get all excited about, as if asking was somehow too strong a response to looking.

Her mother's bedspread looks pretty ragged when Hannah hauls it into the living room light—pale-green chenille with tufts worn down to almost nothing. It is something familiar, though. She adds a vase for flowers. A calendar, perhaps. She'll stop and buy one at the Franklin Bookstore on the way. She folds underwear and panty hose and socks into a stiff, old blue suitcase she finds on a shelf in the hall closet. What else? Her mother has smart slacks, tops, and inappropriate dresses, most in need of dry cleaning. Her gardening and housework clothes are threadbare and baggy, sad old things from twenty years ago, life all washed out of them. The nurse told Hannah she would provide her with a list of appropriate clothing. She sticks in one pair of slacks and two tops. It will have to do for now.

Hannah is dismayed to find the Franklin Bookstore is no more. Where it should be is a store called Cuddly Collectibles. A dry cleaner is on one side and an empty storefront on the other. Hannah stares at teddy bears in the window and feels disoriented, a palpable sense of loss. All through high school, Hannah loved talking to Mrs. Long, the owner and mainstay of the bookstore. Mrs. Long was a reader, and Hannah would quiz her about new books, look longingly at their shiny dust covers. She would never get to read these at the Franklin Library; acquisitions were often up to two years behind the current new crop. Mrs. Long offered her a part-time job once, but she was in twelfth grade and already working too many hours at the library. A second job was tempting but, with her schedule, impossible. Besides, she would spend too much of her paycheck on books. Hannah wonders what has happened to Mrs. Long, if she is still alive. Everyone seemed old when she was fifteen, eighteen. Of course, dress was more structured in those days. Unmarried young women wore certain clothes and married women wore certain clothes. Unmarried women had to transfer over gradually, some remaining stubbornly individualistic, wearing out-of-date, flamboyant things, crazy old spinsters with no style. Thank goodness for the seventies. Mrs. Long could have been in her late thirties or forties. That would make her eighty or ninety by now. Hannah hopes she won't find her at Sunset Lodge, especially not where her mother is going. Every time she thinks about it, she feels exactly as if someone has tripped her, that unexpected whack off balance, of trying to find where reality exists.

When she says who she is to the receptionist at the Lodge, the woman nods and rings for Mrs. Sanderson. "Mr. Preston apologizes that he can't be here to show you about," Mrs. Sanderson says when she appears. "He was called to a meeting but he is expecting you and your mother at one."

Hannah is holding the suitcase in one hand and in the other, a large shopping bag containing the watercolor picture, a wild flowers calendar, and a marker, the latter two bought at the dollar store. She left the bouquet of flowers, the bedspread, and the vase in the car for a second trip. Hannah isn't expecting a tour; she simply wants to see the room and try to get things a little organized, a little homey. The word homey bounces back at her, almost bringing tears to her eyes. She blinks and tries to will numbness.

Mrs. Sanderson has an organized and formidable air. She marches Hannah to the elevator, telling her that there are two controlled access areas, one on the lower level and one on the third floor. Her mother will be on the lower level where there is a fenced-in area, accessible from the TV lounge, for clients wishing to go outdoors. Like Kindergarten, Hannah thinks. Like a prison compound.

Outside the elevator, at the end of a hall with a highly polished but worn tiled floor, Hannah sees a door with a window. She follows behind Mrs. Sanderson, sheeplike, knowing this now will be her path, the only access to her mother, to what is left of her mother's life. The door is heavy; the glass has wire screening between the two back-to-back panes.

"The number is seven, four, two, star," Mrs. Sanderson says, punching and speaking at the same time. "You let yourself in; a nurse will let you out."

Hannah notices she doesn't seem to check if someone is waiting on the other side. No one is, thank goodness.

"If someone is waiting," she adds, as if reading Hannah's thoughts. "Just shoo them away." She waves her hand back and forth to demonstrate. "It's not difficult."

For years afterward, Hannah will remember the smell, not a

foul smell but pervasive, that imperceptible sloughing off of aging skins, day by week by year. No amount of cleaning solvent, floor wax, or air freshener could eradicate it. The wing itself is pleasant, the halls extra wide with arm railings and posters. The lounge has a large-screen TV and plants. Hannah gazes at the occupants, some in chairs, a few in wheelchairs. Several smile when they enter the room, one old woman reaching out her hand to Hannah. "Elly, I never thought you'd come to get me."

Mrs. Sanderson pats her on the shoulder. "Elly's busy right now," she says almost sharply. "She'll be back later." This seems like a terrible lie to Hannah, and she wants to ask Mrs. Sanderson why she would say such a thing. Why lie to the poor old soul? The woman sits back again and stares dully at the floor. Apparently Mrs. Sanderson doesn't feel an explanation necessary as she whisks Hannah back out into the hall.

"Your mother's room is down here, number 126."

The room is small but has a large window facing south, the drapes are what Hannah would call nondescript tasteful, pastel shades, not quite patterned, not quite abstract. They do contain a green, however, perhaps a little darker than the bedspread but the same tone.

"Your mother is fortunate to be getting a private room," Mrs. Sanderson adds, watching Hannah look about the place. "Most are doubles; this one just happened to be available."

Because someone died, Hannah wants to say to her. For someone so obviously straight forward, such prevaricating seems out of place. Hannah looks for picture hooks and seeing none, asks if she can hang pictures on the walls.

"You brought pictures?" Mrs. Sanderson asks. A rhetorical question, as she immediately continues, "I'll get Maisie Johns to get you a hammer and nails, unless you brought some."

"No," Hannah says, wondering if this is a test, if the highly organized would have thought of such details, and that she, Hannah, has now been relegated to the less-organized caregiver, likely to forget things in the future.

"Someone was going to give me a clothing list," Hannah says, suddenly remembering. She wants to add touché but doesn't.

"Maisie has all the pertinent information. I'll leave you in her competent hands." Mrs. Sanderson leads Hannah into a central, windowed-off area with desks and computers and filing cabinets. A harassed-looking nurse or nurse's aide looks up from her data entry. "Be with you in a minute," she says. "I just have to finish these round reports."

The place is terribly cluttered with piles of papers stacked between coffee cups and boxes of tissues. Someone's costume jewelry earring is pined to a bulletin board containing a poster advertising Elder Care Seminars, a list of toxic shock symptoms, and the telephone intercom directory. It could be an office anywhere, except for the smell.

Maisie Johns is friendly and helpful, a different kettle of fish, as Hannah's mother would say. "Your mother, Edith Norcroft. She's coming in this afternoon, and lucky for both of you, a private room."

Hannah nods and asks for a hammer and nails. They are provided along with the dreaded clothing list, as well as an information sheet for caregivers and visitors with patients in the closed-access wing. After she has hung the picture and calendar and put the marked clothing away in dresser and wardrobe, Hannah sits on the bed to read both sheets. The clothing list is intimidating, calling for a half dozen of almost everything except shoes and slippers. The information sheet says no valuable jewelry, money, or documents. No pets. Visiting hours between 11 a.m. and 8 p.m. Times for crafts, church services, etc. Hannah remembers the flowers and bedspread and jumps up to get them. The room number is

126 and the entry code is seven-forty-something plus star. She can't remember. It hits her right between the eyes. She can't remember. Someone else is in the office now, one of the side windows pulled open next to her desk.

"I just wanted to double check the access entry number," she says as casually as she can. "Seven forty…?"

"Seven forty-two plus star," she says without looking up.

Short-term memory versus long-term memory, Hannah thinks as she walks rapidly down the hall. Fear of reprisal, embarrassment, or both aid and abet long-term memory. She won't forget again.

COLLEEN V

COLLEEN HURRIES from the elevator, intending to stay only a short time with her dad. It's Thursday afternoon and she wants to be home before the boys troop in off the school bus at four. Maureen appears from nowhere and plants herself squarely in the way.

"Guess who Mom saw downtown," she says, tapping her fingers on a clipboard she's carrying. She leans closer to Colleen. "Moira Jackson. Remember her?"

Colleen nods, trying to think of a way to end this conversation before it starts.

"She's got one up on Ms. Norcroft in the glam department. Mom said she had on enough jewelry to sink a ship." Maureen rolls her eyes. "Mrs. Bradley, down the street from the Jacksons, said Moira's back from New York. She's into the movie producing business—may be checking out Franklin for her next film."

"Fascinating stuff, Maureen," Colleen says, glancing at her watch. "This is one of those days, you know?"

Maureen nods and heads for the nursing station. "Well, you won't have to worry about Mrs. Norcroft anymore," she calls, almost as an afterthought. "She's been transferred to the Lodge."

Too bad, Colleen thinks, hurrying past her empty room. It was lovely chatting with Hannah's mom even though she's not sure Mrs. Norcroft had a clue who she was. Always pleased to see her, though, and Colleen thinks how unfair it is that she would be the one to go senile. Mrs. Norcroft, always dressed to the nines, for years walking to work no matter the weather. Colleen used to spot her striding along when she was driving Art to work in the mornings, usually some long colorful scarf streaming out behind.

Colleen hears Bill Milligan even before she gets to her dad's room, that tight little English accent a dead giveaway. It's a bit early in the day for Bill, and Colleen hopes to God he hasn't slipped her dad something to drink. She takes a deep breath and walks in.

"Ah, Mrs. Pinser," Bill says, standing like some butler in a movie. He steps back and waves a hand toward his chair. "Please sit down"—as if she's a visitor in his damn house. He always does this, even at her dad's. She can't actually say anything about it; he's so polite but it bugs her. She sits without taking off her coat. Frank is in a leather-backed armchair, looking better than he has in months. No suspiciously spiked juice glasses in sight, and when she smiles and leans over to give her dad's shoulder a quick squeeze, he still smells like hospital.

"Bill's been playing over at the Lodge," her dad says, sounding almost interested. Colleen stares at the floor, waiting for the kicker.

"Sing-song on Thursday mornings," Bill says, pulling up another chair. "I told Frank he should come over and check us out. Pretty lively group there now. Stanley Middleton can still hit the high notes and Hilda Brown is a natural for harmony."

"Old Stanley at the Lodge?" her dad says, slapping his knee. "Goddammit, imagine that. Never thought he would end up there."

"Classy rooms, too, I'll tell you," Bill goes on. "All the comforts of home."

Colleen wonders if Bill may be on her side, if he knows what's up and is actually helping them along. Has her dad said something to him? She doesn't know what to say. If she agrees, she'll look guilty and she sure isn't going to disagree.

"But do they have a bar?" her dad asks. He taps the chair arm with two fingers. He's hardly shaking at all.

"Pub night, last Saturday of each month," Bill says. "They've asked me if I'll play at that too."

"That's it?" Her dad snorts. "One goddammed night a month?"

"You're feeling better, then?" Colleen says. She knows the comment is a bit off the track, but it's better than nothing.

"Doctor says I can't go home," her dad says, staring at her. He grips the chair arm, knuckles white. "Says I couldn't manage, not for six months or so. For one thing, my damn feet are swelling. Probably this hospital food—some tasteless, salt-free diet they've got me on now."

"I see." Colleen nods wearily. She didn't know about the swollen feet or the diet. She should talk to Dr. Montgomery.

"Bill thinks I should try out the Lodge."

"Till he gets back on track," Bill adds. "I told him, all those cute young nurses, restaurant meals. Not a bad deal."

Colleen is not good at this kind of beating-around-the-bush. She needs a script. She stares at the floor again.

Bill gets up. "Well, Mrs. Pinser," he says. "I must be off. Pick up a paper." He pulls on his topcoat, adds his Sherlock Holmes hat. "Think about it, Frank," he says, as he heads out the door. "You could do worse."

"Should I get you some juice, some more water?" Colleen jumps up as soon as Bill leaves.

"You two in cahoots?" her dad asks.

"No, I swear it," Colleen says, sitting again. She grabs a tissue and blows her nose. "I had no idea he was playing at the Lodge."

"Started after I came in here," her dad adds. "He got a call from Stanley."

Colleen starts clenching and unclenching her hands, hardly aware she's doing it. At home, Steve tells her to stop, says she'll turn into a hand-clenching old lady.

"It's all right, Colleen," her dad says, after too many minutes silence. "I know it's a done deal. The doctor as much as said so. Call one of those damn nurses, will you? I have to go to the can."

Colleen almost asks if he wants her to help, but except for steering him into the bathroom or bedroom when he's drunk, she hasn't put her arm around him or stood close to him in over twenty years. She is not at all sure she can. Instead, she nods and jumps up again, out the door, then leans back in. "I'll get someone," she says, "and then I have to leave."

Her dad nods back, turning away, tense, his knuckles locked and still white on the chair arms, as if bracing himself against attack. The window light picks up a wetness on his cheeks. "Anything else, Dad?" He shakes his head defiantly. "Just call a damned nurse, will you?" Colleen races to the nursing station and, thank God, someone is there. "Mr. Miller," she says, "in 245. He needs help to the washroom." When she sees two women waiting for the elevator, she bolts past and takes the stairs.

Once outside, she stops near the hospital doors to button her coat, looking up and down the street for Bill Milligan, wondering if she should run after him. Then what? A heart-to-heart with old Bill? Thankfully, the street is empty. She knows zip about Bill Milligan, really. Not even where he lives. Does he have a wife, kids? His piano playing is okay, not a patch on her mom's, but then she was the best. All those bratty students week after week, year after year. Who knows, maybe one of them is famous by now. Colleen and her sisters all went through learning to play. Lillian, of course, had to be perfect; Heather, until she left, refused to do anything she was told, and Colleen, even though she hated it, tried because she didn't want to hurt her mom's feelings. She couldn't think straight about anything when she was in the house, let alone plunking away at boring scales. Home was mostly a place to get away from—over to Hannah's whenever she could wangle it, Hannah's mom always puffing away, a chain smoker, that's what she was. Colleen never thought about why her own dad didn't smoke; most of his cronies did. After a weekend poker game, Madge always complained the place reeked for days.

Colleen has never asked her dad about smoking, never really talked to him about anything, for that matter. He played sax in some band before he met her mom. She was sure there was no saxophone in the house. He probably sold it to buy booze or pay the rent, because he used the rent money for booze. He was a souse even before he met her mom, and there were tales of him drinking himself under the table at parties.

Colleen isn't so quick to judge now. They were young and in love, sure they could make a go if it after the Depression. Three babies in four years, and then the war put a damper on that—her dad signing up in 1940 when she was still in the oven.

A number of times, Colleen remembers her mom telling how her dad and his buddies all got drunk before going down to the Franklin Armories to enlist, Frank roaring into the house three hours later, blasting out "God Save the King." He'd have a steady job now, for sure. How her mom had coped, Colleen has no idea. She already had two preschoolers and Colleen was born only a month after Frank left for England. Bridget, Colleen's grandma, was so crippled up with arthritis by this time that she couldn't even get down from Toronto to see the new baby. With gasoline rationing, no one went far during the war, anyway. Her dad never did get onto the frontlines. In 1941, a company payroll clerk in his regiment waiting in London for posting orders, he came down with some awful rash—nerves they said, and he lay around for most of the next year and a half in a military hospital until his discharge came through in January 1943. Her mom always ended the story by saying Frank wasn't cut out for the army, too soft in the heart.

Today her dad wasn't even ticked off, didn't even yell at her. "Thanks Bill," she says out loud to the empty street.

When Colleen gets back to her car, the Buick she is sure was parked next to her is gone, but the rear right bumper of her car is dented, as if the Buick backed out and, for some reason, lurched forward. No note on the windshield—nothing. Ordinarily, Colleen would freak out, sure it was somehow her fault, that she shouldn't have parked there in the first place, that it would cost some awful amount to get it fixed, that they never had enough money, that if only she'd gone teaching, she would have a pension now and no money problems. Ordinarily—but not today.

It's only a bump, she says to herself. And the car's already fifteen years old. Nothing can get to her now. She sees her dad in the Lodge singing "I Only Want a Buddy Not a Sweetheart" with Bill thumping on the ivories. She feels giddy, ready to throw a party, go on a baking spree. At home, she takes a fast shower lathering herself with bodywash until the whole bathroom gets aromatherapy. Listening to make sure her two eighteen-year-olds haven't already landed in, she streaks down the hall, puts on her V-neck pantsuit, big loop earrings, and high heels—sexy, but not too. If the twins were away, she'd go for candlelight at dinner, stripping down a bit after dessert, pulling Art into a slow dance—Chris de Burgh. As it is, she puts on Gordie Lightfoot full blast and, pouring a glass of wine, starts making an apple pie.

"Whoa," Steve says, half an hour later, dumping his knapsack and gym bag on the kitchen floor. "Company or what?"

Colleen is browning the breasts for chicken cacciatore. A hot-apple-pie smell fills the kitchen.

Cal appears a few moments later, knapsack over one shoulder, mail from the roadside box in his hand. He drops the letters on the kitchen table. Colleen knows they are both checking her out, wondering what's up. "Someone coming over?" Cal asks, pausing at the stairs.

"Just us." Gordie is singing "Cotton Ginny," and she really wishes they would both skedaddle so she can dance a bit.

Cal takes off, but Steve slides into a kitchen chair, pretending he's sorting mail. Two peas in a pod, she and Steve, that mirror thing, flattering but, still a worry. She sees the same dark side in him, and it isn't from his home life. Besides that, he reads her like a book.

"How was your day?" she asks, chopping an onion.

"Not as good as yours."

"I want to wait until supper to tell everyone."

"You won the lottery?"

"Don't I wish."

"Something to do with Grandpa?"

"Maybe."

"That's a switch."

"Want a snack? There's chocolate cake. Take a piece up to Cal if you're going."

Steve cuts the cake and leaves. Colleen knows that he knows she won't tell, besides he doesn't like Lightfoot.

She hears them upstairs kidding around in the room above her, Cal already playing a computer game. They'll probably mention her off-the-wall mood, and Steve will say the clue is Grandpa. Her dad—who thinks he'll be sailing back to his own place later, when his arm is better. Never mind what he thinks or why. Just enjoy it. Especially tonight. *We'll cross that bridge when we come to it.* Art says this, but her mom did, too. There is some truth in her dad saying she's like her mom, like her and not like her. Fifty percent of children of alcoholics either become alcoholics or marry one. Well, I haven't and I didn't, she says to herself.

Gordie's into the "Canadian Railway Trilogy" and Colleen

dances around the kitchen, singing at the top of her lungs until Steve thumps the floor and shouts, "Keep it down, will you. We're trying to study up here." Even over the music, she can hear their computer game, the whizz and screech of some shoot-and-bang they're into—and the two of them having a good laugh at their mom, out of her mind over some old folk singer from the seventies.

BRITANNIA THEN

A MONTH INTO working at the Britannia, Hannah felt she had the routine under her belt. It was Thursday and, even though Colleen told her to stay away from the place on her day off, she slipped back in on her way to the library. The hotel was always semi-deserted in the afternoon. Salesmen and laborers were not yet back from their daily grind, and Daisy, who filled in as desk clerk for her husband on Rotary Lunch Thursdays, was snoring discreetly in the back room, nylon-stockinged legs propped up on an extra chair, radio blaring, ledger book open on the accounting desk. Astrid was always out afternoons and Charlie probably up napping in his room. Hopefully, Larry was out with his friends.

Hannah came to retrieve the overdue library book she had stashed on a shelf outside the pantry above the employee coat hooks. The so-called pantry was a roughly closed-in section under the back stairs leading up to Charlie's room behind the main second floor hallway. Even in semidarkness, Hannah noticed the photos thumb-tacked above the hooks. Two almost identical shots of Hannah and Colleen and Charlie in front of the steam table: Charlie's birthday celebration last week after everyone left—Charlie standing between the girls in the ridiculously too-large shirt they bought him, Astrid's five-dollar-bill gift in one hand, each of them rolling a sleeve up over his wrist before they said cheese, and Charlie with a closed-mouth grin looking pleased and slightly embarrassed. Astrid had promised the girls each a photo. Hannah pulled one down and tucked it into her pocket.

Afternoons the place was always too quiet, the rasping squeak of the swinging kitchen door echoing over the stainless steel counter and across cold stove burners. Hannah listened to her own breathing. As her hand reached for the book, floorboards above creaked—probably Charlie. Hannah was reading about Bernardo boys but hadn't gotten up enough nerve to quiz him about them.

More creaking: two sets of feet shuffling, struggling.

"You were in my room." Charlie's high-pitched voice.

"So what?"—the response sullen, with an adolescent crack.

"Where's my money?"

"Shut up, old man."

"Girls said my money is my money."

"Those dumb waitresses?" A snort, undeniably Larry's.

"Give it back."

Hannah slipped up against the wall, heart pounding. No one else was within earshot and she knew it was Larry. Ever since the dining-room episodes, Hannah had avoided him at all costs. His oversized hands still figured in her nightmares.

"I know you've got it, dammit. Hand it over." It was the most Hannah had ever heard Charlie say at one time.

More shuffling, grunting, and then Charlie's voice gurgling, a body crashing down the stairwell, crumpling at the bottom, one gnarled hand flopping into view, nicotine-stained fingernails curling and slowly relaxing onto the worn kitchen floor—a final gasp and quiet.

"You lose." Steps receding along the boards above, a door shutting. Stifling silence.

Hannah lodged herself in the back corner of the library, legs tucked under the wooden table, knees shaking. Feigning concentration, she tried desperately to read. *Girls said my money is my money.* She and Colleen both told Charlie that. Now look what happened. She should have gone back and alerted Mrs. Mourand, but she couldn't. She knew if she looked at Charlie and he was dead, she would faint. What would that have solved? For starters, it could have implicated her. What if there turned out to be a trial and, because they found her there, she had to testify? What if it was written up in the *Franklin Standard?* Mourand would fire her for sure. How would she get another summer job in Franklin? Her reputation would be ruined. Her mother's reputation. Her mother could even lose her job.

Hannah shivered and stared at her overdue book, *The Bernardo Children: A Forgotten History.* Several dozen hopeful young faces on the black-and-white cover photo stared at her from in front of a nondescript brick building. She breathed in and out and turned each page, slowly, trying to seem casual, even though her hand was cold and unsteady. The book's photographs, the shadowed shelves on either side of her, anything she concentrated on for more than two seconds blurred into those nicotine-stained fingers, letting go, shutting down, resting open-palmed. Dead.

She had no idea how long she sat there, trying to blank out her mind, trying to read a line or two. Mrs. Rankin, pushing the wooden cart piled high with books, tapped her on the shoulder as she passed. "Library closes in five minutes, Hannah. Time to go."

Colleen had planned to cut out fast and lounge at the beach. With Hannah off for the day, it was impossible to get her regular two-hour break, even though Charlie had helped her by scrubbing down the counter and resetting the tables. If she hurried, she could get her bathing suit on downstairs, grab an hour of sun and sand, and be back at the hotel for 5:30.

Just as she was heading out the front door, she felt that messy wetness in her panties. Damn. Her friend had arrived two days early, the curse her mom called it—the curse of white uniforms and bathing suits. So much for going to the beach. Thank goodness she'd stashed some supplies in the employees' washroom.

She tiptoed along the silent hall past Mrs. Mourand sawing one off. If Daisy saw Colleen, she would be stuck there for at least fifteen minutes getting advice she didn't need and being asked questions she'd rather not answer. Daisy had a *National Enquirer* mind.

About ten minutes later, when Colleen was about to grab the bathroom door latch, more than relieved that there was no blood on her uniform, zipping up her pedal pushers, she heard voices echoing down through the heating vent, not from the kitchen but the next floor up—angry, muffled voices on the landing where the back stairs came down into the kitchen, one of them high-pitched. Charlie? She stood frozen, hand on the cold metal. Mr. Mourand and Charlie?

"Where's my money?"

"Shut up, old man."

"Girls said my money is my money."

"Those dumb waitresses?"

"Give it back."

She heard sounds of pushing, shoving, and then something, someone, crashing down the stairs, landing right above her head: a gurgling, gasping sound, and then nothing.

Someone on the landing saying something. Footsteps moving away. The faint sound of a door closing. Silence.

Colleen kept staring at the ceiling, sure she would see blood dripping through any minute. There was someone else right above her, tiptoeing across the kitchen floor—that familiar squeak of the swinging door into the dining room. More silence.

Colleen stayed absolutely still, terrified someone would come down into the basement, find her there. When her own breathing became so loud she couldn't stand it, she took slow careful steps along the hall, thankful the floor was cement, pulling herself along the railing two steps at a time, whispering to herself, "Two more and now two more…" She inched herself around the door frame until she could see down the hall, her heart pounding so hard she was sure it would echo. No one. Giant silent steps past Daisy, still snoring. Ordinary steps now. Colleen pretended to check her lipstick in the big fancy mirror. She made it to the front door and stood inside, staring as a car passed. A fly buzzed and she watched it bat against the glass pane. Once outside, she tried to pull herself together, to look as if nothing was wrong and get across the street. She mustn't run, mustn't look terrified in case, later, someone said they saw her running from the hotel, running from the scene of the crime.

What she should have done was wake Mrs. Mourand or find Astrid. Cramps were already making little knife pains in her gut. Something awful had happened, a fight or worse. *Girls said my money is my money.* Charlie. Someone crashed down the back stairs—pushed by someone else at the top. He was out cold for sure. But if she had gone and found him, they might blame her and she'd lose her job. Besides, the Mourands lived upstairs and owned the place. Mind your own p's and q's her mom always said. She stopped at the end of her street and looked back. Just last week she and Hannah lectured Charlie about how he had rights, that he shouldn't give his cigarettes or anything else to that arrogant big fart Larry. The girls knew it had happened already, and it wasn't fair. Charlie had nothing but the few cigarettes Astrid gave him each week, a little cash from her month-end paycheck.

Colleen ran, her mind in a blur, pounding until full-blown cramps and nausea brought her to a slow walk. Two blocks from her house, she leaned over someone's white picket fence and threw up.

At 4:10 that afternoon, Colleen called in sick, telling Moira

Jackson that she had come down with the flu. Moira assured her not to worry—that there had been an accident.

"What kind of accident?"

"Charlie must have fallen down the stairs," Moira said. "He's dead."

Colleen started to sob.

"The hotel dining room is closed, in any case," Moira went on, "so there's no reason for you to come in. It's a real shame."

A faint click.

"Colleen? You still there, honey?" That's funny, Moira thought. She must have hung up.

Sometime between 4:15 and 4:20, Sarah Finn—ignoring Sergeant Brown's sputterings—burst into the hotel. Daisy had phoned her, and Sarah, who excelled during emergencies, made tracks over to the hotel. No one saw her slip out the back door, returning with her shiny blue Austin, which she parked in the back alley. A few minutes later, she escorted Daisy Mourand, shoulders slumped and shaking, head covered with a shawl, into the still running car, back to Sarah's and into a safe haven.

At 5:00, when Hannah walked back along Main from the library, knees shaking, a town police car was parked in front of the hotel, lights flashing. The front of the hotel was cordoned off with three rickety sawhorses and some dirty looking rope. Sergeant Harry Brown, belly jiggling out over his police belt, waved Hannah across the street when she attempted to walk down Victoria toward the lake, her usual route home. She had deliberately chosen this route before she left the library, her rationale being that if anyone was watching her and saw her avoid the hotel, it might raise suspicions.

"Hotel dining room is closed this evening, Miss. There's been an accident."

"An accident?"

Sergeant Brown grimaced and told her what happened.

Numbness kept her composed. She nodded and kept going.

Hannah couldn't eat any supper that night and told her mother she thought she was coming down with stomach flu, that Vivian at work had it, so she'd just lie down and read.

A small crowd had gathered in front of the hotel, mostly late-afternoon shoppers, some school children on the way home, but when nothing happened, they gradually dispersed. Clientele who came back to the hotel for supper chatted briefly with Sergeant Brown and left. Everyone, of course, speculated.

In one of the back booths of Roamer's Restaurant and Confectionary, a group of regulars gathered to discuss the matter. It wasn't often that an event of such dramatic significance occurred in Franklin, especially on a weekday afternoon.

Any mention of Mr. Mourand always carried a certain aura of ambivalence. On one hand, he had done wonders for the town, everyone agreed to that. The Britannia had helped boost sales in all the little stores up and down Main Street. On the other hand, little was really known about him, and what was known was not particularly flattering. Questions arose, for instance, as to why, if the Mourands were so well-off, they were living on the third floor of the hotel. Granted they still owned property down in Ohio, a family cottage apparently, not that Mourand himself ever went there. Summers, his wife and the hotshot kid always disappeared for a month, but not Mourand. He guarded the hotel seven days a week, twelve months of the year.

No one knew anything much about Charlie, either. He'd always been part of the Britannia as long as anyone could recall. Stanley Garret said he'd seen him a little drunk once a month in the Britannia Men's Room, likely after he'd been paid. Harold Clark said he often saw him behind the hotel smoking but had never seen him in any Franklin store buying cigarettes. Earl Pinser figured Charlie probably had a heart attack, poor old fella. Either that, or he took a dizzy spell and fell down the stairs. That he could have easily been close to eighty, they all agreed. The owner of the restaurant, Donald Roamer, known as Doc, said he didn't really give a damn one way or the other, that it was near closing, and he'd like them all to get the hell out.

The women, of course, had an entirely different set of stories. That evening, Mrs. Rankin told her husband George she worried about those poor girls working such long hours at the hotel, that Daisy Mourand was not a good role model, and the cook so rough and ready she wouldn't notice a ruckus if she heard one. Maybe old Charlie was drunk and fell down the stairs. No one knew anything about him, and heaven's knows, with all that alcohol in the place, anything was possible. Mrs. Long closed the bookstore half an hour early, and as soon as she arrived in the door, even though her cat, Jeremiah Puddle, was mewling pathetically at her feet, she called Sarah Finn. Mr. Finn told her quietly that Mrs. Mourand was near a nervous breakdown and that she was presently at the Finns' and likely staying the night. His abrupt tone of voice discouraged further details, and Mrs. Long thanked him politely and hung up.

The next day, none of the staff at the hotel asked questions. Hugh Mourand was at the front desk, looking particularly dapper in his pinstriped suit. He seemed preoccupied, head down when anyone passed by. Hannah and Colleen arrived for the morning breakfast shift as usual. Vivian seemed a bit bossier, and Astrid looked haggard, great black circles under her eyes as if she hadn't slept. Charlie's stool at the far end of the prep counter was empty, and without asking, Colleen and Hannah and Viv pitched in after dinner: dishes, cleanup, everything. It didn't take that long as the dining room was unusually slow, with only five or six customers all evening.

Larry was never seen again. No one seemed to connect this with Charlie's death, not even the staff at Larry's high school. School records were strictly confidential, of course, and if Mr. Staples, the principal, knew anything, he wasn't talking. Rumor had it Mourand sent his son off to a military school down in Ohio. He still had plenty of connections there. Larry was a brilliant student; Franklin teachers did talk about that. Of course, it was announced at the final June assembly that Mourand sponsored a basketball scholarship for the high school, which may have determined what anyone would or wouldn't say.

Whatever Colleen Miller and Hannah Norcroft thought or felt, they kept it to themselves. Anyone who noticed they looked thinner and tired most of the time, like Mrs. Rankin, said it was the job that was doing it to them. Those long hours, six days a week—it was enough to wear anyone out.

Daisy Mourand was never terribly well afterward, and Mr. Mourand hired Moira Jackson full-time. She told anyone, whether they asked or not, that she had aced her Special Commercial exams at high school to work the front desk and be Mr. Mourand's private secretary. She prided herself at being a Marilyn Monroe look-alike, an over-sixty-words-a-minute typist, and the loudest gum cracker in her class that year. She certainly livened things up at the Britannia, and later, after Mrs. Mourand was gone, people claimed she was seen climbing into Mr. Mourand's big black Lincoln late on Friday nights. He kept it parked in the back alley, not well lit but still visible from the side street. Sarah Finn insisted Deandra developed cancer and that Mr. Mourand sent her to an exclusive health spa in New York State. Most people were sure she had suffered a nervous breakdown after Larry was sent away. It was common knowledge that she couldn't live without the boy, her dear and only Larrykins. Mrs. Finn categorically denied this and railed at anyone who suggested any truth in the rumor—so much so, she didn't get elected the following term.

Astrid, probably the most affected with no one close to talk to, started drinking soon after. It wasn't noticeable for quite awhile, certainly not before the end of that summer. She was a big woman and could hold her liquor. Jake, the barman, always slipped her the odd drink, just as she slipped him leftover roast beef and chicken legs. Moira Jackson, who was even worse than Mrs. Mourand as a gossip monger, maintained the two of them were in the Ladies to all hours, especially on Saturday nights; and after Jake's wife died, Astrid moved in with him.

No further investigation was made, and the autopsy results recorded by Dr. Allister, Rotarian and friend of Mourand's, were never questioned. Charlie Elliot was not on the list of Franklin's noteworthy citizens. Most people, frankly, had never heard of him or, if they had, could not remember why. Besides, the economic slump had dodged them after the war and the town had bigger fish to fry. The economy was on the rebound. Postwar Franklin was more concerned with promoting tourism and two cars in every garage.

HANNAH/COLLEEN I

WHEN COLLEEN finally meets up with Hannah, it's all out of whack, wrong time, wrong place: Zellers, less than a week before Christmas, the store still packed in spite of the fact it is after nine at night.

Colleen, who has sweated it out at the hardware store for twelve hours straight, hopes to get in a little last-minute shopping. Originally, she thought of waiting until tomorrow, beating the crowds and showing up at the 7 a.m. opening, but there's not a chance she'd pull herself out of bed at that ungodly hour.

Now, trying to remember what it was that was on sale that she wanted, she's sure she looks out of it, her polyester, no-wrinkle pantsuit streaked with dust from boxes pulled from too-high shelves, her nail polish chipped from gift wrapping parcels and counting out screws and bolts from bins. Why anyone would be buying screws a week before Christmas is beyond her. She thought it was coal they put in stockings for a joke.

This morning at the hardware store, the rush started right at nine and customers were pressing their noses to the glass door even before Art unlocked. In the rush, she left her duffle coat on a chair in the back room. At lunch, one of the part-time teenage employees, had obviously dumped pop on it then piled newspapers on top. She didn't notice this until, pulling on the beige coat at the end of the day, she found a motley, orange-colored newspaper pattern on one sleeve and partway down the front. As she said to Art when he pointed it out to her, "Frankly, Scarlett I don't give a damn."

Her arms feel like lead weights and all she has eaten since this morning is a chocolate bar and cream cheese bagel, gulped down in the back office during the two lulls when fewer than ten people were in the store at once. As she rummages through her purse for her precious list, she feels someone staring at her.

Hannah is rushing to buy a small Christmas tree to take to her mother in the morning. She left the staff party as early as she could diplomatically maneuver herself out. Scanning shelves and walking too quickly, she almost plows into a woman head on—someone tired and frazzled. And familiar. "Colleen?" Hannah says, hardly believing it. "Colleen Miller?"

"Hannah?" Colleen gulps, snapping her purse shut. She pats at her half-gray hair, wondering if it, too, is covered in store dust. "Hannah Norcroft?" There she is, wearing a longish skirt, a suede outfit under a fancy capelike coat, shiny, straight brown hair flipped at the ends. And thin. My God she is thin.

They stare awkwardly at each other for a few moments.

Colleen, in spite of being exhausted, comes to first. "A couple of months ago," she begins, "Maureen at the hospital said she had seen you. I hope you don't mind, I visited your mom a few times." Instant sidetrack. Would Hannah have heard her dad yelling? Hopefully Maureen didn't mention anything about his past sobering-up stints. Colleen flashes a theater smile. "My dad was just down the hall."

Hannah can't hide her embarrassment. She has hoped all along that no one she knew would see her mother in such a pathetic state. Especially not someone she went to school with. "Yes, yes," she says, as breezily as possible. "Mother had a little stroke, but she's better. And your dad?"

"He fell and broke his arm," Colleen says, going into fast forward and edit at the same time. "My mom's been gone for a while so Dad has decided to hang out at the Lodge for a few months." It sounds good, maybe a bit general, not that Hannah will likely catch on.

"My mother is there, too," Hannah adds, trying to decide the vaguest way to word it. What if Colleen asks what wing or what floor? Hannah feels sweat between her shoulder blades, anxiety creeping up from behind. Her mother is well on her way to senility. She is her mother's daughter. She could easily follow in her mother's footsteps. Someone at school has already suggested this.

"It's a joke, Hannah. I meant it as a joke." Hannah didn't and doesn't see the humor.

"We should get together for coffee," she says to Colleen, mainly as a diversion. "When do you usually visit your dad? Weekends?" Stupid question, Hannah. She's right here in the same town. She can visit him whenever she wants.

"Sometimes." Colleen notices how uptight Hannah is. How could she forget? High strung and uptight, never standing still, talking too fast. "Dad will be at our place for Christmas, of course." She says it without thinking. This hasn't even been decided, ye Gods, and why did she add, "of course," making herself sound like a pompous ass.

"What about tomorrow?" Hannah asks, seeming to ignore the comment. "I'm here, staying at Mother's until the day after Christmas." Make it sound casual, thinks Hannah, not, I'm trapped at my mother's, stuck in this time-warp town, spending Christmas Day with Mother in "controlled access" and making the best of it. "Unless you're too busy, that is." Why did she say this? Because long ago we were friends, and even though it's obvious we have nothing in common now, let's anyway, for old time's sake.

Four days before Christmas, what can Colleen say? She works at

the store ten hours a day. She has a trillion things to do with everyone coming home. She's dog-tired and never goes out for coffee.
"I've been filling in at the store," she begins, instead. "Christmas
rush and everything."

"We could wait until the new year," Hannah says quickly—a
momentary exit sign flashing on and off. "I'm sure you'll have family
home for the holidays." Hannah turns to go.

"Hannah, no," Colleen says in a rush. "I'll tell Art we're getting
together for coffee, that we went to school together, worked together
at the Britannia, and that I haven't seen you in a dog's age. There
are three of them at the hardware store besides me. The place won't
fall apart if I leave for an hour."

"Pinser's Hardware Store?"

"Art Pinser is my husband."

Hannah grins, her face taking on a younger look, impish
almost, and she leans into the end of Colleen's cart. "Mar-i-on,
Madame li-brar-ian," she sings.

The Music Man, Colleen almost squeals. "And Moira Jackson.
Remember her?"

"She was…doing props," Hannah says, "among other things."
She laughs. "Oh God, Colleen, it's been a long time."

The Music Man, Franklin Theater Guild. One of those out-of-
the-blue connections—like yesterday. A nasal sounding voice cuts
in on the PA. "The store will be closing in fifteen minutes. Thank
you for shopping at Zellers."

"Tim Hortons?" Colleen says quickly. "On Garland, just off
the expressway. Did you come in to town that way?" There are a
couple of things Colleen really needs to buy.

Hannah nods. "Tomorrow at ten? You'll be able to get away?"

Colleen nods back and watches Hannah march off, shiny hair
swishing, coat flowing out behind.

As if to set Colleen off first thing, they sleep in the next morning—because one of them, and in her muddled state she has no idea who, pushed the wrong button or didn't push one at all. Colleen wakes and, seeing light coming through the curtain, bolts to a sitting position. Her clock radio glows at her—7:42.

Today Colleen has to be ready to go to the store with Art for 9:00. The twins, out late last night, have wangled use of her car so they don't have to get up for the early bus to school. After their first and only class that day, they are due at the store by 10:00. Good plan unless they're late, in which case she won't be able to leave. She should have told Hannah 10:30. Colleen can't bring herself to phone Hannah, not so early. It would seem like a last minute thing and look as if Colleen isn't interested. Hannah might cancel. Colleen attacks her closet, pulling out three or four outfits, throwing them onto the bed.

"I thought you two were meeting at Tim Hortons," Art says, watching her as he buttons his shirt.

"We are," Colleen snaps, "but I don't want to look like some old washerwoman."

She looks at the blue top but it's too flashy, especially for the store. She was going to wear a red sweater with her Christmas-tree earrings, but now she thinks that would be too gaudy, cheap looking. She needs something more elegant, something she could wear if she weighed thirty pounds less. She sits on the bed, a familiar weight pressing against her chest. Chest wall pain the doctor called it. Anxiety. You should relax more, Mrs. Pinser, especially at your age. That really ticked Colleen off—at your age. What age? Rocking chair age? Fat old matron age? Tears run down her cheeks.

Art sits beside her, his arm firmly around her shoulder. "Whatever you wear," he says quietly, "you'll look wonderful. Really."

Colleen stiffens. It's all very well for him. He loves her, that forever blessing/curse. Didn't her mother sound off about it enough when she was alive: You're so lucky to have a good man. "Yes, yes," Colleen says, jumping up. "And we don't have much time. We're late and I haven't made the lunches and…"

Art sighs and leaves the room. She hears him downstairs, opening and closing the fridge, probably checking the state of lunches. The boys could buy lunch, but Steve, especially, won't. He saves every cent. She looks in the closet again and finds a black jumper she hasn't worn for ages, straight up and down with silver buttons, slimming if she can get into it. And a black turtleneck sweater and silver earrings. Why is she doing this? They will probably have zip in common after all these years. She hardly saw Hannah after that summer at the hotel. Different friends. Different plans. Different lives.

As she screeches into the parking lot fifteen minutes late, Colleen sees Hannah's silky head at one of the window tables. Colleen is starving with no time for breakfast at home and no time for anything once the store opened—almost a dozen customers working over the shelves when she left, frantically picking up items, often putting them back in the wrong place. Cranky last-minute shoppers ready to be ticked off, especially if what they wanted wasn't there. And always a shoplifter. Art went on a prayer and a song at this time of year. Everyone was too busy to keep tabs on who came in and out, what bags they were carrying.

Colleen waves to Hannah as she pushes open the big glass doors. Hannah smiles and waves back. She is reading, probably something high class.

"Don't rush," Hannah calls, heading for the counter. "I waited to order. Had any breakfast?"

Colleen shakes her head.

"Me either. We should have something decadent. What would we have ordered at Roamer's? Remember Roamer's?"

"Restaurant and Confectionary. Best chocolate éclairs in town." Colleen glances at Hannah. She even looks thin in her jogging suit. One of those exercise fanatics, Colleen thinks, probably runs miles every day.

"They're not that good here," Hannah says. "But the cinnamon raisin buns are M'm good."

"M'm good, M'm good, that's what Campbell's soups are, M'm good," Colleen sings right behind her. Hannah turns and they have an attack of teenage giggles. The woman at the counter is not impressed.

Cosmo, Colleen notices, as she sits across from Hannah. She's reading *Cosmo*.

"Do you ever buy this?" Hannah asks, stabbing at it with her forefinger. "Same old propaganda recycled every fifteen to twenty years; only twenty years ago, I believed it. What about you?"

"Pam, my daughter, used to get it all the time," Colleen says. "That and *Elle*. She spent a fortune on magazines the summer she landed her first real job."

"She's grown up now, Pam?"

"Married with a daughter, Emily." Colleen hears herself inhale. "They live in Sudbury so we don't see them often." Colleen doesn't want to get into the Mother Hubbard list of child naming. Their older daughter, Janet, her husband and two kids in Guelph. Artie, the eldest, still a swinging bachelor and selling real estate in Costa Rica. That's a sore point with Art, not that he ever mentions it—not in so many words. Then the twins, great at the store but neither is into the small-business thing long-term. Both of them out of the nest after this summer. The whole thing is too complicated, too boringly domestic. Hannah wouldn't have a clue, wouldn't want to. Colleen, the brood sow—that's what her dad called her after the twins. Colleen looks at Hannah's manicured nails. "What about you?" she asks.

Hannah presses her fingers together and stares out the window. Where to begin? Her career and teaching make her sound pompous, too academic. Her private life is an undiscovered soap opera, Peyton Place revisited. "I've been teaching English in a Toronto high school," she begins guardedly. "And I have two small books of poetry published." Sure-fire diversion from her personal past.

Colleen reacts predictably. "Books published? Hot damn. Franklin girl becomes bestselling author."

"Not exactly," Hannah says, smiling. "Not many people read poetry."

"But you did," Colleen went on. "I remember—every poetry book in the school and then every one in the town library. Way to go. Where can I buy them?"

Hannah tries not to sound cynical. "They were for sale in a few Toronto bookstores, years ago, in the late sixties. I still have copies at home."

"But you've kept writing?"

Another sore point—after the pregnancy, her thesis, teaching, marking, years slipping into decades. "I've written a bit. Mostly at home. Scribbled on bits of paper here and there." She stops not knowing what else to say. People don't like too much detail, especially about something as esoteric as poetry writing.

"How long have you been teaching?"

"One more year to retirement. I can't believe it, not yet. It seems as if I've been teaching forever."

"Things are so different now," Colleen says. "It's been so much tougher with the twins. Everything fast forwarded. They think they're grown up before they get to high school."

"You have twins?" Hannah asks, leaning forward. "How wonderful. A daughter in Sudbury and twins. There must be a huge gap between the two. The twins—boys? girls?"

"I think you were in our store," Colleen says quietly. "Steve waited on you."

"That good looking, red-headed young fellow? He's one of the twins?"

Colleen nods. "Cal is quieter; he does more work in the back."

"Then I saw Art, too," Hannah says, remembering, puzzle pieces falling into place. "I thought I remembered seeing him in the hospital but I dismissed it. I saw both of you in the Clarence Ridley wing."

"Oh, look at the time," Colleen says, jumping up. "Got to get back—Christmas rush and all. When are you leaving for Toronto?"

"I'm not sure. I'll visit Mother in the morning, I guess, and then head out. Why don't I call you the first weekend I'm down in January? I'm aiming for every weekend, providing the weather isn't too awful."

"Love you and leave you," Colleen says leaning over to give Hannah a peck on the cheek. "Merry Christmas to you and your mom."

Hannah watches her rush out to the parking lot and disappear. Three kids. Well, at least three. She watches a young family at the adjacent table—young being the quintessential word. The parents look like teenagers although they're probably in their twenties. How old was Colleen when she and Art married? Why is this important? She vaguely remembers a wedding invitation, during first-or second-year university. She used it as a bookmark for one of her textbooks, made comments at the study table about her former high school friend, flippant, smug comments made from that barely dry vantage point when the screen is mostly skyline. She sees it every semester in the graduating class, baby birds ready to fly straight into the sun. Some of them do. And thrive on it.

Like she did, does. Anyone looking at her would think she has made it, even down to Russ. The chic thing for a woman to do these days is have a younger lover. Not that she planned it that way, not this last one at least. A wave of loneliness spirals through her. Russ is in Europe with his parents, somewhere in northern England, all of them stomping through the moors, warming themselves in fire-lit pubs. She was supposed to be there, too, to get to know his parents. That's what Russ had said. With whatever connotations that meeting held—none now. All of it idle chaff in the wind, scattered in the twinkling of a TIA.

The young father picks up his baby as Hannah moves toward the door. She hears him singing something, the baby chortling and gurgling, infectious, optimistic sounds that follow her out into the parking lot.

COLLEEN VI

SHORTLY AFTER 5:30 the following evening, someone from the Lodge calls the store and asks for Mrs. Pinser.

Colleen is trying to help a snobby woman decide between two Christmas serving dishes in the Giftware section. "You're sure these are both microwave safe? I don't see anything on the back that says so."

Steve appears beside her, quietly trying to give her the high sign.

"I'm sure," Colleen says. "They're both Chartney Ware, both microwave safe."

"Someone from The Lodge is asking for you, Mom," he says quietly. "NB I think."

"If you'll excuse me," Colleen says quickly. "Steve will take over, won't you, Steve? She wants info on Chartney Ware." Colleen hurries into the back room hearing the woman still bitching and still not convinced.

"I'm terribly sorry about this, Mrs. Pinser," a worried-sounding voice says, "but your dad, Mr. Miller, is temporarily missing."

Colleen's throat tightens. "Missing? How can he be missing?" It's been a long day.

"He went with a group in the Bunny Bus to the mall this afternoon," she went on. Someone young and frazzled, Colleen can tell that much. "Charlene was with them and she didn't do an accurate head count before they left."

"What time did the bus get back to the Lodge?" Colleen asks. She doesn't want to believe this, that her dad is missing. "Maybe he's in someone else's room," she says. "Wandering around the halls maybe?"

"We've looked, Mrs. Pinser. They should have noticed at supper, but we're short staffed and several of the girls are filling in because it's so close to Christmas." Her voice breaks, close to tears.

"Are you in charge?"

"The supervisor's due in any minute for the evening shift. I'm a nurse's aide."

"Should I go to the mall to look for him?"

"We've already phoned Mall Security, and they say he isn't there."

Colleen feels her shoulder muscles tighten, her throat go dry. He's found some crony and waltzed off to a pub. Christmas—the season from hell. "He didn't have much money so I don't understand why…"

"Charlene says he went into the bank with his pension check."

"His pension check? Are you sure?" The tightness in her chest squeezes again. She takes a deep breath. A month ago, they sent in forms to have his check put into direct deposit. Obviously, this check got through and was forwarded with his other mail to the Lodge.

"Yes Ma'am. Charlene says he was bragging about surprising his family with big Christmas presents."

"Right," Colleen replies. "Well, he's obviously met someone and gone off to celebrate so we'll just have to track him down. You tell your supervisor I'll get back to her as soon as I make a few phone calls."

Colleen looks through the one-way glass from the office into the store. Five or six more people are there now, Art and the boys going from one to another, answering questions, opening boxes to show off product, all of them, including her, totally whacked and on automatic. Now this. She can't bring herself to go out into that hubbub to tell one of them. She's suddenly been put on mop-up duty, again. Bloodhound to the rescue, again. Two days before Christmas. Pam and Janet and all of them are already at the house fending for themselves, not that they're helpless, but Colleen would like to be there—told them she would leave the store by 7:30. "No matter what," Art said. Artie was arriving the next day, flying in from Costa Rica. Her whole brood home for Christmas. Yeah Christmas. Blow up Christmas. She's going to bawl and mustn't. She has to rally, gird up, make a list of the pubs in Franklin and phone each damn one. He has to be somewhere.

A few minutes later, she finds out that pubs—of course, what was she thinking—are not listed in the yellow pages. Under Hotels, there are the two main chains: the Britannia, now a Vintage Sundown Inn, one more, and then a series of 1-800 numbers. She feels Art's hand on her shoulder.

"Trouble?"

She takes a deep breath and swallows. "It seems Dad is missing."

"Missing? How can he be missing?"

"That's what I said to the tearful young thing who just phoned." Colleen puts her hand up and rests it on his, determined to keep a hold on herself. "He went with a bunch to the mall this afternoon and they didn't notice somehow."

"Even at supper? What kind of a shoddy place is this?"

"Please, Art, I don't know, and right now I have to work out how to find him. You can be sure he's living it up at some pub, doing that getting-drunk-out-of-his-mind-before-Christmas thing."

"Dad?" Cal is at the doorway. "Someone wants to know if the warranty on a snow blower covers paint chipping off the blade cover."

"Go, Art," Colleen says. "I'll manage here."

Art leans over, his warm, whisker-rough face pressing against her. He squeezes both her shoulders. "We'll close early," he falters. "I'll help you find him."

Her shoulders stiffen more as his footsteps fade. The great all-demanding store must carry on. She knows that, accepts it, but right now the way it consumes all of them makes her see red. Blow the wretched place up: Colleen in military army fatigues, cat walking from the back alley after midnight, explosives all in place. She has thought about it more than once over the years. So here she is alone again, coping with yet another damn situation out of control. What else is new? She knows she could phone Pam and Janet, that they would come roaring in, her feminist knights drawing their swords and charging forward. But it's two days before Christmas, and her grandchildren will be wound up tighter than bowstrings, racing around the house; their parents will be sitting around with wine and munchies, living room stove blazing—all back there in the nest she worked so hard to build for all of them. No. She'll do this herself, like she always has. It's her problem, not theirs.

She attacks the white pages, finds Franklin, first column the A's, and runs her finger down and up, left to right, page by page. Thank God Franklin isn't any bigger. The Ambler Motel. Does it have a pub? She better check. The Britannia. Not likely he would be there, but if he is, Art will have to go in. Years ago, when she was still in the occasional theater production, the cast often went there after rehearsal. Colleen wouldn't even walk past the damn place if she could help it. She'd cross the street a block before Victoria, march past on the other side of Main.

She turns the page, Catcher's Cafe and Bar, and the next page. In the end, there are nine places not counting restaurants that serve alcohol, unless she has missed some. The print is much too small in phone books these days, even with reading glasses. At home she always gets Cal or Steve to look up numbers for her.

Even before she dials The Ambler Pub, the first place on her list, Colleen knows that anyone who answers will assume she is checking up on her husband and will, automatically, cover for him. She, therefore, needs a script, as ad-libbing under stress is not her thing. Writing it is another matter. She has to pull the words out one by one, stewing over what to leave, what to cross out, adding two or three words, and then taking them out. Art sticks his head in the door and she waves him out with her hand. They all know it's better to leave her, let her cope with this rerun alone: her battle, her disgrace. She recopies the lines and dials the first number.

(In a fake older voice) "Good evening. This is Mae Westbury speaking. Could you tell me if, by any chance, you have a Mr. Miller there? An older guy, wavy white hair. Cash is no problem as I remember, and he's probably buying his friends another round of draft." (If he isn't there) "Thanks then and Merry Christmas to you." (If he is there) "Tell him, will you, Merry Christmas from an old friend just back in Franklin."

Colleen knows her dad, and this is the only way to go. If they tell her dad who called, he'll be gone in a flash no matter how wasted he is. First and foremost, no cat and mouse games the night before Christmas Eve. Get him out of wherever and back to the Lodge. ASAP.

At 6:45, after too many fake cheery conversations with holiday-pumped bartenders and desk clerks, Colleen hits gold.

The Salamander Café on Highway I toward Port Turner. Why hadn't she thought of it? Right on the highway, only a couple of miles past the mall—the place to go in the fifties but, now, handed over and down through too many owners and too close to the wider, so-called better Highway I, its big front windows have been filled in, the whole front of it ugly concrete block. An old has-been, good for nothing but rounds of draft, meals down to bare bones, front counter and stools empty.

Even on the phone, the background din drowns out any extra chat.

"Good evening. This is Mae Westbury speaking. Could you tell me if, by any chance, you have a Mr. Miller there? An older guy, wavy white hair."

"Yer lookin' fer Frankie Miller? Some days he's here, some not. You his wife?"

"An old friend from his high school days."

"Well if yer after his money, yer too late. He's spent most of it."

"Tell him Mae raises her glass for a damn good holiday."

"Yer not goin' to join us then? He might have enough left for a draft or two."

"Tell him I'll see him at New Year's and God bless."

Colleen is shaking so much she can barely put the phone down. She gets this scene in her mind: She's old, totally gray, an afternoon tea drinker still scheming, scribbling little scripts so when they phone, she can lie to her well-into-middle-aged children, where she's going, where she's been, without realizing it, taking on her father's role, spending her pension check the first week, going on bus tours or playing bingo with her friends.

Cal sticks his head in. "You okay, Mom?"

"He's at the Salamander." Colleen jumps up. "Could you phone the Lodge and tell them not to worry, he's on his way back?"

"Good as done."

"And can you and Steve hold the fort?"

"Hey, we're pros." He disappears as Colleen gets herself to the coat rack.

The bartender or clerk or whoever he was may or may not pass on the message. If her dad's drunk enough, he won't think anything of it. He'll laugh it off, order another round. It may niggle at him, though. Why would an old friend call him at the Salamander? More likely his do-good daughter or someone from the jailhouse Lodge.

Would he think like this, Colleen wonders? She has no idea what he thinks about other than some sentimental longing for a wife he mostly ignored all his married life. And his next drink.

"Colleen?"

Art's there with his coat on, guiding her out the back door toward the car. The winter lake wind cuts through coat seams and she feels goose bumps on her skin. Art, all too aware of how frantic she is, manages not to go through his usual down-to-the-last-speck window scraping routine and, instead, squirts masses of washer fluid onto the frost-filled windshield.

"The Salamander," she whispers as they bump down the back alley toward the street.

"Cal told me."

"What if he's gone before we get there?"

"He won't be."

"He used his pension money. Damn the bank."

"Someone slipped up. It happens."

"If I had a gun, I'd nail him. First him and then myself—"

"Colleen. We'll get through this. He'll be back at the Lodge. An hour from now, you'll be with your grandkids."

"I'll be in great shape for grandkids."

"I talked to them earlier on the phone," Art says. "They're so wound up, especially Emily."

Colleen watches Christmas lights, people walking, piles of cars as they pass the still-crowded mall. Art drives carefully down the black road, slower than Colleen would, his steadiness only a little annoying, but mostly comforting.

Three cars are parked in front of the Salamander. One has to be the bartender's, one the cook's, if he's still on, and the last, whichever drinking cronie was clever enough to bring Frank here. Easy mark Miller. Still misses his wife, poor guy, being it's the holidays and all. Cheer the fellow up. Help him spend his money.

Stale beer and cigarette stench hits them as Art opens the door, a hurtin' song wailing out from a radio. The place is empty except for a table in the back corner where five men sit, laughing and chewing the fat. Light flashes on and off from a muted TV behind them. The bartender is nowhere in sight.

Colleen leans against the doorframe, her father's white head glistening above the others. Art squeezes her hand and strides toward the group.

"Goddammit," Frank slurs loudly, looking up. "Art Pinser, my esteemed son-in-law."

Art leans over the table, talking quietly so that Colleen can't hear. No fuss. No waiting. Frank pushes his chair back, weaves to a standing position, salutes, and manages to drape his good arm over Art's shoulder. As if they're buddies.

Colleen bolts for the car and slips into the backseat.

"So I said to the bartender," Frank cracks as Art opens the front passenger-seat door, "Where the hell are the dancing girls with walnuts in their navels?" He snorts and belches loudly. He hasn't looked in the backseat but Colleen is sure he knows she is there.

Art gets in and starts the engine. "Pretty cold night, eh?" he says as they wheel out of the dark lot.

In spite of the fact that Art has just successfully corralled her father, his remark gets Colleen's goat. Good old Art, forever and always the fence-sitter. No bawling her dad out, no questions asked, might as well be a taxi driver picking up a fare.

"Pretty damn cold in the backseat," her father snorts. "How's the Gestapo back there? Making sure I get signed, sealed, and delivered back to the jailhouse Lodge?"

Colleen grinds her gloved fingers into her palms; Art turns on the car radio. The voices of two singers crooning "I'll Be Home for Christmas" fill the car. Her dad joins in on "you can count on me" and then laughs until he starts coughing.

Art turns the volume down. "Bad cough," he says. "Got a cold?"

"Damn secondhand smoke," her dad slurs. "Gets me every time." His head is dropping now. Any minute he'll be out.

Colleen watches dark fields, darker tree branches. Everything blurs. Last week in the paper, police somewhere out west were accused of dumping drunken First Nations people at the edge of town in below-zero weather. After more than one corpse was found, family members became suspicious. An investigation was currently underway. It would be so easy, someone drunk, asleep—just pull over and roll him out. Guilt sweeps over her even before she thinks it through. Art's hand reaches back to comfort her, and she pulls away, unworthy, sins of the father racing through her veins.

By the time they reach the Lodge, Colleen has pulled herself together. She creates her wife-of-town-businessman look for the woman at the front desk who treats their arrival as if they were back from a regular outing. Either the woman knows and is keeping quiet or doesn't know and is being polite.

"A wheelchair for Mr. Miller?" she repeats, smiling. "There should be one down the hall, next to the lounge."

"Would you let them know on the second floor?" Colleen says smiling back.

The woman nods and dials as Colleen hurries out.

It takes a few minutes to get Frank out of the car and into the wheelchair. He half wakes up, tries to steady himself with his cast-covered arm, staggers against Art and almost knocks him over. Colleen rushes in with the chair from behind, buckling her father's knees so that he falls onto its seat, cursing in full voice.

"Shh," Colleen snaps, steadying the chair as Art gets her father's feet onto the foot pads. "You'll wake the dead if you keep that up."

"Goddammed bunch are half dead anyway," Frank snaps back. "Christmas at the morgue, for God's sakes. That's what you're taking me back to."

The automatic glass doors close behind them, and thankfully, Frank is quiet. Asleep again.

The fact that he has had to share a room hasn't bothered Frank as much as Colleen thought it would. He likes to gab and doesn't seem to care about the lack of privacy. His roommate, an overly tidy little man, is sound asleep, snoring in short, windy spurts, every few breaths, a high-pitched wheeze in between.

Art follows Colleen out of the room, or rather runs after her. "Shouldn't you call someone," he pants.

"I've already told them," Colleen snaps. "He's asleep, anyway. What time is it?"

"Just after 7:30."

"So Janet and Pam don't have to know. It's as if we've closed the store and we're on our way home."

"If that's what you want," Art says wearily, patting her arm before turning the key in the ignition.

Colleen nods and thinks hard about butterflies—the colors in their wings, the way they glide.

HANNAH VI

LATE MORNING the day of Christmas Eve, Hannah sits in her mother's front room, hand sewing red-velvet ribbon strips to adjacent corners of a colorful Christmas napkin—a bib for her mother, part of a place mat and napkin set purchased at Zellers, an impulse buy along with too many Christmas ornaments and two artificial trees, one small and a larger one for the house. Why? Because there has always been a tree in the house at Christmas. Because the thought of being here alone in her mother's house with no tree amplifies her self-pity to an almost audible level. Two trees. An utter extravagance except that, so close to Christmas, they were marked one-third off. She has no idea, really, whether or not her mother even cares about a tree now. Or ever did for that matter. She always had a real one when Hannah arrived home over the years. Where it came from or who brought it into the house, Hannah has no idea. "Tree's up," her mother would say, waving her hand almost dismissively in the tree's direction—a signal for Hannah to put whatever small presents she had under it, add them to the few already there, nestled in the white sheet crumpled strategically around its base. Large presents would not do—too extravagant, too ostentatious. "For heaven's sakes, save your money," her mother would say. "Don't go spending it foolishly on me."

Hannah finds the old decorations tucked away on a basement

shelf behind the water heater. Everything neatly packed in a still amazingly resilient octagonal department store hatbox and a large Campbell's soup box with the happy-little-girl insignia smiling at the soup can. Christmas decorations, small fragile balls, hand-painted with sparkle over the paint, likely applied when the latter was still wet, and red string threaded through and knotted around each arched metal loop. Several dozen balls, all different—from where? What store? What city? What decade? Hannah makes a mental note to research this when she returns home.

And the lights. These lights have been used since Hannah was a child and so must be at least fifty years old. Two boxes, smallish by today's standards, with detailed instructions on the bottom of the box explaining that each string is in series and, therefore, when one lamp burns out, the entire string will go. Each "lamp" is screwed into a solid-looking plastic housing with two cotton-covered wires, red-and-green-striped, like an old fashioned barber's pole, thread-ing from its base. Directly beneath, a red wooden bead slides up and down to pull tight onto a tree branch when decorating. Both sets seem safe enough, although when she tries them, neither lights up, and after a frustrating twenty minutes of bulb switching and replacing, she manages to make one set operational. Her impulse is to take this set to use on the tree for her mother, but then, worry-ing that they might be stolen, she keeps the single set to turn on for memories' sake.

All those stilted Christmas mornings before and after she left home: just the two of them. A roasted capon with red currant jelly, not cranberries the traditional condiment, as she discovered much later. Red currant jelly—bought at great expense until Hannah discovered Colleen's mom made the stuff from their own berries. Hannah, who was in high school at the time, tried to buy some of the jelly for her mother, but Mrs. Miller insisted on it being a gift, going on about how wonderful it was that Hannah was

Colleen's friend, as if Colleen were some outcast. Right in front of her—Colleen agreeing, grateful to be in collusion with her mother's pronouncements. Much later Hannah realized Mr. Miller's behavior was the cause, that his drinking was some kind of pall over their heads. Beautiful, effervescent Colleen—boys flocking around her and she swatting them off like so many flies, determined not to get involved with anyone, heart set on a glamorous career. And then, before she was twenty, married to Art Pinser—himself a contradiction—flamboyant looking with his flaming red hair, but also shy, intense, heir to the hardware business. Colleen went to Teachers' College. Hannah's mother sent Hannah Colleen's graduation picture from the *Franklin Standard.* But did Colleen teach? Does it matter now? She's the one with children and grandchildren—a wonderful warm family all home for Christmas. Hannah will not wallow. Never has.

A knock on the door jolts her back to reality. Hannah peers through the front window. It's the postman, or rather the postwoman. She waves. Hannah waves back and unlocks the deadbolt and chain.

"Too thick to go through the mail slot." Ms. Postperson grins. "Thought it might be a Christmas present."

"Thanks." This wouldn't happen in the city, Hannah thinks.

"How is Mrs. Norcroft these days?" Loaded question, only the woman doesn't realize it.

"She…she had a stroke about a month ago," Hannah begins. What to tell this person? Why would she want to know, anyway?

"A stroke? Oh, I'm so sorry. She was such a dear lady."

"I'm her daughter," Hannah says, feeling again exposed.

"I know." The postwoman beams. "She talked about you all the time: your teaching in the city, your poetry. Well, Merry Christmas to you and hello to Mrs. Norcroft from Cath. She'll know who I am."

Hannah watches her leave, her footsteps slosh-sloshing in the wet snow.

To everyone else, then, her mother is a different person, someone friendly, chatting to neighbors, the postwoman. Hannah is again struck with nostalgia for things lost: moments, situations, all that mother-daughter togetherness found in greeting cards, if nowhere else. Right now, she longs for the impossibility of having been a voyeur, a proverbial fly on the wall, watching her mother's life. How did she spend her days? How did she cope with her own inadequacies, her regrets? Did she ever try to find her husband, Hannah's father? And her sexuality. Repressed? Never realized and eventually forgotten?

The envelope. She has almost forgotten what she is holding. Something too thick to go through the mail slot. A fat brown envelope addressed to Hannah from Winnipeg, Manitoba. Aunt Harriet. Hannah slams the front door and races to the kitchen table.

A pile of photos and a card fall out of the ripped-open envelope. She thumbs through the photos, searching for the one Aunt Harriet mentioned on the phone: you and your mother just back from the hospital. When Hannah finds it, she gets up and moves to the kitchen window. Her mother looks so young, sitting primly on what must be Harriet's sofa, her legs crossed demurely at the ankles, with her, Hannah, a blanketed little package in her arms. The adoring look on her mother's face, staring at her newborn, says it all. Hannah feels a huge lump in her throat. She stomps over to the table, puts all the pictures in a row, like cards, face up, and then rearranges them according to family. Five of her mother with herself, a couple of close-ups showing her little prune face, eyes tightly closed. Memories of her own baby flood back, the two times she held him, blanket-wrapped and asleep, the ache inside her, so great she could barely focus, willing herself to hold, but not acknowledge, what she had produced, this child she had finally, after so much struggle, given birth to. The release form she had signed, hand shaking. Silent discrimination. The husbandless woman. The hussy who abandoned her child. She can't even remember now what arrangements Anthony made. A private room, thank God. Money was no issue with Anthony. She remembers wondering if he had done this before, if he had a string of children by promising young grad students. Anthony's seed scattered abroad. Not likely. The cost would multiply, become a burden, even for well-heeled Anthony. Sacrifice wasn't one of his strong points. Image and success were. She remembers only that the baby was whisked off somewhere to someone, and she was left to make the best of it.

Hannah shoves the pictures of her mother and her baby-self back in the envelope and picks up the card, a Christmas card with a note neatly penned on the inside: *So wonderful to make contact with you after all these years. Here are a few pictures. I've written on the back of each. Carol and family here for a few days. They send regards. Love, Aunt Harriet.* Carol—a daughter—Hannah's cousin. Hannah runs a finger along the remaining pictures. Two children likely under ten, arms akimbo over bicycle handles, the girl obviously younger, grinning and probably pleased that her two front teeth are missing. Hannah turns the picture over. *Brian and Carol, summer 1952.* Another, a young man leaning rakishly against a parked motorcycle. *Brian. Not long before his fatal accident, August 20, 1959.* Hannah stares at the picture. A motorcycle accident? How old would he be? Eighteen? Nineteen? An unexpected wave of rage runs through her. Damn her mother. Why didn't she tell Hannah about this family, her only relatives? And now, now it was too late. Her mother's computer has crashed, files irreparably scrambled.

If her mother kept Aunt Harriet's address all these years, perhaps she wrote occasionally to her sister and brother-in-law. Letters secretly typed at work, evenings probably, on the shiny black Underwood No. 5, dusted regularly and kept on a small oak typing

table, varnished wooden filing cabinet to its left. Funny how details
remain. Hannah was only allowed into her mother's workplace a few
times. Up a set of wide stairs and to the left along a dusty hardwood
floor to the second office where her mother was ensconced at her
secretary's desk, Mr. C.R. Lumsdon, Chartered Accountant, behind
a closed door on her right. He was a kindly round-faced, round-
middled man, meticulous in dress and exacting in expectations.
"He's fair," her mother always said. "And fussy down to the fourth
decimal." This was as close to humor as her mother ever came. If
her mother wrote letters at all, and Hannah, in all the years she
lived at home, never saw evidence of this, she might have written
them by hand, right here at this kitchen table after Hannah went
to bed. She stares at the tabletop as if looking for evidence, a dab
of ink from her fountain pen, the ghost of a rejected word tossed
carelessly aside.

When she was growing up, Hannah couldn't imagine her
mother writing a letter—writing anything except business reports.
She would have nothing to do with Hannah's school work once
Hannah was in high school. "It's your responsibility," she always
said, if Hannah ever asked her to look something over before or
after it was marked. "Your responsibility and your business." A
double-edged comment, lines distinctly drawn.

She could ask Aunt Harriet about letters, but not now, not
when Carol and family were there for a few days. Carol would
likely be in her fifties, but younger than Hannah. Married of course,
probably grandchildren running about, which only made Hannah
think of Colleen, her house filled with laughter and anticipation.

On the way to the Lodge, Hannah decides that even though it is
the day before Christmas, she will track down Mrs. Sanderson. A
week after her mother was admitted, she fell in the hall lugging an
oversized armful of clothes still on hangers, heading toward the

controlled access door, obviously hopeful of escape. Efficient and ever accurate, Mrs. Sanderson called Hannah at school to report that because Edith Norcroft took it upon herself to move some of her personal effects into the hall, with the supposed intent of leaving, she fell and/or suffered another TIA. In consequence, Dr. Fulton, the resident physician, advised a wheelchair. Her mother has not walked since.

When Hannah arrives at the Lodge at eleven, she catches a glimpse of Mrs. Sanderson disappearing down one of the main floor halls. "Mrs. Sanderson," she calls. "If you don't mind, I have a few questions."

Mrs. Sanderson marches back, giving Hannah her I'm-in-a-hurry-so-don't-take-too-long look.

"I was wondering when I could see Dr. Fulton to discuss my mother's situation."

"The doctor is booked three months in advance," Mrs. Sanderson replies firmly. "You will have to put your name on the list like everyone else."

Hannah nods and can see this isn't the time or place. Catching the ephemeral Dr. Fulton has, so far, proved futile. He is either coming in later, on some other floor, or has just left. "I could do that at the nurse's station?" she asks, smiling politely.

"That would be the place," Mrs. Sanderson says, turning to leave.

"One more thing." Hannah adds quickly.

Mrs. Sanderson turns back, her mouth a ruler-straight line. She is not used to being interrupted, Hannah thinks.

"Do you think my mother would enjoy spending Christmas Day in her own home?"

Mrs. Sanderson's response sounds textbook accurate but is less than satisfactory. "It usually follows," she says, "that a resident recently removed from her own premises, and frequently in a confused state of mind, is best kept in a stable and constant environment." She gives Hannah a curt nod and marches off.

This doesn't, of course, answer the question, not directly, and Hannah is still wondering. It would be nicer for both of them if they spent Christmas in the usual place. A conundrum. Hannah lets herself into the controlled access wing, thankful no furtive-looking resident is lurking by the door.

Edith sits facing the big hall window, slumped in her wheelchair beside another resident slumped and asleep. She is wearing her red Christmas blouse, already christened with breakfast remnants, her hair in need of a set again. Instead of her jaunty sweat pants—Hannah had purposely bought two good black pairs—Hannah is horrified to see her mother wearing a fuchsia-and-green flowered skirt, obviously open at the back and hitched up over her wrinkled knees and calves, white sports socks and shoes an incongruity below.

No nurse or aide in sight as Hannah briskly wheels Edith back to her room. "Who dressed you today, Mother?" she asks, as they glide past the empty nursing station toward 126. Not that she is expecting an answer. In the last couple of days, her mother has spoken only once, and that was to tell Hannah that her shoulders were stiff and she was glad she didn't have to type any more reports today.

Neither pair of black pants is in sight, and Hannah finds only a pale-blue pair, part of a set. The skirt pulls off easily, and Hannah is struck, again, by the indignity of all of this, her mother's thin wrinkled legs, the bulky, oversized diaper, the smell. Dead skin, urine not quite wiped away, age. They do bathe her mother regularly? For a moment, she feels herself implode—helplessness, frustration.

"Used to have good legs," her mother remarks. "Betty Grable legs."

Hannah is rummaging through the bottom bureau drawer one more time, still hoping to find a pair of the missing black pants.

She almost knocks the drawer onto the floor. "We'll get those legs into a decent pair of pants," Hannah says, wishing she had better experience in on-the-spot banter. She never was good at it, not even with close friends. Being with her mother now is like a skewed carnival ride, seemingly stalled indefinitely, then jerking forward momentarily to throw her off balance, almost knocking the wind out of her. Betty Grable legs.

Pulling the jogging pants over those legs and up to her mother's waist proves impossible. Hannah is shocked at how weak her own arms and shoulders are. The whole thing becomes a comedy scene turned macabre: Hannah pulling and shoving, reaching under her mother's scrawny, diaper-covered buttocks, trying to pull the fabric without dislodging the diaper; her mother completely unable to heft up even one iota of an inch, becoming more and more agitated as struggling progresses.

"If you could just lift up the tiniest bit," Hannah mutters, yanking and pulling. Her mother groans, hanging on for dear life to the arm rests of the wheelchair as if Hannah might throw her off. In the end, Hannah is sweating and the pants are a twisted three quarters of the way on. She arranges the red blouse over them as a disguise, then ties the jaunty bib around her mother's neck and marches her back out to her place in front of the window. Getting her to the house on Christmas day would be impossible.

A worried kitchen staffer stands by the lunch tray cart, the sound of plate scraping and shaky conversation drifting from the dining room.

"Oh, Edith," she says, as the two of them come into view. "I was gettin' worried there that you'd run off with someone."

"A quick change," Hannah explains, taking the tray from her. "Thanks for waiting."

"Bye, bye," the woman calls in an annoyingly cutesy voice, giving Edith an adult-to-infant wave.

Much to Hannah's surprise, Edith waves back, smiles even. These gestures, unreasonably, frighten and infuriate Hannah. Is this really her mother? Or has someone or something switched her, removed her? It is as if everything her mother has been and represents has been sucked out of her, leaving a husk with only the faintest echoes of Edith Norcroft left. Washing over this irrational fear, is a sharp flash of anger. Her mother, in her right mind, would never tolerate this patronizing drivel, this outright condescension.

I'm probably being unfair, Hannah thinks, depositing the tray and watching her mother scan its contents. The woman is likely minimum-wage kitchen help and just trying to be friendly. Hannah watches her mother's finger zero in on the butterscotch pudding, pushing the not-too-desirable-looking stew aside.

"It can't be that bad," Hannah says, sitting and putting the smaller spoon in her mother's left hand. Edith has always been right handed down to the core of her being. Hannah remembers her mother sing-songing "left hand, witches curse" almost any time she found Hannah writing. It certainly kept her from doing homework at the kitchen table.

Edith's right arm wobbles now, the hand arcing through the air, dive bombing, like an out-of-control stunt pilot, over the food but not actually into it. After several abortive attempts, she drops the spoon and sticks her finger into the pudding again, coquettishly sampling the fruits of her theft.

Hannah hears herself say "Mother" in an annoyed tone of voice. She hasn't meant to. Her mother recoils slightly, turning her head to one side as if scrutinizing the wall.

"Mrs. Sanderson won't like it if you don't eat your lunch," Hannah says, or rather her voice says. She knows it's a vapid thing to say, unsubstantiated and whiney, like mothers she overhears in the supermarket needlessly threatening their misbehaving children. What is there about her mother's behavior that reduces her to this? She is the one in control, the one who is free; she should be magnanimous, understanding. The four-decade pile of mother/daughter baggage continually reinvents itself between them—a hair's breadth, a gesture away.

Her mother turns back and nods at the paltry stew. Hannah deposits one mouthful after the other, trying to be patient as her mother chews and chews, sometimes coughing and spurting the contents over the tray, the pudding, Hannah. When the stew is half gone, Hannah reverts to the pudding. Her mother beams, opening her mouth twice as wide for each mouthful even as Hannah scrapes remnants from the dish. Two sips of tea and Edith nods, the third is never swallowed and trickles from the corners of her half-open mouth. Hannah pats her face dry, looking up and down the hall for the tray lady and her cart. The adjacent dining room is emptied of its wheelchairs and walkers. Hannah wonders what happens when she isn't there to feed her mother. Does someone else do it, or do they simply leave the tray and then remove it after a set time? She should talk to Mrs. Sanderson about this.

A tired-looking nurse's aide whisks by before Hannah can think of what she wants to say, how to explain what seems to be out of control, too sprawling to get into words. This unreal reality. It smacks of *Waiting for Godot*, surrealistic with no answers, no closure except death. Her mother as Hamlet, except her mother didn't aspire to power, didn't avenge, she simply plodded all her life making decisions she obviously thought were best, not for herself, but for Hannah, always for Hannah.

What she should do is take early retirement and bring her mother home. That would be the noble thing to do. People in other generations did this. The maiden aunt, the eldest sister Sacrificed their years for a mother, father, grandparent. Eighteenth century literature is full of their heroic, selfless lives—usually told from someone else's point of view. Occasionally now, in modern literature, a tale of genuine caring and sacrifice, but as the crowded conditions in even this illustrious institution show, not really the modern trend.

"Ms. Norcroft?" Hannah wonders how long she has been sitting there, staring at her mother's slumped and sleeping form. "I'm here to put Edith to bed."

A young nurse's aide—organized and eager.

"Thank you," Hannah says gratefully. "She fell asleep before she finished."

"She often does," the girl says, grasping the wheelchair handles and turning the cumbersome thing with an experienced finesse. Hannah follows along behind, stopping at the door, defeat weighting her arms and legs and visibly, she's sure, sagging her face.

The young woman pats Edith's shoulder. "She's adjusted very well, you know. I feed her almost every day." Hannah nods, feeling tears close to the surface. She turns to leave.

"Only ten percent of seniors are institutionalized," the aide explains, as if Hannah has asked. "The rest live fully productive lives on their own."

"Thanks," Hannah says before bolting down the hall to the controlled access exit. Was I that transparent? Did I have it written all over me? Such a young thing, but she is perceptive, caring, rattling off text book percentages, still confident she can make a difference.

Outside, snow has covered car hoods and windshields, even the too-black parking lot. No one is about and a snowfall stillness permeates, leveling everything to neutral with only form to define context. If she stands here long enough, Hannah, too, will be covered, melding into this perfection, absolved of duty and guilt—more likely get pneumonia first, she thinks, shaking the snow from her hair and searching in her pockets for a pair of gloves.

On the way home, she plans the rest of her day. Wrap presents.

Two new cassettes she has bought for herself, an elegant dressing gown for her mother, and some more Chopin, copied from tape to tape before she came. She can't help feeling relieved at not being able to bring her mother back here. The furniture's been moved, Hannah's belongings tucked everywhere.

Maybe if I go on a bodybuilding regime for the next year, Hannah thinks, I'll be strong enough to heft Mother out of the wheelchair, into the car, and back out again once we arrive here. Besides that, she would need a ramp. She hasn't even thought of the ramp until she returned home today. She found the snow shovel in the basement, cleared the front and back steps. A couple of wide boards might do it, but what if the wheelchair tipped or ran off track? No one would build her a ramp this time of year. Her conscience continues to prod. Circumstance has, again, absolved her.

What she should do is go for a run, but Russ is supposed to call from England between 2:00 and 2:30 and it's just past one now, six hours later there. Besides, the roads and sidewalks will be slippery. If she was at home, she could go to the Fitness Center, indoor track, like-minded joggers, albeit the day before Christmas. She considered getting herself a treadmill for Christmas, even priced them. Russ talked to his fitness-expert friend who said a commercial treadmill was the only way to go, that all those TV ads were bullshit, his words, and that none of those advertised would stand up to prolonged use. The commercial ones started at $4,500, and Hannah can't justify that amount. She determines she will walk, walking being just as good exercise: a two-hour walk each day. But today has slipped away from her, and after Russ calls, she won't have the energy.

After a bowl of soup she feels suddenly exhausted and decides to take a short power nap before wrapping the presents. Andrea Bocelli's voice is washing over her from his *Sacred Arias* tape when the phone surfaces her from half sleep.

"How are you?" Russ's voice travels like an electric current through her body.

"Fine, I'm fine."

"And your mother?"

"She...she's doing about as well as can be expected. I thought about bringing her here tomorrow but it's impossible..." Hannah hears voices, laughter, the clink of glasses. "Where are you?"

"Downstairs at the inn. There's no phone in our room. You'd love it here, Hannah. It's a seventeenth-century Free House pub, rooms upstairs. We went for two hikes today, morning and afternoon. God, my parents can almost out walk me."

Hannah is determined not to sound jealous. She could give him a dig about being out of shape but instead says, "Doing any research?" One of his reasons for going in the first place.

"A bit." He lowers his voice. "I miss you terribly."

"Me too." Hannah feels her defenses slipping, her coping skills dissolving. She hates to think she needs him, anyone, this much. "Give your parents my best regards," she says, rather stiffly. A Hannah the-English-department-head voice.

"Later," he says, "when things are less complicated, we'll come back here together. Same room. The window looks east into a wonderful walled garden."

"Later," she repeats, blinking tears.

Static interrupts. Hannah thinks she hears him say something else and she shouts a reply. It's no use. They manage good-byes and she hangs up.

Getting drunk has definite possibilities. The phone rings again and Hannah grabs it, hoping Russ has tried a second time, but it's Colleen inviting her over for a Christmas Eve drink. Art will pick her up. Hannah, completely unprepared for this and still stabilizing from Russ's voice, can't think of any logical reason to say no.

"Yes, yes. How kind of you." All sorts of background noise. Kids, adults, sentimental Christmas music.

"I kind of thought you might be alone. I'm not intruding?"

"No, no, not at all."

"Art will pick you up at seven."

"Great, that'll be great."

HANNAH/COLLEEN II

HANNAH RUSHES around getting herself ready before the appointed seven o'clock pickup and, afterward, sits staring at the Christmas tree, pretending to read a poetry book Russ recommended. She hasn't wrapped the presents and doesn't want to start, given she will be momentarily interrupted. At 7:30, the doorbell finally rings.

To say Art Pinser looks tired is an understatement. Tired and haggard. "Sorry I'm late," he offers, smiling briefly. "Three-year-old Emily decided she could climb the Christmas tree."

Hannah smiles back, hoping her apprehension doesn't show. "No problem," she says. "I'll just get my coat."

The inside of the car smells, and even in the dim interior light, Hannah sees what is probably dog hair on the passenger seat. She sits gingerly and buckles up. Overly sentimental Christmas music blares from what Hannah recognizes as an Easy Listening station. Once past the town limits, Art thankfully turns it down a bit.

"Colleen says you're a high school English teacher," he says after they have turned north on the Spider Lake highway.

Hannah has no idea where they are going, the dark pavement disappearing beneath them, headlights channeling into wet snow. "For more years than I care to remember," she comments. "Where do they all go?"

Art nods and they drive on, the music whining away, the car, obviously an older model, rattling occasionally. Hannah tries to think of something to say, but she's not good with strangers, and the thought of approaching a house full of them only intensifies her inability to socialize, especially in this awkward situation. They turn off the highway, finally, and head east along a twisting country road into a tunnel of darkness. Hannah looks over at Art's profile, trying to remember what he looked like forty years ago. Art Pinser, the redheaded rake. Not much of that left now.

He glances over and smiles. "It's not as far as it seems," he says reassuringly. "Fifteen minutes north of the highway." He pauses, as if working over what to say next. "Colleen is really looking forward to seeing you," he says finally. He says it convincingly enough, but then withdraws into his driving.

Hannah nods again wondering why he would say this. Did Colleen prime him before he left to pick her up? Had they been sitting around hashing over old times, remembering Hannah in her high-strung, nervous-as-a-cat high school days? Art wasn't even in high school when they were. He was older, at least seven or eight years older, out of high school and working at the hardware store— all his life like his father before him.

The car slows and turns abruptly, and Hannah sees the outline of a large stone house, two and a half stories with dormer attic windows, set back in a grove of trees, Christmas lights spiraling from several of the smaller conifers. They wheel past a glassed-in sun porch, its windows outlined in twinkling, multicolored lights, to a large, tiered deck, still cluttered with summer furniture, long-dead annuals in plastic planters, and a rusting barbeque. The minute they stop, Colleen, wearing a frilly Christmas apron, pushes open one of the French doors and stands waving frantically as if they have just returned from stormy seas. Hannah waves back and feels the same momentary giddiness as in the donut shop, giggling in line. A brief time warp, exhilarating but ephemeral.

Colleen has no idea why she did this, invite Hannah to their friendly madhouse, tonight of all nights. But that's exactly why she did, figuring Hannah would be alone in that dismal little house she grew up in, worrying about her mom, missing out on parties and God knows what fun in Toronto. Did she have a man in her life? Was she ever married? Hannah has lived such a different life, teaching, making good money, all kinds of successes, a sort of Murphy Brown teacher type. She has zip in common with Art Pinser's wife, broodmare of five, once a dusty Miller. And yet, that infernal *but,* they had connected—Madam librar-i-an—at Zellers. Imagine her remembering? And in the donut shop. What it made Colleen feel, she wasn't sure. Young? Hopeful? She wanted that feeling back, to sit in a quiet corner drinking coffee, laughing over all those wonderful old moments. Behind her, two of the kids are playing tag—through the living room, up and down the stairs. Someone in another room can't find the scissors and someone else yells that they're getting low on wrapping paper. This isn't the time or place, but spur of the moment has set the scene, and so she'll do what she always does—make the best of it.

Hannah takes a deep breath. Inside everything is chaos. Two large dogs bound to greet her, and Art, noticing Hannah's nervousness, steers them out through the doors. Someone takes her coat and sits her down on a chair, removing first a teddy bear and broken cookie. The Christmas tree in the corner spills out over adjoining furniture and almost touches the ceiling. It must be at least eight-feet high with presents piled under, around, into branches, more on an adjacent chair. The same radio station blares out an almost unrecognizable version of "Silent Night." Hannah takes a deep breath.

Colleen appears pulling a pajama-clad child by her chubby arm. "This is Emily," she says, grinning. "All ready for bed and Santa."

Emily is Colleen's pride and joy. She looks so much like Pam did at that age. Just holding Emily, Colleen feels younger, this warm little body, the reward for her struggles all these the years. Shane and Taylor had the same effect on her when they were small. Colleen soaks it up like a sponge.

"Me want Franklin," Emily says, peeking shyly from behind her grandma's long skirt.

"I doubt if Hannah has read the Franklin books, dear," Colleen murmurs, taking the child up in her arms. "Franklin the turtle, not Franklin the town." She laughs. "Big with the under-fours. Even a TV show."

Hannah smiles weakly at Emily and says, "Franklin books."

"It's the doll she wants," Colleen says, turning to go. "There's a writer who must be making a bundle. I'll be back in a min. We're off to bed and lullabies." She hopes Hannah doesn't feel too lost. These moments with Emily are few and far between: her silvery belly laugh, her hands around Colleen's neck. Like shooting stars, there, and when you blink, not there.

A younger version of Colleen, with boy-short, curly auburn hair, hands Hannah a glass of red wine. "We're out of white," she says, holding her wine glass aloft as she drops to the floor at Hannah's feet. "And we didn't realize it until too late. Hi, I'm Pam. Emily's mom. That's Jake, my better half, over there." She lowers her voice. "He's checking out the records, trying to find something better than that tacky radio station."

Hannah smiles. "You a stay-at-home mom?" she asks, hoping this is not an inappropriate opener.

"Don't I wish." Pam rolls her eyes. "I'm teaching fifth grade this year. Who knows what or where next year. Mom says you teach high school English. In Toronto?"

"Charles R. Fenshaw."

"Fenshaw? Oh my God, I don't believe it. Jake, Jake, honey?"

Pam waves frantically at her husband. He ambles over and Hannah realizes, even though she doesn't recognize him, that he must be a former student.

"Recognize this lady?" Pam says. An awkward question for both of them.

Hannah puts her hand out. "Hannah Norcroft," she says smoothly. "Fenshaw, but I don't remember the year."

"Ms. Norcroft?" Jake looks slightly embarrassed.

Hannah stabs at a date. "The early eighties, I think."

"Seventy-nine. Grade ten English, first semester. Don't tell Pam how bad I was. English was definitely not my bag, not that year."

"He's a chartered accountant," Pam offers, possibly in his defense. "Numbers, numbers, and more numbers." She giggles. "I need another glass of wine." She jumps up and is gone.

"Janet," Jake calls over the music and noise. "Come and meet my high school English teacher."

Hannah finds out that Janet and her husband, Paul, their two kids, Shane and his sister, Taylor, and her best friend, Paula, are here for the holidays. The latter seems a bit odd to Hannah, who finds out later that Paula's parents are in the middle of a messy divorce and Paula needs a safe haven. Hannah is also informed that the kids are upstairs with Cal and Steve playing a computer game.

"Five less bodies," Janet says over the din. "You'd never know it from the noise."

The dogs are let back in and make a beeline for Hannah, almost knocking her wine glass to the floor. When she whispers to Jake that dogs make her nervous, that she was once bitten when running, he banishes the creatures to a back room somewhere.

"You're a runner," Jake says, returning to pull up a chair and sit next to Hannah. "Pam and I are running the Massey marathon next summer. You could join us."

"I'm flattered but I'll probably have to pass. Not enough time. You know how it is."

Colleen finds her empty wine glass and pauses in the living room doorway. Two lullabies and a book didn't begin to calm Emily down, and in the end, she called Pam to take over.

Jake and Hannah are leaning toward each other, obviously into some intense conversation. "Bet you've been talking about running," Colleen says, leaning over the two of them to interrupt. "Am I right?" She smiles and shoos Jake away. "My turn now, and we need someone to bring us more wine. We'll be in the dining room." She ushers Hannah through a set of sliding doors, pulling them shut behind her. "A little P and Q," she whispers, sitting heavily in a chair. "Will I live till morning?"

What Hannah notices first is the clutter. It wasn't as obvious in the living room, overflowing with people and presents, but here, the long cloth-covered dining room table is still crumb-ridden from supper and piled with wrapping paper, open magazines, and in the middle, a poinsettia that cries for water.

Colleen pushes things back, nonchalantly brushing crumbs to the floor, making enough table space for the two of them. Janet's husband, Paul, slips in with a wine bottle and towel over his arm. "Ladies?" he says brightly.

Colleen pats the towel in a motherly way. "Yes, yes, Paul. Two glasses, if you please." She holds Hannah's glass first, then her own.

After Paul leaves, Colleen sighs and wipes her brow. "Welcome to the Pinser zoo," she says candidly. "Good thing we live in the country where there's no noise bylaw."

Hannah shrugs. "It's wonderful," she replies, "so many of you and all related, all together for Christmas."

"Ten now and four more to come in the morning. I do wish Artie had told me he was bringing a girlfriend. You never know what their sleeping arrangements are. I gave them a double bed, but you never know."

Hannah feels like a reluctant voyeur. "Artie? Where does he fit in?"

"Artie's our oldest. Living down in Costa Rica for the last five years, selling real estate," Colleen continues, "making a bundle. The kids are working on a trip for us there in June." She catches her breath, looking wistful. "Our thirty-fifth."

"Your thirty-fifth wedding anniversary?"

Colleen nods. "Hard to believe, eh? Never mind. Enough about me. How's your mom? The house? When do I get to read that poetry?"

Hannah feels the third-degree bare-bulb routine pressing down on her, fight or flee, modified to talk or take off, with departure a much safer option. "Mom's doing about as well as can be expected," she says cautiously. "How about your dad?"

"He's…he's not great," Colleen says unexpectedly. Two glasses of wine and she's going to blab. "He…ah, got away from them at the Lodge yesterday, well actually at the mall, that Bunny Bus outing every week. Some mix up, I don't know. Anyway, when they took a head count at supper, he wasn't there."

"How could they lose him?" Hannah looks horrified.

"He lost himself. Took off. Found some drinking buddies. We tracked him down around seven. At the Salamander."

"The Salamander? It's still there?"

"A dump now," Colleen says. "Nothing like what it used to be when we were in high school."

"The Salamander," Hannah says. "Down from the drive-in along that gravel road."

"Where you and what's-his-name had your famous date."

"My mother nearly killed me."

"You were grounded for ages."

"Almost the whole summer," Hannah says, looking away. "That summer in Franklin."

"A million years ago," Colleen adds. "Way back in 1955."

The year seems to hang between them, and they both listen to background chatter and noise.

"Your dad," Hannah says finally. "You were telling me about your dad."

"Well, he was drunk. We found him and took him back to the jailhouse lodge, as he calls it."

"Colleen, I'm so sorry."

"At least it wasn't the Britannia. Art would have had to go in there."

Hannah looks puzzled. "You both went to get him then?"

"Drunk-dad rescue," Colleen says bitterly. "Art's good at it now."

"This has been going on for a while?"

"Oh yes, nothing much has changed with my dad over the last forty years."

"And you've stayed here?"

"Pinser's Hardware Store, part of Franklin since 1912."

"You deserve a medal."

"You think so? I never thought of it that way."

"What about your sister?"

"Lil has retired in Luxembourg. Married for the third time. Hit gold, literally. The guy's loaded." Colleen takes a long swig from her wine glass.

"Luxembourg," Hannah says. "So you don't see her often."

"I haven't seen my sister in almost twenty years, but it's all right, you know, because I have this." She waves toward the living room. "My wonderful brood."

Hannah has suddenly had enough. Details of Colleen's life boil and churn around her, unresolved anger and so much pain. All of it stabbing at her, demanding a response. She doesn't want to know any more about Colleen, not tonight and possibly never. "I hate to be a party pooper," Hannah says a little too quietly, "but it's getting late and I haven't even wrapped Mother's presents yet…"

Colleen jumps up. "And here I am blabbing on to you about my pathetic little life." She yanks open the sliding door. "Jake? Could you drive my dear friend Hannah home?"

Hannah puts her hand tentatively on Colleen's arm. "I didn't mean…"

"No, no. It's all right. Really it is. Two glasses of wine and I tell all. Good thing my family keeps me on the straight and narrow." She gives Hannah a hug. "I'll get your coat."

On the way back, Hannah and Jake discuss running, and by the time they arrive at her door, her anxiety is down to a tolerable level.

The house is dark and wonderfully quiet. She has a momentary guilt stab over Esmeralda, her cat. Personal door greeter, keeper of her heartstrings. Next-door neighbor Annie checks in on her more than once a day, Hannah knows, feeds her and makes sure the radio is still on. Hannah thought of bringing Esmeralda here but she is a miserable traveler, howling as though being tortured. Once a year to the vet and back is the most Hannah can tolerate.

She lights a couple of candles and the Christmas lights, pours some eggnog, puts on a Jane Coop cassette, *The Romantic Piano,* and sits on the couch. Maybe it wasn't as dismal as she remembered, her Christmases at home. Everything in its place and a place for everything—another of her mother's maxims, so ingrained in her that, even here, she has automatically put everything somewhere, out of sight, in a corner, behind the door. Her life compared to Colleen's seems idyllic. All those people in that house, as big as it was, and her dad, running away from the Lodge to drink at the Salamander. Her odd comment about the Britannia, as if she wouldn't set foot in the place. Why would it bother her, for heaven's sakes? She was off shift that afternoon, down at the beach tanning. Hannah shivers and hugs a pillow. As long as she's in Toronto, it is easy to keep Larry Mourand and Charlie, the whole mess, at bay in her distant past. Here it's another matter.

The visit turned out to be about as she expected, Colleen so sweet, but it was too chaotic, too many people. Who knows what Colleen has had to put up with over the years. How could her sister never come home? And what about their mother? She remembers Colleen saying her mother wasn't alive, as if to justify her father's being at the Lodge. Colleen ending up a mother to them all. And how many children? With Janet and Artie, five—five children, three grandchildren.

The piano melodies sift through her, and when Jane Coop begins "Lebensraum," Hannah leans back savoring the poignant melody, so full of longing, with the bass chords beneath, the melody soaring. Hannah finds her notebook and a pencil. This cocoon of her own making is necessary, whether here or back in Toronto. She needs this tranquility in order to survive. Hannah picks up her glass, raises it to the small cluster of twinkling colored lights. "Here's to Christmas Eve 1995," she says, lifting it higher. "Here's to what we all make of our lives."

BRITANNIA NOW

ALTHOUGH ALLAN SEARP has been at the *Franklin Standard*
for less than a year, everyone knows he has his eye on the Editor-in-
Chief job. He has worked his way up from Obits and County Court
to News and Features, no small feat in such a short period of time.
His first project in the new year is to finish a series of articles on the
Britannia Hotel, a growth-of-the-town-as-tied-to-the-vicissitudes-
of-business series. He's been working on the project for the last year,
having started it when he was a cub reporter at the smaller *Calston
Chronicle*, a paper covering news east of Franklin. As his immediate
family knows, the series began as a journalism assignment when he
was still a student at Ryerson Polytechnic University in Toronto.
Landing a job at the *Standard* means he is busier, being all over
the county most weeks, but he still has enough time to work on it.
Living at home helps, even if it means listening to his dad complain
almost every night about the paper and its bad grammar and lack
of local editorial input. His father, self-educated, with a thriving
carpentry business, often takes his red pen to the paper's articles and
then gives them to his son to take in to the office. That they never
make it to the Managing Editor's desk is understandable.

On the job, Searp is brash and smart with endless contacts
and energy. While in school, he picked up a leather gaucho hat at
a secondhand thrift store, and it has become his trademark. He sees

himself going beyond the *Standard,* maybe staying there five years and then on to a city paper.

The Britannia articles begin at the hotel's opening in June 1926 and end with its present rejuvenated state as a Vintage Sundown Inn. Last fall, Searp pitched the series to his boss, giving him outlines with titles and word counts. Max Reginald, the managing editor suggested they could run one article a month for six consecutive months, beginning in January and ending just before the Britannia's birthday celebrations on June 20.

The first three articles, "Birth of a Twenties' Dream," "The Depression Years," and "New Life During the War Years," have already been fairly well documented in a disjointed and difficult to follow history of Franklin called *Gilder's Glorious Franklin.* This resource, combined with microfiche of the *Standard's* predecessor, *The Franklin Tribune Weekly* and subsequent *Daily,* gave him enough information to create the three solid articles, which are now basically finished. He has the last two articles, "From Metric to Mini Skirts" and "One Small Town, One Large Legacy" in point form and knows he can easily get more than enough local input for each.

Serious research problems, however, have appeared with the fourth article, "The Postwar Boom Days." No one he talks to remembers Hugh and Deandra Mourand who took over the hotel in November 1946.

When he goes to the County Assessment Office the week before Christmas, the woman at the desk recognizes him.

"Allan Searp," she says, reaching out to shake his hand. "You won't remember me, but I'm May Quigley. I used to bowl with your mom back in the eighties. You're doing well at the paper. I've read several of your articles."

Searp straightens his hat and grins. "I'm looking for registration information about the Britannia," he says. "She changed hands in 1946."

"That would be on microfiche," she replies, "That's quite a ways back, 1946. It'll take me a few minutes."

She disappears into one of a number of rows of tall shelves spaced across the room behind the counter. Searp looks around. Near the door, an artificial tree glows with lights and decorations, a splash of color to brighten the utilitarian walls. He's never searched a real estate document before and has no idea if it will contain anything useful or not.

"Here we are," she says, bustling out from behind the counter. "This way." She leads him to a row of cubicles where individuals, likely real-estate types, are laboriously scrutinizing screens.

"It's a Bell and Howell," she says, patting the machine. "The instructions are posted and it's easy to use." She hands him an open envelope. "The fiche is in here—two hundred entries, so you'll have to hunt a bit."

Searp feels his hand shake. This could be the first clue.

The document finally appears, and he pulls a spiral notepad from his knapsack and turns to an empty page. *Charge/Mortgage of Land* is across the top of the document. *Principle amount: twenty-five thousand dollars.* He knows already that the dollar exchange then was two to one in favor of the US, so any bank would have been eager to deal with Mourand. He scans further down. *Chargor: Mourand, Hugh William. Chargor's Address: 821 Moonglow Rd, Cleveland, Ohio* and beneath, *Chargee: Dominion Bank, Franklin, Ontario.* He writes both down quickly and, taking the microfiche from the machine, hurries back to the desk.

"That was fast," the smiling Mrs. Quigley says. "Merry Christmas to you and your family."

"Thanks," Searp replies, tipping his hat. "I've gotta run." Which he does, literally, out to the parking lot and into his car. Cleveland. It makes sense that Mourand wouldn't have a legal Canadian address at that point. They were new arrivals, and he already knows from an old *Franklin Daily* article that the hotel was purchased in November 1946. He drives across town and goes to the Bell Telephone office. Unfortunately they don't have a Cleveland phone book and suggest he drive to a larger center. He checks his watch. It's nearly noon. He has an article to finish and hand in before four.

COLLEEN VII

CHRISTMAS MORNING is the usual zoo. Emily wakens at 4 a.m. and again at 5:30, the second time jumping up and down in the hall, shouting with gusto, "Santa here, Santa here" until, one by one, everyone appears bleary-eyed and gathers around the tree. Cal and Steve, who were out partying, retreat immediately to the darkened dining room opposite, heads on the table. Janet and Pam, closely followed by Jake and Paul, slip directly into the kitchen. The children gather by the tree, Emily ensconced between Taylor and Paula, with Shane attempting to see names on presents. Art and Colleen, who have only been in bed a few hours, come slowly downstairs. Art has left the tree lights on, and Colleen pauses at the bottom of the stairs to momentarily breathe in her brood, their hair and faces sparkling with flecks of light—like stars, she thinks sleepily. Art nudges her and they traipse over to sit on the couch, Colleen hoping she won't doze off. Jake bursts in from the kitchen door carrying an armful of wood, a plaid shirt over his red tracksuit, a red-checkered cap on his head.

"Deck the halls with boughs of holly," he sings cheerfully, as he dumps the wood by the Franklin stove. "Well come on, isn't anyone going to join me?"

"Deck halls, deck halls," Emily squeals, jumping up. "Sing, Daddy, sing."

There's a groan from the dining room and the rest laugh.

Pam waltzes in with two cups of coffee.

"Taste this," she says, a big grin on her face.

"Smells good," Colleen replies before she even tastes it, and then, "Exceptional. A new brand you brought with you?"

"Merry Christmas," Pam announces, pulling a box from under the tree. Shane and Taylor and Paula and Emily flop down at her feet, grinning. "We know what it i-is," they chant.

"You open it, Art," Colleen says, nudging him. "I need more java."

Art puts his cup down and picks up the box. "Light as a feather," he chuckles, balancing it with one hand.

"Better not drop it," Jake cuts in. "It might break."

Art tears off the paper revealing its contents. "General Electric Deluxe Coffee Maker," he reads.

"This coffee," Colleen squeals. "You used it to make this coffee."

"We gather you approve," Pam adds laughing. "I told you perked coffee was better."

"More presents," Emily says, jumping up and clapping her hands. Taylor nods and mouths something to her. She grins at everyone and singsongs, "We want presents, we want presents."

Paul appears wearing a Santa suit, the beard drooping half off. "Ho, ho, ho," he booms, sticking his thumbs into his oversized belt. "Merry Christmas."

"You not the real Santa," Emily says, stomping her foot. "You my Uncle Paul."

"Santa's helper," Pam replies, scooping her up. "We'll sit on the floor, over here." She moves to an empty spot not far from the tree.

Paul makes his way to the tree and the ritual begins.

Colleen watches them all with delight. She knows she spends too much, but right now, it's worth it. They all ooh and ah and she lets it soak in, basks in everyone's delight, the camaraderie, the hugs.

This is what she and Art have done, they have created this, and it's in technicolor with panoramic sound. She needs this on Christmas Day, needs this wonderful jumble to keep her Christmases Past at bay. Even though she's been away from them for almost thirty-five years, they always manages to slip in at some point, tuning in like some unwanted black-and-white movie suddenly there on the TV. Her dad hung over and grouchy, her mom dolled up and determined to make the best of it, the tree small, presents sparse, and Colleen hoping for miracles, waiting for the next bomb to go off.

Shortly after one, Artie, looking tanned and always more handsome than Colleen remembers, bursts in with his beautiful coffee-skinned girlfriend.

"Merry Christmas, everyone," he announces, grinning. "I'd like you all to meet Celestina." As each family member comes forward to say hello, it's clear Celestina speaks little English. Pam, who has been to New Orleans once, manages a few Spanish phrases, while the rest of them just grin and say who they are. When Emily comes over, she shyly takes Celestina's hand, looks up, and says, "You look nice, like chocolate."

When Artie translates this into Spanish, Celestina squats down and gives her a big hug.

"I need recruits to get presents out of our car," Artie says, guiding Celestina to a spot on the couch. Everyone has shifted around and Janet brings the newcomers coffee. Shane and Taylor race outside and return, laden with boxes and bags and the whole present routine goes into act two.

"It took us over an hour to pick up the rental car," Artie says, trying on the sweater Colleen and Art have given him. "The airport was a zoo."

By now, Emily is sitting on Celestina's lap and she claps her hands, singing, "Zoo, zoo, all the animals at the zoo."

"Zoo?" Celestina asks, looking puzzled.

Everyone laughs and Celestina looks embarrassed and Artie translates. It's a pattern that repeats itself too many times over the weekend. Celestina does her best, but it's clear she is finding it all quite difficult. Colleen wonders what her family is like and how this must be very different from Christmas in Costa Rica.

Everyone disperses for a while, and at four, as turkey smells begin to sift into every room, Cal leaves to pick up Grandma Pinser and Colleen's dad. He returns with only Art's mom. When Colleen quietly asks, Cal says Grandpa told him he wasn't up to their madhouse bunch and was eating at the Lodge.

Colleen pretends it doesn't matter and admires Grandma's new black pantsuit and red silk blouse. "Bought especially for the occasion," she says, hugging each family member in turn, asking pertinent questions or making interesting comments. Colleen always marvels at her graciousness, glad in a way her dad copped out. He is always a loose cannon at the best of times.

The children crowd in beside their great-grandmother as she carefully opens her presents, watch as she meticulously folds the wrapping paper from each. Afterward, she brings out her knitting and sits by the fire. "You all just carry on," she says. "I'm fine right here."

Colleen stays and chats with her while the kitchen and dining room crews take over. Someone, likely Pam, has organized them all, and they scurry back and forth, setting the table, chattering and banging pots in the kitchen.

Art is into some intense discussion with Artie, and Colleen hopes it won't end with them jawing at each other—the old-buck, young-buck routine. When they still lived at home, Janet and Pam teased their dad and Artie about it, especially at dinner. Artie was a bottomless-pit teenager, thinking nothing of three pieces of pie at dinner, if he could wangle them. They'd start trying to outdo each other, moving from who could eat more pie to egging each other on about the dumbest, most unimportant things. Pam or Janet or both would go into their paw-paw, snort-snort, lock-horns chant. The males paid no attention, of course, and when things heated up too much, which they usually did, the girls left the table. Colleen, the good little wife and mother, stayed, trying to work things out. Interrupting enough to make them stop and listen, however, meant she had to yell, getting red in the face, at which point Art or Artie or both would tell her to calm down, saying they couldn't understand why she was upset, that her saying they were shouting was a huge exaggeration. Simply healthy male give and take. It didn't help her that Pam and Janet always took off before the sparks flew and were never there to stick up for her.

She hears the odd word now, and knows they are arguing again, likely about Artie's Costa Rican job, the glamour of it, from Artie's point of view, the lack of a future in it, from Art's point of view. Grandma Pinser has dozed off in front of the fire and Celestina sits on a chair nearby, thumbing nervously through a magazine, obviously tuned in to their brittle tones.

"Why don't you show Celestina your Star Trek collection," Colleen says at last, glaring at Art.

"Star Trek," Celestina repeats, eyes lighting up. "Mr. Spock, very seee-rious." She pulls her ears up and tries to look fierce.

"Grand idea," Artie says, jumping up. "*En mi habitación, Celestina. Vamos. Vamos.*"

Celestina giggles and they head up the stairs.

Colleen realizes it's so much easier for Celestina in Spanish, and she's already noticed it bugs the rest of the kids. Colleen is sure Celestina must feel uncomfortable with them, the way they live, their middle-class life, and especially how they all babble in English, probably too fast. Celestina speaks slowly and carefully and is terribly polite.

"I don't see why he can't talk to her in English," Art says after they leave.

"I don't see why you two have to argue," Colleen replies, picking up wrapping paper and stuffing it into a half-filled bag.

"We weren't arguing," Art says. "We were discussing things."

Christmas dinner is a magazine-feature affair. Before they sit down, Art insists that Paul, who is the family photographer, take pictures of the table; Grandma Pinser says grace, and everyone talks and eats until there is little left. Colleen is always amazed at what good cooks her family have turned out to be—even Cal and Steve, whose specialty is fudge.

After supper, Art and Artie are into it again, the two of them still hunched over the dining room table after it's cleared, Celestina smiling weakly and fiddling with her napkin.

"Why don't we go for a walk?" Colleen says, waving to the front door.

"A walk?" Celestina repeats, looking confused.

"*Dar un paseo*," Artie translates.

"*Si, si,*" Celestina replies, jumping up.

They wave good-bye to Grandma Pinser as Cal maneuvers the car past them on the snow-covered lane. Early evening shadows darken the snow and Christmas lights twinkle from the two spruce trees on the lawn.

"I guess there's no snow in Costa Rica," Colleen says finally, trying to think of something to say.

"Snow," Celestina says, looking pleased. She points to it and nods. "*En la montaña,*" she replies.

"Montaña," Colleen repeats, wondering if it has something to do with the US.

Celestina squats down and draws an inverted triangle in the snow beside the road. "Montaña," she says again, pointing to it.

"Montaña," Colleen repeats, trying to copy her accent. She points toward the sky. "High up in the montaña."

"*Si, si,*" Celestina says, smiling shyly at Colleen. "*Si, si, Señora.*"

When they return, the two Arts are on opposite teams in a Trivial Pursuit game around the dining room table. Colleen sits in the other room, sorting presents and stuffing more paper into the bag, while Celestina moves in behind Artie, rubbing his shoulders and watching. After a few turns, Artie yawns and rubs the back of his head against her.

"I think we've had it," he says, getting up. "That ten-hour flight is taking its toll."

The others nod, and the game, already in high pitch, continues. Colleen hears a few snickers and notices the look on her husband's face. She won't admit to feeling a little uncomfortable about them sleeping together. She worries, momentarily, what affect it might have on Shane and Taylor and then lectures herself. She offered, so what does she expect?

Later, when she and Art are getting ready for bed, Art says a little sharply, "You didn't tell me they were sleeping together."

"You didn't ask."

"I have to say," he says, sitting heavily on the bed. "It disappoints me."

"Is that what you two were talking about?"

"When?"

"Before and after supper."

"Not really."

"No," Colleen says, taking a deep breath, "what you were arguing about was why your oldest son won't come home and run the hardware business."

"We weren't arguing."

"Art," Colleen says, sitting down beside him, "Admit it. You want him to be the third generation of Pinsers to carry on the great hardware-store tradition."

"I don't see much future for him down there in a foreign country," Art says wearily.

"What you need to tell him," Colleen continues, putting her arm around his shoulder, "is that you've worked in the store since you were a teenager and run it since your dad died, just over thirty-five years ago."

"I'm not sure that's necessary."

"Art, I worry you know."

"You're good at that, I have to admit." Art pulls the pins out of her hair and runs his fingers through it.

"I don't want you following the same route as your father. You should slow down. Sell the business or, at the very least, get someone else to take over."

Art pulls her onto the bed and runs his hands over her night-gown-covered breasts. She pushes him away and sits up again. "I've been trying, for the last two years," she continues, "to get some sense into your head. You know our oldest son couldn't care less about hardware, never has. Don't you remember the ridiculous excuses he came up with to get out of working there through high school?"

Art pulls her back down and nuzzles his face in her neck. "It's getting late," he says. "Let's not talk about it." With one hand, he reaches over to turn out the light and with the other, runs his hand up between her legs.

Pam and Janet and families leave the day after Christmas; Artie and Celestina say good-bye early Tuesday. The store has its annual week-after-Christmas sale with Art and Colleen staying every evening to work on year-end inventory. When they arrive home late Thursday evening, Colleen is too tired to check the answering machine, and when she finally notices it blinking and listens to the message, it's almost ten.

"This message is for Mrs. Pinser. Your father, Frank Miller, is scheduled for hospital tests Friday morning. Please call Eileen before five today to schedule his pickup time."

Colleen has a slice of take-out pizza in one hand, a diet cola in the other. She's so exhausted she has to play the message twice to get the day right. Art is already on his second piece of pizza and absorbed in the *Franklin Herald*.

"Tomorrow! They want me to drive Dad to the hospital for tests tomorrow."

"Who does?"

"Someone from the Lodge."

"What tests?"

"How would I know? You heard the message." Colleen says this knowing he goes stone deaf whenever his eyes hit a page.

"What time?"

"Tomorrow morning, and I was supposed to call before five about a pickup time."

"We'll manage then. Don't worry."

That good old "don't worry," one of Art's best comebacks. "What if it's eight in the morning?" Colleen fumes. "Why didn't the dumbo call me at the store? I've told them enough times. They think I just sit around here doing nothing. Mrs. Pinser—afternoon soap opera queen."

"Colleen, you're tired."

"Your point?"

"We'll work it out in the morning."

"I'd call them back right this minute if I thought it would do any good, but I'll get some no-brain night staffer."

"Another piece of pizza?"

Colleen knows she's gearing up for a fight; she also knows she is too stressed out to follow through. Art doesn't put her off on purpose, and after more than thirty years, she's almost used to it. It simply never occurs to him. "I know you don't," she says aloud, not meaning to. He gives her a look but doesn't ask, and she squeezes his shoulder as she reaches for more pizza.

She looks at Art sitting slumped in the chair, obviously over-tired, dark circles under his eyes; they've been there for months. He stands suddenly, leaning a moment, steadying his hand on the chair arm, and then sits again.

"You all right?" Colleen asks.

"Little heartburn." He grins at her. "Ate the pizza too fast."

"Heartburn. Right." Colleen rushes over to him and, straddling his legs, cradles his face with her hands. "Tightness of the chest? Nausea? What else? Art, I don't want to lose you."

Art pulls her forward and nibbles at her ear. "I'm tired. We're both tired. All I need are a couple of Tums and your sweet bod beside me."

"You always say that."

"It's true."

"You're sure?"

"Positive."

Colleen thinks about making a fuss, of insisting they go to Emergency to spend the night in the Heart Unit, not sleeping until everything checks out normal. It's happened twice before and they haven't told the kids, not even the twins, both times arriving home before they were up in the morning. She also knows Art will prob-ably want to make love. He always does after this happens, as if getting inside her pushes the fear away. She'll agree, partly because the old thump and grind still, most of the time, distracts her and, at its best, sends her into temporary float-away heaven.

As they climb the stairs, she again hears Art's offhand comment from years ago about his own dad likely "dying in the saddle." Colleen had to ask what he meant. Her proper mother-in-law, would never have told anyone, and Art said Bill, his ne'er do well brother who showed up for the funeral, was the source.

As they slip into bed, Colleen tries to suppress her anxiety. Art snuggles against her and runs his hand under her nightgown to her already hardened nipples, which never seem to worry. She closes her eyes and pulls him toward her.

The next morning, Colleen makes it to the Lodge by 8:20, stopping for a donut and coffee on the way. Her dad, pale and in a wheelchair, is dressed and ready to go.

"You're on the ball this morning," she says, not asking about the wheelchair, trying for cheery and hopeful even though she fears the worst.

"No damn breakfast," he replies. "And the nurse insisted on this thing." He slaps the wheelchair arm.

"Not too steady?"

"Took a downer getting into bed last night. Almost pinned the poor little nurse under me." He slaps the chair again. "Great chance, and I just felt too punk to do anything." Colleen smiles realizing her dad's sex drive is still alive and well, if only in his memory.

As she wheels him to the outside door, he dozes off, his stubbly chin falling on his chest, fingers slackening on his trouser knees. Not his own trousers either. When she asked on her last visit, he said his own pants didn't fit any more. "Too damn tight around the waist." When he was first admitted, she had left the required three pairs of labeled pants. Were all his pants too small around the waist, or just one pair? And why? She meant to ask and forgot. Today, they have a deadline. Maybe she can find someone when she brings him back later. He's skin and bones now, her dad. He must be bloated or something.

On the drive to the hospital, he falls asleep again, and she remembers a dog they had, years ago, part husky. The kids called him Polar Zone, PZ for short. He went everywhere with Pam and Janet, even following Artie back into the bush, all of them with tales of PZ this and PZ that. He was half-blind and bloated at the end, his gut distended and hanging down. The vet said it was his spleen.

"He doesn't have much quality of life," she remarked, shaking her head. "It might be kindest to say good-bye." Colleen was horrified and suggested PZ might just die of his own, that they might come down one morning and he would be gone. "Don't count on it," the vet cautioned. "His spleen could easily burst and that's something you don't want to deal with."

She brought him home again, but he started bumping into things, falling several times a day, staring at her in that trusting dog way. She was the human; she should fix it. In less than a week, Colleen called the vet, who came and took the dog away. Afterward, she walked round and round the house yelling and crying. Cursing the universe—the unfairness of it all. The awful pain of deliberately ending a life, signing a paper, watching the van drive off.

In the waiting room, she looks at her dad now, his bloated middle, his fly zipper straining and not completely pulled to the top. He never was a natty dresser, but these poorly fitting pants made him look like an old bum, someone pulled out of a back alley.

"Mr. Miller?" A nurse holding a clipboard sticks her head in the open doorway.

Frank snorts and rights himself. "Alive and well," he says, trying for a smile, pulling himself up as if he was still in control.

"He'll be about an hour," the nurse says, slipping behind the chair. "We're doing the whole spectrum."

"The works," her dad quips, waving to Colleen, seeming to take it all in stride.

Colleen nods and watches the nurse briskly wheel him out. She hadn't thought it would be the whole spectrum, whatever that means. Why, she has no idea. Obviously, once they have him in here, they will want to make sure they cover everything. An hour. Not enough time to go to the store and be useful, too much time to sit and read more out-of-date magazines.

She goes for the cafeteria and a Danish, which she doesn't need and coffee, which she feels is necessary. She is barely settled at a table for two, away from a bunch of nurses and aides all talking shop, when Maureen Downey stands beside her, coffee cup in hand, looking more tired than usual.

"Colleen? You alone?"

"Maureen. Sure." Colleen waves at the empty chair. She hopes Maureen won't ask about her dad or Art or anything too personal. Stress always lowers her defenses.

"How's everything?"

"Not bad."

"Seen Hannah Norcroft lately?"

"We had coffee together before Christmas."

"Did she tell you her mom's in controlled access at the Lodge?"

"I knew her mom was there," Colleen says, feeling uncomfortable. Maureen is fishing, leading up to something.

"And your dad?"

"He's…he's there. At the Lodge, I mean. On the first floor."

"You'd think she'd take her mom home with her to Toronto. Being a teacher all those years with no family, she must have scads tucked away."

"She has one more year to retirement," Colleen says, wondering how much of the Danish and coffee she has to eat before she can excuse herself. She wonders if Maureen says the same thing about her, why she doesn't take her dad home. Art Pinser's wife. Probably just works at the store to put in time.

"You and her were real close in high school."

"For a while," Colleen says. She has taken too large a bite of the doughy Danish and has a sharp pain in her throat. She takes several rapid sips of coffee.

"Worked together a summer waitressing at the Britannia."

Colleen nods. The lump has gone down, leaving the pain still in her throat. Her eyes water and she ignores it, afraid Maureen will think she is crying. For what? Lost friendship with Hannah? Lost high school days?

"Weren't you two working there the summer that old guy died?"

"What old guy?" Colleen goes into instant acting, looking puzzled now as she sips her coffee.

"You know. He worked in the kitchen or something. Some people thought he was murdered."

"Really?" Colleen raises her eyebrow, opens her eyes a bit wider. "If I remember, that's not what the papers said."

Maureen leans forward as if right on the edge of an important secret. "I remember my parents talkin' about it. How he was drunk or done something awful to get himself in trouble. Someone must have pushed him down them stairs."

"Old Charlie?" Colleen stands up. "I don't think so. Look, Maureen, this memory-lane thing is great fun but I have to fly. We should get together sometime. A fifties reunion." She squeezes Maureen's shoulder. "Catch you later."

The elevator is empty, thank God, as Colleen feels like she might throw up and has to hold tightly to the safety railing when liftoff occurs. Maureen Downey of all people, talking about poor old Charlie as if it were common chitchat. She and how many others? Ready at the drop of a hat to jump back almost forty years, link Colleen and Hannah with that day. That July afternoon in 1955. July what? She has no idea. It must have been near the end of the month, several weeks after Hannah started working. Hannah, lucky thing, missed it all.

Funny, no dumb, how you never get over some things, Colleen thinks as the doors slide open. An instant after Maureen leaned forward exploding her little bomb, Colleen is down there in the hotel basement, hearing Larry's threats, looking up at the cobwebs as Charlie's body flopped down onto the floor above, even though at the time she wasn't absolutely sure. Charlie's body and a faint gurgling sound, his last breath. The usual sets of eyes look up momentarily from their magazines and conversations as she sits heavily in a green vinyl chair in the waiting room, pretending she is fine.

Over the years, she has pushed the guilt away whenever anything reminds her. Before she married, she flung herself into love with Art, sure that being with him would save her from her demons, and afterward, she wrapped herself in housework and babies, endless days of non-ending chores. It still works most of the time. Right now she thinks fiercely about her dad, his tests—whatever they are—what they will find out, and more down to earth things like remembering to pay his utility bills by the end of the month.

She picks up a women's magazine that promises to help her reorganize her investments for a higher return, lose ten pounds before summer, fill out a questionnaire to find out whether or not "he" is faithful. Between almost every page, she remembers: The dark circles under Astrid's eyes; the fact that Larry and Mrs. Mourand were never seen again; Hannah, except for her great boobs, losing weight, spending more time in the library, telling Colleen how she wasn't cut out to be a waitress. And she wasn't. She dropped things and forgot things and was so serious about everything in life.

"Mrs. Pinser?"

Colleen jumps up, the magazine falling at her feet. "Yes?"

"Your father is waiting beside the nurses' station. And the doctor, in 207, wants a word with you."

Colleen hurries after her, sure she is walking right into some booby trap, some awful news.

"Dr. Warton," he says, standing to shake her hand over his desk, bare except for what she figures is her dad's file. He's young, Dr. Warton. Good looking with a firm, warm handshake. Colleen hates talking to new doctors, especially about her dad, trailing the Millers' dirty laundry across the floor again. Her mother's voice echoes inside her, gives her a stiff upper lip, makes her pretend there's nothing to hide.

"He's doing reasonably well," the doctor begins. "My examination reveals what I suspected, an enlarged liver and edema, fluid swelling, especially in the abdominal area. The ultrasound and CT scan show obvious liver scaring. I'm sorry to be the bearer of bad news, but your father is in an advanced stage of cirrhosis of the liver."

Cirrhosis of the liver? The rest of it is a blur of medical gibberish.

"Damage to the liver," he says, leaning toward her and speaking quietly, almost as if he's chatting about grocery prices. "It happens over a period of years, usually due to drinking too much alcohol, but…" He pauses and then continues. "It can also follow certain unrelated diseases. In any case, there is little we can do at this point, other than make him as comfortable as we can."

Colleen knows she has gone pale and her breathing has sped up. He's so matter of fact about it. The new breed of doctor, expecting her to be, already to some degree, informed. She nods and looks away.

"What about siblings?" he asks, as if hoping there would be someone else to help her get through this, even though she is here alone.

The question startles Colleen. What to say? There are and there aren't. One lost, one too far away. Why is he asking this? More bad news?

"I didn't mean to pry," he goes on, "but I do notice that you have been the only one listed as a contact, and that usually means an only child. It's always difficult in these circumstances."

He smiles, and Colleen feels herself slipping. From Charlie to her dad. One tiny step. "I…I have an older sister but she's not here," she blurts out, turning away. "That is, she doesn't live here in Canada, I mean."

Dr. Warton shuffles the papers and clears his throat. "I ruled out doing a needle biopsy of the liver. Because of his general health and age, he's not a good candidate for a transplant." He stops, looking like he cares but is, perhaps, a little weary. "I'm afraid I have to tell you that the prognosis isn't good."

"His chances?"

The doctor nods. "You can contact your sister?"

"Yes. Yes."

"They can make him comfortable at the Lodge, but the report is that he's a bit confused at times, and if he wanders again, we'll have to transfer him to controlled access." He says it almost as if he expects her to pass this threat on to her father. As if it's her job.

"Have you told my dad this?" Colleen knows she sounds ticked off. Shock to anger. She wants to be angry, wants to shout it at him. This young doctor—does he have any idea? Does he know how impossible her father has become over the past years? Jekyll and Hyde, one hour to the next. Not likely. Not very likely. As if Colleen could tell her dad anything. Or Art. Or any of them.

"We have advised him to stay put, that if he wants to get feeling better, he needs to follow Lodge rules."

"I see."

"You're not convinced?" The doctor closes the file and stands.

"My dad has always pretty well done whatever he wants."

"My card," Dr. Warton says. "In case of an emergency."

"Big deal," Colleen continues at the dinner table, as she puts down her coffee cup. "He gave me his card." She tosses it in front of Art. The twins ate early and are already upstairs, supposedly studying.

"Dr. Thomas D. Warton (BA, MD, MMD)." Art reads, picking up the card. "Went to school with Artie, same year. Remember?" He holds the card at arm's length, admiring it, and Colleen knows he's onto an if-only trip. If only they had more cash put away, saved the baby bonus instead of using it each month, Artie might have stayed in university instead of leaving, giving up, getting bored, whatever it was he did. Art, again, blaming himself for the huge fight they had before Artie took off to university, ridiculously blaming himself for the boy quietly switching from commerce to political science without telling his dad. A big slap in the face, saying no to becoming an educated merchant, no to the family business. The dad wanting for his kid what he never had himself, without finding out what it really was the kid wanted in the first place. He never really wanted to go to university at all. He had, and still has a burning desire to make a buck, a million bucks, in part, no doubt, from watching his parents' thirty-year struggle to break even.

"Little Tommy," Colleen says, suddenly remembering the skinny kid with glasses, part of Artie's weekend gang—eager little boys, fishing back in the creek after school, and a few years later, driving off in the van or truck, Colleen holding her breath until they were safely home. "Tom Warton, won all sorts of awards at commencement. I wonder why he's practicing back here?"

"Why not?" Art says in his why-not-Franklin-it's-as-good-as-anywhere-else voice.

"That's why he made a comment about Lillian," Colleen says suddenly. "For God's sakes, he wants me to get in touch Lillian."

"It's that bad?"

"Cirrhosis of the liver. Advanced. You know what it is?"

Art nods and reaches to take her hand.

"He gave me a line about how it might be from something other than drinking. So polite, so straight down the middle." She squeezes Art's warm hand. Her dad, in his final days, weeks. This responsibility she has had for as long as she can remember, even when her mother was alive, will end. Stop. All the years tumble against her like a deck of cards. All the bad blurs, and she surprises herself remembering a few good things, a word here, a moment there.

She wipes her eye with the back of her free hand.

"You all right?" Art asks.

She laughs and wipes her eyes again. "I was actually remembering a couple of good things," she says. "Whatever would make me do that?"

"Do we have Lillian's phone number?"

"In Luxembourg? I'm not sure. It might be in the old blue address book."

"Didn't the kids call her on Christmas Day?"

"Lillian? They called Lillian? What on earth for and why wasn't I in on it?"

"I think you had gone to bed. Christmas day or the day after. To thank her for presents. The kids were up very late. Cheap-rate time." Art tells it as if it happened only a few hours ago.

"Why didn't you tell me?"

"I thought I had."

"What did she say?"

"I don't know. Janet talked to her a bit and then Pam."

"And no one bothered to tell me. My sister. I've hardly said two words to her in the last ten years."

"Pam said she would fill you in but then, remember? Emily came down with that fever."

No one told her. Damn them. Everyone keeping quiet in case it ruined her holiday.

Lillian. They talked to Auntie Lil, who sent ridiculously expensive presents from Luxembourg that no one could use—Hawaiian shirts (from her latest trip) that the boys wouldn't be caught dead in, board games (from her latest trip) with instructions in French only, so that no one could play. Lillian, who sent only a two-line Christmas note and who never actually asked about Frank, whether he was dead or alive, for God's sakes. Why should she call Lillian? To let her know their dad is dying? See if she wants to come home to watch him breathe his last—all of them standing in some movie-scene group around his bed, remembering the good times?

"Colleen?" Art puts his hand on her shoulder. "I'm telling you now because her phone number will be on our last bill. We can look for it there." Art gets up and heads for the sideboard where they stack old bills, paid and unpaid.

"So someone must have had her phone number in the first place," Colleen says, following him. "Who had her phone number?"

"I think Pam did. Or maybe Janet." He's rummaging through the pile now, trying to save the day, find the bill.

Colleen stomps back to the dining room, stacks dirty dishes, slamming them hard enough to make a racket, not caring if one breaks. So let him find the number. She'll call Lillian when she's damn well ready.

HANNAH VII

SUNDAY AFTERNOON and Hannah is marking essays. One week to go before, thank God, spring break. The phone rings.

"I just decided to take the proverbial bull by the horns and come to visit." Aunt Harriet's cheerful voice. "To see my dear sister. March 8th to 16th."

"That's…that's wonderful, Aunt Harriet."

"No fuss now. I know it's your school break and other than visiting your mother in Franklin, I'll be here and there. I've got a cousin in Citadel I haven't seen for some fifty-odd years and an old teaching compatriot who's moved to a farmhouse near Marborough—writing up a storm, and getting published too."

Hannah takes a deep breath. Information overload. "You taught?"

"Only until I married but we've kept in touch, Sadie and I, and I'm so looking forward to seeing you and everyone after all these years. It's my first trip since Clarey died, and I have to say, I'm as giddy as a school girl."

"It will be wonderful to meet you, at last," Hannah says, marveling at her aunt's enthusiasm.

"The flight gets in just after 4:30 on Friday the eighth, and I'll be wearing my navy trench coat."

"I'll be there," Hannah replies.

Every evening following, Hannah, who knows she is a tidy freak but pretends not to be, has rearranged and uncluttered her relatively pristine Toronto house over and over: putting this over there, that in the cupboard, standing back to change one picture for another, tearing off the guest-room bedspread, replacing it with the rose-colored duvet she bought earlier in the week. Even polishing an old silver tea service from her mother's front-hall table. Inside each blackened piece, she finds decades of buttons and pennies and paper clips vying with dust, even a burned-out light bulb. As she furiously scrubs at the blackened surfaces, Hannah turns each over looking for some clue as to its origin, deciding, finally, that either someone gave Edith the set after Hannah left home or that her mother kept the set hidden. Hannah knows that had she found it, especially in her teens, she would have asked, pestered her mother. Rescuing it on her most recent visit, Hannah brings it back with good intentions, intentions never carried out until 10 p.m. this evening.

School is out at two tomorrow, and there's the traditional get together at Plutarch's Pub afterward. Good excuse not to go. Julia will make a fuss and get over it. Russ is on his final rewrite and incommunicado anyway. The worst part will be taking Harriet to Franklin, to her mother's shabby little house. If Hannah had some warning, she might have wallpapered, bought a new couch, replaced the kitchen chairs. Everything sagging at the knees, smelling of age, in spite of her repeated cleaning sprees over the past few months.

It's after 2 a.m. when Hannah finally puts the polished silver tea service out onto the sideboard. Reluctantly, she leaves the piles of essays on her dining room table. She doesn't have a computer at home, has resisted, even though Russ teases her and calls her his sexy technophobe. She has a perfectly good electric typewriter that suits for letters and poetry. She can't move the essays. They are in strategic, after-first-reading piles. One last check in the spare bedroom. The brocade throw, rescued from the Victrola at her mother's, now adorns the three-legged bedside table, cigarette burns carefully mended, water stains to the back. The rose-colored duvet was chosen to match petals scattered throughout the brocade's intricate pattern. The second English countryside watercolor painting, brought earlier from her mother's, now hangs over the bed. For Aunt Harriet. Their origins are still a mystery. Something her mother bought? A wedding gift, perhaps.

All of this, the polishing and reorganizing, fends off the anxiety-ridden excitement vacillating through her. Until now, there has only been her mother to measure up to, and for almost fifty-five years she has failed, whether for substantiated reasons or for fabrications of her own short comings. One blood relative to give her furtive hugs, tut-tut impartially over whatever she said she has done or not done, and now, here she is—instead of climbing further out on another precarious branch, she is inching deliberately to the trunk to embrace a voice which sounds so real, so interested in her, seemingly with no strings attached. Hannah is not at all sure how she will deal with it.

Hannah arrives at the airport with her usual fifteen-minute leeway and checks the incoming screen. Flight 237 from Winnipeg, on time, scheduled to land at 16:47, gate 39. As she makes her way through the crowds, Hannah grimaces and subtracts to get the real time. Anthony was big on international time and, even after all these years, it rankles her. Arrogant cock-sure Anthony, screwing her every chance he had, even on his desk. What a stupid little fool she was, but then he did teach her a thing or two, and now with Russ, it definitely comes in handy. Drive your man into a state of frenzied ecstasy. She could write an article. Whoa. Stop this, Hannah thinks. Not good for the libido. Stupid international time.

She sits at the far end of an empty row of seats across from the gate, strategically positioning herself away from as much animated conversation as possible, and finds the packet of photos in her purse. There are no remotely recent ones of Aunt Harriet but she is sure she will recognize her. Medium height, most likely plumper now than in these early pictures, and with her now-gray hair up in a chignon. This much Harriet mentioned. "Clarey loved my long hair, and after he went I thought of cutting it, even before the funeral, of putting some with him in his pocket perhaps, but I couldn't bring myself to do it, and afterward, every time I looked in the mirror, I felt him behind me, so I've kept it long."

The romanticism of this overwhelms Hannah. She has already started two poems about it, trying to define this unknown quantity, this idyllic relationship, and has given up, hoping that after she spends time with Harriet, she will gain the needed insight.

Hannah looks up to see the carousels turning and people with postflight daze moving to check for luggage. Navy trench coat, she says to herself, edging through the usual accumulating crowd of hopeful greeters—navy trench coat and gray hair up in a chignon.

Aunt Harriet forgot to mention the large red-felt hat, floppy at the edges, almost completely covering her upswept hair. The round-faced woman who strides toward Hannah, dark brown eyes scanning the crowd, bulky suitcase banging against her stocky legs, momentarily reminds Hannah of Paddington bear.

"Hannah?" the woman says, looking up at Hannah who is about to move out of her way.

"Aunt Harriet?" Hannah says, realizing now who she is.

"Why yes, yes, dear." She drops the suitcase and embraces Hannah, giving her a long, warm kiss on the cheek. "My, my," she says, standing back. "So much like your mother when she was young. Rake thin and those wonderful blue eyes."

Hannah takes the suitcase and they weave through the arrivals crowd. She still feels the kiss on her cheek and Harriet's warm arm linked tightly through hers.

"Did you have a good flight?" Hannah feels tongue-tied. Self-conscious.

"For my first-ever flight it was dandy, just dandy. I sat beside the nicest young man. On a business trip. Something about grain elevators, those ugly new metal ones. Of course, most of the wooden ones I remember are gone now." She laughs. "Mind you, I didn't mention that to him. Could you find a washroom? I was terribly nervous about leaving my seat in the plane."

"There should be one just up ahead," Hannah says, feeling a lump in her throat. She hates leaving her seat during a flight, avoids it like the plague. "Right over there," Hannah says, stopping. "I'll wait here with your suitcase."

She watches Harriet stride toward the door, plump but solid, obviously used to regular walking. Like her mother in the old days. No time for maudlin self-pity, Hannah thinks sternly to herself. Harriet's suitcase reminds her of the one she used to pack her mother's clothes for the nursing home. An antique, solid construction, sewn together with matching leather strips. Pre-plastic and vinyl, probably a 1940s vintage.

"Here I am. Good as new." Harriet taps Hannah's arm and smiles up at her. Hat in hand, her silvery gray hair is twisted up and around into a coiled knob at the top of her head. Even with that extra half inch of hair on top, Harriet is still a good six inches shorter than Hannah.

"I had to park my car on the third level," Hannah says once they're through the automatic doors. "Do you want to wait here while I get the car?"

"Goodness, no," Harriet replies, giving Hannah's arm a friendly squeeze. "Sat enough on the plane. I need to get the kinks out."

Getting out of the airport and onto the highway takes all Hannah's concentration. It's rush hour and the merging lanes are a nightmare. After a lane-changing Camaro obviously fueled by

testosterone almost cuts her off, Hannah pushes in her Andrea
Bocelli tape, hoping Aunt Harriet won't mind. To Hannah's surprise,
Harriet hums along with the Shubert, a high warbly hum, perfectly
in tune.

"You know," Harriet says wistfully at the end of the piece, "Your
mother and I used to do that one."

"Mother and you...sang?"

"Ah, yes, the Jennings sisters. Church dos, celebrations, that
sort of thing."

"How old were you?"

"Edith was a young lady, seventeen or eighteen, and I was
pretending to be." Harriet laughs, a little silvery laugh. "No teenagers in those days."

"In Winnipeg?"

"Why yes, dear. Didn't your mother tell you?"

"I did find out I was born there, but Mother...Mother..."

"Wouldn't talk about it?"

"Hardly a word all the time I was growing up. For a long time
I took for granted that I was born in Franklin. I never gave it a
thought really, until I found my birth certificate."

"In the red-velvet chocolate box?"

"How did you know?" Hannah has to concentrate on driving,
eyes on traffic, the speedometer, the rearview mirror. Her knuckles
whiten as she grips the wheel.

"I helped her pack," Harriet says quietly. "We stashed the box
away in the bottom of something."

"The wicker laundry basket."

"That's it," Harriet says, pulling out a tissue to pat her nose.
"He was so romantic, her Harry," she continues. "Romantic and
irresponsible, I guess." She turns her head and dabs her face again.

"My father? I know so little about him. I used to make things
up when I was small, that he was waiting for me somewhere, that

I would visit and find him—handsome as he was in his army uniform."

"Our parents were pretty strict," Harriet said, after a few moments silence. "Strict, and with high standards concerning marriage. Your father, Harry, was a wild one. He sang too, but pop stuff, Crosby and the Ink Spots."

Later, Hannah will remember every word, every syllable of this conversation—hoard it like gold. "Mom used to listen to them all the time. Old seventy-eights. I found most of them at the house in Franklin."

"Yes, well, he swept her off her feet, did Harry. They eloped, and you arrived seven months later."

The Andrea Bocelli tape has ended. Traffic noise does nothing to fill the silence that follows. Harriet fidgets with her tissue; Hannah stares at the license plate of the car ahead. Seven months. She knows she weighed over eight pounds.

"A month after you were born," Harriet continues, "your father signed up to go overseas—brought her the box of chocolates a few days before he left."

"Valentine's Day?"

Harriet nods.

Questions multiply, hoards of them spilling out until Hannah bangs the wheel and inhales sharply, forcing herself to concentrate on driving.

"This probably isn't the best time to be telling you this," Harriet says. "We could wait…"

"No, go on. I'm fine. Please go on."

"I remember our parents, your grandparents, arguing at night, Mother trying to convince Father you were a preemie, Father categorically denying her weak logic. His anger hung in the house for days, weeks. Especially when Edith moved back home."

"After my father left for overseas?" Hannah is slowly piecing it together.

"A private's basic pay was a dollar thirty a day," Harriet said, smiling for the first time since the conversation began. "Not enough for you and your mother to stay in their little flat on Mercer Street."

"A dollar thirty a day." Hannah realizes she knows as little about Canadian history as she does her own.

"Seems unbelievable now," Aunt Harriet remarks, "but it sure beat what it was like during the Depression."

"Why did Mom leave Winnipeg?" Hannah whispers. "How did she end up in Franklin?"

"Your grandfather was an accountant. One of his McGill classmates had a practice in Franklin." Harriet stops and sniffs, just slightly, turning her head to momentarily gaze out the window. "It was a stormy time in our household," she continues, head still turned. "Your mother…your mother was headstrong…"

"Still is," Hannah adds, laughing nervously. "Always has been."

"Edith moving back added insult to injury as far as my father was concerned," Harriet continues. "And you, bless your heart, disrupted everything. Night feedings, diapers in the bathroom, mother spending too much time with you."

"Was he jealous?"

"Could have been part of it, I guess. He was angry, barely spoke to any of us, spent longer and longer hours at the office. I was sure Edith would get a job; I heard her talking to mother about it—she'd wait until you were three months old, see if her old boss would take her back."

"She was working, then, before she married?"

"Oh yes, MacCartney and MacCartney, barrister and son. Your mother was a whiz of a typist."

Hannah has purposely stayed in the right-hand lane. Again, she almost grinds to a halt behind an aging cement truck, its slowly revolving tank periodically spewing water and bits of gravel against her windshield. "But she didn't," Hannah says, turning on the wipers again. "She didn't get that job."

"Didn't get the opportunity as far as I remember," Harriet says. "I came home from school one April afternoon to find Mother in tears. Edith was to leave the following week for Ontario; Father had come home at noon with a letter confirming employment from Mr. Cecil Lumsdon in Franklin, Ontario, and a train ticket."

"I see." Hannah hears her mother's voice now. That reserved, pulled back, tut-tut consequences voice.

"Even after all these years, I remember it as unfair, unspeakably cruel." Harriet's voice is shrill, her shoulders rigid. "Mother said later that Father felt Edith would be a bad influence on me."

Hannah nods, and in spite of the traffic noise, silence momentarily separates them again.

"I was so sure Edith would get a job and that all summer I would be able to babysit. Told all my second form friends I was an aunt now and would be tending my niece all holidays."

"Second form?"

"Oh yes, I always forget. I was fifteen, dear, so that would put me in the tenth grade. Am I correct?"

"You were fifteen when Mom and I left?" Hannah feels even more overwhelmed and isn't sure she can keep driving. Trauma at fifteen. She looks ahead. Where is that turnoff?

"Such a romantic, impressionable age," Harriet continues. "Don't you find that, dear, with your students? My goodness, we carried our hearts, no, the whole world, on our sleeves in those days. All our wonderful boys going off to war."

"And so Mother and I left and that was it?" Hannah knows she sounds clipped. It's a well-worn distancing tactic. "You never heard from us again?"

Harriet either ignores it or doesn't notice. "Mother kept in touch by letter," she goes on, "but she had to be secretive. As soon as Edith left, Father disowned her and forbade us to so much as mention her name. Later, after I was married, Edith and I corresponded, but she always painted a rosy picture, the stiff upper lip handed down through our family."

"Only another fifteen minutes," Hannah interjects, relieved to see the Avenue Road turnoff sign. She doesn't want to hear any more. Not right now. Her head spins with questions and her chest hurts. Anxiety. She grips the wheel and smiles bleakly in Harriet's direction.

"I've probably done enough rambling," Harriet says, putting her hand momentarily on Hannah's arm. "Silly old aunt, but it's so wonderful to actually see you after all these years."

She nods off then, the hand closest to Hannah with its sensibly cut nails holding her hat, the other gradually slipping down by her side, her head turned away so that the chignon with its twists and knots glimmers silvery in the approaching headlights. She rests with that trust of someone who has never been behind the wheel, someone who is totally confident of arriving at her given destination, unaware of pileups, maniac passers, and eighteen wheelers roaring past on either side.

As soon as they open the front door, Hannah realizes she has forgotten about supper, about having anything ready. When she suggests going to a restaurant, Harriet asks if she has any soup. "It's what I'd do at home," she says. "Good old Campbell's, it's sure to hit the spot."

While Hannah dithers over everything, including crackers or buns, Harriet sits quietly in the living room reading a *National Geographic*. "Such wonderfully detailed articles," she says when they sit down at Hannah's two-seater table in the kitchen.

"Hope this is okay," Hannah says, pouring soup into Harriet's bowl. "I use my dining room table as a desk and it's beyond clearing at the moment."

"Lovely, just lovely. Umm and this tomato soup, dear, it's delicious. You must have given Campbell's a boost."

"A can of tomatoes and some basil," Hannah says, getting buns from the micro. "Mother always did it this way."

Hannah sits and attacks her soup, knowing she can't, at the moment, say one more word. Nostalgia and regret sweep over her, nostalgia for not sitting here with her mother chatting like this, which she never did, as her mother never came to this house. When Hannah first bought the place and was so excited about it—the back yard, the French doors out to her deck. Her mother asked about getting there on the bus or train. They even set a date; her mother bought a ticket. The fateful weekend coincided with Russ hearing that his first book had been accepted. Hannah foolishly assumed her mother wouldn't mind postponing her visit. In the following months that metamorphosed into years, it became one of those paramount issues hauled up into conversations at the slightest pretext—that man she was seeing, muted references to her promiscuity. During the last few years, the subject disappeared, lost with everything else in her mother's encroaching confusion.

"Microwave ovens are so amazing," Harriet says, buttering one of the warm buns. "Clarey bought me one three Christmases ago."

"I'd probably starve without it," Hannah replies. "I don't seem to have much time for cooking."

"Your mother was a good cook."

"She always said studying was more important than cooking, and she'd shoo me out of her kitchen."

"Wise of her."

"I'd have to agree."

Nostalgia washes back, apparently over both of them, eliminating conversation and reducing sound to polite mandible crunching and the odd scraping across a bowl bottom.

"You must be tired," Hannah says, jumping up. "I'll show you where your bathroom towels are and your bedroom."

"This picture," Harriet says, the minute Hannah turns on the bedroom light. "Your great-grandfather Charles Jennings painted this picture." She runs a finger along the roughly hewn wooden frame.

"My great-grandfather Jennings?" Hannah stares at it in amazement.

"There were two, as I recall. I sent mine to your mother after father died. Edith loved those paintings so."

"The other one is at the Lodge in Mother's room," Hannah whispers.

Harriet pulls her suitcase onto the chair beside the door. "I'll tell you all about that tomorrow, dear," she says, snapping the metal fasteners open. "I think we're both a bit tired."

"You're right," Hannah manages. She pulls down the coverlet and fluffs the pillow. Harriet embraces her when she stands, a full, warm embrace, a kiss brushing Hannah's cheek. Only after she leaves and rubs the spot, does Hannah feel the saltiness left with it.

BRITANNIA NOW

BY THE SECOND WEEK of March, with three articles already in print, Searp has the fourth sketched out, and if he doesn't get some solid information about Larry Mourand in the next three weeks, he will have to make do without. He's asked for an extension, and his editor says they could probably run it the following week if necessary. Not surprisingly, Mourand's fifty-year-old Cleveland address is no longer valid. Larry would likely have been in eleventh grade. Now, there are both public and Catholic high schools in Franklin but he's not sure about forty years ago. When he mentions this to his mom, she says she's pretty sure there was only one high school in the fifties, although she thinks she remembers the Catholic kids going to their school until the end of grade ten.

"Call your Aunt Franny," she says. "She's been teaching at Harvey George Public School since 1965."

He'd forgotten about Aunt Franny. His dad was the youngest of five, and the only aunt they were close to was Aunt Maureen, his dad's oldest sister. Her daughter, Sharon, babysat him when he was little.

Aunt Franny laughs when he asks about Franklin schools in the fifties. "There was Franklin High," she says, "and St. Albert's Catholic Church school and I think your mom's right. Kids went to the Catholic school until the end of grade ten."

"Franklin High," Searp says. "Would you know anyone who taught there in the fifties?"

"You're working on another one of those newspaper articles, aren't you?" Franny quizzes.

"Yes, I am," Searp replies, hoping this won't jeopardize getting the information.

"I think Wilfred Staples was principal of Franklin High back in the fifties," she says. "I'm pretty sure he's at the Lodge now, and he might remember."

Searp has never been to Sunset Lodge and he takes it in stride, noting there might be the seeds of an article or two in the place.

"Allan Searp from the *Franklin Standard*," he says to the receptionist. "I'm looking for Wilfred Staples."

"Are you going to interview him?" the receptionist asks, looking impressed. "Such a lovely gentleman. A reader, he is. You'll likely find him in the library, just down this hall a few doors."

Searp thanks her and locates the room. A white-mustached man in suit and tie sits by the window, reading.

"Mr. Staples?" Searp asks, striding toward him. Several other residents look up as soon as Searp speaks.

Wilfred Staples gives Searp the once-over. "Well, you're certainly too young to have been one of my students." He smiles and puts down his book.

"Allan Searp, *Franklin Standard*," Searp says, extending his hand.

"Ah, yes," Staples replies, "the young fella who's writing those Britannia articles."

"Three down and three to go," Searp adds. "Do you mind if I sit down?"

"Pull up a chair, lad. There's one over there."

Searp brings the chair and removes his hat as he sits.

"A gaucho hat," Staples says with a wry smile. "You fancy

yourself a cowboy?"

Searp laughs. "Not exactly, sir. I've had it since college—picked it up at a secondhand store. I figure it brings me luck."

"Luck comes with hard work, young man. Hard work and perseverance."

"That's why I've come to see you, sir." A better lead in I couldn't have written, he thinks.

"Well now, and what is it you think I can do for you?"

"I'm looking for information about Larry Mourand."

"Mourand?" Staples stares out the window a moment and turns back.

"Yes, sir. He would have been at your school in 1955."

"Eleventh grade," Staples says, nodding. "Smart lad, good looking. His father had the hotel, then, did he not?"

"He did." Searp remains cool-headed and focused. Staples may have the missing link.

"A bit of a troublemaker as I recall, didn't fit in too well."

"I understand he left your school that year, and I was wondering…"

"Where he was sent?"

"Exactly."

"A military school in Ohio, as I recall. I wouldn't remember the name, though." He gives Searp a scrutinizing look. "I have to assume this has something to do with one of your articles."

"It does, sir."

"And does this help you in your quest?"

"It's another missing link," Searp says. "Would you remember anything else?"

Another pause. "Mourand set up a basketball scholarship for the school," Staples says, "it's still being used today."

"He was a generous man," Searp adds, hoping for more.

"He was indeed."

Wilfred Staples doesn't say so, but Searp can tell the interview is over. "It's been a pleasure talking to you," he adds, extending his hand.

"Likewise," Staples replies. "I'll look forward to that article."

Searp spends Monday at the Toronto Reference Library researching Ohio military schools. He laboriously contacts each one, only to find few of them go back as far as the fifties. In his brief conversations with school receptionists, he does find out they are schools for moderately troubled boys. Tackling US military schools again he finds an article in an old *Atlantic Monthly* that says they were wildly popular until the Vietnam War, after which hundreds closed. Another dead end.

When he talks to his dad about Mourand and his son that evening, Searp Sr. suggests getting hold of Al Turner, a friend of his grandfather. "If your Mourand was an American," he says, "he likely drove a Lincoln or a Cadillac. Al had the Ford Dealership in those days, Al Turner Autos, right on the main drag. It was in its glory days when I was a kid. Can't remember who had the GM dealership. Never the twain would meet in those days. You were either one or the other."

"And where would I find Al Turner?" Searp asks. "At the Lodge?"

"No, no. He's not in that place yet. Likely still hanging around the dealership. It sells used cars now. Martin's Motors."

"I've seen it," Searp replies. "Thanks, Dad, I'll check it out tomorrow."

Searp figures if this lead fizzles out, he going to go with what he's got.

Fred Martin, the owner of Martin's Motors smiles when Searp asks about Al Turner. "He's that guy in back"—he points through the door behind—"smoking his cigar and jawing with one of the young salesmen. Shows up every morning like clockwork. Kind of a fixture, you might say."

Searp finds garage interiors fascinating. He hasn't a mechanical bone in his body but the places always intrigue him. This place is like all the rest, an overriding metallic oil smell, assorted equipment neatly lined up like soldiers on the floor, shelves and shelves of parts. He's a bit of a neat freak himself so this always appeals to him.

Turner and the young salesman are heavily into some technical discussion and completely ignore Searp when he approaches. Another given in these places. Searp shuffles his feet and tries to get a word in edgewise between zero to sixty times relating to the latest car models. Finally Turner looks up. "If you're looking for a used car," he says, slapping his knee, "you're in the wrong part of this establishment." Both men laugh, and the salesman puts his hand on Searp's shoulder. "Turner's an old timer around here. What can I do for you?"

"Allan Searp, *Franklin Standard*," Searp replies. "It's Mr. Turner I'd like to chat with."

The salesman stands and offers Searp his chair. "I should be out on the floor, anyway," he says with a grin. "I'll catch you later, Al."

"So you're the hotshot grandson I've been hearing about. Your granddad and I share a pint at the Legion from time to time."

"I've been working long and hard on this series I'm doing about the Britannia," Searp replies, "and I hear from my dad that if Hugh Mourand drove a Lincoln, he might have brought it in here for service. Back in the fifties."

"The fifties. That's a day or two ago." Turner smiles and puffs on his cigar. "I remember Mourand well. Yes, he drove a Lincoln, a Continental, and he brought the beast in here." He pauses. "Had his Model T, stored right over there." He points to the back of the shop.

"A Model T? He was into antique cars, then, was he?"

"Just the T as far as I know. He'd show up every Sunday morning to give her a good polish—when his wife and the boy were at church."

"The Anglican Church?"

"Yes it was. Your granddad's right. You're sharp all right."

"The Model T," Searp says quietly. Don't rush him, he thinks, don't interrupt.

"He was almost as proud of it as he was the boy. Had great plans for that kid. Course that was before…" He stops and stares directly at Searp. "All this stuff I'm telling you, you using it for one of your newspaper articles?"

"It's mainly research," Searp replies. "Backstory to help me understand what was going on."

"There was a lot going on," Turner snorts. "Most of it behind the old man's back."

"The boy was a bit of a wild one?" Searp asks.

"More than a bit if you ask me, and when the old guy was pushed down the stairs, that was the last straw."

"The old guy?" Searp is in his element now.

"I can't remember his name. He worked in the hotel kitchen. Mourand was pretty sure his son did it. No hard proof, mind you, but he sent him packing back to the US, to some fancy military school. Last we saw of the kid."

"It must have been tough on his mother," Searp says.

"She went right off the deep end," Turner replies. "Last we saw of her too."

"Did Mourand come here after that?" Searp asks. He is getting nowhere, all this information he already knows.

"I remember him coming in all excited when the boy made it into university," Turner says.

"Do you remember what university?"

"One with a fancy sounding name. It seemed important to him. He sold the hotel about a year after that and went back himself."

"To Ohio?"

"Guess so."

"Thanks for your time, Mr. Turner." Searp stands to go.

"Some magazine had an article about a Mourand," Turner says as an afterthought. "I was in Sloan's when I saw it."

"Recently?"

"Before Christmas, I think. I was looking for something to give my own grandson. He's into hunting and I figured..."

"Do you remember the magazine's name?" Searp cuts in. "*Newsweek? The Atlantic?*"

Turner shakes his head. "You're the reporter, you should be able to track that down."

"Thanks, Mr. Turner." Searp's out the door and running. He doesn't even bother to get back in his car and sprints the five blocks back to Sloan's. He was at the Reference Library. Why didn't he look at current magazines? It never occurred to him Larry Mourand would be prominent—if it is Larry.

Searp finds the magazine at the back of a pile, bottom row, in Sloan's extensive magazine section—a December issue, *Business USA*, Mourand's name on the front cover: *Real Estate Magnate Mourand Seals Another Deal.* He flips to the first page of the article and as soon as he reads the name Larry Mourand, he buys the magazine and sprints back to his car, wishing now he hadn't left it at Martin's. He parks down at the marina and reads the article.

Larry Mourand wheels and deals in real estate and is based in New York City. His office, Mourand Estate Properties Inc., is in the Chrysler Building on the east side of Manhattan. Searp's pulse races. He throws the magazine into the backseat and hightails it back to the newspaper office, where he contacts Information and gets Mourand's office number. He knows it's a long shot that he'll get to talk to the man, knows there'll be at least one if not two dragon receptionists guarding the man's lair.

He tries anyway, and when he says he's a Canadian newspaper reporter, a receptionist tells him curtly that Mr. Mourand is unavailable and he should call back.

He does, almost every day for the next two weeks, with the same result. He toys with saying he's from the *New York Times* but knows bullshit begets bullshit, and it might backfire. By Thursday, with only one week to deadline, he knows he better just finish the article the way it is.

When he arrives home late Thursday afternoon, exhausted and somewhat discouraged, his Aunt Maureen has dropped in for a visit.

"Your mother tells me you're having trouble finding someone who worked at the Britannia in the fifties," Aunt Maureen says before Searp has time to say hello.

Searp slumps into a kitchen chair and nods, helping himself to a date square his mom has provided with tea.

"Colleen Pinser," Maureen says, putting more sugar in her tea. "She would have been Colleen Miller then, of course, her dad was a drinker and her mom taught piano." Maureen taps the teaspoon on her cup. "And Hannah Norcroft."

"You know these women?" Searp says. "Are they still living here?"

"Pinser's Hardware Store," his mom adds. "Colleen married Art Pinser. She was a looker when she was young, and could sing too."

"Her dad was in special care last month," Maureen adds, "and she's finally got him into the Lodge. Stubborn old fart if there ever was one."

"And Hannah Norcroft?" he asks.

Maureen snorts. "High school teacher in Toronto," she says. "She's been down here the last couple of months getting her poor old mom into the Lodge—swished in and out of the hospital like Miss America. Apparently she and Colleen had coffee together, but for the life me, I can't imagine what they would have in common."

"Colleen Pinser," Searp says, pulling out the small notepad he always has in his pocket. "I could get in touch with her through the store."

"I'd completely forgotten she was at the Britannia until Maureen mentioned it," his mom added.

"In 1955?" Searp says. "You're sure she was there that summer?"

"Are you questioning your aunt's memory?" Maureen gives his arm a poke.

"No, no," Searp says, grabbing another date square. "Great seeing you, Aunt Maureen. I've got to cover a Chamber of Commerce meeting at 5:30."

"What about supper?" his mom asks.

"I should be back by seven in time to grab a bite before I leave for the Town Council meeting."

"He never stops running," his mom says to Maureen.

"Keeps me fit," Searp adds, giving his mom a peck on the cheek. "Thanks for the info, Aunt Maureen."

Why is it, Searp thinks, as he starts his car, that crucial information always shows up just before deadline?

COLLEEN VIII

THE CALL COMES at 2 a.m. Sunday, in the middle of a snow-storm, the week of Spring Break. Art answers and passes the phone over to Colleen. "It's the Lodge," he mumbles, before rolling back and pulling the pillow over his head.

Mrs. Pinser, we have your father in the ambulance on his way to the hospital.

Colleen sits, instantly awake and immediately shivering. "He's fallen again?"

"Vomiting blood. Disoriented."

"Emergency?" She's on her feet now, searching with her free hand for yesterday's clothes.

"They'll probably take him straight to Intensive Care."

"I'll get there as soon as possible."

Art rolls to a sitting position and turns on the bedside table lamp. "Is it bad?" He looks gray in the half light, totally whacked out.

Colleen, always at her best in a crisis, snaps into coping mode. "He's fallen again," she says coming over to smooth Art's rumpled hair and turn off the light. "I'll probably just have to sign something. You go back to sleep."

"Are you sure?"

"Positive."

"I think it's storming," Art says, lying back down. "You'd better take the van."

Thank God for four-wheel drive, Colleen thinks as she wheels through bumper-high drifts on the long, tree-clad laneway. Unpredictable March. A couple of days ago, the snow was almost gone. Tonight, much of the back road has been swept clear by a high wind, but once on the highway, salt and slush coats the pavement, the few cars and one cube van that pass smack wet, brown snow over her windshield slowing her down, making it hard to see. She notices headlights tunnel closer and closer behind. She peers into the snow-swirling night, her eyes jumping back and forth between the appearing and disappearing yellow line along the pavement's edge and giant snow swirls ahead. "Get off my butt," she mutters, and as if on cue, the driver pulls his exhaust-smoking car out to pass. Right on the big curve before the long hill down into Franklin. Colleen holds her breath and slows even more. Once past her, he fishtails back and forth, hitting gravel on the right shoulder, and skidding in a half circle into the oncoming lane, brakes screeching to a stop as she inches by.

He waves and holds up a beer bottle.

A dozen what if's pound her as she white-knuckles the wheel, determined to keep going no matter how much her hands are shaking. Another damn drunk driver. She could have been tomorrow's accident news. Like her mom. The driver would have made it. If Art had been with her, he'd be dead too. Both of them on their way to what—the bedside of her dying dad, to watch his bloated form breathe its last? Why? For some reason, she has never figured out, she has to play the good daughter role to the bitter end.

Street lights at the bottom of the hill help her see, and once she passes the Franklin town limits, the swirling snow and high wind stop, leaving only flurries in a light breeze. They plough more in town so there's less slush. The van is warm now, and Colleen sits a few minutes in the hospital parking lot, staring at the building, this place so wanting to save everyone, keep everyone alive—so clean and organized, and yet so many times unable to understand. Her hands still shake a bit and she takes a couple of deep breaths before opening the van door to lean into the sharp cold. Fifteen or twenty steps to the front desk, a couple of minutes at least. Plenty of time to get ready, change into the good daughter once again, ready to do and say whatever is proper, to be helpful and caring the way she was taught.

It seems months ago that she talked to young doctor Warton, listened to him explain cirrhosis of the liver. Not even three months. A fast, downward slide, a day-to-day falling apart. Her dad started seeing things and people, civil war dudes and Mickey Spillane types, pulled up no doubt from the days when he used to read whodunits. Then there were insects—bugs he kept telling them were crawling over his skin, ants and beetles he slapped at and scratched until they put soft mittens on his hands. They had him tied into his wheelchair now, and for the last couple of weeks, he didn't know who Colleen was, didn't even call her Madge.

Her dad is white as a sheet, tubed up with intravenous and a catheter. His bloated gut sticks up through the sheet and blanket as if someone pumped up a large balloon inside him.

"He's been drifting in and out," the nurse says, pulling a more comfortable than usual chair up close to the bed. "We have kept to the Health Care Directive from the Lodge. They aren't equipped to deal with hemorrhaging. The intravenous is only for dehydration. Are you alone?"

Colleen nods and sits down knowing she is still shaking, still cold, even with her coat on. There is no other bed in this room. They've brought her dad here to die.

"We've got fresh coffee on," the nurse says. "Cream and sugar?"

"Double cream, please." Colleen starts to undo her coat and stops.

"I'll get you a blanket." The nurse smiles and is gone.

The Health Care Directive. It wasn't that long ago that she made herself fill it out—one of those heavy-duty things; she even needed two witnesses. She asked Maureen and their lawyer, Carl Broomfield. At the top of the first page, three headings: *Life Threatening Illness, Feeding, Cardiac Arrest*—each with the same two words: *reversible and irreversible.* Under these were worse choices going from full support to no support. How she felt about her dad, the years piled up with so much crap and anger, to say nothing of the fact that other than making sure he had food in the house and clean clothes, she didn't know him, didn't want to, made sure she stayed out of his way—all of this seemed to melt away as she stared at this cold, necessary medical form. As it was, she spent an entire afternoon worrying over every question, every choice, wishing the impossible, that he could have filled the form out himself. Never in his right mind—he would have thrown it across the room. "Goddammed forms," he always said about anything that even looked like a form. "Nobody's going to tell me what to do."

Colleen notices that the nurse pulls the door partway shut when she leaves, and she is sure this was done on purpose, first of all, to tell anyone in the hall that the room is occupied so stay out and keep your voice down, and second, the fact that it's not completely closed lets the nurses hear, in case she or her dad needs help, calls out.

The nurse returns with coffee and a blanket, and tucks Colleen in. "You an only child?" she asks, pausing at the door.

"One sister," Colleen replies, holding the cup to warm her hands. "She's out of the country."

"Always happens," the nurse says, nodding. "The one closest by gets stuck with everything. Should be a special place in heaven for those close by. Even better, a big cash reward." She smiles and leaves.

"Madge?"

Colleen turns too fast, almost spilling her coffee.

"It's Colleen."

"Where the hell am I?"

"In the hospital."

Her dad has not opened his eyes. A shudder runs through his body and he runs a mittened hand over his face. "Colleen?"

"Yes, Dad."

"This time I am packing it in."

"I don't know." Colleen can barely get the words out. He seems to know who she is.

"Those damn older sisters of yours."

"Lillian?"

"Where are they? Thought they'd all be here…" He coughs and holds his abdomen…"to watch the old man die."

"I…I didn't come here to…" Colleen can't go on. Her acting skills, all the usual ways she protects herself, are slipping, falling away.

"Not you. Goddammit." Her dad grabs the metal sides of the bed and turns to stare at her.

"You stuck it out even after Madge." His hands fall limp and he drifts off.

The coffee cup rattles as Colleen tries to take another sip. This is not how she thought it would be—her dad being so with it. Guilt washes over her until her stomach heaves. She stands and walks to the door and back. She is not going to barf here in this room; she is not going to barf, period. She should have asked Art to come with her.

Her dad makes a gurgling noise, and Colleen sits instantly. Twice he opens his mouth slightly as if to say something and twice he drifts off. Colleen feels numb again, better than throwing up she thinks.

The nurse sticks her head in the door. "Everything all right?"

Colleen nods.

"There's a buzzer there. Just press it."

Colleen nods again.

"Who the hell is that?" her dad whispers.

"The nurse."

"Where am I?"

"At the hospital."

"Where's your mother?"

Colleen hunches over and looks at the floor. What can she possibly say? How can she deal with everything this question asks?

"Are we alone?"

"Yes," Colleen says quickly. Better question.

"They've all gone, then?"

"Who?"

"They were at the foot of my bed, staring."

"They've gone." It's like acting without a script, Colleen thinks. A totally weird, real-life improv.

"There's a will," her father whispers. His breathing is slower now. A lot slower.

Colleen leans over him, putting her hands on the metal bedside.

"A will," her father says again with great effort. He jerks his hand through the air and it bangs against Colleen's. Cold fingers close over hers.

Colleen doesn't pull away, watching as if she were someone else as he hangs on.

"Handyman's…haven," he whispers after a long pause. "Case of…twenty-four." His breath comes out in funny little sighs, longer and longer pauses between. His hand slides down. Colleen listens and waits. The room falls away, only his breathing, less and less, until it stops. The room snaps back, bright lights, metal bed, blue-green drapes. Her dad is no longer there. Eyes closed, lips slightly parted. Gone.

The next day, with everything in chaos and most of the family back home except for Artie, whose flight arrives in Toronto at nine that evening, Lillian calls from the Franklin train station. Suppertime. Colleen is in the kitchen, filling the teakettle. Still numb but coping, mainly because her family has rallied.

"Aunt Lillian's on the phone," Pam sticks her head in the kitchen. "She's asking for you, Mom."

"Hello," Colleen says, taking the portable phone in one hand as she continues to fill the kettle with the other.

"I cannot find a taxi driver who has the intelligence to know where you live."

"Where are you?"

"At your quaint little train station."

"In Franklin?"

"I certainly hope so."

Colleen manages to not drop the kettle. She covers the receiver and walks shakily into the dining room, feeling as if someone knocked the breath out of her. "Aunt Lillian is at the train station," she half-whispers. Everyone is talking at once.

"Who?" Cal says. They seem to be getting over the telling of a joke; Cal and Pam are wiping their eyes, all of them trying to be serious, trying to look concerned.

"Aunt Lillian," Colleen repeats. "She's here."

There's a hush as everyone tunes in to what Colleen says.

"Where is she?" Art says, standing. "Should I pick her up?"

"At the train station." Colleen hands the phone to Art and walks from the room.

There are no extra beds; the TV couch is all that's left for Artie. Colleen slips into the downstairs bathroom and turns on the light. A Franklin Turtle doll is sprawled beside the unflushed toilet, a wet face cloth in the sink.

Lillian. She had written to her not long after her talk with Dr. Warton. Lillian hadn't written back or phoned to say she was coming. How like her just to land in, like the Queen of Sheba. Colleen tries to remember the last time she saw Lillian. She didn't make it home for their mom's funeral. Why was she bothering with this one?

She breezed in when Colleen was pregnant with Pam, thirty years ago; Artie and Janet were still preschoolers. Colleen and Art were, at the time, living in a little bungalow on the outskirts of Franklin, not enough furniture and never enough time. Lillian, smoking with a cigarette holder, highly put out when Colleen said she couldn't smoke in the house. Worse, when Colleen said it was Art's rule.

"Wouldn't you know," Lillian said, shaking her head. "You poor dear. Married to a dictator."

Colleen couldn't believe this, that Lillian would say such a thing, and she made a point of saying how wonderful Art was, how kind and helpful, horrified that her dear never-hurt-a-fly Art could be called a dictator. No smoking in 1964—he was way ahead of his time.

Lillian went on. About everything.

"Such a darling little house," she said as she picked her way through the children's toys. Janet who was three and felt quite grown up appeared first, her four-year-old brother Artie, shyer, close behind. When Colleen said who Lillian was, they raced over and Lillian held them off with one hand while pulling two huge lollipops from her purse with the other—suckers much too big for their small mouths. Colleen kept away from candy, especially hard candy, as spit out bits always ended up stuck on something, usually the seat of a chair. Janet and Artie squealed happily and sat on the floor, slurping and smearing candy dye across their faces.

Lillian perched on the edge of the crumb-laden couch in her

white shift. "So wonderful to have a young family," she said, patting
her every-hair-in-place beehive, "so fulfilling. Lucky, lucky you, with
another one on the way."

Colleen did ask about Lillian's second year teaching at the
Luxembourg International School, but all she wanted to talk about
were semester-break visits to Paris and London. *Ah* the Eiffel Tower
and little bistros and *ooh* the pubs in London. And the theater—
how Colleen would love the theater.

Colleen remembers Lillian not giving her a hug or even once
touching her. She does remember laughing afterward, telling Art
that maybe Lillian thought pregnancy was catching like chicken
pox or mumps. She also remembers watching the taxi roar off,
Lillian waving out the window, her just so nail polish gleaming in
the sunlight, Janet and Artie pulling on Colleen's baggy maternity
dress. The young mother in the shoe.

"Mom, are you okay?" It's Pam at the bathroom door.

Colleen flushes the toilet and turns on the tap. "Fine," she calls.
"Out in a min."

Pam slides an arm around Colleen's waist and leads her back
into the dining room. "Coffee," she says, pulling out a chair. "We're
taking over."

Colleen watches them rush about. Her wonderful brood. She
hears the car start, wheels crunch on the gravel driveway. It will take
Art at least twenty minutes to get there, a good five to load Lillian's
luggage, and then twenty back. An hour. She has almost an hour
to get herself ready.

Eight-year-old Taylor, looking more and more like her mom,
carefully brings Colleen a plate of goodies: butter tarts Colleen made
earlier in the day, Oreo cookies brought by Pam, banana bread made
by Taylor's dad, Paul. A new breed, these modern families, share and
share alike, even baking. Colleen thinks it's wonderful, even envies
them, but wouldn't want to share her kitchen on a regular basis,

especially not baking. Art cooked a meal once in a blue moon, but there were so many other jobs around the house, things Colleen was hopeless at, and so they carried on like Art's parents had—You do this and I'll do that, like fifties sitcoms, her daughters said. It wasn't, but there was no use arguing.

Colleen gives Taylor a hug and takes some banana bread. Everyone else has left the table now, plates and napkins whisked away, Pam and Janet and the men busy in the kitchen. Getting ready. They know Lillian is used to service.

"Cal's showing Shane how to play the Sims," Taylor says. "I get a turn next." Taylor gives her grandma a hug and races off. Computer games, Colleen thinks, these grandkids, another galaxy. Her family, the friendly aliens.

Steve appears with a mug of coffee, turns a chair, backwards and sits opposite his mother. "You all right, Mom?"

"A bit numb and trying not to be, I guess."

"Damn inconsiderate of her to land in with no warning."

"I wrote her a couple of months ago, after I talked to Dr. Warton. I said she should come home, that he said your grandpa wouldn't last much longer."

"Well, she just made it for the last act, didn't she? Two days from now, it will be history."

"Luck, I guess. Coincidence." The cup rattles as Colleen returns it to the saucer. She wonders if she is going to be one of those old ladies who shakes. Stress, she says silently to herself. I am under a certain amount of stress.

"We've booked her into the Britannia," Steve says quietly.

"Who did?" Colleen stiffens. Would they want her to visit Lillian there?

"Pam did," Steve goes on. "Aunt Lillian can't stay here, so Dad's going to take her there first. You've got an hour and a half, at least."

"The Britannia," Colleen says, as casually as she can manage.

"A Vintage Sundown Inn, now. Should be good enough for her."

"Yes, I'm sure it will be."

They all hear the car, the doors open and close. Lillian's voice going on and on as Art shows her up onto the deck. They have apparently stopped, Art pointing things out: the maple sugar grove up on the hill, the cedar swamp, how many acres they own. Dear Art. He would never brag on purpose, but he is doing this for her, letting Lillian know they have been successful over the years, have amounted to something.

Pam gives Colleen a hug. "We're all here," she says quietly. "Lots of support."

Colleen pushes a strand of gray hair back and tugs at the too-tight waistline of her skirt, her favorite Christmas skirt, long and swirling, good for hiding her spreading hips. She hasn't bothered with makeup and thinks she must look awful, like the wreck of the Hesperus, her mom would say. Wrong thought at the wrong time.

Everything spills out inside her head: things she and Lillian did, things they didn't do, what it might have been like to have a real dad, a TV-family dad; it's ridiculous, but she's into it now and she can't stop—the normal family life she longed for, her mom dead too soon, pets long gone and buried in a grave site near the old apple orchard, birds and chipmunks she tried to save and couldn't, the roadkill she still stops to move into the ditch. All of them dying, dying…

Pam leads her, sobbing, into the kitchen.

"Take a deep breath," Pam says, and then, "group hug." Paul and Jake join Pam and they surround her, their warm arms and bodies holding her, trying to make her feel safe. "We're all here," Pam says again. "Remember that."

"Come in, come in. Long time no see"—Janet's voice, laughter all around. "Let me take your coat."

Colleen breaks away and forces a smile, her showtime face. "Okay. I'm okay," she says. "Just a bit of overload."

"Where's that wonderful sister of mine?" Colleen hears Lillian say.

"Here I am," Colleen replies, pushing open the door. "The one and only."

"Little sister," Lillian says, grabbing Colleen's two shoulders. "Haven't you weathered well." She gives Colleen a peck on the forehead.

Colleen has forgotten how much taller Lillian is, taller and a good deal heavier. Thirty years with a pound for each, Colleen thinks. It must run in the family.

"It has been quite a while," Colleen says. On-stage chat. There and not really there. "Sit yourself down, Lil. Bet you won't say no to dessert and coffee?" She motions toward the dining room. Art has done his disappearing act, and Colleen knows he has politely excused himself and beat it to his upstairs office.

"Oh, I shouldn't," Lillian says, patting her middle. She stops halfway across the living room, looking things over: Colleen's family picture collection on the mantle, the Pinser chairs refinished last month and not yet paid for. On into the dining room. Lillian walks with an air, always did, even before she had money. "Shouldn't but will," Lillian adds, laughing. "Story of my life." She glides into a chair, crossing one leg, adjusting the skirt of her expensive-looking suit. She gives everyone the once over, smoothly, sure of herself as always. "Just look at this family of yours. Let me see now, Pam, yes, and Janet, and where is little Artie?"

"Upstairs," Pam says, trying not to giggle. "Playing computer games with our kids."

"Grandchildren. Don't tell me. Shane and Taylor and Emily, right?"

"Right on," Jake says, appearing with a teapot. Paul is behind him with the coffee.

"And these waiters? They have to be…Jake and…Paul." She looks up at them. "Or is it Paul and Jake? I do keep track of you all, Colleen's wonderful family."

Pam, who is behind the now-seated Lillian, rolls her eyes and disappears into the kitchen. Janet, still in the living room, follows her. The dashing waiters sit, one on either side of Aunt Lillian.

"How flattering," she says, patting her hennaed hair. "A gentleman on either side."

"So, how are things in Luxembourg?" Jake asks.

"The only place to live," Lillian intones. "The world at your fingertips. Shops, theater, restaurants par excellence."

"You retired from teaching…last year, wasn't it?" Colleen says, trying to be part of the conversation. Why, she isn't sure. Lillian has always talked at people, not really to them.

"Last year," Lillian goes on. "They had such a lovely retirement party for me and then Edward surprised me with a Mediterranean cruise."

"How is Edward?" Colleen asks. She's never met the man, never even a photo all these years.

"Dear Eddy." Lillian pauses and taps her nail on the table. "Still trots off to that office every day, too many investments, never enough time. You know how it is. He manages tennis once or twice a week—and he sends his condolences. Our villa sprouted a plumbing leak and he had to hurry off to supervise fixing it."

"Your villa?" Jake has moved cups from the sideboard to each place at the table.

"Just a tiny one," Lillian says, "on the Seine." She laughs and coughs, a crackling chest cough.

If she's stopped smoking, Colleen thinks, it must be not long ago.

"Coffee or tea?" Paul says, holding up the coffee pot.

"Ah, yes, always the quintessential dilemma," Lillian says. "I'm so terribly fond of both. Let's see, I think I recall my little sister makes superb coffee." She moves her cup a little. "I'll have coffee, black of course, the only way these days."

Pam marches in and slides a plate of butter tarts onto the table.

"*Pièce de résistance*," Lillian says, rolling her eyes. "Butter tarts. Homemade, I can tell."

Colleen nods and passes them to her sister.

"Another of your culinary achievements? So domestic, even after all these years."

"Hey, Janet," Paul calls out. "Bring in some of my banana bread, will you? I'm being upstaged by my mother-in-law." He winks at Colleen.

"How do these new-age men do it?" Lillian half whispers to Colleen. "Dear old Eddy can't boil water."

That moment of silence follows, everyone sipping and munching. Art's mom always says it's angels passing over. Colleen wishes Rosie was here, but she knows this whole funeral business has been and will be hard on her, taking her right back to her own dear husband's funeral. Colleen asked her to come for supper, but Rosie said she needed to rest up for the funeral. Janet waltzes in from the kitchen and slides into place on the far side of the table beside Pam.

"The funeral," Colleen says, a little too quietly, "the funeral is at Weller's Funeral Home, Saturday at two."

Lillian puts her cup down, uncrosses her leg, stares toward the window, "The funeral, of course, we must ultimately arrive at the funeral."

Colleen watches—the slight twitch of her mouth, her hands, though, perfectly still.

"Your dear husband told me," she begins. "I was expecting a hospital visit."

"He…he died early yesterday morning…at the hospital."

"You were with him?"

Colleen nods.

Lillian folds her napkin and places it on the table. "That property will be worth a bit, you know. All those upscale places along the street." She turns toward Colleen waiting for a reply.

"Property?" Colleen is trying to figure out where Lillian is coming from.

"I told Art he simply had to drive me past it on the way here." Lillian sits back, smiling. "Déjà vu or what? The house, not exactly in prime condition, but if we negotiate things to our advantage—I do wish Eddy was here—we should have a decent little sum between us."

Colleen nods, wishing she had at least seen the will before her sister arrived. "That damn sister of yours"—Frank's slack face stares at her, pulls her back to the hospital room.

"You do have his will, I assume."

"His will." Colleen tries to think of what to say. She blinks, feeling ten years old again with Lillian, arms on her hips, demanding to know this or this. "I don't have his will…here."

Everyone stops moving, no clinking cups, no chair squeaks.

"He has a will?" Pam says, running her fingers back and forth through her short hair. "I don't believe it."

"He…he told me yesterday. At the hospital. Just before…" Colleen loses it and turns her head as tears blur the room.

Janet, closest to her mom, jumps up and wraps her arms around Colleen from behind. "It's been a pretty harrowing few months," she says, pressing her head against Colleen's. "Mom's been on call pretty well twenty-four hours a day."

"I'm sure you have," Lillian says, reaching out to pat Colleen's arm again, "but we do have to get on with things, don't we, and reading the will is surely the first step."

Colleen nods—a deep breath, clenched fists, tears stop. She may not have class and clothes and villas, but she does have self-respect. She can carry on no matter what. In spite of Lillian. Because of Lillian. No matter what she asks or says.

"You know where it is, I presume."

Last straw—just like when they were kids, pushed against the wall—make something up. "In the house," Colleen says straightening up. "We haven't found the exact place yet."

In the pause that follows, everyone moves slightly, sipping coffee, taking another bite, rustling a napkin. "Another butter tart, Aunt Lillian?" Jake says, "or some of my brother-in-law's famous banana bread?"

Lillian shakes her head and hammers on. "The sooner we find it the better, don't you think? I'm not here very long."

"Tomorrow before the funeral perhaps?" Janet says, easing herself out into the living room. She makes a high sign to Colleen from behind Lillian's back and mouths, "I'll get Dad," before disappearing.

"Yes, yes." At this point, Colleen has no confidence in her own voice, no idea whether she sounds sincere or not. "Whenever. You pick a time and I'll be there."

Pam, as if on cue, takes Janet's place, arms twined around her mom. "Only so many places in that little house it could possibly be. Shouldn't take long."

"Tomorrow then," Lillian says. "I'll meet you at the house. Is ten too early?" She stands as if ready to leave.

"Ten is fine."

Cal produces Lillian's fur coat and holds it for her.

"You're not going to have one of those awful receptions are you?" she says, slipping it on. "Tea and little cakes in some dismal church hall?"

"I…I thought we'd all come back here."

"One small blessing," Lillian says. "I'm sure we'll be the only ones, anyway."

"Dad had some friends," Colleen hears herself say. She still has to stick up for him, smooth things out, put on a good front. Even to her own sister.

"Friends, meaning drinking buddies?" Lillian asks, coldly. "If you're counting on drinking buddies, half the town should be here."

Janet calls from the kitchen. "Dad says he'll be down in a minute."

"Yes, yes," Lillian says. "It's been a long day. The airport was dreadful. Did I tell you? I stood forever before a taxi came." She pats Colleen's shoulder as she moves past. "My dear little sister, Colleen. Always setting things right, making the best of it. Just like Mom."

"Well," Art says, appearing in the doorway. "You two catching up?"

Colleen nods, knowing she couldn't possibly open her mouth. Just like Mom.

"Here you are then," Lillian says brightly, smiling at Art. "Colleen's dear husband on call to escort guests off in the family chariot again."

"The chariot's rusty but reliable." Art smiles. "A bit like me, I guess."

"Witty, your husband," Lillian says, taking Art's arm. "Witty and such a good man. I can see that. Sleep well, everyone."

Colleen listens to the car drive off. Lillian, the battering ram. The more things change, the more they stay the same—big sister, the oldest, used to getting her own way. She left home a week before her nineteenth birthday—Colleen was in grade six—off to Normal School in Marborough. After that, two years teaching grade school; it must have been somewhere in the city. She stayed with Grandma Larken who was in a wheelchair, housekeeping and cooking in return for room and board. Tough going; it had to be.

Colleen tries to remember if Lillian ever came home during those two years. Not at Christmas, that's for sure. Christmas was the season from hell wrapped in fancy paper and pasted-on smiles. Worst time of the year.

Lillian had high enough marks for Normal School, out and away. That was her motto. So why is she back here now, sniffing around for the will, talking about dividing things up—fair is fair and all that?

Colleen knows exactly what she is going to do—wait until Art gets back and while she's waiting, fire her resolve with memories of her disappearing sisters. Lillian, at least, stayed and graduated from high school. Heather, one year younger, was more volatile, arguing with both parents over everything, always pushing the limits. Seventeen-year-old Heather, beatnik impersonator, singing with a local rock and roll band on weekends, skipping school for out-of-town gigs. Colleen had a better voice; Heather had more nerve. That Saturday night, Madge left the porch light on, sure her daughter would trail in thirty minutes or so after the evening bus stopped in Franklin. Heather called from the Toronto bus station. "Off to New York City," she explained, "with the Big Beat Slingers." Never to be heard from again. How many nights did Colleen sit with her mother, handing her tissues, mopping her face with a cold cloth, working through the what-ifs for the hundredth time.

"You all right, Mom?" It's Steve. Colleen realizes everyone else has slipped upstairs. The kitchen lights are off; the house has that night feeling.

"Waiting for your dad," she says, reaching out to take his hand. "I'm okay."

"That's what Pam and Janet said, but I wanted to be sure."

"Thanks."

"See you in the morning."

Colleen watches him disappear into the front hall and upstairs.

To say Lillian has no right to her share is wrong. To think that she deserves some burns in Colleen's craw like too-hot coffee. The will. They must follow whatever it says in the will.

She and Art leave the car at the back of an apartment parking lot, three blocks from the Miller house. Colleen stares straight ahead as they walk side by side, their heels clicking on the night-dark sidewalk. Art hasn't said what he thinks of her plan. Colleen is driven by necessity, drenched in it so that there is nothing else, not her past-tired body crying for sleep or any thought of how much strength she will need to get through the next day. She is a blood-hound with the trail in sight.

"Shine the flashlight over here. No, more to the left." Colleen checks again, behind and to each side, before turning the lock. They have seen no one. No late-night dog walkers. No teenager sneaking home. No Lillian.

Art doesn't say she's being ridiculous, that Lillian wouldn't come pussyfooting around, trying to get in tonight. Colleen is not sure. She sees this as a cut-her-off-at-the-pass-before-she-finds-out measure.

"Remember, no upstairs lights on," Colleen says as they slip into the back porch, Colleen pulling the door quietly behind.

Art immediately trips on a loose beer bottle, and Colleen's flashlight beam locates empties shoved against piled-up cases of twelve and twenty-four. Colleen sighs as she unlocks the inside door. The smell of stale beer and pee hits them in the kitchen. Colleen puts her hand over her nose. "We should have worn masks," she whispers.

Art is already at the basement stairs turning on the light. The forty-watt bulb throws a shadow, making every step seem narrower than it is. Colleen has never gone down here, not since high school, and has forgotten how unsteady the steps are, how steep. Feeling momentarily dizzy, she clutches the wobbly railing to steady herself.

Ever since the Britannia, she avoids basements, all basements, and even at home has always let Art or the kids carry down and fetch up preserves and stuff from the freezer. One of the many good things about a large family, no one ever noticed or asked why. Here, Art has always been the one to check the furnace and the water pipes. Colleen is struck by the hundred dust-filled cobwebs swaying between beams, the decades of dirt coating the floor.

Handyman's Haven. The door is partly open, a large cobweb woven between the latch tongue and the jamb. Colleen still wonders if they are on a wild goose chase. It's hard to believe her dad actually made a will.

"You said it was down here?" Art asks, behind her in the semi-dark.

"In the case of twenty four. On the window ledge."

Art pulls out a beat-up looking business envelope, luckily not sealed. Colleen squeezes his coat shoulder and tries to stop trembling.

Art gingerly pulls out the paper from inside. A shaky hand, smudged and uneven.

"It's handwritten. Does that count?"

"Yes," Art says, looking it over. "He's signed it, so it's legal."

"You're sure?"

"Positive."

Colleen reads aloud, her voice shaking: "I Frank Miller, being of sound mind and body, do will to my daughter Colleen Pinser this house and all its contents. Dated and signed this day, October 14, 1995." His signature trails down the page, Bill Milligan's neat-as-a-pin signature beneath. Colleen turns quickly and stares at the dark basement wall. "Put it back," she says. "You can put it back."

She hears Art tuck the envelope into the case of twenty-four. She feels numb. "Thank you," she says hoarsely. "I wish I could have said thank you."

Colleen doesn't remember climbing the basement stairs, Art steering her through the kitchen and out the back door. She remembers being cold, her teeth chattering, her feet moving one after the other, the damp night wind smacking her face, her wrists, the back of her neck. When she stumbles, Art puts his arm around her waist. "We're nearly there," he keeps saying. "Only a few more steps."

The car heater blasting on high doesn't help. "You've had quite a shock," Art says quietly. "Hang on. We'll be home in a jiff."

When they pull up to the house, Art jumps out and walks her up the steps, his hand under her elbow, his arm across her waist, helping her inside, sitting her on the couch and covering her with a blanket.

Janet appears first, then Pam, and a moment later, Paul, Jake, and the twins—all in their dressing gowns, all hovering, all talking at once.

"Where were you?" Cal says, looking worried.

"What happened?" Pam asks.

"Did you fall?" Steve blurts out.

"We found the will," Art says behind them. "In Handyman's Haven."

"You went to the house?" Pam says in her teacher voice.

"Why didn't you tell us?" Steve adds.

"What did it say?" Cal continues, squatting down beside her.

Colleen opens her mouth to tell them but only little squeaks come out, little squeaks and tears. She puts an arm over her face, embarrassed.

Art pushes through and leans over her. "She'll be all right," he says with his back to them. "It was a letter. He left her everything."

Everyone stops then and, as if rehearsed, stands listening—to the room, the air, to each other's breathing.

Janet recovers first. "You damn well deserve it, Mom." She pushes in beside Art to give Colleen a hug.

Everyone starts talking again, telling her how great it is, how she should be so happy, how they're glad the house is hers.

Colleen feels a weariness pulling her backwards; her eyes won't stay open.

"Thanks," she hears herself say. "Thanks, all of you."

The next morning at five to ten, Colleen sits alone in the car in front of the house, chewing her fingernails. Everyone has told her over and over that there isn't a chance Lillian will go hunting for long, not after the first whiff. All Colleen has to do is hunt around a bit and then bring the will up from the basement. It's the next part that terrifies her—Lillian reading the will and what she will say after. On the other hand, what can she say, all things considered. A taxi pulls in front of Colleen's car. Lillian waves.

"Looks even more derelict in the light of day," Lillian comments as Colleen unlocks the back door.

"I'd better warn you," Colleen says before she opens it. "It's pretty rank."

"I'll manage," Lillian replies as she follows Colleen past the beer cases. "It's the forty-year time warp I'm concerned about."

"Forty-four years," Colleen says quietly.

When she opens the inside door, Lillian reacts as Colleen expects.

"What kind of a putrid stench is this?" Lillian says, putting a hand to her nose.

"First or second floor?" Colleen asks. "We can open windows."

"How could he live like this?" Lillian says, kicking at a towel on the hall floor.

The towel resists moving, and Colleen realizes it's stuck on the bloodstain. She maneuvers her sister to the bottom of the stairs. "Probably easier up there," she says. "I'll look down here."

Colleen hesitates in front of the basement stairs as she hears

Lillian pull out drawers, dumping stuff on the floor. Do it, she thinks. Do it before she notices and decides to come with you. Colleen inches her way down, purposely keeping the light off, treading gingerly on each step, feeling her way along the rickety hand rail, faint light from a basement window lighting the dirt-stained floor, into Handyman's Haven. Back upstairs, she slips the envelope under a pile of letters on top of the piano and then sorts through flyers and unopened mail on the kitchen table.

"I need a break," Lillian announces sooner than Colleen expected. "Air and a cigarette." She marches past and outside.

Colleen waits until she sees Lillian walking toward the back fence, lit cigarette in hand, and, pulling out the envelope, follows her.

"I found it," she calls, waving the envelope.

Lillian takes a drag and butts out the cigarette. "Well," she says as soon as Colleen is beside her. "Going to open it?"

"You can." Colleen hands it to her and turns away.

"Wouldn't you know," Lillian says as she begins to read. "He's left it all to you."

"Are you sure?"

"Read it." She hands the page back. Lights another cigarette.

Colleen looks and the words blur.

"I should have known. Good little sister. The one who stuck around."

Colleen's hand shakes as she folds the letter and tucks it into her jacket pocket. "That's unfair and you know it is. You know nothing about me. Nothing."

"You're still easy to bait."

"Didn't think you'd remember."

"Touché."

"You don't need the money," Colleen says, her hands jammed into her pockets. "Whatever it's worth."

251251251251251251
251251251251251251

"And you do?"

"It would be…helpful."

"Well, you know what they say. They're either good in the sack or good on the job. You can't have both."

Colleen catches her breath and turns toward the house. "I'm locking up," she says, barely managing not to spit at her sister. "We can go now."

Lillian is right behind. "I can see I'm rubbing you the wrong way. It's not my intention. I'm a bull in a china shop, Eddy tells me often enough. I just thought will, division of property. It's not that important to me." She pauses.

Colleen is on the back stoop, keys in hand.

"Look," Lillian goes on, "I'm finding this difficult too. Probably more difficult than you. I'm the one who left."

Part of Colleen would like to kick Lillian—right in the face. It's one of those feelings that begins and ends in the same moment. Just as well. "You've made yourself a good life," Colleen says. "Why would you care?"

"Same reason you do." Lillian sits heavily on the back step. "It brings everything back. Mom and high school and…"

"You didn't even come home for her funeral."

Lillian looks up, tears in her eyes. "I didn't get the message you sent until the day of the funeral. The school was moving to a new location, phones were down, mail nonexistent. I should have called, I know, but everything was in such chaos, including my next-semester job."

Colleen sits beside her sister, feels her own lip trembling. "It's been pretty rough, you know. Let me say that again. It's been hell most of the time."

Lillian slips her arm around Colleen's shoulder. Colleen stiffens.

"Remember the lemonade stand?" Lillian says. "You were a star at getting customers."

"We were saving up for the Toronto Exhibition." Colleen remembers suddenly—how they dragged a card table out of the house, mixed lemon juice and sugar and ice cubes from the fridge.

"And we had to have the whole thing put away before Dad came home, so he wouldn't mooch our money."

"We were dirt poor," Colleen says. "I didn't have a clue."

"How could you? Besides, no one had money then, no one we knew, at any rate."

A car honks on the street and, in front of them, a robin lands on the dead grass to peck, turns its head sideways to stare at them, and pecks again.

"We used to sit here every spring watching for the first robin."

"And here it is," Lillian says, almost smiling.

"There you are, there you have it, there it is, boom, boom," Colleen sings. She looks at Lillian and grins.

"There you are, there you have it, there it is," Lillian sings back. A raspy cigarette voice.

They jump up at the same time, singing together:

"If you like it or you don't
If you will or if you won't
There you are, there you have it, there it is, boom, boom."

Two sideways hip bumps, gales of laughter, until Colleen has tears in her eyes. A momentary hug. Both pull back, stare at one another, and sit—almost as if what just took place, didn't.

"Where did we learn that?" Colleen asks.

"Mom, I think." Lillian replies. "She used it as a diversion when we asked for something she couldn't give us."

"And we didn't get to the Exhibition, did we?" Colleen says, wiping her eyes. "It was the summer I was in grade three. Grade four?"

"Mom was so sure we could go in on the bus and stay over-night with Grandma Larkin." Lillian snorts and goes for another cigarette. "Mom lived on hope and wishes, I was skeptical, and you, the eternal optimist, were sure it would happen."

"But it didn't." Colleen buries her head on her knees. "Like everything else. It didn't."

"Hey," Lillian says, giving Colleen another quick hug. "You've done all right little sister. What a family. Hearts of gold."

"They'll be wondering what's taking me so long," Colleen says, jumping up. "Want a ride back to the hotel?"

"I think I'll walk," Lillian says. "I'd forgotten how close it was, how small this whole town is." At the car, she takes Colleen's hands in hers. "What are you going to do with all the stuff in there?"

"Most of it goes to the dump. Janet and Pam said they would help me sort through everything."

"I don't have a picture of Mom."

"We can probably find one. Might be when she was younger."

"That's okay."

"What if she's with Dad?"

Lillian turns away. "I...I don't know."

"They didn't set out to screw things up," Colleen says. "It just happened."

"Send whatever you can find." Lillian leans forward and gives Colleen a peck on the cheek.

Colleen hugs her and they stand crying again until Lillian breaks away. "Enough," she says. "Shades of Mom. No use crying over spilt milk." She squeezes Colleen's arm and strides off down the street.

The funeral is a sad little affair. Only five people show up besides family and Lillian. Lillian rushes in at the last minute after they are already lined up and waiting. She's dressed in a smart black suit and reeking of perfume, both probably expensive. Art, who always has sneezing attacks from the stuff, smiles and moves over so Lillian is beside Colleen. Lillian gives Colleen's arm a squeeze but says nothing. Minutes later, they walk one by one to the front four rows of the funeral chapel, past Bill Milligan, his wife, two others Colleen doesn't recognize, and the last person she ever expected, the bartender from the Salamander Café. His slicked-back fifties haircut, gleaming in spite of the toned-down lighting.

The service is short and to the point. What is there to say about her dad? During an earlier visit to the funeral director, Colleen scraped up a few details—that he played sax in a Toronto band when he was young, that he went overseas but didn't fight in WW II, that he married and had three daughters, and most recently, that he sang with Bill Milligan's group at the Lodge. The United Church minister, called on to officiate by Art's mom Rosie, made this pathetic bit of information sound quite wonderful. So much so that, afterward, Colleen asks him for a copy to put in the Memorial Record book, open and waiting for autographs outside the chapel doors.

In the foyer, Bill Milligan shakes her hand and introduces his wife, a large woman who dabs her eyes with a cloth hankie. He also introduces Stanley Middleton and Hilda Brown, singing buddies from the Lodge. They both hug Colleen and say how wonderful her dad was, what a great voice and always so cheery. Colleen, numbed out but still able to talk, nods and smiles and makes the right comments—an actress, center stage.

Soon after, Lillian hugs everyone good-bye, saying she hopes they'll all come to visit in Luxembourg, that she's is sorry her flight back leaves so early in the evening. From the funeral parking lot, Colleen watches her stride down the street, the black suit shrinking like a movie scene fadeout.

That evening, alone in the almost-dark living room with everyone gone and most of the dishes picked up, Colleen thinks about

Lillian again. Not the hoity-toity Colleen thought she was. For a moment she wonders if, before Lillian left home, Frank had pawed her, if that was why she never came back. So many lost days, lost years, lost Mom. And now a lost dad. She should be happy, jumping for joy. But here she is, alone in the dark, tears dripping one by one onto her funeral dress.

Art appears with two small glasses of brandy. Colleen hasn't heard him come down the stairs. She holds out her hand and he sits beside her, handing her a glass and slipping his arm around her shoulders.

"Two weeks," he says firmly. "I want you to stay away from the store for two weeks. Rest a bit. Do something about the empty house."

Colleen nods and slowly sips her brandy.

HANNAH VIII

THE MORNING AFTER Aunt Harriet arrives, they move from room to room, identifying and naming things, Jennings things and Taigg things. Over the years, whenever Hannah visited Franklin, her mother often suggested she might as well take this or that piece of furniture, never saying they were family things, rather that they were of no value to her, that Hannah might as well make use of them. Formerly meaningless items are suddenly charged with family history, her history. The standing lamp was a wedding present—her grandparent's wedding. The beautifully detailed side table was made by Harriet's husband's uncle—Taigg furniture, a big item in Bristol, England at the turn of the century. The tea service had been Grandma Gladys Jennings's pride and joy. Hannah retrieves a steno pad and follows Harriet like a reporter, asking questions, getting the spelling right.

The biggest revelation is the brocade throw. "I noticed it as soon as I woke this morning," Harriet says, running her fingers over its surface. "Imagine it lasting all these years."

"Another family heirloom?" Hannah has already scribbled brocade throw and underlined it.

"No, actually. I think Mother was given it by a neighbor—for some good deed or other. I remember it being on the back of the couch. We played with it, Edith and I, draped it over two dining room chairs and pretended we were princesses in some exotic land, Arabia most likely. I was silly over camels. It started with one of those Sunday school pictures of the three wise men and went on from there." Harriet pauses and walks slowly back into the living room. Morning sun streaks across the deck, the wind loosening a few wet leaves to tumble down the steps. "I wasn't as headstrong as my sister," she continues, "but I always considered my ferreting out the watercolor and throw a deliberate coup."

Hannah sits on the couch and beckons Harriet to follow. "You make it sound like a Bond movie."

"Ah yes," Harriet replies, fluffing the pillow before she sits, "Auntie Bond at her best—my first and last rebellious act. Mother unearthed a trunk…"

"It's in the basement in Franklin," Hannah says excitedly.

"From England, your grandmother's family when they emigrated in the late 1800s."

Hannah writes, *trunk, late 1800s, Grandma Jennings's family, England.*

"That trunk filled, too quickly, with Edith's clothes," Harriet goes on, "most of which she couldn't yet fit into, a few baby things, some old pots and dishes from the back of mother's cupboards." Harriet stops again and squeezes Hannah's arm. "How did she manage, my poor sister?" She pauses, staring into space.

Hannah, worried that nostalgia would steer the conversation elsewhere, clears her throat. "The brocade throw," she prompts. "How did…?"

The pressure on Hannah's arm increases. "The night before Edith left, I couldn't sleep. Sometime after the hall clock struck midnight, I tiptoed downstairs, carefully took the throw from its accustomed place along with one of the watercolors from the living room wall." Harriet pauses, eyes twinkling. "I wrapped the throw carefully around the picture and managed to wedge it into the lid of the chest. It was already out in the front hall and I was lucky, I guess, that the lid was arched and deep, that they hadn't already locked it."

"No one noticed?"

"Mother did, but not until several days later. I had taken another picture from my bedroom and put it beside the remaining watercolor. Noticing details in a room was never my father's forte. I knew that, counted on it. Mother's only admission to my act of duplicity came on cleaning day the following week, when she asked me to go upstairs and fetch the afghan from the front bedroom, Edith's room, to put in the throw's place. She never mentioned the picture."

"So, my grandmother was...wise and perceptive."

"She was."

"But if mother only had what was in the trunk, how did all this furniture end up here?" Hannah's head is throbbing again and she keeps feeling tears edging to the surface.

"After father died," Harriet continues, staring in the direction of the floor lamp, "Mother stayed on in the house for a winter. We worried about her and were relieved next spring that she decided to sell and find a smaller place. She chose what each of us would have and shipped your mother's lot to her in Ontario."

"What year would that have been?" Hannah asks, trying for a measured tone, sure she is almost squeaking.

"Why 1969, dear, the year after our father departed this earth."

Silence again, at which point Hannah checks her watch. It's after eleven—time to change gears and head for Franklin and the Lodge. Harriet insists they go to an A&W on the way out of Toronto. Hannah, increasingly apprehensive about this first visit, has only a salad, while Harriet munches happily through a Mama Burger and fries. By the time they're on the highway, Hannah is well beyond conversation, the looming trauma building as the miles tick by. Fortunately, Harriet is soon asleep, head against the passenger window, hands on her lap, loosely holding the edges of her Paddington hat.

Harriet meeting Edith again after all these years—it could be a movie, Hannah thinks. One of those art films, poignant and a bit disjointed. Harriet wakens as they slow down and move into the Franklin turnoff lane but she remains unusually quiet, even after they wheel into the Lodge parking lot. Hannah has no idea what to expect. Earlier, when she had tried to tell Harriet that her mother wasn't really herself, that her thought patterns were, to put it mildly, out of kilter, Harriet patted Hannah's arm in what comes to be a familiar gesture. Pat, pat. She's my sister, nothing can change that. She'll remember. Pat, pat.

At the access door, they have to fend off dear old Mrs. Stillings, wringing her hands with the usual, "Oh, Elly, I'm so glad you've finally come." Harriet gives her a pat and says what a pretty dress she's wearing. Mrs. Stillings beams. Hannah would never have thought of saying that—a diversion, simple and reassuring. Pat, pat.

Edith is not in her room, and when Hannah races to the nurses' station to enquire, Maisie Johns cheerfully tells her to look in some of the adjacent rooms. "Your mother has become mobile," she says, looking pleased. "She's been wheeling herself up and down the hallway. Try another room. Sometimes they borrow each other's stuff. It's so cute." Her mother, dropping in on someone, borrowing something? From a stranger? Every time Hannah visits, she is hit with another left curve. She adds this to the accumulating list.

Edith, in her wheelchair, is rummaging through the dresser drawer of a thankfully empty room, two doors from her own. In one hand she clutches a tag-eared copy of *Screen Secrets*, a thin trail of drool from the corner of her mouth, betraying concentration. Hannah smiles and hugs her mother, so conscious now of her bird-bone frame: no fat, no muscle, a TIA survivor's lot.

As soon as they appear in Edith's room, Harriet embraces her sister, rumpling her hair and saying "my Edith," over and over.

Edith stares at her for several seconds, then reaches out shakily. "Mother, Mother dear, how kind of you to come."

"Now, Eadie," Harriet replies, pulling a chair up beside her. "It's not Mother, Eadie. It's Harriet." She says it cheerfully, without a hint of disappointment.

Edith nods, tears running down her face.

Hannah isn't sure she can stay. She desperately wants to, to eavesdrop silently in the background, watch these two—her mother and aunt—feel connected. She watches from the doorway, her hand squeezing the doorjamb.

"I flew in from Winnipeg, Eadie, just to see you. So many years. Do you remember the brocade throw?" Harriet puts her palms together and, elbows up, moves them back and forth, turning her head slowly from side to side, humming an exotic, faintly familiar tune. "We were Arabian princesses, remember? And when Mother was in a good mood, she let us use her jewelry case." Then Harriet, like a well-practiced magician, pulls a long string of beads from her coat pocket and strings them around Edith's neck. Edith beams, fondling the beads, staring wide-eyed at her benefactor.

"Partridge," Edith says after several moments' silence.

"We had a good time on Partridge Street, didn't we?" Harriet leans over and adjusts the beads, letting her hand rest momentarily on her sister's cheek. "I dream of Edith with the light bro-own hair," she begins in a high, warbly voice.

"Borne like a vapor on the summer air." Edith joins in, her voice the clearest Hannah has heard in months. "I see her tripping where the bright stre-ams play, happy as the da-i-sys that dance on her way…"

Hannah bolts. Down the hall, past the nurses' station, into the lounge, thankfully deserted, the big-screen TV intoning yet another cheery household product. She stares out the large picture window into the so-called exercise area, cordoned off with chain-link fencing. When she asked about it, soon after her mother arrived, someone told her the door was permanently locked, that the area was not presently in use. Even over the TV's product eulogizing, Hannah still hears faint strains of "I Dream of Jeannie." She sees in her mind's eye two little girls adorned with clip-on earrings and strings of beads laughing under a brocade chair tent.

Harriet visits the Lodge every day for three straight days, Hannah dropping her off at ten in the morning and picking her up shortly after four. When Hannah comments on the long days and how grateful she is that Harriet is willing to spend so much time with her mother, Harriet laughs and squeezes Hannah's arm.

"We're having a lovely time," she says. "I show her photos and we sing a bit and, maybe I shouldn't tell you this…" She turns to Hannah, looking almost coy. "I've introduced her to my soap opera, *As the World Turns*. Now you don't have to tell me it's lowbrow." She laughs again. "But I've been watching for so many years now, and I think she enjoys it."

As the World Turns? Hannah can barely believe it.

"Soap operas aren't what they used to be, dear," Harriet says definitively. "They're…modern and…quite racy."

Then she changes the subject and Hannah can tell there is to be no more discussion or comment; for a moment she can even see, in Harriet, her mother, jaw set and deliberately changing gears.

So be it, Hannah thinks, and a millisecond later she feels a lightening flash of clarity, one of those forever earmarked realizations—it's all right when Harriet reacts that way. It doesn't make Hannah angry or defensive because there is no baggage attached. Harriet has a perfect right to say what she thinks. If Hannah could only sever the baggage, toss it away, she could be so much more compassionate with her mother.

Midweek, Hannah drives Harriet, in a blinding snowstorm, to Marborough, following a hand-drawn map along country roads north and west of that city to Sadie Cameron's farmhouse. Harriet and Sadie shared a year of teaching in a two-room school near Brandon, Manitoba beginning in September 1943, when the boys were fighting and dying overseas. Sadie, only two years older than Harriet, looks a good ten years her senior. They both squeal like young girls as Harriet rushes from the car, though. Sadie, who insists Hannah stay for lunch, has a wonderful old house full of antiques, art and, of course, a prominent display of her five published books. The conversation vacillates between writing and teaching, and by remaining virtually silent, Hannah learns even more about Harriet, especially during those two teaching years. Hannah leaves the two of them planning a hike down into the back fields and, ever amazed at her aunt's resilience, promises to return by Saturday at ten to drive her back to see Edith one more time before leaving for the airport.

Hannah doesn't check her mail when she unlocks the door and turns up the heat in her Toronto house. Esmeralda demands food and attention, and Hannah, still in information overload from her chats with Harriet, puts the Brandenburg concertos into her cassette player and lets Glenn Gould play his magic, slowly pushing everything into the background, everything except the room, the kettle starting its boil, heat from the radiators permeating the chilled air.

The reprieve ends when she notices Aunt Harriet's sensible woolen scarf fallen down behind one of the living room chairs. "So that's where she left it," Hannah says, fishing it out. Harriet hunted for the scarf before they left, noting the damp lake air and raw March wind made Ontario seem colder than it really was.

Esmeralda purrs against Hannah's leg. Hannah sits on the floor, pulling the scarf back and forth, running its fringe along the carpet. "Do you think I should phone her and tell her I found it?" she says, watching the cat pounce on the scarf. She winds the soft material around Esmeralda and picks her up, nuzzling her face into the creature's purring back. "She'd like it if I sent you as well." She puts the cat down, trailing the scarf back and forth again.

So many things about Harriet: her love of cats and classical music, and her unquenchable zest for life, in spite of losing a teenage son, a loving husband, to say nothing of her having spent over half a lifetime estranged from an older sister she obviously adores. Idealizes. How strange to hear her talk of "my Eadie" in their growing-up years. What irreparable damage was done to her mother, sent away with a new baby to an alien land where she fended and made do, giving all, and at the same time, withholding all, so that Hannah missed so much, so much. Hannah, of course, said none of this to Harriet, confident she gave nothing away. She always spoke carefully of her mother, divulging only what she hoped was neutral and positive. "She always made sure I had plenty of time to study and we always had enough to eat, a good car." She told Harriet about her high school friend, Colleen, and how she had met up with her again after all these years. Nothing about the Britannia, though—an unnecessary detail with too much baggage.

Esmeralda's claw brings Hannah back to reality. "Too rambunctious," she says, sucking her finger and retrieving the scarf. "No more playing with you." Esmeralda hightails it to the kitchen and mews pitifully.

"Poor starving kitty—hasn't eaten for at least an hour." Hannah follows and finds an unopened package of Kitty Best dry cat food in a bottom cupboard. Opening packages has never been Hannah's forte, and as she struggles with the easy-zip closure, her gaze absently falls on the letters stuffed under her purse. "Kitty first," she says to the purr machine, rubbing frantically against her ankles. "Then my mail. Who knows, maybe a letter from a tall, dark stranger."

The return address on the letter, buried between a pizza flyer and the phone bill, leaps out at her, becomes, in an instant, wrought-iron numbers over an outside transom. Seven thirty Chapel Street. The polished-wood smell, even inside the vestibule. His hand on her shoulder, his voice assuring her they were alone, that his wife was away, out of the city—all weekend.

Almost thirty years ago—1965. That numbers could evoke so strong an image amazes her. She laughs and rips open the envelope. "What on earth would you be wanting from me, Professor Anthony Hendricks?"

BRITANNIA NOW

ALLAN SEARP barges into Pinser's Hardware twenty minutes before seven on Friday evening, ready to interview Colleen on the spot if she's available. He's tried the NYC number twice today with the same generic response, and now he's counting on this, his last hope for a live lead.

Art, who closed the store Wednesday afternoon because of the funeral, and is now behind filing invoices, has had a bad case of heartburn all day. Consequently, he has closed early but hasn't taken the sign down or locked the door. Ever since the big mall opened between Franklin and Port Turner two years ago, except for Christmas rush and the summer sidewalk sale, business on Fridays nights hasn't been worth diddly-squat, as Art says to anyone who will listen. Even with a March thaw and clear sidewalks, there's rarely a soul in sight after five.

"Mr. Pinser?"

Art is bent over behind the front counter, sorting invoices piled in some random out-of-date order, probably because the high school co-op student was tidying. "Yes, yes," Art says, straightening up.

"Allan Searp here," Searp says, thrusting his hand over the counter. "*Franklin Standard*."

"We don't need any advertising this month," Art replies wearily. "Budget's all used up."

"Oh no, Mr. Pinser. I'm not with advertising." He flashes a smile and whips out his card. "News and Features. I'm writing a series of articles on the Britannia Hotel. She's seventy this summer."

"Our grand old lady at Victoria and Main," Art replies with a nod. "Seventy this year."

Searp leans conspiratorially over the counter. "And did you know that on Thursday, July 21, 1955, an employee, Charlie Elliot, fell or was pushed down the hotel's back kitchen stairs and found dead?"

"You don't say?"

"My research says that your wife, then Colleen Miller, worked as a waitress in the dining room that summer. Would she be here now?"

"No, no," Art says. "She usually only comes in mornings."

"I'd like to interview her about the incident."

"1955. She would have been fifteen." Art scratches his head. "I know she worked there, but it might not have been until the following year."

"She's never talked about it, then?"

"About what?"

"The murder."

"I don't recall any hotel murder in the fifties, that summer or any other." Art frowns.

"The newspaper article called it an accident, but the whole thing sounds fishy to me. I've done quite a bit of research and have a different conclusion to the whole affair."

"Wouldn't something like that be easy to track in the *Franklin Standard?* It was around in fifty-five." Art turns to put the invoices back into their pile.

"There was supposed to be an autopsy, but it was never reported in the paper." Searp adjusts his hat and carries on. "Paper says the old guy is buried in Fairgrove Cemetery out on Clark Road."

"And you think my Colleen knows something about this?"

"It's a long shot," Searp says. "I do know the so-called accident took place during the afternoon."

"I could ask her."

"Would she be in on Monday morning? I'd like to talk to her. Get a feel for the hotel at that time. The owners then, the Mourands, are long gone. My aunt went to school with Colleen. Maureen Searp? Maureen Downey now. She nurses at the hospital—says she'd talked to Colleen several times when her dad was in the special care unit."

"Colleen might have mentioned her."

"When would be a good time to drop in?"

"Pardon?"

"To talk to your wife. Mrs. Pinser."

"I…I don't know, really. I guess she'll be here Monday morning."

"Monday morning, then. At ten." He dashes for the door. "Thanks a heap, Mr. Pinser."

Art follows him and turns the dead bolt. "Reporters," he mutters. "Always think they've got something by the tail."

Art arrives home Friday night exhausted, falling asleep on the couch right after supper. Late Saturday afternoon, right after Art arrives home from the store, Paul and Janet and the kids drop in on their way to visit Paul's parents in Ottawa. Sunday, the twins have a noisy gang over and Art camps out in his office, rap music and videos not being his cup of tea. Colleen is sorting through stuff in the attic and they barely see each other all day—until suppertime.

"Just remembered," Art says over tea, the twins upstairs supposedly hitting the books. "Some young reporter, Searp I think his name was, dropped in at the store on Friday, asking questions about the Britannia Hotel. He wants to interview you."

Colleen's stomach tightens. "Me? Why would he want to talk to me?"

"Something about that old guy Charlie. He died in an accident? Way back in fifty-five. I wasn't sure you worked there then."

"What did you say to him?"

"Who?"

"The reporter, for God's sakes."

"You don't have to get riled up over this."

"I'm not. I'm just asking."

"I told him you'd be in the store on Monday morning."

"For an interview?"

"I think he said at ten."

Colleen jumps to her feet—so fast the chair slams backwards to the floor. She's out in the hall almost before it lands.

"Colleen, where are you going?" Art stands in the living room doorway, watching as she yanks her coat from the hall closet.

"We need milk for the morning."

"You want me to come with you?"

"No." The door slams and Art stands scratching his head. "I think," he says out loud. "I must have said something wrong," Back in the living room, he sits wearily and, for a long time, stares at the mantle crowded with pictures and memories and say-cheese smiles.

HANNAH/COLLEEN III

COLLEEN SLAMS the car into drive and roars down the driveway through the slush, anger and fear pouring through her until only the basics keep her going. Stay on the road. Use your turn signals. Brake only when you have to. A stroke of luck that the highway is empty; the speedometer being way over the speed limit. By the time she reaches the first row of town streetlights, she comes to her senses a little and slows down. Art has no business setting her up like that. Damn nosy reporter. Damn Art. What did he say? Oh, my nice little wifey would be happy to talk to you. What is this reporter getting at? They always have an angle, usually some ax to grind. She tries to remember how much she has told Art over the years, a comment here or there. Not the whole thing, she knows that. No one knows the whole thing.

It all flashes back. Pulling the chain to turn off the bathroom light, Larry Mourand's threats, a thump above her, a voice gurgling, absolute quiet, how the basement stairs creaked, dusty sunlight in the hotel foyer, her escape. Has Art ever asked her to explain more than the *Franklin Standard* version she always tells him? It happened before she even met him. He might have read about it if he was reading the paper in those days. He was such a stud, he probably couldn't have cared less. Over the years, Colleen has made a point of pushing traumas back, tucking them away: her dad's ongoing drunkenness, their money troubles, that summer at the Britannia, what Larry did. Murder. She kept her cool when Maureen Downey and she talked in the hospital cafeteria—Maureen saying her family chatted about it like everyday gossip. Stuck in between pass the salt.

It hits Colleen now, one of those sudden flashes. Maureen Downey was a Searp, one of a large family that lived up on Spider Lake somewhere. This reporter, Allan Searp, is most likely related to her, a nephew or second cousin. And now he's tracking her down, moving in for his big scoop.

Quite deliberately, Colleen turns toward the beach. She slams on the brakes in the usual spot and watches snow-rain coat the windshield. Jumping out of the car, she half trips on the cement steps leading from the deserted brick walkway to the beach. She stomps across wet sand, stopping at the water's edge to stare toward the horizon, the wind smacking icy waves onto darkened shore.

Everything from the last few months piles up. Her dad's death, her rich sister Lillian, the mess in her dad's house, the fact that she's never done anything important in her entire life, the fat slob she's become, how she's trapped and always has been. No way out. Well, this is the last straw. The one that breaks the camel's back. Fists clenched, she wades into the shallow water, icicle cold waves stabbing her ankles, pain shooting up through her calves. She won't have to talk to anyone about anything ever again. Catching her breath, she wades further. No damn way she'll talk to a reporter. Never in a million years. Damn Maureen. Damn Art. Damn everyone. "Two minutes," she whispers. "It takes less than two minutes." She knows she'll have to wade in further and throw herself forward. Lights twinkling from the walkway behind her blur. She feels distanced from everything, almost not here.

Behind her, in the park, a dog barks. Out of the corner of her eye, Colleen sees its small four-legged shape jump from the brick walk onto the beach. It charges for the water, a long leash dragging behind in the wet sand.

"Taffy, come back." Colleen turns to see someone up on the walk, a dark shape against the light. "Taffy?" The dog races into the water slurping up mouthfuls, racing round in an ever-increasing circle into deeper water, wild with its freedom.

The girl calls again, panic increasing in her voice. The dog couldn't care less, jumping and circling until it yelps, suddenly, as if it has stepped on something or twisted its leg. Yelps and submerges once and then again and again, staying under longer each time.

Colleen snaps into rescue mode, out of the water and down the beach to where she sees the thrashing animal. Back into the water up over her knees, gasping from the cold, grabbing for its leash. She hears the girl shrieking "Taffy," as she reaches under once more. The dog has obviously tangled itself. The girl is closer now, yelling, "Taffy, Taffy, I'm coming."

Colleen finally manages to grab the small creature and pull it out. It coughs up water as she untangles the leash from its front legs, places her hand on its wet, shivering body.

"Thank you. Oh my God. Thank you." The girl pulls off her coat and bundles the animal inside, pulling it up into her arms, crying and laughing. "You silly, silly dog."

Colleen is soaked now, her feet, her jeans up to the knees, the bottom of her coat. "He was tangled in the leash," she says, backing up, getting ready to take off.

"How can I thank you?" the girl says, coming closer. The dog whimpers. "He might have drowned. Oh my God, he might have drowned." She holds him tightly to her chest.

"It's okay," Colleen replies. "Take him home. Get him warm."

"You too," the girl says, grabbing Colleen's arm. "You're wet too."

"I'll be fine," Colleen hears herself say. "I'm okay now."

Waiting for the car to warm up, Colleen can't stop shaking. Her feet and calves have almost no feeling. Smart-ass, she thinks to herself. All that's going to happen now is that you'll get sick. She drives slowly down Lakefront Road, thinking she'll wait until she dries out a bit before heading home. *You're not setting foot in this house until you're dried out.* She hears her mom pushing her dad back outside, telling him to throw up in the backyard, get himself dried out. Even in the winter. "Get yourself dried out, Colleen," she says, giggling as her teeth chatter. "Don't set foot in that house until you're dried out."

Driving along Lakefront Road always makes her think of their little bungalow—their first house—up on the north side of the city. Almost every Sunday afternoon, after Janet and Artie woke up from their naps, they bundled them into the car and drove along here, half the houses still unfinished, no trees. "When our ship comes in," Art would say, "We'll get a fancy house down here. In the ritzy section." The people who did are in the pink now; these properties are sky high. All of them so close together, so tidy. Lights twinkle across their large, perfectly cut lawns, out of their price range even twenty years ago when they bought in the country.

The dreaded interview surfaces as house lights come into view from a familiar, much smaller house. Colleen slams on the brakes and stares through the windshield at the little clapboard bungalow, set back from the street, its garage sticking out so that the front door is safe from the lake's east wind. Here, nearly at the end of the street, lots and houses are smaller, built before the sixties building boom; and this house—Hannah's house—is one of them. But is it Hannah's house? The house number is missing, fallen off like some of the paint. Art would say it's seen better days. The sensible thing to do would be to go back to the highway, to the corner store—where she can check in the phone booth, call first. A shiver runs through

Colleen, then another. She can't go into a store looking like this. And what will she say to Hannah? Where were you on Thursday July 21, 1955? Lucky stiff was on her day off, likely at the library. More shivering, but this time it won't stop. Colleen puts her head on the steering wheel. "Do it or don't do it," she says out loud. She pulls into the driveway.

Since she returned from visiting her mother that afternoon, Hannah has been sorting through boxes stashed under her bed. She feels exhausted and emotionally drained but can't seem to stop. The boxes are a revelation, five of them in all, grade eight to twelve. She remembers only a few of the things saved: in the grade eight box, a booklet honoring the coronation of Elizabeth II in Westminster Abbey, June 2, 1953; grade nine, two third-place ribbons for field day; grade eleven, a program from *The Music Man,* autographed by the cast. She left the grade ten box to the end, avoided it for fear it might contain something from that summer at the Britannia. It doesn't. Once all the boxes are pulled out, she decides she may as well vacuum the who knows how many decades of dust up from underneath. When the vacuum nozzle catches something and goes into a high-pitched whine, she yanks out the wand to clear it. A photograph, half bent, sticks out from the nozzle.

Now she is out in the kitchen staring at the picture—Hannah and Charlie and Colleen standing in front of the steam table— the vacuum still running in her bedroom. On the back is written *Charlie's birthday, July 12, 1955.* She presses out the crease as best she can and holds the photo up to the light. "Poor old Charlie," she whispers. "Poor dear man." She stashes the photograph in her mother's red address book and runs to turn off the vacuum. Darkness has closed in and she looks out the window at drizzle haloing the streetlight. Even though staying put is tempting, Hannah knows she should get in her car and drive back to Toronto tonight. If she stays, the kicker, as always, is getting up at five to keep ahead of the morning rush hour.

She pays little attention to car headlights in the driveway. Being almost at the end of the street, people have always used this driveway as a turnaround. When the doorbell rings, Hannah gets up grudgingly. "Idiots," she mutters. "Can't they see house numbers in the dark?"

"Hannah?"

"Who is it?" Hannah talks through the chained door crack, city instincts on red alert.

"It's Colleen," she says, teeth chattering.

Once inside the vestibule, Colleen bursts into tears, head down, her wet feet pooling water on the floor.

"My God, what's happened?" Hannah says, rushing to get a chair, pushing it behind Colleen's legs so she sits automatically. "Here, let me get your shoes off. Sand. You've been down at the beach. Your jean are soaked, too, and the bottom of your coat."

Colleen says nothing and keeps holding her breath, as if to stop crying, emitting childlike hiccups every few seconds.

"Someone attacked you, chased you back to your car. Right here in Franklin." Hannah is on her knees and leans over, embracing Colleen, pressing her face against Colleen's salty, wet cheek. "It's all right, Colleen. You're going to be all right."

"It's…it's not what you think," Colleen manages to say, pushing Hannah back. She turns her head. "I…I was down at the beach and there was this dog…"

"You were attacked by a dog. Were you bitten? Here, we need to get those jeans off. I'll get you my dressing gown." Hannah leads Colleen into the living room and disappears.

Colleen struggles to pull off her jeans, her arms stiff and slow. She's making a fool of herself. And she is so cold. This room hasn't changed though, she thinks. In forty years, it's still the same—the same silk lampshade, the same old lumpy couch. She balances awkwardly, pulling off one sodden pant leg and then the other. And the Victrola—afternoons, she and Hannah playing old records, giggling and laughing over lyrics, crooner's voices. They were still on the upside of life, nothing but plans and possibilities. Colleen rolls her jeans into a ball, watching water drip onto Hannah's clean floor.

"Don't worry about the water," Hannah says, rushing in to trade a terry dressing gown and pair of sweat pants for the wet jeans. "You can't hurt these floors." She takes off again and is back almost immediately with a blanket. "Curl up on the couch," she says. "We need to get you warm as soon as possible."

Colleen tucks up under the blanket, pulling in her knees so she wraps her arms around them, shoving an icy cold hand between each thigh and calf. She presses her face down onto her knees and listens to Hannah already in the kitchen putting on the kettle.

"Brandy," Hannah calls, opening and closing cupboard doors. "I'm putting brandy in your tea."

They sit for a few minutes saying nothing, and as Colleen feels the brandied tea slide down her throat, her body slowly warming, another wave of reality hits her. She must look ridiculous, like a drowned rat, blubbering like a baby—attacked by someone, by a dog. She could tell Hannah that. Save face like she's been taught. *Keep the bleeding arm behind her back and smile.*

"I...I have to tell you something," Colleen says, finally, after she can't stand the silence anymore or Hannah's quiet sip-sipping, never looking up, squeaking back and forth in that old rocking chair. It ticks Colleen off and, at the same time, impresses her that Hannah can do this, as if they're just two friends having a cuppa.

Hannah looks up. "Take your time," she says quietly.

Colleen takes a deep breath. "This has nothing to do with now," she begins, "running around down at the beach like an idiot, getting myself soaked."

"You're not an idiot."

"I feel like one, especially now."

"It's certainly not what I see—mother, grandmother—God, it's hard not to be jealous."

"You? Jealous of me?" Colleen inhales sharply and stares at Hannah. "Ye Gods, what have I done? Not much compared to you: career, glamour, published poetry. I can't hold a candle to that."

"The grass is always greener, I guess," Hannah replies. "Here, I'll get us more tea."

"Could I call Art?" Colleen asks, as soon as Hannah is in the kitchen. "I told him I was just going for milk."

"The phone is right there," Hannah calls. "On the table behind you."

Art sounds relieved to hear Colleen's voice. She tells him how she rescued a dog and that she's at Hannah's, almost as if Hannah was down at the beach, too, as if she might have told Colleen to come and get warmed up at her place. She leaves out everything else, knowing Art won't ask, knowing he will wait up for her, knowing, and not always willing to admit, how much the man loves and depends on her.

"The dog was all right, then?" Hannah says, handing Colleen her second cup.

Colleen nods. "I'd better stop after this," she says, toasting the air. "I'll be all over the road with any more."

"You were saying," Hannah says, after another uncomfortable silence.

Colleen puts the cup down and sits up straight. "Okay. The bull by the horns. The summer you worked with me at the Britannia."

"Good old 1955."

"Where to start?" Colleen whispers. "That oversexed brat Larry Mourand, he tried to feel me up more than once."

"You too?" Hannah white knuckles her cup, stares past Colleen.

"A bloody Peeping Tom to boot." Colleen shivers. "I had to replug that hole over the basement washroom mirror almost every day."

"The first time," Hannah says slowly, "I heard him breathing—he must have been standing on something behind the wall. I bolted for the cubicle to change."

Colleen twists the end of the blanket, pulling it more tightly around herself. "And I was so sure it was only me he was after."

"We didn't talk about personal things in those days."

"When did we have time?"

"Who would have listened?" Hannah drains her cup and puts it down. "We weren't exactly in a position to squeal on the boss's son, were we?"

"The day old Charlie died, you were off and I…"

"I was in the kitchen." Hannah stands and walks slowly toward the couch. "Plastered up against the coatracks." She sits and grabs a faded satin-covered pillow, hugs it flat against herself. "I'd left my library book on the shelf."

"I was downstairs in the washroom," Colleen whispers. "My period had arrived and I went for a fast repair job."

"All these years," Hannah says, putting her hand on Colleen's shaking arm, "I thought I was the only one."

"Me too." Colleen hears a clock ticking somewhere; the kitchen tap is dripping.

"You know," Hannah says, jumping up and heading into the kitchen. "This is more than a strange coincidence." She comes back with a red address book open. "Here." She hands Colleen the photo.

"The three of us. Oh my God. Where did you find this?"

"Under my bed, would you believe? Today—behind a bunch of keepsake boxes."

"Poor old Charlie," Colleen whispers.

"I've hashed it over a million times," Hannah says. "Why didn't I tell someone? Go to the police?"

"Who would have believed us?"

"No one, and our summer jobs would have been kaput."

"I know."

"Is that why you kept quiet?" Colleen stares at Hannah, still not sure she believes what she has heard.

"Yes and no," Hannah says reluctantly. "I...I knew they wouldn't believe me, that Mourand would say I was lying, trying to get his perfect son in trouble."

"Arrogant son of a bitch," Colleen says, pounding her fist on the sofa. "Thought he could do whatever he wanted."

"Everyone knew that."

"Astrid? Do you think Astrid knew?"

"Astrid knew more about everything than we did," Hannah added. "But she needed her job too. The Britannia Hotel was big business in Franklin during the fifties. Mourand wouldn't have tolerated a scandal."

"So we all shut up and let that over-sexed dick get away with it."

"Sins of omission," Hannah says quietly.

"What?" Colleen says warily. She's not sure what Hannah means and isn't in a mood for fancy language.

Hannah pushes herself out of the rocking chair and paces. "I'm saying exactly what you just said but I don't think he got away with it. Mourand knew what his son was like. I remember Mrs. Long at the bookstore—I know it was before summer holidays—talking to someone about that spoiled brat of a Mourand swaggering down the main street like he owned the place."

"You remember that?"

"The same way we both remember all the gory details. Larry was sent off to a military school."

"You think so?"

Hannah nods. "Someone told Mr. Lumsdon, Mother's boss, that Mourand sent him back to Ohio, to a school that would straighten him out. I remember Mother saying good riddance to bad rubbish. She didn't usually say things like that."

"So even though we're not off the hook, we are," Colleen says.

"In a manner of speaking, I guess." Hannah looks at her and sighs. "Maybe we were smarter than we thought," she says. "We did what we had to do under the circumstances."

"Come on, Hannah," Colleen says. "We were scared shitless and needed the money so we didn't blab."

"Would it have made any difference if we had?" Hannah says, sitting beside her. "It was the fifties. We were powerless."

"Do you really think so?" Colleen hands the photo back and jumps up. "It must be some kind of an omen, finding it."

"Meaning?"

"A reporter from the *Standard* wants to interview me tomorrow at the store. Ask questions about Charlie." Colleen sits again and wrings her hands. "About what happened."

"An exposé?"

"I don't know, but I can't talk to him, I just can't…"

"We'll do it together, then." Hannah puts her outstretched palm over Colleen's knuckles.

"Both of us?"

"Will talk to the reporter."

"What about school, your classes?"

"I'll get a sub for the morning. I can do that."

"You were there," Colleen says almost to herself. "I can't get used to the idea. You were actually there."

"I could say the same thing."

"It's like some far-fetched story," Colleen says, squeezing Hannah's hand, "I guess truth is stranger than fiction. Right? You're the smart one, the poet. We were both there. Truth stranger than fiction. Dammit." Colleen is crying again—crying and pounding the arm of the sofa.

Hannah waits until she stops and hands her a tissue.

"Not any stranger than me finding the picture." Hannah picks up the photo and inhales sharply. "I still have nightmares," she says, in a barely audible voice. "His hand sticking out beyond the doorframe, fisted, and then slowly opening. A small, sort of strangled breath out, and then, silence." She puts the picture back inside the address book and snaps it shut.

"What will we tell the reporter?" Colleen asks.

"We'll say we heard someone but have no idea who it was."

"I don't think I can do that," Colleen says, wringing her hands again. "I'm lousy at lying."

"Did you see anything?" Hannah asks.

"How could I, from the basement?"

"Colleen," Hannah says, slapping the address book down on the side table. "It won't do any good to tell now."

"But we were there. We heard him…"

"Okay. Suppose we tell the reporter, spill our guts out to him. Do you think he's going to treat us sympathetically? Is he going to say, there, there, you were poor young girls, products of the fifties when teenage girls were powerless, of course that's what you did?"

"I…I don't know."

"He'll plaster it all over the front page of the *Standard*: *Youthful Witnesses Withhold Evidence* or *Witnesses Break Forty-Year Silence*."

"You make it sound like the *National Enquirer*," Colleen says.

"One of the city papers might even pick it up. Who knows?"

"And that might affect you? Your teaching?"

"I hadn't even thought of that. I doubt it, and besides, that's not the point." Hannah stares intently at Colleen.

"So what is, if it's not that it's going to smear us all over the place?" Colleen blows her nose loudly and shivers. "I think Art said it was part of a series, the history of the Britannia or something."

"The most exciting part. The only dramatic part," Hannah cuts in. "You think that reporter won't play it up? Make the most of it?"

"I…don't know."

"I thought you were good at acting."

"Not without a script."

"Then I'll do most of the talking," Hannah says, getting up.

"But it's me he wants to talk to." Colleen jumps up and paces. "I can't do it, I…"

"Maybe you…you have laryngitis from rescuing the dog." Hannah cuts in. "I'll give him a story. You nod."

"Is that honest?"

"It's necessary."

The phone rings.

"It's Art," Hannah says, holding her hand over the receiver. "He wants to know if he should come and get you."

Colleen throws off the dressing gown and dives for her coat.

"She's just leaving," Hannah says, nodding. "We started reminiscing and lost track of time."

"Milk," Colleen says as she pulls on her wet shoes. "I was supposed to get milk."

"Wait." Hannah dashes into the kitchen. She reappears with Colleen's jeans in a plastic bag and a carton of skim milk. "Unopened and right from the store."

Colleen waits a few minutes to let the car warm and wonders what she will say about the milk. No one drinks skim. They never buy this small a carton. The twins will back away like it's radioactive. Art will take it as yet another sign that what he said to the reporter—setting up the interview—has, for some unknown reason, pulled the rug out from under his beloved wife.

Nothing. They will basically tell the reporter nothing. Hannah made it sound so easy. She must be used to dealing with crises at school, smoothing things over. In her gut, Colleen is still not sure it's the right thing to do, the honest thing, at any rate. And if they do tell and the whole thing is blown up in the paper again, forty years later, what will people say, especially at the store? People come in to chew the fat with Art every day. Will he, too, smooth it over, or will he come home and ask questions? Will she have to spill the beans to him after all these years? And if she does, what good will it do? Get yourself home, she says to herself. You can't do anything about it right now.

As soon as she opens the door into the house, everything comforts her, the clock ticking, the furnace coming on, everything in her house—Art upstairs waiting. She feels suddenly so tired she can barely kick her shoes off, afraid to sit in case she won't be able to get up again.

Art already has the bed turned down, lighting dimmed. His study chair creaks and he's there to help her into the room, gently undressing her and pulling on a flannelette nightgown. He tucks her in and she feels heat from the electric blanket right down to her toes.

"I made hot chocolate," he says, kissing her forehead. "It's in the micro."

Colleen nods and tries to listen to his footsteps going down old stairs, tries but feels herself drifting. She doesn't remember him coming back into the room.

BRITANNIA NOW

ON MONDAY MORNING, just before Searp leaves from his office to interview Colleen Pinser, he tries the NYC number one more time.

"One moment please," the receptionist says. "I'll put you through to Mr. Mourand's secretary." Searp taps his fingers on the desk. He doesn't have much time.

"A reporter from Franklin in Canada," the secretary repeats. There's a pause. "Mr. Mourand will speak to you. One moment please."

Searp grins. Luck at last.

"A reporter from Franklin?" booms Mourand over the phone. "Takes me back a few decades. How are things in that sleepy little town?"

"Fine, sir, just fine. I'm writing a series of articles about the history of the Britannia Hotel."

"And so you should be. I was just telling my secretary the other day how my daddy pulled that place up by its bootstraps and put it back on the map."

"You lived at the hotel with your parents, did you not?"

"I did, even started high school there."

"The summer of '55? Were you here then?"

There's a pause and Searp hears a female voice interrupt. The secretary. Searp waits as sweat trickles down his back.

"Sorry about that," booms Mourand. "You were saying?"

"Were you living at the hotel the summer of 1955?"

"I spent every summer down on Lake Erie—family cottage, lovely old place."

"A hotel employee, Charlie Elliot, was found dead in the hotel that summer of '55," Searp continues. "Would you remember that?"

"Young man," Mourand replies. "It was a long time ago, but I can assure you I know nothing about that. I wasn't there that summer or any other summer."

Searp thinks he senses a certain sharpness in the man's voice but he can't be sure. "Thank you sir," he replies. "I won't take any more of your valuable time."

"Give my regards to Franklin," Mourand adds, sounding magnanimous. "Best of luck to you, son."

Searp sits for a few minutes letting the reality of Larry's statement sink in.

He was not there. He says he was not there. If no one saw him, there is no proof he was there.

When he arrives at the store, Art ushers Searp to a cramped back room sporting a small table and several chairs. He is surprised to find two women waiting for him.

"My wife, Colleen Pinser," Art says. "And her friend, Hannah Norcroft." It's easy to tell from his Aunt Maureen's description which is which. Colleen is wearing a thick turtleneck sweater, the room smelling of Vicks, her eyes puffy, as if she's having an allergic reaction or has come down with a cold. Hannah has a city look to her and is more self-assured.

"Pleased to meet you," Hannah says, extending her hand. "Colleen has come down with a major dose of laryngitis, and I volunteered to do most of the talking."

Searp sits at the table and pulls out his spiral note pad. "I've been writing a series on the Britannia Hotel," he begins, "and I am hoping you can give me some information about the summer of '55."

"We'll do our best," Hannah says, crossing one leg and staring directly at him. "What exactly is it you want to know?"

"I was told," Searp continues, "that Mrs. Pinser, then Colleen Miller, might have been in the hotel the afternoon of July 21st."

Colleen, who looks momentarily like a rabbit caught in the headlights, manages to croak, "Afternoons off."

"We had every afternoon off," Hannah says, smoothly. "And it's a bit of a tall order asking us to remember one particular afternoon from over forty years ago."

"This was the afternoon Charlie Elliot was found dead at the bottom of the kitchen stairs."

"Mr. Searp," Hannah says. "I realize you are, with good journalistic intentions, looking for the truth, but what do you hope to prove with this line of questioning?"

"I think there was more to it than the newspaper report revealed. I think there's a cover-up, that his falling down the stairs wasn't an accident."

"And you're wondering if we, somehow, saw what happened that afternoon?"

"I am."

"Have you done any research, Mr. Searp, as to what it was like to work at a hotel in the 1950s, especially if you were young female staff?"

"Without being rude, Ms. Norcroft, I do have to say you are not answering the question."

"We did not see what happened, Mr. Searp, that afternoon or any other afternoon, for that matter. We were lowly waitresses, badly paid, often harassed." Hannah leans closer to Searp. "If we hung around when no one else was there, we could be accused of theft or who knows what."

Searp tapped his pencil on the paper. "Mrs. Pinser, you agree with Ms. Norcroft's statement?"

Colleen croaks "yes" and nods.

Searp notices, however, that her hands are shaking.

"I've talked to a number of people about this," Searp goes on. "And it has been suggested that Larry Mourand, the hotel owner's son, might have been involved. Do either of you know anything about that?"

"Larry Mourand," Hannah says. "We did see him from time to time. He was an arrogant teenager that summer, around sixteen as I recall."

"And you didn't see him the afternoon the old guy died?"

"Most definitely not," Hannah replied. "Anyway, if it was July 21st, it would be summer holidays so he could have been anywhere. How would we know?"

"He lived with his family on the hotel's third floor, so I thought…"

"Isn't that what is called conjecture, Mr. Searp?" Hannah sits back and stares intently at him. "We are telling you what we know. Neither of us saw Larry Mourand that afternoon or any other afternoon for that matter."

"I guess that pretty well sums it up, then," Searp says, standing to leave. He turns at the door.

Colleen has a coughing attack and Hannah gives her a tissue.

"Thank you ladies," Searp says, and nodding to Colleen. "I do hope your cold gets better."

Back in the car, he puts a big goose egg on the page in his notebook. He'll finish the article this evening. He still thinks there was more to it than either woman revealed in their short conversation. It's frustrating, and he'll have to decide how to word his interpretation of the incident. He's smart enough to know he can say so much and no more, not if he intends to stay here for the next five years. Franklin is still a small town; the Britannia still carries an aura of its past glory. Tarnishing that image would not, politically, be in his best interest.

HANNAH IX

LATE ON TUESDAY afternoon, Hannah sits at her dining room table, marking tenth-grade creative writing assignments, most dreadful, a few so-so, and one promising. This student reminds Hannah of Colleen at that age, not so much in looks as enthusiasm, magnetic personality, chutzpah. It comes out in her writing. A Leo, she is certain. Hannah tries to remember if Colleen is a Leo. A beaten-down Leo, to be sure, especially last Sunday night. What was she doing down on the beach in the drizzling rain? The dog story sounded a bit too pat. Easy to speculate, of course, and she did grow up in a stormy household, not that Hannah remembers ever seeing evidence, but people talked, discreetly, behind closed doors—even her own mother. Don't you stay over there if her father's been into the bottle, she would say. No telling what he might do. Hannah doesn't remember Colleen's sister, but Colleen certainly made a different life, prolific and, perhaps in the end, most fulfilling. Art is an unknown but he does seem like a decent man.

And the interview? It was obvious what the reporter was after. Of course, no one except Larry would have known what actually happened. Maybe Charlie did just fall down the stairs. Larry did take Charlie's money and Charlie did protest. At the time, it sounded like Larry pushed him but it was impossible to tell.

Now, she wishes she hadn't agreed to go out to lunch with Colleen. At the Britannia no less. She and Colleen don't really have much in common. How could Hannah, for instance, tell Colleen about Russ. Or her pregnancy.

The letter, she remembers. I still have to do something about that letter. Tea first. While the kettle is boiling, she retrieves the letter from under her jewelry box where she stuck it two weeks ago; she determines that when she reads it this time, she won't feel faint—won't have to lie down, won't get a blinding headache.

March 17, 1995

Dear Hannah,
The several decade gap in our communication does not mean I have forgotten you. To the contrary, I have, prominently displayed in my office, your two well-crafted books of poetry and have heard, over the years, of your ongoing success as a high school teacher.

I am writing to request a meeting with you about someone of great importance to both of us, namely, our son, Carter.

Could you, at your earliest convenience, please call my home and book an appointment with my secretary.

Yours,
Anthony (416-837-4291)

The second reading is almost as overwhelming as the first. Her gut reaction is to give it the red-pencil treatment and send it back. She does scribble in a few comments.

Dear Hannah, (much too familiar—Ms. Norcroft, please)

The several decade gap in our communication (what communication? I remember almost none unless tactile communication counts) *does not mean I have forgotten you.* (Please!) *To the contrary, I have, prominently displayed in my office, your two well-crafted books of poetry* (the least you could do, I'm sure) *and have heard, over the years, of your ongoing success as a high school teacher.* (I didn't know you had added stalker to you accomplishments. Or voyeur. Or both.)

I am writing to request a meeting with you about someone of great importance to both of us, namely, our son, Carter. (How kind of you to mention his name, and here I've been, for the last thirty years, calling him you-know-who to all my friends)

Could you, at your earliest convenience, please call my home and book an appointment with my secretary. (I'll think about it…)

Yours, (presumption beyond belief)
Anthony (And what did you say your last name was?)
(416-837-4291)

This brings only momentary satisfaction. Carter. She never would have called the child Carter. If she is going to do anything, she shouldn't procrastinate any longer. Their son. Another bloody presumption. Genetically alpha and omega, amen. All men. Always men. Men always win. Her mother again, which only brings back that bitter-gall feeling, that acid-in-the-chest sensation. A mother is someone to confide in, to lean on, to share with—not. Not her own mother. She might have been, given the chance, would have tried. Would have… Tears fall on the page, blurring some of the edit. I should buy a waterproof pen, she thinks, mopping it with a tissue.

Someone to talk to, right now, would be a definite advantage. Someone to list the pros and cons, rationally, without all her emotional baggage. Lemon Time tea with a shot of Scotch—the best she can do, given it's too late and too dark to go running. She'll go to the gym in the morning. They open at six. She'll pump some iron with the big guys, enjoy them enjoying her. They're such a silent bunch, no worry of being chatted-up.

"Okay Esmeralda," she says plaintively, from over the top of her teacup. "Whoever can I talk to?" The cat leaps down from the back of the couch, always hopeful that there might be food. She purrs her way around each of Hannah's ankles and sits for a detailed paw wash. "You're right on the top of my list," Hannah says, walking her fingers down the cat's back. "Only one small problem: communication. That bug-a-boo, communication."

Hannah moves to the couch, knowing the cat will follow. Her warm, purring body has a meditative effect, a tactile Om engine.

Julia, she thinks, stretching her legs out so the cat can lie on them—great colleague and chitchat confidante, but not good at the serious stuff. Hannah remembers a few years ago when a colleague was in a car accident, Julia couldn't even deal with a hospital visit.

Russ is out. Imagine calling him for a heart to heart. It's about an old lover. I had his child. Oh, sorry. Thought I'd mentioned it. She rhymes off several more names, but each one seems too busy, too preoccupied, and not suitable. The next stage, of course, is, oh my God, I don't have any friends, not real friends, the kind women are supposed to have. One more cup of tea but no Scotch, not if I want to work out in the morning. If only she could think of Anthony as someone she doesn't know. She doesn't, really—has no idea what he has done during the last thirty years. His wife, grandchildren, the fact that he must be about the same age as her mother. She certainly didn't think about that thirty years ago. If she wasn't so impaled by the past, the meeting could be quite interesting. She knows she has weathered the years well, that her exercise and diet and probably her genes have kept her looking a good ten years younger than she is. In a perfect scenario, it would be satisfying to have Russ go with her, or she could hire an escort, have him pretend. A stand-in. Great idea, but the stuff of fiction not reality. She could never pull it off.

"It's too late, Esmeralda," she says, draining the last drop, scooping up the cat as she stands. "We'll deal with it tomorrow."

The following afternoon, Hannah waits in her office until everyone leaves. She hears the industrial vacuum whirring down the hall. It seems safer to phone for a meeting from here, more neutral. Whatever is said, or isn't said, won't linger the same way as it would in her own house. She will feel less violated.

Her hand shakes visibly as she dials, waiting what seems an interminable length of time for an answer. One ring, two, three. My luck, she thinks. I'll get an answering machine.

"Professor Hendricks' residence." A professional voice, tidy, with overtones of protection.

"May I speak to Professor Hendricks, please," Hannah says, parroting the tone.

"Whom may I say is calling?" More reserve, getting ready to fend off.

"Hannah Norcroft. Ms. Norcroft." With a heavy emphasis on the Ms.

"One moment please. I'll see if he's available."

Hannah holds the receiver away from her ear. Muzak it is not. Schoenberg, she thinks, grimacing, twelve tone theme and variations. A fast way to eliminate telephone solicitations.

"Hannah, my dear. So good of you to call."

Only the shaky age in his voice prevents her from spitting out some feminist epithet. "In response to your letter," Hannah says, as tersely as she can manage. She is shaking visibly, holding the receiver with both hands.

"It would be best if I told you in person."

"I see." The shaking has progressed down to her knees.

"Could you manage Friday at four? I'll get Mrs. Arthur to make tea."

"Friday at four," Hannah repeats, "will be fine."

"I'll look forward to that, my dear."

Hannah hangs up without saying good-bye. She sits for a long time, staring at her bookshelf, a professional library accumulated over the past thirty years, a visible buffer zone between everything Anthony represents and her pain. She feels the wound bleeding again now, that impossible tear in her soul, bound so tightly over the years by books and time, teaching and deadlines. She can't believe she is willfully doing this: exposing herself, her past, her vulnerability. Who else would do such a thing, be such an idiot?

Colleen, she thinks ruefully, but her situation was different. The interview was foisted on her. The obvious parallel tweaks at her. Colleen. Someone she doesn't know very well, someone who would be sympathetic, would probably have a more objective take on the situation. Out of the question. She has never blabbed to anyone, ever. Especially not this.

Hannah feels dizzy when she stands, has to steady herself a few moments before going over to her bookshelf—one of her self-made comfort zones. She runs a finger along the top row—old books, books from university—and pulls out Hardy's *Far From the Madding Crowd*. Why, she has no idea. Hardy never particularly appealed to her. As she flips through the yellowed, paperback pages, she finds a card, embossed and formal-looking:

Mr. and Mrs. Frank Miller
wish to announce
the marriage of their daughter
Colleen Nora Miller
to
Arthur Terrence Pinser
on Saturday June 15, 1960

The paper airplane folds are still there—study hall, second year. She cringes, remembering her self-righteous pomposity: in retrospect, the irony of her holier-than-thou pronouncements.

In her gut, Hannah knows that whether or not she talks to anyone before Friday, nothing will change. Unless she cancels the appointment. Which she won't. Can't. She feels her heart pound, her chest constrict. She sits down and does some deep breathing. In out, in out. It doesn't help. Somewhere I have Colleen's number, she thinks, grabbing her purse from the floor. In my address book? No. I wrote it down on something after she left Sunday night—to call on Monday, see if she was okay. "A" for good intention. She picks through the debris in her purse. A Pizza Palace takeout flyer. That's it, she thinks. She checks her watch: 4:37. Colleen might still be at the store. She isn't. Art answers and says she's likely at home.

As she dials the second time, the receiver shakes against Hannah's ear; she tightens her grip, waiting while it rings once, twice, three times. Once more and she'll hang up. It's a crazy idea anyway. Whatever is she thinking?

"Hello?"

"It's Hannah, and...I need some advice."

"Hannah. Of course, what is it?"

"I'd rather tell you in person. Could you come over to the house, say, around seven?"

"You're back in Franklin, then?"

"I'm still in Toronto."

"Oh…right, well, drive carefully."

"Thanks, Colleen."

"No problem. I'll be there."

For the second time within the hour, Hannah hangs up without saying good-bye.

COLLEEN IX

COLLEEN STARES at last week's copies of *Franklin Standards* spread out on the dining room table. Her parent's house is now officially empty. The trauma of cleaning it out, even with Pam and Janet and Art and the boys helping, nearly drove Colleen around the bend. The smell was the worst, and even now on sunny days, Colleen goes over to open windows. Air the place out—tone down the embarrassment of opening the closed door to a real estate agent, only to be hit in the face with that awful stench. Art says she may be exaggerating a tad. Colleen doesn't think so.

News still travels fast in Franklin, and a day after phoning one real estate agent, two more call, all dying to sell the property. The fact that the place is a dump, run-down, in need of who knows how much repair turns out to be a selling point. It's easier to tear down. The property is worth a bundle—hot. Colleen hasn't had so much attention since high school when two or three guys would often go after her for a date at the same time. She feels that same heady power, the forty years slip-sliding away and she with the world by its tail. In control. In demand.

Now that she faces that a ball-and-chain, bulldozer knock down of the house will soon happen, she gets all sentimental. About everything. She wonders if the house her grandparents lived in, in Toronto, is still there. She makes a point of driving past the house that belonged to Art's parents, a two-and-a-half-storey brick house, lots of trees. After Art's dad died, Rosie only stayed in it two winters. The following spring she put it up for sale. Too much upkeep, she said, too big and too costly to heat. She seems happy enough in her place at the Seniors' Residence. Colleen doesn't know if Rosie ever goes back to look at the house. She doesn't ask. But it is there to look at—something to show for all the years, all the hardships, good times and bad.

How often has Colleen said she can't wait to knock her dad's place down once her dad is gone. Flatten it. Hire a band to play while the bulldozers crash and roar. This is the best thing, she says to herself, and she imagines a medium-sized building, Flannigan Place, named after her mom's side of the family, a small gold piano on a plaque over the doorway. I could make it a condition of sale.

She soon finds that the real estate agents already have clients lined up. The property is large enough for a three-storey apartment building, a small condo complex. They hint at a bidding war; it seems this property has been watched for the last ten years. Colleen is scanning the week's newspapers, supposedly to get a feel for the market. What she's been doing, however, is daydreaming about her pot at the end of the rainbow and what she will do with it: pay off their house mortgage—a mind-boggling step—never to worry again if there will be enough money in the account each month. That cash-flow devil always on their backs. Top priority. Next, get a newer model car. Every time something goes wrong with the Chev, they go through the same patter. How much to fix it? Usually under five hundred. How much would it be worth as a trade in? Not likely more than a thousand. Can we make monthly payments? Not at the moment. Get the old Chev repaired. She and Art have talked about a newer car, even test-driven a few after the hardware store has had a good month, but something always happens and the car goes off the list. Set up trust funds for her grandkids. To do that she would have to invest the money, not pay off the mortgage, and forget about the car. Her one trip to talk with a bank person left her feeling totally out of her depth and stupid. The interest earned wouldn't be worth a tinker's damn.

Her kids ask when they call. A phone call from one of them every night since the funeral—general and chatty but always with that are-you-all-right tone.

"What about yourself?"

"Hadn't thought about it, really."

"Well, you should."

"Paying off the mortgage would be for me, for both of us."

"What about taking a trip? Or going to a spa?"

"A spa? I don't know. I'll think about it."

"When we were kids that always meant no."

"It all depends on how much I get."

"I'll ask again when you find out."

Today, she almost doesn't answer the phone, in case it's yet another real estate agent. It turns out to be Debbie Matthews of all people. Colleen hasn't talked to Debbie for umpteen years. She was in the Franklin Theater Guild way back when in high school, and so it seems, still is.

"Colleen? I'm calling from the Guild—for Moira Jackson. You remember Moira?"

"Moira," Colleen says. "That takes me back a few years."

"There was an ad in the *Franklin Standard*: a call for extras in her movie. You must have seen it."

"I heard she was in the movie business."

"Well, she called me about Guild members getting first dibs."

"Why are you calling me?" Colleen says, feeling stunned. "I haven't done any acting for years."

"Colleen, she especially asked for you."

"She did?"

Debbie lowers her voice. "She says she has a tiny part with 'you' written all over it."

Colleen takes a deep breath. Moira Jackson. A film part. She stares at the Real Estate Section in front of her. This is insane. There must be a mistake.

"Colleen? You still there?"

"You're sure she asked for me?"

"She remembers you from high school. All those shows you were in. Who cares what she said? You should be tickled pink."

"I don't look much like I did in high school," Colleen says with a snort.

"She knows that. Said she's seen you at the store a couple of times."

Colleen feels her head spinning. At the store? She's been in the store? When?

"Colleen, I have to know. You'll love it. It sounds like a peach of a part."

"I don't know if I'd have the time."

"This Saturday at the Legion Hall, 2 p.m." Debbie is playing it up, always thrilled to organize and obviously flattered to be working with the apparently famous Moira. "Come on, Colleen."

"I should check with Art," Colleen falters. "And the twins."

"Look Colleen," Debbie says, lowering her voice. "This is an amazing chance. I'd give my eyeteeth to do it, but she wants you. You'd be a fool to say no."

Colleen thinks about everything she still has to straighten out over the house...

"Yes?" Debbie cuts in after a moment. "Did I hear you say yes?"

"When is it again?"

"Saturday, 2 p.m. The Legion Hall."

"Okay," Colleen says, feeling sucked in and a bit giddy.

"Fabulous. See you Saturday."

Colleen stares out the window to the hill behind the house. It's cold today, one of those March winds. In another month, when she walks the dogs, everything will be greening up—grass, old apple trees. This spring will be different from all the others. Who knows, maybe she'll have scads of extra time. If she took this part, maybe no one in the family would even notice. Dream on, she thinks. I must be out of my mind saying I would go.

Moira Jackson. Someone should write a book about her. Tough and independent, especially at the hotel. Most of the time, she ticked everyone off. Daisy was understandably suspicious of her, and Astrid picked on her any chance she got. Probably because Astrid worshipped the ground Daisy walked on. When loaded comments were tossed around, Colleen never said much. She needed her job too much, but a couple of times, she remembers getting Moira out of the line of fire. Besides, in spite of their differences, Colleen knew she and Moira were in the same boat.

Moira's dad often came over to play cards with Frank's buddies. Often as not, halfway through the evening, when the empties piled up, Mr. Jackson picked a fight and stormed out, swearing and kicking the door as he left. Colleen always listened from the top of the stairs—heard the men make comments about his poor damn wife and kids.

Colleen checks the time. A habit drilled into her over the years: waiting for kids to get off the school bus, waiting to pick someone up from music, sports, whatever, always waiting for Art to come home from the store. It's 4:30, still time for a cup of tea.

When the phone rings again, she is holding a too-full teacup and doesn't get to it until the fourth ring. It's Hannah, and afterward, Colleen sits and stares out the window. The stone wall along the driveway is falling down; it has been for the last twenty years. Falling down and still there—still keeping the peonies in place.

Something God-awful has happened to Hannah. Maybe, after

the interview, the reporter found out that she was in the hotel kitchen. Or maybe something has happened at her school—a shooting, kidnapping. Whatever it is, Hannah is driving all the way to Franklin, just to talk about it. Colleen takes her tea back to the kitchen and dumps it into the sink. Only one thing to do when things are in disaster mode—work it off.

Art arrives home early to find Colleen has pulled everything from the bottom cupboards and is scrubbing furiously.

"Early spring cleaning?" he remarks, slumping into a kitchen chair to flip through bills and flyers.

"You're early," Colleen says, appearing from inside the cupboard. "Anything wrong?"

"Dead this afternoon so I closed early."

Colleen sits on his lap and traces the wrinkles on his brow. "You're sure you feel okay?" she asks. "I don't remember the last time you came home early."

"Just a little tired, I guess. Didn't seem much point staying. Not one soul on the main street."

"There's spaghetti sauce heating in the microwave and water simmering for pasta. When the boys get here, the pasta needs ten minutes."

"You're going somewhere?" Art looks puzzled as Colleen whips things back into the cupboard.

"I'm meeting Hannah at her mom's house. She's driving down from Toronto. Must be some kind of emergency. I'll eat when I get back." She kisses his brow. "Put your feet up and don't do the dishes."

HANNAH/COLLEEN IV

HANNAH HAS put on an extra sweater, pulled the curtains, and turned up the heat, but in spite of this, she is still cold. After arriving at her mother's house at 6:15 and parking the car in front of the garage, she seriously considered putting it inside, keeping the house lights off and not answering the door when Colleen arrives. She forgot the garage is more than half full of stuff, some of it accumulated by her mother, most of it discarded by Hannah.

She pours herself a Scotch straight up and drinks too much of it, too quickly. It burns down her throat and reminds her, momentarily, of Gordon Ellis and her fifteen-year-old self at the drive-in. "Of course I've had a drink before," she says out loud. If she wasn't so upset, this would be funny.

How to begin? Where to begin? Is there a beginning? She could start at the end and work back. The good old flashback method, a tried-and-true novelist's approach. If she had time or had thought of it before she left Toronto, she could have typed it out like a little Hardyesque drama, full of pathos with maudlin detail—handed it to Colleen and left the room while she read. And then what? Walked back in? Faced the music? The thought constricts her chest so that she has to take long, deep breaths. She never has been good at facing things and can't believe, as she sits and stares at the Victrola, the faded drapes, the worn rug, that she has actually put herself into this position.

The doorbell rings once, twice, every small vibration stabbing into Hannah's spine. After the third ring, she stands and walks slowly to open it.

"Oh my God," Colleen says, embracing her before the door is even shut. "I can't believe you drove all the way down from Toronto." She bustles in carrying a cloth bag and her purse, dumps both on the couch, and produces a round, colorfully decorated tin container. "Comfort food," she says, patting it. "And chamomile tea." She pulls off her coat and hurries into the kitchen. Obviously in take-charge mode. Hannah follows and sits at the table.

"At home," Colleen chatters as she fills the kettle, "We always say if Peter Rabbit's mother used chamomile tea, it must be good for us."

After a prolonged silence, Hannah pulls the words out one at a time, as if her throat is constricted, frozen. "I…I'm…so…glad… that…you're…here," she begins.

Colleen finds a teapot and mugs and places the opened tin container on the kitchen table. "Shortbreads and Nanaimo bars," she says, putting the teapot beside it. "Do you want sugar?"

"Scotch."

"Great idea." Colleen scans the counter, gets up to look in cupboards.

"On the Victrola," Hannah manages. Colleen disappears and returns, efficiency personified.

"Okay," Colleen says, after she pours tea and Scotch and sits down. "Whatever it is, it must be awful, and I've had my share of awful over the years." She takes a Nanaimo bar and pushes the box toward Hannah. "So shoot."

"I…I have a son."

"A son?" Colleen's eyebrows go up and down. "Okay."

"But I've never seen him."

Colleen watches Hannah clamming up. Like Pam, Colleen thinks, like Art. Both of them have to be pushed against the wall before they can spit anything out. There must be more. Hannah's likely holding back the clincher. Colleen's been down this road so many times with Art. She takes another Nanaimo bar and holds the box out to Hannah. "Janet made these; they're from the funeral."

"The funeral?"

"My dad."

"Your dad? Oh, Colleen, I didn't even know."

"How could you know?" Colleen leans toward her. "March 3rd, around four in the morning. Funeral was on the sixth. Everyone rallied round."

"I'm so sorry."

"It hasn't really sunk in yet. I still think I should be traipsing up to the Lodge to see him."

Hannah pours some more Scotch into her mug. Colleen adds tea.

"It's a funny thing, this getting older," Hannah says, taking a sip from her mug and then looking over its top. "You'd think we'd learn from our mistakes, get a little wiser."

"Too soon old, too late smart," Colleen says, watching Hannah. A tear pings into Hannah's mug; she turns her head.

"You were telling me about this son of yours."

"I have a meeting with his father tomorrow. I've made an appointment. I'm not sure I can keep it." Hannah hugs herself and leans toward her knees, head still turned away.

"He asked you to come?"

"In a letter. It arrived during spring break."

Colleen hasn't a clue what to say. It's like a sitcom. Giving up a child. When? How old is he?

Hannah gets up and paces from the counter over to the kitchen window, back to the counter. "I want you to know," she says, lean-ing against it, fingers white-knuckling its edge, "I had no choice. Professor Hendricks called the shots."

Colleen nods. Professor. First clue. "When you were in university?"

"Grad school, first year, 1965."

"Sixty-five? The year before Pam was born. He'd be twenty-nine. Is he married?"

Hannah turns and faces the counter. "I don't know," she says, almost inaudibly.

"You could be a grandmother."

"I could." She turns back, cheeks wet, face tight. "I don't know why I wanted to tell someone. I can't tell my mother."

"She doesn't know, then?"

Hannah shakes her head.

"You should go," Colleen says, in a rush. "Maybe he wants to tell you something important about your son. Maybe your son has been trying to get in touch with you all these years."

"Someone, his father's relative in England, took him," Hannah says a little less shakily. "When he was a baby. He's still there, I guess." Hannah sits down again and takes a long swig of tea. "I'm getting loaded. I won't be able to drive back."

"Can you go in the morning?"

"I've done it before."

"What time is your meeting tomorrow?"

"Four in the afternoon."

"I'll light a candle."

"You think I can go through with it?"

"You have to. Think of your son trying all these years to find you, his mom."

"You're terribly dramatic, do you know that?"

"Always have been."

"Is it nice being a grandmother?"

"The best."

Hannah finishes her tea. "I'll look forward to it."

"You can do this." Colleen takes the mugs to the sink, a second trip for the teapot. "I know you can."

"Thanks," Hannah says, taking Colleen's hand. "Even though it was awful, the telling, I mean, I feel better somehow."

"Hey, that's what old friends are for." She gives Hannah a hug. "You're sure you'll be all right?"

"I'll manage."

"I promised Art I wouldn't be too long," Colleen says, hurrying into the living room to grab her coat. Hannah follows and flops down on the couch.

"We still haven't set a lunch date," Colleen adds, covering Hannah with an afghan she finds over the back of the rocking chair. "Want a wakeup call in the morning?"

"The alarm is permanently set for 5 a.m." Hannah says sleepily. "I'll be fine."

Colleen lets herself out. The wind is up; more snow is likely on the way. Wretched March, going out like a lion. She barely makes it up to the speed limit by the time she gets to the highway. Everything spinning round and round, her life, Hannah's life, what she knows of it, the little Hannah has told her. No one's life is what it seems, that's for sure. It's all on top, and underneath, it's another whole kettle of fish—her life as much as Hannah's, except Hannah's seems, in a way, more complicated. A son. Hannah has a son. It seems amazing, the last thing Colleen would have imagined.

As soon as she pulls the car up in front of the back deck, Colleen knows something is wrong. The inside door is open, too many lights on. She hears the phone ringing as she hurries in but is too late, and the answering machine cuts in. "Art?" she calls, throwing her purse on the floor. "Art, are you here?" Later, when she thinks back, it was a stupid question. She had the car. The twins had the van and were out for the evening. The dogs, Tiff and Miranda, both banged into her at the door, noses against the backs of her legs, whimpering. She races up the stairs two at a time and stands panting, holding her side. The bathroom light is on; the radio playing. "Art?"

The phone rings again and she grabs the receiver from the hall table, knocking the phone onto the floor. "Mom? Mom, is that you?"

"Pam?"

"Dad's had a slight heart attack. He's in Emerg. Janet and Paul are on their way."

"A heart attack?" Colleen sits on the top stair. "When? When did this happen?"

"Sometime after seven. He said you hadn't been gone long."

"This is awful. I shouldn't have torn off. How did he..."

"He called 911 and then me. Maybe you should get a taxi to the hospital."

"I'll be fine. Talk to you later."

Colleen hangs up and runs down the stairs, scooping up her purse. She's halfway into town when she realizes she hasn't grabbed her coat. "Art," she keeps saying, tears running down her nose. "No, Art, no." All the while knowing that whatever has happened, all the wishing and bawling won't change it. She speeds ahead, eyes glued to the dotted line, there and not there, there and not there, like a heartbeat. Ker-thump, ker-thump, ker-thump. It slows as she slows, turns into a steady hum with the solid line, and then disappears altogether when she turns into the hospital parking lot. Colleen catches her breath and hurries from the car through the fancy automatic doors, unaware of the cold March wind.

Cardiac Unit. First floor. She stops outside the elevator, tries to psych herself up for the worst. She's been here before, those secret nights no one else in the family knew about. A row of beds all with heart monitors, oxygen, one nurse always in the room. A *Family Only* sign on the door, everyone talking in a whisper.

At the nurses' station, some young nurse tells her they're running tests and would she like to wait in the lounge. The lounges in this hospital are all the same and, for a moment, after she sits down, she can't remember where she is. Special Care, Emergency? No, it's the Cardiac Unit.

They haven't had enough time together, not real time. Days, decades, years piled against one another until it seems only yesterday she was back at the beginning, waiting for her life to happen.

Before Art, boyfriends came and went, but never to her house. She had a whole raft of reasons why no one could pick her up, changed them to suit each date. Like being in a play. Every boy was a leading man, someone to impress and have a good time with. Being serious wasn't in the script until Art crashed into her life. Literally. Backstage at the tech rehearsal of *The Music Man*. Colleen was in the chorus with a small speaking part and a one-line solo. It was 1957 or '58, she can't remember for sure. She lived for rehearsals, knew all the songs and almost everyone's lines off by heart.

It was as if it was meant to happen. She was back stage waiting for the women to finish "the chicken chorus," as it was dubbed. Moira Jackson, who was helping with props, and Lorne, one of the backstage crew, were having another argument about the props table. Lorne said it was in the way at intermission when they did scene changes; Moira insisted it wasn't. Colleen moved further into the shadows. Arguments reminded her of home and always gave her a stomachache. Art was tiptoeing a large scenery flat to the other side of the stage. The quartet was singing again and splat, he banged right into her, knocking her sideways. By an amazing stroke of luck, she managed not to fall onto the props table. Art, who couldn't let go of the flat, mouthed sorry and kept going. Even as she ran for her entry, shoulder stinging, she noticed his red hair and muscles. Too old, though. One of those guys building sets in the back of Pinser's Hardware. Later, during a break, he apologized again, said he hoped he hadn't hurt her shoulder. Most guys wouldn't have bothered. He said he watched her on stage, that she had talent. Colleen barely remembered their first chat, but much later, Art told her she was gorgeous and sexy, a real turn-on.

They saw each other in several more shows, but it wasn't until grade twelve when she was Maria in *The Sound of Music* that he actually asked her out. She was flying high on rave comments about "Sixteen Going on Seventeen," and then at the cast party, Art never left her side, dancing and talking the whole evening—well she did most of the talking, even mentioned her dream of going into theater.

The following week, it was Hannah who told her who he was: Earl Pinser's son, the hardware Pinsers. Standing in front of their lockers at school, she teased Colleen saying he was likely old enough to be her father.

A week later, Art phoned to see if she would like to see *St. Joan*, a play coming to Franklin the following week, put on by a touring company from Toronto. She couldn't let him pick her up at her house. The Pinsers lived on Logan Avenue, trees and brick houses and everything perfect. She couldn't let him meet her parents, her dad would be half cut and her mother would know right away how old Art was and who he was. She told him she was working at the library, sorting books after it closed, forgetting she would have to convince Mrs. Rankin to let her to stay late, in the end saying she had to finish a school project. Colleen was so excited she forgot about going home afterward.

The production was amazing, like nothing she had ever seen. The sets, the acting, everything. She cried, and Art slipped his warm, sweaty hand over hers. Afterward, because she felt so full of pain and words and Art being so close to her, she let him walk her home—right up to the door. Luckily the house and street were quiet. Colleen stood on the darkened front step, holding her breath, feeling like she was a whole chain of firecrackers waiting to go off. When Art leaned toward her, he barely touched her lips—a polite, reserved sort of kiss, that was it. One little kiss, just like in the movies. He might as well have grabbed her and given her the works. She didn't admit it, not until a long time after, probably not until he proposed to her, when they both knew she was pregnant.

"Mrs. Pinser? You can see your husband now."

Colleen jolts upright and follows the nurse, her heart thumping as if it's twice its normal size. The nurse quietly places a chair beside the bed and motions Colleen to sit.

Art is asleep, breathing with oxygen, his heart-monitor screen ticking out a steady rhythm, intravenous in his arm. Other than looking a little pale, he's still Art. On his forehead, that curl of nearly gray hair, several strands still highlighting red, bristle on his face peppered pale blond and gray. Colleen sits quietly and takes another deep breath, hoping she won't cry. All her life she's been a crier; it doesn't seem to slack off with age. Art snorts and opens his eyes.

"Colleen?"

She leans over and puts her cheek lightly on his chest, her arms pressing against his. "You're going to be okay."

"You bet I am." His hand strokes her back. "Sorry. Must have given you an awful scare."

"Don't say sorry." She takes both his hands in hers. "The kids are on their way home, even Artie."

"Heck of a way to get them all back," he says grinning at her.

Two nurses appear, one with clipboard in hand. "Sorry to inter-rupt. Hourly check."

Colleen slips out into the hall as they close the curtains around him. Lights are dimmed, the hall is night quiet. Colleen leans against the wall with questions racing at her. How will they manage? Who will run the almighty store? Will Artie stick around?

"You can come back in, Mrs. Pinser." A nurse at the door. "He's doing very well, not to worry." She gives Colleen's arm a squeeze.

They've cranked the bed up a little. Art has more color in his cheeks.

"The ambulance came in a flash," he says, as she sits down. "Said they were on their way back into town."

"Lucky," Colleen adds.

"And some new drug they gave me sure did the trick." He smiles at her. "Guess I'll have to slow down a little."

Colleen nods. She knows if she says anything it will come out in a torrent: the store, the debt, the struggle, everything from beginning to end like a fat old elastic pulled and snapped back.

"Could you call Mom?" Art says, putting his hand over hers. "Better wait until morning, though."

Colleen nods again. Another cross for Rosie to bear. Her voice will have that quiet in it, and she'll sigh once or twice but never cry. She'll probably say something she hopes will make Colleen feel better. She's an amazing woman. When she thinks about getting old, Colleen wants to be like Rosie, husband long gone, drunkard son, who knows where, and yet she still serves tea, smiles and talks about something good, something worthwhile. "I'd better go," Colleen says, pushing herself up. "So you can sleep."

"Jake knows the password," Art says, pushing himself up on his elbows, "and the store keys are on the hook in the hall."

"You just rest," Colleen replies, kissing his forehead. "And don't worry."

HANNAH X

BY NOON on Friday, Hannah's hangover headache from the night before has moved to her sinuses. Two English teachers have called in sick, and when only one supply teacher is located, Hannah has to endure an introduction to *Macbeth* with a raging-hormone ninth-grade class. At three, when she checks her home phone messages, Russ's voice, sounding somewhat strained, says he's on his way to New York for two days and absolutely has to talk to her when he gets back on Sunday. She returns the message and says that's fine. Drop in anytime. She means to put it in her appointment book, then immediately forgets, her four o'clock meeting with Professor Anthony Hendricks overpowering all. Afterward, she plans to pick up a pizza and watch old movies all evening, possibly all weekend. Give herself time to rally: no phone calls, no contacts, no one.

Getting to Anthony's involves driving across town. She avoids the expressway, knowing it will take longer but not caring. She even considers arriving late. With still five minutes to spare, Hannah parks where she parked thirty years ago and walks the three blocks to Anthony's house, not because she doesn't want to show off her late model, sporty car, not because she fears anyone seeing her, but because she needs a run at it, a one-step, one-heartbeat-at-a-time run at it.

The house looks exactly the same, a bit down at the heel

perhaps, paint curling on a window ledge, bushes overgrown, but then she wouldn't have noticed that sort of thing thirty years ago. Before she rings the doorbell, she consciously battens herself down, pulls on her Plexiglas aura for protection, becomes her mother, skeptical and distant. She barely hears the doorbell.

"Ms. Norcroft?" The woman who opens the door is less intimidating than on the phone, a bit dowdy and sturdy looking. "Come in. The professor is expecting you."

In spite of her preparation, déjà-vu almost immobilizes Hannah: the mahogany side table in the front hall, where she momentarily sees a summer hat, straw with long, yellow ribbons. Her dress had been yellow, too. The balustrade, curved at the bottom with its Persian carpet runner, brass stair rods twisted like licorice.

"This way, Ms. Norcroft." The woman stands by the French doors, her hand on the china knob. Hannah inhales sharply and follows.

The man she sees bears little resemblance to the Anthony she remembers. An old man, bent over in his wheelchair, brown cardigan too large and not buttoned properly. He looks up from a book on his lap, slaps the page, and grins. The grin identifies him. "Hannah." He thrusts out a hand, fingers unable to extend. "Hannah my dear. So good of you to come. Sit down, sit down."

His hand is cold and can't grasp hers properly. She sits on the settee, dropping her purse on the floor at her feet. The carpet here is also the same, not that they ever spent much time in this room.

"John Donne," Anthony says, slapping the book again. "I've been rereading John Donne. Marvelous stuff."

"You wanted to talk to me about…Carter," she says.

"Yes, yes, as soon as Mrs. Arthur brings tea."

Then, Hannah would have felt it necessary to talk, to fill the empty air, to amuse. Now, she crosses a leg and leans back, slowly scanning the room as if looking for something.

"The years have been good to you," Anthony says, watching her.

"Quite," she says. "And you?"

"I'm alone now," he says, not sounding too regretful. "The children have scattered. I'm comfortable here. The university has been good to me; the new arts wing has my name on it."

"Congratulations."

Mrs. Arthur appears with a tray. "Tea," she says cheerily, putting it down on the rosewood coffee table.

"For two," Anthony says. His chuckle immediately turns into a cough—a dry, rasping cough that quickly twists him double. Mrs. Arthur rushes out and returns with a glass of water. Anthony clutches the padded arms of his wheelchair, chest heaving, obviously in pain. Mrs. Arthur leans over him, possibly administering a pill. It's obvious Hannah is not to ask, not to acknowledge the episode.

Like the blip in a film reel, the scene evaporates. Mrs. Arthur pours tea; Anthony pulls his wheelchair closer to the coffee table.

"And how do you take your tea, Ms. Norcroft?" Mrs. Arthur holds the filled cup aloft. Hannah tries to decide if there is a snatch of irony in her voice, a hint, perhaps, that she is not the fallen woman Hannah is.

"Clear please. With a twist of lemon, if you have it." Hannah knows there is no lemon on the tray.

This sends Mrs. Arthur scurrying back to the kitchen.

"I should have remembered," Anthony says, smiling. "That lovely twist of lemon."

Hannah watches, bracing herself, in case Anthony decides to discuss Carter while Mrs. Arthur is still there. Thankfully, she returns with the lemon, pours Anthony's tea with double sugar, and leaves.

"And so to the matter at hand," Anthony says, finally setting his cup down. "On the secretary over there, you will find my address book."

Hannah refuses to jump up immediately. She takes another sip of tea, looks thoughtfully at the cup as if she might ask about its pattern, sets it down.

"The secretary?" she says, as if a stranger to the house.

"Still in the same place."

Old, maybe, but he can still play the game. She retrieves the book and hands it to him, intending to sit immediately, not stand before him, the suppliant student revisited.

"Hannah?"

She has already turned away.

"He looks like you."

She turns back to see that he is offering a photo. She takes it and sits with as much composure as she can muster.

"Last summer," Anthony says. "A holiday at the British seaside."

The young man in the photograph is on a sandy beach, a retaining wall in the distance, his shirtsleeves rolled up, walking shorts, a shock of blond hair parted at the side and partially falling over his forehead, obviously blown by sea wind. The smile is Anthony's; the rest is Hannah. She inhales sharply and puts the photograph on the table.

"I said I would ask," Anthony says, watching her, "if he could contact you."

Hannah inhales again and looks at the photo. "Yes," she says almost inaudibly. "That would be…fine."

"I'll give him your number, then," Anthony continues. "When would be a convenient time for him to call?"

Hannah feels herself grinding to a halt, emotional shut down, power off. "The weekend," she says faintly. "Morning would be best."

"I want to thank you," Anthony says, leaning slightly forward, "for taking time from your busy schedule."

This is it, Hannah thinks. I can leave. Anthony is staring at her, expecting something. A response? A fond comment for old-time's sake? For her to take his hand, extend some gesture of basic human kindness?

She picks up her purse as she stands, clutching it in front of her with both hands, like a shield. "Thank you for the tea," she says. "I need to get a head start on the Friday traffic."

"You are still very beautiful," Anthony says, just before she bolts for the vestibule.

Mrs. Arthur is right behind her. "The professor wants you to take the photograph."

Hannah turns and accepts.

"I know he wouldn't mention it," Mrs. Arthur says quietly, "but his prognosis is for six months at the most."

"Lung cancer?"

Mrs. Arthur nods.

Outside, the late afternoon sun still warms the air. He was a smoker, Anthony, his office rank with the smell. Not the house, though. Apparently Mrs. H. didn't allow smoking in the house. Hannah smoked a bit then, almost everyone did. After she was pregnant, Anthony told her to stop, that it was bad for the fetus. What a joke. His second-hand smoke, his smoke-polluted sperm. Hannah realizes she is still holding the photo. She stops and gives it a once-over. "So," she says, sounding, she knows, like her mother. "Are you a smoker, Carter, or are you part of that new breed?" She sticks the photo into her purse and returns to the car. Health conscious, environment conscious, vegan, granola head—none of the above?

Once out of the sedate residential enclave, she deliberately takes the expressway. It suits her that the traffic is a nightmare: stop and go, horns sounding, everyone in the usual TGIF hurry. She deliberately concentrates on driving, putting the past hour on emotional hold, deal with it later—the necessary art of procrastination.

The phone is ringing when she enters her house and she just manages to catch it on the last ring. Esmeralda purrs against her leg.

"Hannah?"

"Aunt Harriet, how are you?"

"I've been meaning to write. Thank you again for your wonderful hospitality. So many good memories. Thought I'd just call and say it in person."

"Oh, Aunt Harriet, I'm...I'm so glad you called."

"Are you all right, dear? You sound a bit stressed."

"I'm fine, just fine. Hectic day at school and I just came in the door."

"Won't keep you, then. Give my love to Eadie."

"Yes, yes. I'll call next weekend after I visit her."

"Good-bye, dear."

Hannah stands holding the receiver until a recording comes on telling her to hang up. She picks up the cat, strokes her purring form. She should have called Aunt Harriet last weekend. She thinks she remembers saying she would, at the airport. She isn't used to having to check in, be accountable—too many years of independence and family isolation. She's being unfair, of course. Harriet puts no claims on her other than kin and caring. The heart understands this perfectly; the head balks, wants to reject.

The cat squirms and she lets her go, a leap to the floor and into the kitchen.

"So," she says to Esmeralda as she fills her dish, "the quintessential question is—should I tell Aunt Harriet about Carter or not?" She watches the cat crunch away at the food, soon to be content, at peace with the world. If only it were that easy, she thinks. Better to wait. Who knows, maybe Carter won't phone. Maybe this whole chapter will die a natural death. Part of her definitely wants it to, wants the status quo, the before-all-this-happened-what-was-I-doing-with-my-life stability. She knows that this is impossible,

that even if nothing more transpires, everything has shifted like
plates in a fault line, her former stability altered, fissured cracks
delineating its surface.

Esmeralda jumps onto the back of the couch, kneading it and
purring hopefully. A creature of habit, she waits for Hannah to curl
up with the evening paper, turn on the news before supper. Instead,
Hannah changes to go running, does her stretches inside so as not
to inadvertently run into Roger or Annie next door.

Forty-five minutes later, sweat-ridden with most of the angst
run off, she showers and throws on her dressing gown. A glass of
wine, Lasagna Lite, and the VCR. The afternoon quickly dulls to
a faint hum; the evening, initiated by a wrist flick of the remote,
lights up Hannah's preferred escape of choice.

Friday evening, Hannah watches movies until 3 a.m., *Gentlemen
Prefer Blondes* and then *Casablanca*. Saturday morning, the phone
jolts her awake at 10:20.

"Hello?" Not even close to her own voice.

"Hannah Norcroft, please." A precise, English accent. Should
be a giveaway.

"This is she." Slightly more coherent.

"Carter Whemscroft here. Anthony said I could phone."

"Carter. Carter…good morning." Cold water in the face, wide
awake. "How are you?"

"I'm fine. And you?"

"I'm…pleased…to hear from you."

"You have quite an accent." He chuckles. "A Canadian accent."

"I…I have your photograph…from Anthony."

"And I have your poetry. Very good poetry."

"It was written a long time ago." Hannah feels herself seizing
up like an engine out of oil. Any second now and her vocal chords
will quit.

"Suz and I are getting married this summer." He pauses, and Hannah realizes he is as nervous as she.

"We'd like to invite you to the wedding."

"I...I'd be honored."

"In Bristol. We both teach at the Art Academy here."

"Art teachers." She is almost monosyllabic.

"Anthony says you teach English."

"Yes...yes I do."

"You have summers off?"

"July and August."

"Perfect. Our date is August 3."

"I'll be there."

"I'll post a note with more details."

"Do you...need my address?"

"Anthony sent it. We'll keep in touch."

Hannah barely remembers the rest of Saturday. It rains, and she walks to the corner store for milk, sans coat or umbrella, and is soaked. She dials Aunt Harriet twice, no three times, and then hangs up each time after the first ring.

Sunday, she thinks about making a mad dash down to see her mother, even picks out a couple of cassettes her mother likes, then watching the rain still pelt against the front window, decides better of it. She brews some herbal tea instead.

Hannah has deliberately worked to control trauma in her life. Her ideal goal is to exist in a trauma-free zone, 365 days of the year. Given this, she weighs every decision carefully, pragmatically. It occurs to her that, even though over the last couple of months her trauma quota has substantially increased, she feels no less secure. Almost, she is loath to admit, the opposite.

First, Aunt Harriet, a positive trauma, but a trauma nonetheless, especially their initial meeting. Lining up next, the letter and Anthony, a nostalgic trauma, still tinged by betrayal whether real or imagined. The photograph, an unexpected trauma pulling up feelings and implications further augmented by the phone call, Carter, the summer wedding.

The final trauma, that of Russ appearing unannounced on her doorstep Sunday evening is, in the end, liberating. She completely forgot she told him to drop in. The doorbell rings shortly after six. Hannah is in her old sweat suit, no makeup, hair limp from yesterday's soaking.

"Russ, Russ, come in." She grabs his hand expecting an embrace. Instead, he slips by almost shyly, sits at the dining room table, no eye contact.

"Trouble?" Her first thought is his parents.

"I...I have something to tell you."

A small arc of suspicion rises and falls as soon as she is standing behind him. The back of his neck, his shoulders—she wants to massage them.

"Hannah?"

"Why don't we sit on the couch?"

"This is difficult. Sit down." He motions to the chair opposite.

It hits her then, like the proverbial ton of bricks. She backs up a couple of steps. "You...you've met someone."

"My editor." He turns, his face in pain. "I'm sorry. A facile thing to say, I know, but I wanted to be honest. I told Penny..."

"Penny Stratenburg? Koplin Publishers? She was written up in the *Globe and Mail* last week."

"The same."

Hannah is leaning against the back of the couch now, arms wrapped around herself. "I should tell you to go to hell but I can't. Your book will do well."

"Thanks. I...I don't know what else to say."

She turns and grips the back of the couch. "Good-bye. I think you're supposed to say good-bye."

She hears him get up and walk to the door. "I've dedicated the book to you," he says just before the door closes behind him. A couch pillow hits the door a second later.

"Damn you," she yells. "Damn all of you—Russ, Anthony, every last, stinking one."

She paces from one room to another, crying and blowing her nose, resisting the temptation to pick up and smash, especially Russ's picture. She lays it face down on her dresser. A double Scotch. More pacing. When she remembers Carter's picture, she retrieves it from her purse. It looks the same size. She yanks Russ's photo from its frame, breaking off two back tabs in the process. "Carter on holiday by the sea," she says aloud as she sits the frame upright. She throws Russ's photo behind her dresser, listens to it fall part way down and stop. "Maybe I'll fish you out," she says, "in twenty years or so. For old time's sake." She moves the picture frame over to the center more, turns it slightly to catch the light. "My son Carter."

Half an hour later, in from a brisk walk, she retrieves the school video of *Hamlet* from her briefcase and sits down with a clipboard and paper to make notes for tomorrow. "Focus," she says out loud to herself as she turns on the VCR. "That's what you always tell your students. Focus."

COLLEEN X

MONDAY MORNING at 8:30, Colleen pops in at the hospital on her way to the store. Art is out of the ICU and on the second floor, color back in his cheeks, and when she kisses him, he grins and nibbles her ear. Good sign.

"Doctor says it was only a mild heart attack," Art says, "but the kicker is, I have to stay away from the store for at least a month, and then, if I behave myself, maybe part-time."

Janet nods from a leather chair where she's curled up, having driven down from Guelph sometime after ten and stayed all night.

"I'm fine at the store this week, even next week if need be," Colleen says.

"Pam will be here by this evening," Janet adds, "and Artie's already booked a flight, ETA in Franklin Sunday night."

Colleen doesn't ask any questions, like for how long or is he going to help out. It's as if Pam or Janet or all three already have something planned.

The twins, kidding each other about skipping school with a cause, have already divided the day, with Steve taking the morning and Cal the afternoon.

Colleen dashes into the store three minutes before nine. She wonders, fleetingly, what happened on Friday and Saturday when no one showed up and the store was closed. "Tough banana peels," she says, as she throws the *Open* sign in place and telephones Jake to come in early. It's slow, she thinks, thank God, Monday mornings usually are, most people waiting until after lunch to rev up after the weekend.

The day drags to begin with, customer by customer, purchase by purchase. When a shipment arrives at the back, Jake takes care of it, telling her he would rather work behind the scenes anyway. She knows it's because he thinks she can't heft boxes from the truck, up the stairs, and onto the shelves. She feels old age creeping up on her, her fifty-fifth birthday to be exact. Sunday. Surprise, with everyone home. She blinks back tears just in time as Moira Jackson, of all people, waltzes through the door. Still playing the part, a middle-aged Munroe now, but still the same pizzazz.

"Colleen, Colleen, long time, no see." She reaches across the counter, perfectly painted nails, rings galore.

"Moira," Colleen says, changing gears. "The audition Saturday…"

"You took the words right out of my mouth. Good thing I tracked you down. Slight change of plans."

"I…I won't be able to make it."

"Doesn't matter. I have to make a fast trip down to the Big Apple—last minute meeting with my divorce lawyer. How's a week Saturday?"

"I…I don't know. My husband…Art, he had a heart attack Thursday." Colleen straightens boxes on the shelf behind, afraid she'll make a fool of herself.

"And left you running the store? Men, never around when you need them."

Thankfully, Jake calls from the back and Colleen excuses herself. She signs the delivery slip and breathes in cold air from the open back door. She always had a mouth on her, Moira Jackson. She can stuff the part. Who needs it?

"You all right?" Jake stares at her.

"Fine. Fine, Jake." Back at the counter, Moira has picked up a totally ugly serving plate, supposedly the latest thing, one of several a salesman talked Art into. So far, they haven't been trendy in Franklin.

"These are all the rage down in LA right now," Moira says, "twice the price, of course."

Colleen is all set to say there is no way she can take the part, that she has more important things to do, that...

"Sorry about Art," Moira says, placing the plate on the checkout counter. "I'm a bit jaded right now."

"Art's going to be fine," Colleen hears herself say. "Lots of family support."

"You always were a brick," Moira says quietly. "I do remember that."

Colleen nods and rings through the amount. "Would you like a box?" she asks. Tell her no, she says to herself. Get it over with.

"A bag is fine," Moira says. She leans over the counter. "Did that young prick of a reporter bug you about the Britannia?"

Colleen isn't prepared for this. "Why, yes. He...he interviewed us."

"Us?"

"Hannah and me."

"Hannah? Don't tell me. Hannah...Norcroft. Right? Is she still in Franklin too?"

"She teaches in Toronto," Colleen says, feeling totally sidetracked.

"So he dragged her into it, did he?"

"There was nothing to tell him, really," Colleen says quickly. She doesn't want to get into this. Not today. Not ever. Moira probably knows the whole wretched story.

"Good for you," Moira says. "Nosey little bastard, thinks he can boost sales by digging up dirt." She's at the door now. "I'm holding that part for you," she says. "Someone will call you next Friday. Toodle-oo."

Okay, Colleen thinks, so you didn't tell her. You still could. Get the message to Debbie before Friday.

Moira taking on Alan Searp. That would be something to see. What did Moira know about Charlie? Poor old Charlie. Where would he be buried and who buried him? No money. No family. She looks at people hurrying by outside—everyone on their way somewhere—busy, going, doing. And then what? All that struggle and then bang. Gone like Charlie, like her dad. If she only had faith like Art's mom, still going to church almost every Sunday. Years ago, Colleen tried it for a while but it screwed her up even more. Every Sunday there were these Prayers for Forgiveness, with a list of all the things she didn't do and all the things she shouldn't have done during the past week. Colleen always piled on the last month, the last year, often the last decade, so that by the time she went home, she was a total mess, dredging up every little thing she might have done wrong for the past year. It did her absolutely zip good that, at the end of the prayer, the minister said God forgave her. How could this calm-faced minister rattle off so many sins and possible sins and then simply write the whole thing off, saying she was forgiven? Once she got started on her own pile of crap, she added everything she could remember from last week's news: refugees, starving children, bombed-out streets, piling pain on herself until, a couple of times, she had to take off, walk out into the parking lot and sit in her car, faking an earache or something when a worried Rosie finally appeared. Today, the phone rings, cutting short wallowing, her train-of-thought.

Good thing store busyness keeps Colleen on the go, ringing things in, answering questions, trying to be helpful. Jake is good at his job but he doesn't push himself; he always makes sure he gets his coffee break as well as lunch. Around 2:30, Cal breezes in with a takeout sandwich and coffee, shoving it into her hand and motioning her to the back.

Colleen feels herself deflate as she sits, so much so that she has to work at opening the sandwich bag rather than nodding off, head on the table. The food helps, and a few minutes later, Cal appears holding a sheet of paper.

"Came through on the fax," he says. "From Pam."

Colleen reads the note, hand-written on the Rainbow Board's fax cover page: *Deerhurst Public School, Sudbury, Ont: Hope you are surviving the day—see you Saturday—give Dad a hug for me—Pam.* Her kids are amazing. Everyone says that about their kids, but hers really are. She's done her best over the years. That blink from day one to now, her sexy redheaded Art, her babes, this store. All of it still there like shadows, telling her to go on, keep going, that it isn't over yet.

Hardly anyone now remembers the store, what it was like in the fifties. Good thing. Dark and dreary, old hardwood floors so uneven you'd catch your toe if you hurried, terrible lighting, so much stock. Art said his dad knew every nut and bolt in the store, which was fine for him. Neat as a pin he was with his trim moustache, always in a pinstriped shirt, memory like an encyclopedia. Ask for something and he gave the aisle, shelf, and how many were left. Hard on himself and everyone else, especially Bill, Art's older brother who rebelled early—cigarettes at fourteen, whiskey at sixteen, gone by eighteen. Art wore the good hat, did the right thing. Colleen figures Grandpa Pinser ruled them all, set impossible standards, and never was satisfied. One of the reasons Art refuses to do so with his own kids—except for Artie. Somehow Art can't get it through his stubborn head that Artie will never be interested in the business.

Colleen tries to block out anything more than getting through the day, tries, but things still niggle at her—who will look after the store, how will they keep the cash flow going, stock, inventory, what will Artie and the others do about it. They will be scot-free by the end of the summer, the last collateral mortgage payment made. That much she knows. Fourteen years in hock, the price they paid for the Handy Hardware franchise. In September they could, in theory, sell the kit and caboodle, let someone else mortgage their life. Most small businesses are like that in Franklin, "all in the same boat," Art always says.

Before Art, with Art, and after Art. She knows there will be an after but not yet. Especially today, she needs to believe the with and ignore the after.

The new inventory needs entering, she thinks, walking back to look at the boxes just delivered. Cal can do that. He's a wiz with the computer inventory program, how to price and label. The boxes blur, momentarily. Keep things going, day after month after year 'til death do us part. "No," she says out loud. "No."

"Started talking to yourself, Mom," Steve says, right behind her.

"How's Dad?" Colleen pastes on a smile.

"Up and walking the halls, worrying about you, the store."

"What about homework?"

"Hey, we're in control. Don't worry."

"Jake leaves at five. Don't forget the alarm."

"*Mom.*"

"I know. On the ball and in control."

"Times two," Steve says, helping her with her coat.

Colleen tries to hurry across the spring-sodden lawn from the hospital parking lot. Her shoes are too tight and she gets out of breath too fast. Those damn extra pounds. Maybe she'll try WeightWatchers—after Art gets better. Once inside the first set of automatic doors, she spots a *Franklin Standard* news box and stops to scrounge through the bottom of her purse for change. Art hadn't paid much attention to the newspaper for weeks—should have been a clue something was wrong. He always read *The Standard* cover to cover, ranted about council doings, followed the funnies, checked out the obits.

The headline leaps out at her even before she finds enough quarters.

Death at the Britannia—Features Editor, Allan Searp, continues his fascinating six-part series on the history of the Britannia Hotel—See page 5. Her hand shakes so, she drops one of the quarters and has to fish it out from under the news box. Instead of going right to Art's room, Colleen sits on one of the reception chairs, her hands sweaty, fumbling to turn the pages fast enough. She runs her finger along the words as she reads:

"*Part IV, The Britannia's Post-War Boom Days, Death in the Afternoon*

"*The Britannia Hotel purchased and rejuvenated by American businessman Hugh Mourand in 1945 was, by the 1950s, a thriving and viable enterprise.*"

She skips the next few paragraphs looking for the part about Charlie. "*The most noteworthy incident occurring at the hotel in the fifties is, undoubtedly, the mysterious death of one of Mourand's employees, Charlie Elliot.*" Searp quotes from the July 22, 1955, *Franklin Standard* article that "*Mr. Elliot sustained a fatal blow to the head falling down a set of stairs from a second-floor storage room to the hotel kitchen.*" Searp goes on to say that "*if Elliot was pushed or attacked, the culprit escaped unnoticed. Since Mr. Elliot had little in the way of money or personal possessions, it was difficult to speculate the motive for such a crime.*" Colleen notes that he spends another paragraph bad-mouthing the local police force for not checking more thoroughly and mentions the fact that, although the newspaper said there would be an autopsy, none was reported. She slows down now, making sure she reads every word.

"*There has been, over the years, some speculation as to whether or not Mourand's sixteen-year-old son, Larry, had any connection to Charlie Elliot's death. Local residents say the boy was a troublemaker, and it is known he was sent to a military school in the US sometime that summer. Whether or not this was before or after Elliot's death is not known. No one interviewed saw the boy on the premises that day.*"

"He didn't mention our names," she whispers. "Thank God, he didn't mention our names."

The next paragraph, however, stops Colleen short. She has to read it twice to make sure she has it right. "*Mr. Larry Mourand, now a successful real estate broker, interviewed recently by this reporter, says he knows nothing about Charlie Elliot and was at the family cottage in Ohio at the time of the murder.*" The bastard, she thinks. Either he doesn't remember or he's erased it. His dad must have suspected, otherwise why did he send him off to military school? Hannah was right. They didn't see Larry in the building that day and so nothing could be proven. Not even then. She runs her finger down the rest of the paragraphs just to make sure. Hannah's interview plan was perfect. All the more reason to take her out for lunch, dinner even. Live it up. Yahoo.

Colleen waltzes into Art's room, paper behind her back. "You look terrific," she says, giving him a hug. "Where'd the snazzy outfit come from?" He does look better than she expected, sitting there all relaxed, wearing a navy tracksuit she's never seen.

"Steve brought it when he showed up at noon after Janet left for the farm. Said it was from her and Pam."

"Wouldn't you know," Colleen says. "Color looks good on you."

"How are things at the store?"

"Good, good, not too busy."

"I should be out of here tomorrow."

"Artie's arriving Sunday."

"Artie doesn't want to run the store."

"We'll work something out."

"My line," Art says, smiling. He takes the paper from behind her back.

"Wait till you read this," Colleen says, flipping over to page five. She knows it will sidetrack him, get him off the store. "All my worry for nothing. We're home free." She goes and stares out the window. "Think I'll get a coffee," she adds. "Be right back."

The dinner cart is moving down the hall toward her, that hospital-food smell leaking from metal covers over the white plates. Art is eating when she gets back, some kind of stew with a pathetic-looking dumpling and rice pudding for dessert. "Will you last until tomorrow?" she says, sipping her coffee.

"Probably," Art replies, "but they're going to give you my low cholesterol diet. The nurse already warned me. No more apple pie or brownies." He groans.

"We'll both go on it," Colleen says, sitting on the bed. "Maybe I'll end up looking like Hannah."

Art shakes his head. "Too thin, if you ask me."

"Did you read the article?"

"He didn't mention either of you," Art says.

"I know. I was worried and I'm so relieved."

"It would have been foolish of him to mention anyone's name. Happened so long ago and no one cares anyway."

Colleen looks quickly out the window.

"I remember talk about that Larry kid," Art continues, "that he could have been the one who did it."

Colleen nods, trying to look as though it's just another comment. All these years and Art knew? Knew and didn't tell her?

He runs his finger down the newspaper column. "Didn't know there was a Potter's Field in Fairgrove Cemetery, though."

"Potter's Field?" Colleen asks, determined to keep her cool. "I must have missed that part."

"Here," Art hands her the folded page, "paragraph at the bottom of column three."

Colleen reads aloud. "*The official fate of Mr. Elliot lies forever buried with him in an unmarked grave in Potter's Field at Fairgrove Cemetery on Clark Road. Whether a victim of accident or foul play, no one seems to know or care.*"

"I could have told him that," Art says, attacking his rice pudding. "Trying to stir up something where there's nothing to stir."

"Pardon my French," Colleen says, rolling her eyes. "But what's Potter's Field?"

"It's from the bible, I think," Art replies. "The place where Judas died. You know, the one who betrayed Jesus."

Colleen shakes her head. "Well that figures, doesn't it? Sticking the poor old bums and orphans where Judas died. Typical." She tosses the paper on the bed, "The snotty rich blaming the dead for being poor, saying they're no better than Judas."

Art gives her a look and continues to eat.

Colleen fiercely hates anything she thinks is uppity. She hears her mom in her own voice, going on about it even worse than Art on one of his rants. Cal always says she overreacts; Art teases her, calls her melodramatic.

"You and Hannah knew the old guy, right?" Art says, scraping away at the empty bowl for the last rice grain.

Colleen doesn't say anything about that. The kids would. They'd go at him with the starving prisoner routine: scrape, scrape, across the bowl bottom one more time. "He was a sweetie, an absolute peach," she says instead. "Always a smile on his face, never bad-mouthed anyone."

"Do you think the kid murdered him?"

Colleen stares at Art and bursts into tears.

"Sorry, love," he says, reaching for her, stroking her hair.

"I'm just so relieved," Colleen hiccups. "About you, the article…"

"And you're worn out," Art says, squeezing her shoulder. "Go on home. Put your feet up."

"Janet said she'd pick up pizza. Pam should get here by nine."

Art takes her hand. "Have a glass of wine for me," he says. "And Colleen?"

"Yes?"

"We'll get through this."

"I know." Colleen kisses him. "Should I pop in after supper?"

"Watch some TV with the girls; I'll be home tomorrow."

HANNAH/COLLEEN V

THE FOLLOWING WEEK, after listening to three phone messages in three days, Hannah returns Colleen's call.

"The sooner we meet for lunch, the better," Colleen says. "I can't wait to show you the article. Searp didn't name either of us, and you were right, we had nothing to worry about."

"I see."

"And Hannah? I think we should have lunch at the Britannia."

"The Britannia?" Hannah says. "Are you up for that?"

"It will be good for us," Colleen says, "like getting behind the wheel after a car accident."

"Do you have a date in mind?" Hannah asks, she knows, a little too formally.

"What about this coming Saturday?"

"I'm in Stratford that day, checking out a preview performance of *Hamlet*."

"Stratford. Wow, I've never been there."

Hannah knows her life must seem glamorous to Colleen. Seeing *Hamlet* is more school-related than an outing. Over the years, she has seen more versions of *Hamlet* than she cares to remember. "How about the Saturday after, the thirteenth?"

"It would have to be after one," Colleen says. "I'm tied up in the morning. If it works out, I'll tell you about it over lunch."

"That's fine with me," Hannah says, thinking Colleen sounds almost giddy; whatever is happening that morning, must be exciting. "I'll have time to visit Mother before lunch."

"It's a date," Colleen replies.

"Your family's well?" Hannah says, almost as an afterthought.

"Things are better now," Colleen says, completely changing her tone. "Art had a small heart attack last Thursday evening."

"Colleen, no. After you came to rescue me?"

"It happened while I was there," Colleen says, "A minor heart attack, the doctor says, and he's home again and ever so much better."

"What about the store?" Hannah adds, horrified to think this happened while Colleen was comforting her.

"Artie's come home," Colleen says brightly, "to look after things."

Colleen glosses over, that much Hannah already knows. "Well, take care," she says, feeling in overload. "See you on the thirteenth."

Why did I agree to this, Hannah thinks as soon as she's off the phone. Whatever the article says won't erase her distaste of going to the Britannia. Hannah cannot, as Colleen seems to be suggesting, sweep forty years of buried guilt and memories under the rug because of one small-town newspaper article. In Hannah's mind, the Britannia will always be linked to Larry and Charlie, the first a bad taste in her mouth, the second, an ache in her heart.

Besides, Hannah has enough to deal with in her own life right now, not that she said as much to Colleen, not that there was an opportunity. Colleen thinks both of them should celebrate by visiting the crime scene, albeit the room adjacent, to "lunch at the Britannia," Hannah says out loud. It will either close the chapter once and for all or it won't.

Colleen is more than a little relieved to hear from Hannah. She was sure she had put her off, somehow, being too wound up, too theatrical, as Hannah has already told her. Lunch in two weeks will be A-OK, giving Colleen time to check out Charlie's grave. She's working on a plan for the two of them. A good-bye plan for dear old Charlie.

Art's being home all day has turned out to be a mixed blessing. The first few days, he followed her like a puppy, asking could he do this, could he do that, until Colleen ended up snapping at him, often making some crack about him taking a rest. He huffed off to his office more than once with hurt feelings.

Now, almost a week later, they have found a routine: breakfast at the usual time, Art up to his office for the morning, then lunch and doing something together in the afternoon—a walk down the lane or up into the woods with the dogs. "Just what the doctor ordered," Art says each time, grinning and acting like a kid out of school. Colleen bites her tongue and says nothing about money, nothing about the fact that there is damn little left. Artie, who took over the reins without so much as a grumble, takes his dad's salary on paper, giving Colleen some for groceries, paying store bills when the cash flow is short. They laid Jake off so there would be some leeway. Colleen is holding her breath until the house sells, knowing they'll be using it to live on now. After that, she doesn't want to think about it.

Colleen is increasingly uptight about the Saturday audition and, once the lunch date with Hannah is set, she creates a diversion by asking Art if he would call town hall about Potter's Field. She mentions, casually, that she and Hannah want to know. What she doesn't say, of course, is that this is part of her secret plan for Hannah and her, the final scene after lunch at the Britannia. Art, with his business connections in town, arranges a visit to the cemetery the very next day.

Colleen hasn't visited the cemetery since they buried her dad, and she knows Art will write her nervousness off to this and give her extra hugs. She's going to need them. It's not that she ever purposely avoided telling him about where she was when Larry pushed Charlie down the stairs. There was never any real point in telling. It happened before he met her, and he had nothing to do with it. Better, she has always thought, to let sleeping dogs lie.

Art parks the car in front of a spanking new building, white siding and classy looking windows. The cemetery office is looked after by Mel Walters, who looks young, but then anyone under forty looks young these days. On the way over, Art tells her that Mel has recently taken over the job from his dad.

"Dad would have been working here in the fifties," Mel says, lugging a large homemade book from the office storeroom. The front cover looks like a piece of old Beaverboard cut to size. "Dad drew these," he says quietly. "Maps of the different sections—it makes it a lot easier to locate someone."

"Your dad didn't have this fancy new building, though," Art comments. "Worked out of his pickup, if I remember rightly."

Mel grins. "When I told him you two were going to pay me a visit, Dad said to tell you he remembers chasing that red-headed Pinser kid and his hooligan friends out of the cemetery more than once."

"Art." Colleen is shocked.

"Hey," Art says, slipping his arm around her to squeeze her shoulder. "That was in my wild and careless youth."

"Potters' graves are here," Mel continues, turning a few pages. "All numbered. Plots go part way up the slope, over into the back section."

"How would you find someone?" Colleen asks, moving closer to Art.

"See the numbers here?" Mel says, pointing. "Graves were set in rows, about every three feet. If you've got a name, we should be in business."

"Charles Elliot," Colleen whispers. She is sure Mel will ask her about Searp's article, wonder why she is looking for Charlie Elliot.

"Over here in the Register," Mel says, already opening a heavy, leather-bound book on another shelf. "Do you know the year?"

"It was 1955."

"We'll try that one first," Mel says cheerfully. "It could be out by a year either way. People often are."

Colleen has to scrounge around for her glasses and try to keep her cool so she can actually focus on the page. Old fountain pen entries: plot number, death date, name, occupation, place, and cause of death.

"Here it is," Mel says, "number twenty-nine, July 21, 1955."

"*Charles Elliot*," Art reads, giving her a hug. "*Kitchen help, Britannia Hotel, accidental.*"

"Before my time," Mel adds. "We should be able to find it on the map though."

Colleen inhales sharply and Art squeezes her hand.

"I'll show you outside, if you like," Mel says after he matches the number and name.

"I...I don't know. Do we have time, Art?"

"All the time in the world," Art replies.

The letter from England was in a pile of mail from Friday, but as she never looks at mail on Friday nights, Hannah only finds it Saturday, after she returns from Stratford. One of those blue stuck-together envelope letters, tidy but artistic-looking handwriting, the return address: Carter Whemscroft, Bristol Art Academy, Kings Road, Clifton, C49 2QY8.

Her hands shake as she opens it, carefully so as not to rip any of the paper.

Dear Hannah/Mum,

*I must confess, I am at somewhat of a loss over your name—
that is, what to call you. Auntie Bee and Uncle Felix who
raised me have always been my closest relatives. I was sent off
to school at an early age and rarely saw them, but they are
very kind. You will like them, I'm sure.*

*Anthony says I look like you, and I'm keen for a photo. I will
send you one of Suz and me and her cat in my next post. We
took the film in yesterday and it takes a week.*

*Suz and I plan a small wedding since both of us are only
children. She has just her mum. Her dad went to cancer three
years ago and so we waited until this year. Suz feels now she
can move out again, and that her mum can manage on her
own.*

*Hoping to hear from you soon,
Your son, Carter*

Hannah doesn't have a remotely recent picture of herself and
thinks she could ask Colleen next week, maybe outside the Britannia
after lunch.

A dress for the wedding is already an issue and she has been
looking—two chic Toronto stores so far. Clothes have always been
one of Hannah's indulgences. "Fashion plate Norcroft," Julia calls
her. When she mentioned mother-of-the-groom in the first store,
they showed her dowdy looking outfits and made prissy comments
as to what was suitable for the occasion. In the subsequent store,
she said only that it was a special afternoon event, Bristol in June.

The result was better, but nothing really caught her eye.

Lots of time yet, she thinks, putting the letter carefully back in the envelope. Time to get used to the idea. She props the letter up against Carter's picture. His name doesn't sound so strange now. She's actually beginning to like it.

On April 13, even though only Art is home, Colleen puts a *Do Not Disturb* sign on the bathroom door. Just in case. In the shower, she rehashes the morning's audition for the umpteenth time. Moira Jackson is directing a real made-for-TV film, in Franklin, ye Gods, and Colleen—she stands up taller and tries to suck her gut in every time she thinks about it—has a small, speaking part, a paying part, the amount of money being more than Art would bring home from the store in six months. She's still in shock, still pinches herself. But it's true. Colleen Pinser, this middle-aged, overweight, small-town merchant's wife, will be playing, as Moira says, the eccentric and flamboyant owner of a bed and breakfast where a murder takes place. Colleen's part is this woman, Evelyn McGintry, who has a small scene right at the beginning and then again at the end of the film. Moira says that's why the part is so important, why she just had to have Colleen. It's enough to give her a swelled head. Colleen's mom would have said that; her dad would have slapped his thigh and said she had finally made it.

As she rubs the towel across her dimpled thighs, she giggles and does a little side-step shuffle. Good thing there's no nude scene she thinks, looking at her blobby reflection in the steamed-up mirror. The luck of it, the absolute shout-to-the-sky luck of it. Rosie will say a prayer for her when she finds out. Thanks to the Lord. Thanks to Moira more like it. Moira, of course, hasn't a clue how much they need the money and she even apologized to Colleen that it would be slow in coming, that she would only get the five grand when she signs the contract, and the rest not likely until the movie comes out. Five grand. She said it like it was five bucks. Colleen signs the contract next week; she'll get her picture taken, a black-and-white glossy. A glam shot—movie star, hand-on-chin pose. She's going to Toronto with Moira to sign the contract. Moira says she's setting her up with an agent because it's easier that way.

As soon as she stepped in the door and told her family about the audition, Steve started bugging her for her autograph, and Cal said she'll probably be famous in five years. Art didn't say much, but she knows he's tickled pink. Moira says all things keeping on an even keel, meaning the money comes through from her New York backers, the actual filming will get off the ground the first week in June. The rest of the speaking parts have been cast out of Toronto; Franklin Theater Guilders and townspeople can be cast as extras. Colleen doesn't find out until months later that Moira wrote the first draft of the script years ago when she first went to New York.

Forty minutes later, while Colleen is still fussing with her hair, a real estate agent calls to say she has an interested client, and five minutes later, another calls with the same message. Colleen, who is adding beads and bracelets and a touch of mascara, gives both messages to Art. He has been showing the house without her anyway. The first time when they both went, Colleen spent the whole tour apologizing and pointing out flaws. Later, the agent quietly suggested to Art that it might be less stressful for Colleen not to be there.

The afternoon of April 13 is glorious, and Hannah would much rather be going for a run. Only her well-trained sense of propriety keeps her from canceling this luncheon date with Colleen.

The morning with her mother turns out to be a total wipe out. Edith is out pilfering when Hannah arrives, doesn't take kindly to being wheeled back to her room and then promptly falls asleep, head back at a crazy angle, snoring. Hannah plays the Andrea Bocelli tape she brought and hoped her mother would like, and tries to read one of the out-of-date magazines she finds in the lounge. Attempts to rouse Edith proved futile.

The nurse who brings prelunch medication wakes her none too gently, and after she leaves, Edith spits out her half-dissolved pill and brushes it onto the floor. When Hannah starts the tape over, the volume a little higher so her mother can hear, Edith makes a face and puts her hands over her ears. Hannah, who feels herself stretching like an elastic band, tighter and tighter, gives her apologies to the young woman who brings Edith's lunch tray and hightails it to the exit. Tomorrow—she will try again tomorrow.

Once out of the Lodge parking lot, Hannah realizes she still has an hour to kill, to fill, to do something with. She drives down to the west-end beach and parks in the lot overlooking the lake. Farther east, she can see the main beach and marina, both still deserted. Not for long, though. Another month and the tourist season will begin: boats, trailers, the summer side of Franklin. What would Carter think of this? Would she bring Carter here? She did remember the camera and has dressed accordingly in her dark-brown slacks and a tweed jacket. She recolored her hair the previous evening, not so much because it needed to be done but rather it boosted her confidence.

She arrives fifteen minutes early and parks south of the Britannia hotel on Victoria Street, a well-heeled part of the town to be sure. Trees line both sides of Victoria right down to the marina, and the street, designated heritage, is brick rather than regular pavement, with small, elegant tourist shops lining both sides. Hannah walks pragmatically as if new to town, looking for a particular shop perhaps, only at the last minute acknowledging her destination.

The Victorian couple over the front doors have weathered well— she, still the demure wife, he, still the cavalier man-of-the-world.

"*Respite to the Weary Traveler,*" she reads aloud, "*June 29, 1925 AD.*"
When she first worked at the Britannia, Hannah tried to research
this, supposedly the title of an obscure nineteenth-century poem.
After that summer, she changed jobs, worked exclusively at the
library, mind purged of anything connected to the hotel. Now, she
wonders again—was it authentic, or something the flamboyant
Bowen created for his own purposes? Contemplating this helps her
open and close the front door to stand casually in the foyer, glancing
at the dining-room's open French doors. It doesn't look the same
and it doesn't smell the same. She was sure her knees would shake,
that she might feel faint. Nothing. Someone brushes past her and
she moves aside to watch the hotel bustle. A bellhop following two
noisy couples pushes an ornate luggage cart toward the elevators
beyond the curved staircase. The first major alteration, the elevators.
Hannah tries to remember what was there before: a large mirror,
several locked cupboards.

The phone rings continually, the two desk clerks in Bowler hats
and bow ties chat up potential clients, extolling Franklin's location
and shops. She smiles and steps into the dining room. It's harder
here. Everything different but the same, the forty years slipping in
and out of focus, a memory pendulum ticking back and forth. Now
there is a plush carpet and plants, the smell of gourmet dishes, two
windowed doors to the kitchen, the la-di-da section with one big
banquet table, ornate Chinese screens accordioned into each front
corner, obviously pulled across for special occasions.

"May I help you?" The hostess wears a fringed flapper dress,
her short, dark hair gelled in place, a pronounced kiss curl on each
cheek.

"We have a reservation," Hannah says. "Under Pinser, I think."

"Ah, yes," the hostess says, flashing a prospective-tip smile.
"Right this way, please." A window seat about half way back, the
balustrade and Chinese screen behind providing partial privacy.

"Mrs. Pinser called and said she would be a few minutes late. Could I get you something from the bar?"

"Dubonnet," Hannah says, pulling a *Vogue* magazine from her purse. "With a twist of lemon."

"You're a snob," she hears Julia say, when they go out for the occasional TGIF school drink. "Dubonnet"—Julia always holds her pinkie finger up in the air—"with a twist of lemon." An acquired snob, initially a survival tactic, now so ingrained she is, most of the time, unaware of it. *Vogue* magazine has a section titled "Chic for this Summer," an excuse for buying the magazine.

She takes another look around. It's surreal in a way, being here—sitting in the dining room of the Britannia Hotel. She opens the magazine and hopes Colleen won't be too late.

Colleen roars into the parking lot behind the Britannia and slams on the brakes. Late again, story of her life. She grabs a handful of her longish peasant skirt and does her best to hurry to the front doors. Being late does have its advantages. No time to think about climbing the steps and entering. Just do it. She stands for a moment, palms sweating, staring at the grandness of it all. So different and yet frighteningly the same. She's still panting as she barges inside the dining room doors, trying desperately not to look around. She stares at the fancy carpet and immediately tunes in to ice clinking in glasses, plates touching tables, the kitchen door swinging in and out.

"May I help you?"

"Mrs. Pinser. I have a reservation."

"Your guest is already here. Follow me, please."

"Sorry I'm late," Colleen says, flopping into the chair. "Wouldn't you know it? Pam phoned just as I was going out the door."

"Something to drink, Mrs. Pinser?"

"A light beer maybe. Well, no, what are you drinking, Hannah?"

"Dubonnet."

"That's what I want, then. With the lemon, too." Colleen has never tasted Dubonnet. She takes a deep breath and smiles at Hannah. "We're here," she says, "and it's not as awful as I thought it would be. I ran up the steps and didn't even look—would never have done it without you, though. Are you okay?"

"Two kitchen doors," Hannah says, leaning forward, "and much more practical flatware." She picks up a knife.

"Stainless," Colleen adds. "Remember staying late to polish the silver?"

The Dubonnet and menus appear. "We have two specials," the young waitress says. "Atlantic Sole Almandine and Caesar Salad au Poulet."

Colleen has already scanned the prices and is grateful that her credit card isn't maxed out this month. After they order, she pulls the newspaper article from her purse. "Here," she says. "Read it for yourself." She watches Hannah scan the article, notices where she stops to run her finger along a line. "*Local residents say the boy was a troublemaker,*" she reads aloud, "*and it is known he was sent to a military school in the US sometime that summer.*"

Colleen stares at the tablecloth. "He was such an arrogant kid. All I wanted was for him to leave me alone."

"Arrogant kids are products of their family upbringing," Hannah says. "I see it all the time at school. Some kid with tons of bravado, often a troublemaker, waiting to get even. Home life has an immeasurable effect on kids."

"I know," Colleen says, taking a large swig of the Dubonnet.

Hannah, who doesn't pick up on this, continues. "What I mean is, look at the Mourands. His mother was a flake who spoiled the kid rotten, and Mourand? He was using the boy, setting him up to make himself look good."

"Is that how you saw them?"

"Who knows how he treated his son behind closed doors. The

boy was getting more and more out of control. There had to be a reason."

"I suppose so."

"He couldn't have really cared for him not if he shipped him off like that."

"So you think his parents are to blame?" Colleen asks, looking over her glass. "I don't know. It's never black and white."

"Did you read this part?" Colleen points to the statement made by Larry, the adult big shot.

"Would you believe it?" Hannah adds. "Wasn't there? That's an outright lie."

"But it certainly lets us off the hook, doesn't it?"

"It does," Hannah adds, handing her back the newspaper, "at least on paper."

"Your salads, ladies." The waitress deposits two large spinach salads. She smiles and leaves, her young body swaying, the fringe of her dress dancing back and forth.

"She's gorgeous, isn't she?" Colleen says quietly. "And so young." She sighs.

"They're all young," Hannah says, relaxing a little. "I don't mind, most of the time."

As they finish the salad, Colleen notices the *Vogue* magazine. "I haven't looked at one of those in years," she says.

"Here." Hannah passes it over. "Carter," she begins, clearing her throat. "Carter, my son, is getting married this summer."

"And you're going to the wedding?"

Hannah nods.

"Fantastic. It really is."

"I'm not used to it yet, even saying it." Hannah presses her finger tips together, elbows on the table's edge. "I'm…I'm horribly nervous."

"You know what?" Colleen says, again swigging too much of

the Dubonnet in one gulp. "It's okay being nervous." She giggles and leans toward Hannah. "You're nervous and I'm theatrical." As soon as she says it, she is sure that she shouldn't have.

But Hannah smiles and leans back in her chair. "We're not that much different than we were forty years ago," she says, grinning.

The entrées appear and they both dig in. Colleen looks only at her plate, avoiding the windows they cleaned, the balustrade they dusted, anything that reminds her, even though everything does.

"How is Art doing?" Hannah asks after a bit.

"Much better," Colleen replies. "Artie's almost talked him into selling. I don't know. It's a big step."

"Financially, will it be all right?"

Colleen doesn't know what to say. Hannah would probably freak if she knew how much debt they have piled up. "Yes, and no," she says. "It depends."

"I shouldn't have asked."

Colleen leans forward. "Something amazing has happened to me," she adds, "and as off-the-wall as it sounds, it will help, for a while anyway."

"An offer you can't refuse on the house?" Hannah asks. "Pretty upscale on that street now."

"Lots of showings. There'll be a bidding war." Colleen waves her hand. "I can't deal with it so Art's taken over."

"Something else, then?" Hannah looks at her, obviously curious.

"I've got a part in a movie," Colleen says, knowing how ridiculous this sounds. "A made-for-TV movie."

Hannah isn't sure she has heard correctly. She can remember Colleen making things up, fabricating deadlines, obligations. "A movie?" she says in her are-you-telling-the-truth teacher's voice.

"That's where I was this morning. At an audition." Colleen launches right into it. "And Moira Jackson, you remember her? She came back to Franklin to direct, and I have a small speaking part."

"Moira Jackson?"

"I know. Isn't it a hoot? She still has that look, more Dolly Parton now, but right up there with confidence to burn."

The waitress interrupts with dessert menus. "Dessert," Colleen rolls her eyes, "my downfall."

Hannah orders sherbet and tries to connect the conversation: Art to money to the house to a movie. She's still coming to terms with the article.

Colleen orders a double chocolate torte and charges on. "You likely weren't around," she says, "when Astrid took on Moira. After Mrs. Mourand left or whatever happened to her, Astrid used to nail Moira every chance she got."

"The summer we worked here?" Hannah says. Why wouldn't she remember this?

"It started then," Colleen continues. "I don't know—probably on your day off. It was worse in the fall when I worked weekends. Anyway, a couple of times, well maybe more than a couple, I stepped in, you know? Gave her an out. Moira had a rough enough time at home."

"She did?" Hannah has the passing sensation they are talking about two entirely different people.

Colleen nods. "She didn't need more shit at work."

Easy-make Moira. Fastest typist and gum-snapper in grade eleven Special Commercial. Forty years later, a successful movie director—more than a bit far-fetched. "So she picked you because of this?"

"Sort of." Colleen knows she's blushing. "She says I have talent."

"Will you get paid?"

"I'm going up to Toronto with her next week to sign a contract and get an agent."

Hannah lifts her coffee cup. "I guess it's no more far-fetched than me going to my son's wedding in England." She grins and clinks Colleen's wine glass "To your movie and my son," she says. "Both unlikely twists of good fortune."

"To both of us," Colleen adds. "To everything we ever want to do."

Hannah looks at her watch. She should go and try again with her mother. Colleen nods to the waitress for the check. Hannah picks up her purse and remembers the camera. Maybe she'll ask Colleen once they're outside.

"Before we go," Colleen says, putting the credit card on the tray. "A huge favor?"

"Don't ask me to be in your movie," Hannah replies, pushing her chair back. "No stardom for me."

"It's nothing like that," Colleen says quietly. "I want you to come with me to visit Charlie's grave. I've got flowers in the car."

"Now?"

"In fifteen minutes."

Hannah hates surprises, always has. Her immediate reaction is to say thanks but no thanks and leave. Out of Colleen's life, out of Franklin—out.

"I know I should have told you ahead of time," Colleen says. "Nervy. Just call me nervy."

Hannah straightens her jacket as she stands and stares out the window.

"I so much want to do this and I don't know if I can face it alone."

The waitress brings the credit card slip and Colleen signs it.

Flowers on Charlic's grave—such a Colleen thing to do: the grand dramatic gesture. How did she find out where he was buried?

"Art and I went to the cemetery last week," Colleen babbles on. "He knows Charlie was special to us, but that's all. Have you ever told anyone?"

Hannah shakes her head. Tell her it's out of the question, Hannah. Tell her you have deadlines.

"We owe it to Charlie, Hannah. It's something we can do. Especially with Larry saying he wasn't even there."

"Fairgrove Cemetery on Clark Road?" Hannah says, striding for the door.

"The entrance closest to Victoria," Colleen adds. "Park in front of the new, white building at the back." Colleen waves as Hannah turns into the foyer toward the front doors. Hannah doesn't wave back.

Hannah hasn't agreed to do this—doesn't have to. Colleen must know. It's not so much that she doesn't agree with the idea in theory, she thinks as she gets into her car. It's more the presumption on Colleen's part. Flowers on Charlie's grave—what will it prove? The man's been dead forty years. Colleen, the eternal romantic, always wanting to make things right. When she turns left onto Clark from Victoria, Hannah is still ambivalent. She sees the Fairgrove Cemetery sign ahead and knows she must decide. Move into the right-hand lane and signal, or continue on out to the nursing home, the expressway, escape.

Colleen knows she has blown it. She should have told Hannah ahead of time. The look on her face said it all. Jump into it at the last minute Hannah is not. Why did I think she would be this time? Colleen smacks her hand against the steering wheel as she pulls up beside the white building. Mel Walters is waiting outside.

"I can't stay," he says, as she gets out. "But I've marked the grave. I'll show you." He strides off. Colleen grabs the flowers and hurries after him. No time to chat. Just as well.

He walks west from the building to an open space lined on one side by huge old pines. "Along here," he says. "See how the ground dips down every three feet? Each dip represents a grave. I came out earlier and measured off to number twenty-nine." He walks over to a short stake driven in the ground. "Charlie Elliot should be buried right here."

"Thanks," Colleen says, staring at the paper wrapped around the flowers.

"Sorry I can't stay," he adds, and tipping his hat, he strides back toward the building. Colleen hears his car engine start.

The wind has picked up. It whistles through the gigantic old pines above. A train sounds in the distance and traffic hums out on Clark Road.

Colleen unwraps the flowers and bends down to put them behind the roughly cut stake. "We were too young," she says. "Too young, too naive, too scared. But we did care, Charlie. We do, even now."

She straightens up and lets the wind blow across her already wet face. A car door slams. When she looks ahead, she sees Hannah striding toward her, waving, and holding what looks like a camera.

ACKNOWLEDGMENTS

Thanks to everyone at the Saskatchewan Writers' Guild Winter Retreat 2000 where I wrote the first draft, to Joan Barfoot for reading and critiquing two early drafts and telling me I did have something worthwhile to say, to Frances Hanna for her astute comments, to the Red Shoes Writers' Group for listening and giving me support, to fellow writer Sheila Dalton for friendship and support, to my editors Carolyn Jackson, Jonathan Schmidt and Kathryn White for their editorial expertise and, to my family who, over the years, has listened patiently as I described my ongoing writing trials and progress.

ABOUT THE AUTHOR

LINDA HUTSELL-MANNING's writing career spans thirty years and includes poetry, plays, TV scripts, short fiction, and novels. She has taught in a one-room school; worked as a freelance journalist and creative writing teacher; hosted author readings and promoted her work internationally. Linda has twelve published books for children to her credit, including the Wonder Horn Time Travel series. Born in Winnipeg, Manitoba, Linda now lives near Cobourg, Ontario.